Y2K

IT'S ALREADY
TOO LATE

Jason Kelly wrote technical manuals at IBM's Santa Teresa Laboratory from 1993 to 1997. There, walking the hills of Silicon Valley with his colleagues, he learned about the Y2K problem.

Jason left IBM to pursue his career as a freelance writer. He is the author of The Neatest Little Guides, a series of financial books published by Plume. The series includes *The Neatest Little Guide to Mutual Fund Investing*, *The Neatest Little Guide to Stock Market Investing*, and *The Neatest Little Guide to Personal Finance*.

Jason appears frequently on CNNfn to provide investment commentary. He conducts radio interviews across the United States and teaches financial seminars in San Francisco, Los Angeles, and San Diego.

Y2K—It's Already Too Late is Jason's first novel. He lives in Los Angeles.

Y2K

IT'S ALREADY
TOO LATE

Jason Kelly

Jason Kelly Press, Los Angeles

ISBN 0-9664387-0-1

Published in the United States by Jason Kelly Press, Los Angeles.

To order additional copies, visit the Internet at **www.Y2KBOOK.com** or call toll-free **1-800-829-5723**.

To discuss rights to this story, contact Jason Kelly at 818-752-1934 or jkelly@y2kbook.com. To arrange interviews, contact Tammy Delatorre at 818-766-7244 or tammy@y2kbook.com.

Cover design by Seamus Berkeley, www.sbart.com.

Lyrics in Chapter Six are from "I Heard The Bells On Christmas Day," by Henry Wadsworth Longfellow.

ACKNOWLEDGMENTS

Thanks to Michael Reddell, my friend who first introduced me to Y2K on one of our fine walks through the hills around IBM's Santa Teresa Laboratory in San Jose, California. No matter what happens to the world's computers, we'll still be able go for a walk.

The gripping cover was designed by my friend, Seamus Berkeley. At his cabin deep in the Rocky Mountains, he will be safe through the catastrophe and will be able to continue painting.

There were a number of people who stepped forward to help me self-publish, two of whom I'd like to mention. Without their help, this novel would never have arrived in your hands. Tammy Delatorre's editorial comments took the book from a sprawling collection of technical facts and a cast of thousands into its final storyline. Wrenda Searle introduced me to Bertelsmann Industry Services, the best printer I've ever worked with.

I received a great deal of encouragement from the folks in my Toastmaster club, Jewel City 29. From our small meeting room in Glendale, California, I have received some of the best legal, financial, and philosophical advice of my life. When Y2K crashes around us, we can meet on a hillside and speak the days away.

Finally, I return to Tammy Delatorre. After working hard to edit the book, she quit her job to join me as a full-time publicist. Her energy is what has made this book such a success. I could not do it without her. More importantly, I would not want to. We met at the University of Colorado in 1990 and dreamed of one day becoming writers. That day has come, Tammy, and we did it on our own.

*To those who prepare
for life before it happens*

AUTHOR'S NOTE

You are about to read a disturbing story.

It's not disturbing because it has bullets and missiles and riots and human struggle. All of those ingredients form the parts of an exciting read, something you've come to expect from a good thriller. This one is disturbing because it is based on fact and may end up being a true story when the Year 2000 greets us.

When first exposed to Y2K, most people respond with disbelief. I did. It's hard to imagine that something as minor as storing a four-digit year in two digits could destroy everything we depend on in our modern world. But as I kept reading congressional testimony and expert reports, I began to wonder if it could really be catastrophic. I have concluded that it can be.

I don't believe the world will end. It has certainly survived calamities more severe than a computer shutdown. Many people can remember the days when computers didn't even exist. We can survive for long periods without electricity and phones and banks. The characters in this story prove it.

But will you be ready to survive? I hope this story leads you to prepare. I hope you finish this book and stock up on food and store a little cash and buy an extra pair of eyeglasses. You might not need any of it. If you don't, there was no harm in taking the safe route. But if Y2K shuts down the world, you'll be thankful to have prepared in advance.

On page 49, you'll find the S2 Survival Memo. Follow its instructions and suggest to your friends and family that they do the same. Visit www.Y2KBOOK.com on the Internet to learn more about the Year 2000 computer problem.

I wish you the best of luck during these times.

Jason Kelly
Los Angeles
May 8, 1998

1

DEADLY SOLUTIONS

JANUARY 8, 2000

Mark Solvang had never seen a gun pointed at him before. He spent his days in meetings about hardware and software, trying to figure a way to solve the Year 2000 computer crisis. He met with clients in suits all day long. He never saw guns and he never expected to.

His life slowed to that instant, staring across the conference room table. Men surrounded the meeting, grim faced, holding guns aimed at company vice president David Kleewein and the four men from the Department of Defense. Mark had never trusted the military men. He saw the pot-bellied uniforms and wondered if they were somehow behind the invasion. Kleewein looked wide-eyed for answers. Mark wanted to reassure his friend, but all he could do was give a small nod, encouraging Kleewein to cooperate. One man lay dead on the floor already, three bullets in his chest, his blood soaking the carpet. Even with the dead body nearby, Mark could not move his eyes from the pistol in his face. The sharp smell of gunpowder stung his nose.

The Year 2000 had killed power to all of Silicon Valley. The conference room was dimly lit by the company's diesel generators. In the partial light, Mark's eyes remained locked on the pistol but his peripheral vision took in the details of his surroundings.

Photos of Yosemite and the Golden Gate Bridge hung on the wood paneling directly behind the gunman. When Mark founded Solvang Solutions in 1990 with his wife, Margaret, she insisted on decorating with photos of their courtship. Their third date was a camping trip to Yosemite. After two years of weekend wine tasting in Napa Valley, nights in San Francisco, and lazy days in the redwood forests and Sequoia, Mark took Margaret back to Yosemite and proposed to her in the middle of Tuolumne Meadows beside the river. So the halls and conference rooms of Solvang Solutions forever paid tribute to the places that brought the company founders together.

That's what gripped Mark as he stared at the pistol and saw the majesty of El Capitan on the wall. The pistol could kill him in front of the scenes of his courtship.

The gunmen forced Mark and the others through the halls of the executive conference center. They passed the Solvang Solutions logo, a golden S2 on the wood paneling. They marched through glass doors into the tile hallway, turned right, and proceeded past offices that had bustled with activity just a month prior. Now the offices sat vacant in the darkness brought by the Year 2000. All the consultants packed into huge terminal rooms elsewhere in the building where they worked twenty-four hours a day to restore electricity and phones.

Mark never saw the company going this way. He and Margaret started Solvang Solutions in 1990 after years of trying to convince leaders in Silicon Valley that the Year 2000 computer problem would be catastrophic. They sounded like lunatics at their presentations, talking about the end of the world and the need to act fast. Their friends and family said they were crazy to start a company while trying to raise their two new children, Jeremiah and Alyssa. At times, Mark thought they were right.

They nonetheless forged ahead, gathering together some of Silicon Valley's brightest programmers to tackle the Year 2000 computer problem, known in the business as Y2K. It was never supposed to get as big as it got and it was certainly never supposed to attract the kind of attention that brought gunmen to Solvang headquarters. The Y2K problem seemed like such a trivial affair, almost silly. Yet, Mark and Margaret knew that it could bring the world to its knees. Now, ten years after the company's founding, they were proven right.

The computer crisis known as Y2K was a data storage mistake. To save space, programmers in the 1950s and 1960s recorded years as two digits, not four. 1960 became just 60. Two-digit dates seeped into computers everywhere, persisting long after storage space became plentiful.

The moment 99 rolled to 00, the lights went out. Computers did not understand that 00 meant 2000. It could have meant 1700 or 1800 or 1900.

So computers stopped working.

Computers that fly planes. Computers that connect phones. Computers that supply electricity. Computers that guide missiles. Computers that run automobiles.

They all crashed.

Only Solvang Solutions still worked, limping along on its own diesel generators and private satellite network. Thousands of Solvang consultants worked in cities across America and around the world, frantically typing, trying to make headway against the collapse. Mark and Margaret had wanted to prevent the meltdown. But just inside the new millennium, power was out, phones were down, grocery store shelves picked clean, pharmacies looted.

The military was particularly affected. Mark, Kleewein, and the men from the Department of Defense had met that day to discuss an incident in the South China Sea near Hong Kong. Two U.S. destroyers were fired upon and sunk by unidentified warships. Nobody knew why. The Department of Defense was S2's biggest account. The U.S. military sat crippled at ports and bases around the globe. It needed Solvang to act fast.

Walking down the hallway at gunpoint, Mark's fear was overtaken by sadness. His hand touched the tie tack in his pocket, Margaret's Father's Day gift to him in 1990. The black and gold tack displayed a tiny photo of their young family. Margaret had pinned it to his tie on that cloudless June day. "This will always remind you of what's really important in life," she had said. Then she kissed him while the sun highlighted her blond hair. It was the last gift she ever gave to him.

Margaret didn't live to see the company's first full year of operation. She died from lymphoma in 1990. Mark could do nothing but immerse himself in work. Jeremiah and Alyssa moved in with Grandma and Grandpa Solvang in Los Gatos. They lived within walking distance of Mark's home and he tried to visit them as often as he could. Nearly a decade after Margaret's death, Mark still introduced Jeremiah and Alyssa as "our" children, even though they were officially just his children. They would always belong equally to Margaret.

Still touching the tie tack in his pocket, Mark thought about what was really important in life. Jeremiah and Alyssa became an afterthought following Margaret's death. The Year 2000 computer crisis had seemed like the most important project he had ever managed. But at gunpoint, Mark wondered how he could have let a computer problem overtake his life.

The gunmen led them down the stairwell to the basement. They walked through the hallway past the lower terminal room. Mark looked through the glass to his consultants hunched over computers. He saw Susan Levin, the lower terminal room manager. She was a key part of S2's success.

Susan joined the company in early 1991. She was a pretty woman, petite with gentle features. But Y2K had taken its toll on her. Mark saw that she wore sweat pants and kept her unwashed hair under a hat.

During normal times, she dressed impeccably well, often putting her auburn hair in a neat bun, leaving her face and neck completely exposed. Her brown eyes turned up at the corners as if she might have pulled her hair back too tightly. The upturned eyes gave her a sense of fierce intelligence when she presided over rooms full of consultants. She spoke quietly but with confidence. Her terminal room handled Solvang's most important accounts and Susan's name appeared regularly in industry publications. She was a shining star at a fast-growing company.

But through the hallway glass, Mark didn't see Susan's credentials. He saw her compassion, the part of her that few others in the company would ever detect through her upturned eyes and business suits. During meetings with Mark, she was the only one to notice his expression fade from the topic at hand to parts of his mind that were tender and distant. He looked at her once during a tense meeting. She gave him a smile. The chatter of the meeting faded to a distant sound like ocean waves as Mark allowed himself to find comfort in the smile of Susan Levin.

He watched her as the gunmen marched forward. Her small back was turned toward him. He wanted to signal her. She could alert S2 security, who would be able to help. But she didn't turn. He passed the window and let his eyes close.

The procession of gunmen approached the steel door of the diesel supply room. The engines hummed loudly, vibrating the handle as a gunman unlocked it. The rumble from the building's emergency electrical power plant poured from the darkness.

"Everybody inside!"

Mark, Kleewein, and the men from the Department of Defense walked into the tiny room. They turned to face the doorway, the room's only source of light.

Mark felt pain everywhere in his nerves and nowhere, as if he were suspended outside of his body watching the capture of another human. What a pathetic end, was all he could think. In that instant he was not the brilliant president of Solvang Solutions, one of San Jose's most prominent firms. He was not the cover of *Business Week*. He was not a Silicon Valley visionary.

He was a man at last brought to where all men eventually go. The veneers of success peel quickly away from the end of a gun barrel. He felt more human than he'd ever felt, even more human than when his wife died. All he wanted was his life. A second chance to fix everything he failed to fix before that day.

He stood beside Kleewein, shoulder to shoulder in the darkness. The slight touch of his friend soothed Mark as he stared into the faces of men he did not know. They came unannounced and said little. He might never know their identity or intentions.

At that moment, the world could go to hell. Mark wanted to live and to be with his children. He groaned, turning the heads of Kleewein and the nearest guard. His blood strained against his veins. He was a soul about to be released but he was not ready to go. An angry soul is a force to fear. The gunmen couldn't know it, but Mark Solvang carried the rage of a soul owed its life. The rage grew. It carried the faces of his children. It carried the smell of Margaret's perfume, angrily covered by gunpowder. It carried vengeance and it brought energy to Mark, an energy that would see him through anything waiting at the end of this journey at gunpoint.

He flared his nostrils to breathe mightily. His short, black hair remained neat even through the showerless days of the new century. The muscles of his face flexed beneath smooth shaven skin. His magisterial green and silver eyes sliced through any notion of helplessness. He stood with a rigid disdain, not enough to get himself shot, but enough to convey his fury. Enough to assure them that he would not forget.

A gunman pulled the top from a can the size of a hairspray bottle. He rolled it inside the room. The can hissed. They shut the door, leaving the six men in darkness. The air turned sweet.

"It's gas!" Mark said. He moved to the sound and grabbed the can. He tried pushing a finger into the spray to stop it, but the force was too great. "There's no way to stop it."

"Try pointing it under the door," someone said.

Mark scooted to the small crack under the door. Kleewein joined him there, tugging on the handle with all his might. The door wouldn't budge. He tugged twice more, then kicked the handle.

"It's stuck solid," he reported.

Mark pushed the can against the door crack. He tried in vain to direct the spewing gas out of the room. "It's not working," he said. "It's too wide a stream."

"I feel dizzy," Kleewein gasped.

Mark collapsed to the floor. He felt others fall around him. The sweet air permeated the room, winding its tendrils through Mark's fingers clamped futilely over his nose and mouth. He finally let his arms drop to his sides.

Mark saw the faces of Margaret and his children. He saw Susan smiling softly through his troubles. He smelled hibiscus perfume. His eyelids grew heavy, his thoughts drugged. "Margaret," he whispered. Somehow the darkness got even darker.

2

TOWER OF BABEL

JULY 14, 1997, 7:44 AM

"From where?" Mark asked, quickly setting his bag on the desk.

"From Chase."

Chase Manhattan was S2's biggest client to date. The bank discovered Y2K problems years prior when its loan system and trading system needed to project past the millennium to process long-term bonds. But its fixes for that problem were a patchwork of ad hoc solutions from outside vendors and crack teams in house. In 1995, Chase's executives finally understood the seriousness of Y2K and formed Enterprise Year 2000, the firm's preparation project. Steve Sheinheit, senior vice president of corporate systems and architecture, chose four vendors to get Chase back on track. One was IBM's world famous ISSC division, which had started its own Year 2000 office in Chicago. S2 was the second major vendor, and worked closely with IBM. Kleewein flew to Chicago regularly to coordinate with IBM, and to New York with IBM teams to coordinate with Chase. The remaining two vendors, both handling small data migration tasks, were Computer Horizons in New Jersey and Alltel in Arkansas.

"It's the three-year fiscal plans," Susan continued. She tossed a snack bar wrapper into the trash. She always nibbled on snack bars in times of high stress. The stress was her own private exercise routine. It was a successful one, judging from her thin figure. "They can't project to the Year 2000. None of us saw this coming. The manager was in a panic. He said their automated number crunchers fritzed out."

"Get Kleewein on the line with IBM."

"He already is."

Mark looked at the timeline on his office wall. In any other area of the computer industry, five years was an eternity. Not in the Y2K business. "Chase isn't the only company preparing three-year projections. We're going to get a raft of calls this week. Make sure the support center is ready."

By 9:30 AM, Wells Fargo joined the S2 client list. A leader in California banking, it was near and dear to many S2 employees who banked there. The bank's current ad slogan was "Put Your Money Where You Can Find It," referring to its enormous network of branches and ATMs. The Wells Fargo information systems manager who called S2 quipped, "it would be nice if we could find it too."

Later that day, Steve Sheinheit from Chase called Mark, Kleewein, and Susan on the conference phone. He reported that they would survive the three-year projections. "But the Y2K debacle is insidious. These bond projections proved that. Opened a lot of eyes around here. If people knew what a house of cards kept their money, there'd be a run on banks like never before."

"This is a rare moment of candor," Susan said.

"Disasters tend to do that," Sheinheit replied.

"People will find out about the house of cards when it collapses," Mark told him.

"Hey, no talk like that. Let's think house of bricks, house of steel, house of stuff that doesn't collapse."

"House of four-digit years," Kleewein said.

A man dressed in blue coveralls knocked on the open conference room doorway. Debbra Jeffries, the executive secretary, ran up nervously behind the man. "Mark, I'm sorry, he insisted—"

"Mark Solvang," the man said.

Susan leaned to the speaker phone. "Steve, we'll get back to you." She pressed the button.

Mark stood from the table. "Yes?"

The blue-clad man walked to the table. "I have a special delivery from the United States House of Representatives. I need to hand it to you and get your signature here, please."

Mark took a card stock envelope with no return address and signed the courier's slip. It wasn't a regular scheduled delivery. Mark's name was the only one on the piece of paper. The courier thanked Mark, then exited past a perturbed Debbra Jones.

Mark pulled the open strip to dump out another envelope, this one addressed from the House Science Committee. It contained a letter from Congressman Lawrence Petalmquist, Chair of the Technology Subcommittee.

Kleewein and Susan grew quiet as Mark read the letter, then slid it back into the envelope. He sat down and looked at them. "Congress wants to hear my take on Y2K. They want to know about its potential inconvenience to the American people."

"Inconvenience?" Kleewein asked. "That's one way to put it."

"I hope they set aside a few weeks," Susan said.

"They set aside two hours." Mark tapped his pen on the envelope. "Susan, see what you can find in the government Y2K contract file. We haven't been able to land any federal agencies yet. This might be the break we need. I want a full packet of our marketing materials in the right hands before I give this presentation. We don't need the government's money, but they need our skills. This is our opportunity to know that we tried our best to show the government what's coming and that we can help."

Susan nodded.

"You better make this count," Kleewein said. His thick glasses shook with emphasis. The forehead of his enlarged cranium matched the monotone of his voice. Only in times of extreme tension did he resort to inflection. It took months of knowing Kleewein's quirkiness to feel comfortable around him. It took years to consider him a friend.

Mark shot a ferocious look at Kleewein. "I make everything count."

July 28, 1997, 9:30 AM

Mark arrived at the Rayburn House Office Building in Washington, D.C. at 9:30 AM. He wasn't scheduled until 10:00.

He found a seat near the entrance and flipped open his notebook computer. The screen resumed work precisely where he stopped during the plane landing. He typed into the database and retrieved the information he needed. He wrote on a small notepad from his suit pocket: Edwin Pritchett, Undersecretary of Defense for Acquisition & Technology. He closed the computer.

Susan found Pritchett's name on defense contracts she pulled from Lexis-Nexis. She called his office at the Pentagon and discovered that he and a man named Albert Schwager—chief

information officer of the Defense Information Systems Agency—
were in charge of preparing the military for the Year 2000. Pritchett's
secretary invited Susan to mail S2's marketing material. Susan
followed up with a phone call the next week. She told Pritchett
about Mark's presentation to Congress that Monday and promised
a call from S2's founder and president while he was in Washington.
Despite his gruff manner, Pritchett said he looked forward to the
conversation.

Susan met with a different response from Schwager's office.
The secretary said firmly that the Defense Information Systems
Agency was not accepting bids from the private sector. She claimed
that, using its own resources, DISA was on track to fully prepare
the military for the Year 2000. When Susan cited S2's internal market
research indicating that the military was woefully underprepared,
the secretary insisted that S2 was misinformed. Exasperated, Susan
explained that Pritchett's office was eager to receive S2's material
and that Pritchett himself had expressed interest in speaking with
Mark Solvang. The secretary repeated her objections, curtly thanked
Susan for the call, and disconnected.

Mark pulled the phone from his briefcase and began to dial
Edwin Pritchett. A shadow fell across the phone. "If it isn't Mark
Solvang himself," boomed a towering figure.

Mark canceled the call and stood to shake hands. "Congressman
Petalmquist, it's a pleasure."

"The pleasure is mine." He held a faxed copy of Mark's
presentation outline. "We run a bunch of private sector experts
through here. Yourdon, de Jager, Keen, all of them. Your efforts
have not gone unnoticed."

Mark handed Petalmquist the presentation abstract that his letter
requested. The congressman placed his glasses, eyeing the paper
from the top of his six-and-a-half-foot frame. "Tower 2000: The
Babel of our Times." He pointed at the paper. "Isn't this a tad
extreme?"

"It's a real-world report."

"Either that or you're here to drum up business."

"I'm here to drum up attention."

They walked inside the room. Mark felt heads turn fiercely to
eye him. Dressed in a bold navy pinstripe with his short, black hair
combed perfectly to one side, he strode confidently to the front of
the room. He was the shadowy leader from computing's fringe, the

voice from the other side of technology where the future was not lined with endless opportunity. People did not want to hear Mark Solvang's message. They wanted to hear about Microsoft and Intel and portable devices and how in just a few short years America would live like the Jetsons. People did not want to hear about disaster.

While the world marveled at its own progress, Mark Solvang warned that it would end badly. He was hated by droves of business leaders and government officials because he did not hesitate to point out their shortsightedness. To him they were not geniuses. They were people who did what they were told for results that mattered only in the short term. He was hated because he built a thriving company by fixing the failures of more popular companies. He was hated because he refused to consider the possibility that Y2K might pass unnoticed. He was hated, in his opinion, because they knew he was right. In less than three years the world's business and government heroes would be the laughing stock of the century. The ones that lived, at least.

In the back of the room, Albert Schwager took his seat quietly. He was a man of average height topped by curly brown hair parted on the left. Two deep age lines ran south through his cheeks to the corners of his mouth, like rainwater ravines to handle runoff. He motioned his companion to the empty seat beside him.

A prim Chinese man with high cheekbones settled weightlessly to the chair beside Schwager. His eyes peered around the Rayburn House without the slightest bit of interest or emotion. A black freckle twisted from the skin of his upper lip. He parted his lips to take a deep breath. The black freckle rose away from his mouth to reveal gray teeth separated by thick tobacco lines.

Schwager leaned to the Chinese man's ear. "Mr. Chau, that is Mark Solvang."

"The founder of the company?" Mr. Chau asked with a heavy accent. His dark pupils, obscured by low-hanging eyelids, locked onto the proud man at the front of the room.

"Yes, the founder of the company."

Mr. Chau nodded blandly. He'd faced many enemies in his lifetime. All had at one time been proud.

"Ladies and gentlemen," Congressman Petalmquist spoke from the lectern, "we are fortunate today to welcome Mark Solvang. He began his company called Solvang Solutions, abbreviated S2, seven years ago with the goal of preparing the United States for the Year 2000 computer problem. Mr. Solvang is going to deliver a speech to us entitled 'Tower 2000: The Babel of our Times.' Please welcome Mark Solvang."

Mark stepped to the lectern amid doubtful applause. "Good morning. It's my pleasure to address Congress on the Year 2000 computer problem, which arose from the storage of years in two digits instead of four. The current year is 1997, yet most computers know it as just 97. When 99 turns to 00, most computers will crash. You are all here today because time is running out. The end of the millennium is just around the corner. If we do not act fast, we will ring in the new millennium with the mother of all computer glitches."

Mr. Chau studied Mark intently. Albert promised him a transcript of the presentation, but Mr. Chau insisted on taking notes. In his business, how a person speaks is more important than what he says.

"Modern society speaks a common language, the language of computing. Every computer talks to every other computer and, like our forebears, we feel there is nothing we can't accomplish. On January 1, 2000, many computers will not understand themselves much less any other computer. The Year 2000, or Y2K, is our Tower of Babel. At Solvang Solutions, we have taken a two-fold approach to preparing the country for Y2K. First, we sell software called *Solvang2K* that finds potential errors and helps developers fix them. Second, we provide a full team of consultants to make businesses Y2K compliant."

Chinese characters decorated the margins of Mr. Chau's paper, highlighting, categorizing, and dissecting the words coming from the man who might be a difficulty. There was nothing foreboding about the man, this Solvang. Yet, great leaders came in many disguises. So did great enemies.

"We are gravely concerned about the lack of action from government," Mark continued. "No other entity in the world controls more computing power than the U.S. government. Imagine what would happen if every government computer stopped working. No tax collection, no entitlement distribution, no national defense."

Mr. Chau underlined vehemently. He circled a Chinese character beside Mark's last point.

"I want to drive home the impact of a broad-based computer shutdown. Too many people think computers are used only for word processing and cute pictures. They're not. They run our world. When

I talk about the Y2K disaster, I am not talking about losing your ability to type a letter and print it out. I am talking about sitting on a plane New Year's Eve 1999 when the FAA shuts down and the plane's navigation equipment fails. As you plummet to your death, you will finally understand the meaning of Y2K. I am talking about living in Los Angeles when the lights go out and police dispatch systems go quiet and new cars fail to drive and security systems die. As the mob of rioters charges through wealthy neighborhoods and business districts, looting and burning the city to the ground, you will finally understand the meaning of Y2K. I am talking about arriving at the grocery store to find a panicked crowd storming the doors for food. As you are thrown to the ground and beaten unconscious for the small bag of groceries you try to carry home, you will finally understand the meaning of Y2K. I am talking about losing everything you've come to expect as a normal part of your day. I am talking about the return to animal survival. I am talking about the end of your world."

Several members of the audience stood to leave. Mark had seen it before. At this point in his presentation, he could safely be labeled a lunatic, just slightly above the people who preach at malls and bus stations.

"It is too late to fix the U.S. government," Mark said bluntly. He raised his voice for the benefit of those leaving. "Congressman Horn's survey from a year ago revealed that fact beyond question. NASA, one of the most computer-dependent agencies in the Federal government, has not prepared a plan to solve the problem and does not anticipate having a plan completed until later this year. The Department of Energy has not yet begun to address the Year 2000 problem. The Department of Transportation, which includes the Federal Aviation Administration, did not respond to phone calls. The Department of Defense is scrambling to find the best private-sector partners to ready our fighting men and women for the new century. As you can see, the government landscape is grim."

Schwager winced. He knew that Solvang was making inroads with Pritchett. While he doubted that Pritchett would have come across as "scrambling" for the best partners, it was clear that his colleague had given Solvang some room for hope. He would need to tend to Pritchett immediately following the presentation. It made him uneasy to have Mark Solvang and Edwin Pritchett in the same town. He could not let Pritchett hire Solvang as the primary defense contractor.

"All we can do now," Mark continued, "is identify the most critical systems and save them first, a concept known as triage. The government's lack of action is puzzling to me because it is not an organization that relies on competitive superiority. Big business has ignored Y2K because it must survive against competitors in the short term. So the budget that would be used to prepare for Y2K is already depleted. But government has no encroaching competition. Why then isn't Y2K the top priority?

"The fact is, the President needs to step in as CEO of the country and convey to the population just how urgently we need to prepare for Y2K.

"Why hasn't he? His silence is troubling. The federal government's first cost estimate placed the price of Y2K compliance among all government agencies at $2.3 billion. Every quarter since that initial estimate has seen a rise in the projected cost. At S2, we know exactly the reason. As developers dive into their applications and begin pulling apart their systems, they find that the problem is far worse than originally guessed. It's like seeing an ant cross your kitchen counter, opening a cabinet to get bug spray, and having an entire colony of ants spill from the cabinet onto the kitchen floor. The problem seems minute, and it is. But a billion minute problems add up to an enormous threat."

Testing potential fixes, Mark explained, can take as long as or longer than the fixes themselves *and* require more computing power. The cost of testing is often half the total cost of preparation.

"Congress should pass Y2K laws that force government agencies to review schedules of preparation with private firms, and prohibit agencies from purchasing any new equipment that is not Y2K compliant. Such a law would not only help fix government, it would send a clear message to technology vendors that their products need to be ready for the millennium. Federal Y2K laws could cascade down quickly and get the country moving on this issue."

He looked forward into the skeptical audience. "That's all I have today. The American people are counting on their computers for the future. Let's not let them down."

Congressman Petalmquist opened the forum for questions.

"Why do you say it's too late to fix government?"

Mark gripped the lectern. Didn't any of these people read news magazines? "Because there are not enough programmers in the country to locate and repair every problem. Government should have begun work on Y2K in 1977, not 1997."

"What steps has your company taken to help businesses meet their deadlines?"

"Our *Solvang2K* software runs on all major computing platforms and understands major database formats. We stand ready to help almost any computing environment. We are organized in a hub and spoke fashion." Mr. Chau wrote furiously as Mark spoke. He drew a wheel with spokes. One Chinese character identified the center as Solvang's headquarters, another character repeated at the end of each spoke identified remote sites. "As our separate consulting teams encounter problems or breakthroughs, they report everything back to our headquarters in San Jose, California. It's our first and main site, which we call The Keep. There we track every piece of information in our database, which is fully Y2K compliant. Remote S2 sites can access the database at any time for the latest tips and techniques. We've found this setup works very well."

"If this situation is so bad, why aren't we seeing more trouble?"

"Because you're not in the business of Y2K repair. I guarantee that everybody will know about the Year 2000 computer problem long before January 1, 2000. My prediction is that you'll see the most attention paid to banking and investing. We've just recently received panic calls from banks that have encountered Y2K trouble in their three-year fiscal projections. Newspapers love runs on banks. If reporters learn how unprepared banks are for Y2K, it'll make the cover of every paper and magazine in the country. I'm guessing that word will get out soon enough and when it does, people will line up for their money."

"What government agencies are you working with?"

"None yet, and that concerns me. We've sent letters to this committee, every member of Congress, and the technology divisions of agencies, but we haven't heard back. This is my first official contact with government."

"Has S2 prepared a worst-case scenario plan?"

"Yes," Mark said, surprised to hear that somebody could see the reality. "Most of our profits go toward preparing our organization to survive a complete shutdown of the U.S. infrastructure. We operate on a private satellite network and are in the process of establishing private sources of electricity. We have a team of support experts analyzing the needs and systems of every major utility and telephone company in the country, whether they are current clients or not. In the event of catastrophe, we will stand ready to help repair the country one sector at a time." He paused to let S2's extensive preparations sink in. "We anticipate being the only operable company on January 1, 2000 and we intend to use our position to repair the world."

Schwager raised his hand, causing Mr. Chau to pause his writing. The crisis information was new to Schwager and his Chinese companion. "Will you work with the Department of Defense to insure full operations?"

"We will work with any government agency."

"I mean in time of crisis."

"We intend to focus on electricity, phones, and food," Mark answered. "Those seem the most basic supports of society. In case defense becomes a pressing need, we are prepared to shuffle our resources to place national security at top priority."

Schwager's eyes narrowed. He flexed his facial muscles, deepening the ravines in his cheeks. This is exactly what he was afraid of. This Solvang understood everything. He knew what was at risk and he knew that it couldn't be fixed in time. He ran a firm that would not break in 2000 and he ran it with the express intention of fixing the country. Schwager swore to himself that Solvang Solutions would not be allowed to win the Department of Defense contract. It could ruin everything.

"I'm very concerned about the military," Mark added a moment after his answer. "The DoD uses systems and software that are ancient, stuff most of our consultants don't know about. We need to be ready to help the military, so we have assigned a team to analyze its situation. We'll treat it like any other hot spot."

"Hot spot?" Mr. Chau whispered to Schwager.

"Problem area." The Chinese man's face contorted, still not sure of the meaning. "Something he's worried about," Schwager hissed through pursed lips.

"Ah, worried." He wrote a Chinese character on his paper.

"Our time today is finished," Mark concluded. "If you retain nothing else from today's discussion, retain this: the new century will arrive on schedule whether Congress is ready or not. Be ready."

Mark turned down several offers for lunch and finally broke from the crowd of congressmen asking private questions. He found a quiet area of grass outside the Rayburn House. He pulled the notepad from his pocket and dialed Edwin Pritchett. The secretary answered, then transferred the call.

"Pritchett," came the gruff voice. It was the first time Mark had heard Pritchett's voice. The tone came from somebody who had ruined a lot of careers in his lifetime and wouldn't hesitate to ruin a few more. It was the voice of a busy man staring at a long list of tasks still unchecked at midday.

"Mr. Pritchett, this is Mark Solvang. I finished my Y2K presentation to Congress. Sorry you couldn't be there. Would you like to join me for a quick lunch in town?"

"No. I've received your materials and have looked them over. I'm interested in further examining your company's credentials, but I don't have time for lunch."

"Perhaps another time, not that there's much time left."

"No, there isn't. I understand the situation, Mr. Solvang, and I understand your eagerness. I'm just not sure that things are as bad as your literature suggests."

"Then, to be frank, you do not understand the situation."

There was a long pause. "That's rather arrogant."

"I can afford to be arrogant when I'm right, Mr. Pritchett. I can also afford to be arrogant when my company will be the only one operable in less than three years. As you evaluate other firms, ask how they intend to remain in operation when electricity stops and phones are dead. As they sputter for an answer, remember that my company operates on a private satellite network and its own diesel generators. When you are ready to hook up with the firm that will survive Y2K no matter what happens, give me a call."

"I'll do that."

Mark clicked off the phone. He put it into his pocket and watched the procession of congressmen from the Rayburn House to shiny automobiles. They laughed and shook hands and traded cards. A gray-haired gentleman checked his watch before stepping into a limousine. The limo sped off to lunch.

Mark shook his head. What a waste of time. Of all the resources to waste that day, time was the last one Mark Solvang would have chosen.

3

TOO LATE

Pritchett walked the halls of the Pentagon alone. He needed to stretch his legs, get a drink of water, lose some of his pent-up energy. All around him computers hummed. Lights blinked from terminals and printers and security systems. Lower in the building, screens the size of home theaters watched satellite downloads from around the world. In the walls, ceilings, and floors ran 100,000 miles of telephone cable used by the world's largest office building to make a quarter of a million phone calls a day. Computers monitored their progress, tabulated their data, interpreted the results, and stored it where Generals and Admirals and government leaders could get to it faster than ballistic missiles could reach their targets.

He returned to his office, the tidiest one in government bureaucracy. His door read Undersecretary of Defense for Acquisition & Technology. At parties, he took great fun introducing himself as "Ed Pritchett, USD A&T." Then, gesturing to his wife of forty-seven years, he would say, "and this is Mrs. USD A&T." It was as funny as Pritchett ever got. Few people would say they liked him, but fewer still could argue with his results. He was a man with twelve patents and nineteen patent disclosures to his name. Long before buying technology for the Department of Defense, he invented it.

Pritchett never intended to work in government. He shined as an engineer at Westinghouse Electronics Systems Group in Baltimore, leading the radar development division. Private industry treated him well and Pritchett intended to open his own electronics company in the 1970s. Then he was hand-picked to help revitalize the Army's Counter Low Observable program. He accepted and never looked back. His string of successes led to his appointment to USD A&T in 1993, overwhelmingly confirmed by the Senate.

He barely picked up his pen when an all-too-familiar and all-too-annoying knock came at the door. He let the pen fall from his fingers and glared at the blurred shape through the ghosted glass. "Come in!" he blared.

His wide face and broad shoulders gave Pritchett an immovable presence. He stood from behind his desk to extend a wrought-iron hand toward Albert Schwager. Sometimes the world's biggest office building wasn't big enough. Pritchett couldn't stand Schwager. "Morning," he managed.

Schwager nodded. "I've come a long way in analyzing the vendor profiles. I believe our selection will go smoother if I just choose the right one on my own. That leaves you free to assess the needs of the military."

"That's kind of you," Pritchett growled, "but I already have profiles of all major CDC vendors in the country. I'm going to study them tonight." CDC stood for Century Date Change, the government's own acronym for Y2K.

"So you want to choose together."

"That's always been the plan." Pritchett looked sideways at Schwager. They conferred on major contracts that involved both offices. On smaller contracts handled through one office, Pritchett's seniority ruled. If anything, he—not Schwager—would be the sole authority choosing the military's Y2K repair firm

Schwager's eyes hardened and Pritchett couldn't tell what he was thinking. It didn't look good. At last, Schwager spoke. "I think we should choose several vendors. This job is too big for any one firm to handle."

"I disagree," Pritchett retorted. "Teams will get in each other's way. There are firms equipped to handle the military's massive demands. We need a primary vendor who can choose secondary vendors for smaller pieces of the puzzle. I'm leaning toward Solvang Solutions."

"Why Solvang? It's not even a defense contractor."

"They are the best equipped and they're zealots. The company founder, Mark Solvang, just finished a presentation to Congress and called to invite me to lunch. He's convincing as hell. I believe him when he tells me that his company is the only one that will survive the century date change."

Schwager looked edgy. When Pritchett had suggested months ago that they approach firms to assist the DoD in its preparations, he thought he saw Schwager clench inside. It was as if Schwager didn't want to prepare for the century date change.

"Not so fast," Schwager said anxiously. "We should probably take our time choosing the right one. It's important."

Pritchett tensed his brow. "That's the silliest thing I've ever heard. We should choose the right vendor, but we should do it as quickly as possible. We don't have time to waste. As a matter of fact, I'd like to see you back here tomorrow after lunch. We need to narrow this list to a manageable few and schedule visits with each one. I don't know where the hell your mind is, Schwager, but you better either get behind me on this or stay the hell out of my way."

"I'm behind you. I'll see you after lunch tomorrow." Schwager turned to leave.

"Don't you want copies of the vendor profiles?" Pritchett barked after him.

"I've got them already."

Pritchett sat down after Schwager left. Even though he was known as a quick study, the process of reading the stacks of vendor profiles took Pritchett many hours of detailed reading and highlighting. He flipped through the stack of vendor papers, scanning his previously highlighted excerpts of each company's expertise. They explained outsourcing, problem determination, data conversion, and so on. He moved the paperwork aside. He couldn't concentrate. Something was wrong here and it bothered him.

He pressed the speakerphone. "Karen, did you deliver these CDC vendor profiles to Schwager's office?"

"No. Should I have?"

"No. That's fine, I just needed to know."

He looked out the window. Pritchett was not a man prone to getting lost in thought. He was a man of activity lists that started the day with open boxes beside each item and ended the day with a check in each box. He didn't remember checking an item to send vendor profiles to Schwager's office at DISA.

Pritchett's office was the only one to originate a request for CDC vendor profiles. That meant that the only way Schwager could have obtained the profiles to review was by getting copies from

Pritchett. Thus, Pritchett concluded that Schwager didn't have the profiles, but he did have strong opinions on the best vendor choice. So strong, that he wanted to select a vendor entirely on his own.

"Something stinks," Pritchett muttered.

Defense contracting is notorious for backroom payoffs and special favors. Pritchett cracked his thumb knuckles then slammed his fist on the stack of vendor profiles.

He hated backroom payoffs and special favors.

August 15, 1997

Mark entered the executive conference room wearing a collarless white shirt. He emitted beams of energy gliding to the head of the table. He smiled at Kleewein and Susan and the room's two guests, then gestured to Debbra to close the door. The usual collection of S2 managers and lead consultants sat in high-back leather chairs around an eighteen-foot polished oak table. They could not know that Mark intended a major change of direction that day, a change that would meet with outcries and fury. National park photos hung on the wood paneling. Two skylights topped with louvers filled the room with indirect natural illumination.

The President and First Lady were scheduled to speak at the White House Millennium Event at The National Archives that day. Mark chose the event as a good day for Solvang's first industry report and to deliver his news. His executives and managers would begin their day with the grim truth from experts, and end it with glitzy lies from the President.

"Welcome, everybody," Mark intoned. The air vibrated with anticipation. "This is the first of what I'm sure will be many conferences reporting the state of Y2K affairs. Susan, would you like to introduce our guests?"

Susan stood from her seat to Mark's left. The corner of a snack bar poked from the front pocket of her blazer. "Certainly. Our guests today are Kirk Moletta, energy analyst from Baltimore; and Tom Nash, telecommunications analyst from San Francisco. Joining us on the speakerphone are Takayuki Nishida, head of S2 Japan; and Geoff Thome, head of S2 London."

Mark's eyes burned in the direction of Kirk Moletta, signaling without words that the analyst should begin his presentation.

Moletta's thin frame rose from his chair. He wore a brown suit with a wide brown tie and a brown pocket square. He pushed wire rim glasses to the top of a very long nose, then touched his fingertips together while gathering his thoughts.

"Let me set the tone for this gathering right away," he said in a slow, mournful voice. He chose his words carefully, as though cataloging each phrase in his mind before letting the words loose in the conference room. "I spoke this morning with the directors of the Nuclear Regulatory Commission, Donald Cool and Thomas Martin. They said that none of the country's 107 nuclear power plants will be ready for the Year 2000. Therefore, the NRC will have no choice but to shut them down. Without going any further into my presentation, that simple fact guarantees that the nation will lose twenty-five percent of its power grid, forty percent in the northeast."

"Explain the power grid," Mark said.

Moletta took a deep breath, almost a gasp. He nodded his gaunt face. "The U.S. power system is divided into nine regional grids. The overall grid system was developed to let utilities easily trade electricity from where supply is cheapest to where demand is highest. The two western grids are an interconnected system of eighty-eight utilities and more than 112,000 miles of transmission lines. The weakness of the grid system is that a problem in one small area can bring down a huge portion of the country. That happened in summer of 1996 and earlier this year."

"Then why have a grid system at all?" Kleewein asked in characteristic monotone.

"Because it's an efficient way to distribute the nation's power. If each part of the country needed to build power plants to meet peak demand, we'd have power plants that sat idle most of the time. So we have an extensive web of 500-kilovolt transmission lines that connect in Nebraska."

"Seems like that should be able to handle the power distribution," Susan remarked.

Moletta's droopy eyes settled on her face. "Most of the time it can. But the demands placed on the power grid will escalate between now and 2000 because the energy industry is being deregulated. People in Los Angeles will be able to order their electricity from North Carolina. You will choose your power provider just as you choose your long distance company. The grid will be needed to distribute all that custom ordered power from faraway regions. I'm sure this room can appreciate the Year 2000 vulnerability of a computerized power network facing the highest electricity demands in history. Clearly, we have a problem."

Mark gestured for Moletta to take his seat. "Clearly. Thank you for that summary, Mr. Moletta. Solvang currently has contracts in place with Pacific Gas & Electric and Con Edison. We're working both coasts. We will be seeking more energy clients in the months ahead and forming emergency teams to prioritize and repair utilities once the millennium hits."

He turned to Tom Nash and gave a gentle nod. Nash leapt from his seat in a bright burst of clothing and a salesman's smile. He fired folders in every color of the rainbow to his audience around the table. He could have been the fire to cremate Moletta's corpse, so stark was the difference in their styles.

"It's an honor to drive down here today," he sparkled. "I've provided each of you with full reports so you can reference what I'm about to share with you. Your packets will provide more detail on the telecommunications industry than you could ever want to know. With a group as smart as this, I decided too much information was preferable to too little."

He took a breath. Mark half expected him to fall over from hyperventilation. "I guess I'll follow Kirk's lead and tell you the grim reality right up front. AT&T has 500 million lines of computer code to search for Y2K trouble, MCI has 300 million, Sprint has 100 million. British Telecom has 350 million. Every major telecom company is aware of Y2K now and has implemented its best effort to prepare. In our view, none will make it."

An S2 manager raised his hand. "Phones have been around longer than computers. It seems that some semblance of telecommunications could survive a Year 2000 meltdown."

Nash nodded vehemently. "Absolutely correct. The basics of phone communication don't require computers. A couple tin cans and a string can work. But the problems with modern telecom systems lie in switches and routers. Network switches are the hardware that connect your phone and the other phone when you make a call or somebody calls you. If you're calling far away, the chances are good that your signal will utilize several switches. If you're calling up the street, you'll probably use just one."

"And all modern switches are digital," Kleewein said.

"Precisely correct. Up until the 1960s, switches used relays that weren't very smart. A new system from Bell Labs introduced the world to digital switches that work with equipment from carriers to bring advanced services like call forwarding, caller ID, call waiting, and such. The drawback to these digital switches is that they're computerized, and that means they're Y2K vulnerable. Not only do they connect calls, they also record the begin and end time of every call. Because phone lines cross boundaries between time zones, the switches need to stamp every call's beginning and end with a year, date, hour, minute, and second."

"What are the chances of fixing all of the telecom industry in time?" Mark asked.

"Zero." The manic expression wiped from Nash's face. "There's no doubt that the phones are going down in the Year 2000. You won't read about it in the paper because the phone companies are keeping quiet, but you can be sure that you won't be making any phone calls on January 1, 2000. Maybe not even by January 1, 2001. It sounds absurd, but that's how pervasive the problem is. There are more than fifteen million pieces of equipment to be fixed and not a single company has started. We have only two-and-a-half years to go. That's six million pieces replaced a year, half a million each month. Forget it."

"But can we replace some of the pieces to guarantee partial operability?"

"No. It's a linked chain. It doesn't matter if my neighborhood switch is working. If yours is not, we're out of luck. There might be small areas of the country that can call across the street to each other, but for all practical purposes you should just assume that the telecom industry will collapse at midnight on New Year's Eve 1999."

Mark nodded. "Thank you, Mr. Nash. Solvang has contracts in place with Lucent, Nortel, and Siemens. We're trying to work with the major carriers, but I'm not hopeful. They have in-house teams. We will form midnight task groups to respond to emergencies. They will get to work immediately following New Year's Eve 1999."

Debbra escorted Kirk Moletta and Tom Nash from the conference room. The room sat silently while the door shut and Debbra returned to her seat.

Mark cleared his throat. His forehead pulsed in thought, poring over the conclusions surrounding them. It was as good a time as any to make his announcement. He braced for the response. "We are rapidly approaching the day when we cannot take on any more business. You just heard the harsh reality of power and phones. Either industry could keep our entire company busy full time for a decade. We don't have a decade and those aren't the only industries. We need to consider these facts carefully. It's time to prioritize and focus on our core strengths. We can't save everybody. We must choose who rides in our lifeboat."

"These industries are essential," Kleewein said.

"Yes, but others that we are considering are not."

"Such as?" Susan said.

"Such as the Department of Defense."

"Mark," Kleewein said, "the DoD is coming here on Monday. Shouldn't you have thought of this earlier?"

Susan glared at Mark. "Not only should you have thought of it earlier, perhaps you should rethink it period. Defending the nation is vitally important. You've said so yourself."

"It is important, but not as important as getting power and communications operational across the country. If power is out, distribution is down. That means no food on grocery shelves. What's the point of defending a country that can't eat?"

"What's the point of having food to eat if you do not have a country?" Kleewein asked, allowing his normally robotic voice to rise in volume. "Mark, this is a radical shift in your priorities. You have said in the past—and we have all agreed—that national defense is critical."

"But the defense industry's leaders haven't listened to us and I'm not sure that I trust them."

Susan stood, veins pushing through her neck. "They are coming on Monday! They *have* listened to us. After years of writing letters and making phone calls, we finally have their attention. Now you've decided you don't want it?"

Mark rocketed from his seat, face red and his own veins bulging to reach hers. "I have decided we can't save everybody! Is that clear? We can't save all the electrical companies, all the phone companies, all the grocery stores, all the airplanes, all the traffic signals, everything else that makes society work, and still have enough left over to get the U.S. military ready for a battle that probably won't happen. I want to save everybody, but let's be logical. It is better to completely fix a handful of critical industries than to try fixing everything and fail across the board."

Now Kleewein stood. The rest of the consultants and managers in the room sat wide-eyed as the executive team poised like boxers at the head of the table. "There's no disagreement over that part, Mark! There never has been. What we're saying is that defense is part of the handful we need to fix. When you find a chicken and egg situation there is no choice to be made. You need to figure a way to save both. That's where we find ourselves. We need to feed and shelter the country while at the same time defending it. There is no point having one without the other."

Mark lowered himself to the chair, palms down on the table in a calming pose. Nobody breathed. Susan and Kleewein sat. Mark leaned forward, gazing the table's length. His voice came like the careful instructions of a father teaching his son to shave. "I am not abandoning our stated objectives. I know why Margaret and I founded this company. I can't forget that. What I am saying now is that we need to strongly weigh the military's needs against our resources. We need to act prudently with all new clients. If we assess the military's needs and decide that we can handle them, fine. If not, we should allow ourselves the option of turning them away. Can we at least agree on keeping our minds open?"

It was not really a question, of course. It was rhetorical. He was the president. If he told them all to stand on their heads, they would eventually do it or they would find other jobs. But Mark Solvang lead by consent, not by force. It was a skill he learned from Margaret.

Nobody replied, but heads nodded around the room. "We're in this together for the best we can accomplish. Let's not dilute our strengths." He looked at the television. "Who has the remote?"

Kleewein clicked it. All eyes fixed on the screen to watch the President speak at the White House Millennium Event. After the usual platitudes, President Clinton, whose administration wanted to build a bridge to the next century using the information superhighway, broached Y2K.

"Now, as the millennium turns, as we have all seen from countless reports, so do the dates on our computers. Experts are concerned that many of our information systems will not differentiate between dates in the twentieth and the twenty-first century. I want to assure the American people that the federal government, in cooperation with state and local government and the private sector, is taking steps to prevent any interruption in government services that rely on the proper functioning of federal computer systems.

We can't have the American people looking to a new century and a new millennium with their computers—the very symbol of modernity and the modern age—holding them back, and we're determined to see that it doesn't happen."

Kleewein turned off the television. The conference room emptied without a word.

Mark sat at his desk late that night. His phone message light blinked furiously at him. His email folder listed dozens of messages needing his attention. The fax basket at the corner of his desk had reached capacity. Even three hours of steady progress through the workload seemed fruitless.

"Do you ever go home?" came Susan's voice from the doorway.

He lifted his eyes from a memo. "Not at this rate," he answered dreamily, still thinking about the memo. He leaned back in his chair and gestured for her to have a seat. "Are you making any better progress in your office?"

"Sure, but we're not supposed to be here." She looked across the table at him, a familiar expression in her brown eyes.

"We're not?"

"No," she said in a resigned voice. Her auburn hair sat in a tight bun atop her head. The shiny surface caught gold light from Mark's desk lamp, giving her a cozy look against the wood paneling. "It's Friday night. We were going to have dinner."

Mark's eyes closed. "You're right. I'm sorry, Susan."

She tossed a snack bar on his desk. "A girl can't live on these, you know." She smiled thinly.

"There's still tomorrow night," he tried. "We'll be working during the day, but we should take the night off."

"I'd love to. Think you'll be able to make it?"

"Come on, now," he said. "You know I need you."

She stood and walked to the doorway. "I know this corporation needs me. I'm not so sure about you."

AUGUST 18, 1997

Pritchett looked at the diesel smokestack protruding from The Keep, Solvang's San Jose headquarters. He was sure the company had been ridiculed for that, and equally sure the company had stood its ground. The business numbers indicated a firm that knew how to prove its ideas in the marketplace, and to shrug off naysayers.

He exited the rear seat of the Lincoln, followed by Schwager. Neither had spoken much on the flight or the short drive from San Jose Airport. They were forced by circumstance to spend time together. It boiled Pritchett's blood to recount the journey that brought him to the nation's best Year 2000 repair firm accompanied by a colleague he hated.

The two men were charged with assembling a successful century preparation strategy. Pritchett had been barking up and down the military ladder for years about needing to prepare for the century date change. It looked promising for a moment under the Bush administration, but was eclipsed by Gulf War activities. Only in early 1997 did the Army finally release a memo placing Y2K at top priority. The new Secretary of Defense, William S. Cohen, underscored the importance of keeping America's warfighters efficient and agile with equipment that won't let them down. Shooting guns and firing missiles was not as easy as it used to be. Modern planes, ships, radar, tanks, satellites, submarines, and even ground vehicles rely on computer chips.

Pritchett was not a man to despair. Yet, the task before him was truly overwhelming. The DoD had managed to make a mere 302 computer systems compliant with Y2K. That left more than 7,000 to go, and little of that effort was even combat related. Most of the systems getting attention were administrative. Vast amounts of energy were focused on bill paying, contract management, the logistics of moving warm bodies from Base A to Base B, and other details of running a military. An entire force of officers did nothing but analyze the viability of commercial off-the-shelf software and hardware. It had seemed to Pritchett from day one that paying bills was not nearly as important as the ability to shoot guns and fire missiles, but such is the way of a bureaucracy. It tends to its own existence before it tends to the reason it exists.

Pritchett would never say so publicly, but he doubted very much that they could make it in time. He stood in the warm California sun, staring at the diesel smokestack of Solvang Solutions. If any company could save America's fighting forces, it was this one. S2's marketing literature was the best he had reviewed. It didn't hard sell anything. It explained in excruciating detail how devastating Y2K would be and the steps that S2 was taking to save important companies. Mark Solvang's down-to-earth way of communicating appealed to Pritchett's own humble beginnings. Bootstrappers had a special place in Pritchett's heart, and this Solvang fellow seemed like one. Pritchett was most intrigued by the company's own preparations to survive a worst case scenario. That showed great foresight, an important trait to military planners.

Nonetheless, Pritchett would choose the military's contractors by the facts, not by emotional gut reactions. Good literature was one thing, good business was another.

Mark Solvang stood majestically in the center of the front lobby. His green and silver eyes projected a fierce intelligence, heightened by his aquiline nose. He wore a crisp black four-button suit with a black tie. His black hair caught the morning sun, fresh and ready to impress.

Pritchett shook hands firmly, noticing Mark's tie tack photo of himself with his wife and two small children. Pritchett had never seen such a tie tack before. The photo was rendered in classic black and gold with the date 1990 etched at the bottom.

"Mr. Pritchett and Mr. Schwager, welcome to Solvang Solutions. I'm Mark Solvang."

"A pleasure," Pritchett growled. He didn't want to appear too soft. Government contractors needed to know who was boss from day one.

"We finally see The Keep," Schwager said.

Mark nodded once, allowing a curt smile. "Gentlemen, I'm prepared to give you a quick tour of The Keep. I know that you are reviewing other vendors. You should know up front that we may already have enough work to keep us busy. After the tour and your presentation, we can discuss whether we are in a position to help you."

Schwager snapped to attention. "Are you saying that you don't want our business?" His voice rushed past his lips. He turned quickly to Pritchett and then back to Mark. "If you don't want our business, then we'll be going. There are plenty of firms that would kill to work with us. We are, after all, the United States Department of Defense."

Pritchett watched Mark during Schwager's verbal thrashing. Mark's face calmly looked at Schwager. Pritchett thought he detected a glimmer of amusement in the president's green and silver eyes. Mark remained quietly indifferent, as if to say to Schwager, "The door is right behind you. Thanks for stopping by."

Pritchett put his hand in the air, glaring at his colleague. "Hold on, Mr. Schwager." He faced Mark. "Mr. Solvang, I have the final say in this matter. I understand that your company is being pursued at the last minute by the largest and best paying corporations in the world, but the government can pay equally well."

Mark gestured for the two men to accompany him. "It's no longer a matter of money. It's a matter of time, Mr. Pritchett. Even with our capabilities, there is a limit to what we can accomplish in the time we have left." They walked through S2's corridors. They saw employees hard at work in cubicles, managers in offices, conference calls taking place, printouts taped to walls, heated meetings around computer monitors, and one employee asleep under his desk.

"Take this man, for example," Mark continued. "He probably hasn't been home in a week. Around here, sleeping at the workplace isn't a sign of laziness, it's a sign of extreme dedication. It's only 1997 and we're already working around the clock."

Pritchett noticed countdown clocks on several walls, the red numbers underscoring Mark's point. The digital readouts displayed 865 full days until the Year 2000. It seemed like such a long time at first glance, but it was not.

As they walked and talked, Pritchett detected something odd about Schwager. The point of their visiting Year 2000 repair firms was to assess the capabilities that each firm offered. Every question, every observation should have been focused toward that end. But the direction of Schwager's questions didn't indicate a curiosity in Solvang's capabilities. He seemed almost more interested in Solvang's limitations. The difference wasn't in the wording but in the way he asked, the way he seemed to memorize the location of every stop, the way he squinted his eyes. The creases on his cheeks flexed and folded as he absorbed all that Mark explained. Schwager carried a digital recorder in one hand. A small red light told Pritchett when it was on.

They stopped at the satellite control room and at the diesel room, both of particular interest to the military and both explained while Schwager's recorder blinked.

"Solvang Solutions is capable of continued operations even in blackout conditions. We can supply our own electricity at this, our main headquarters, and at each of our outposts around the country and overseas. Every S2 location is connected to our private satellite network. Because the satellites themselves are powered by batteries and solar cells, our diesel power on the ground is all that we need to maintain communications."

Schwager's cheeks glistened in the artificial light, the creases in his face becoming small aqueducts. Pritchett saw Mark look strangely at Schwager as he spoke. The self-sufficiency of Solvang was its distinguishing hallmark, made very bold in its literature. It was the first characteristic Pritchett noticed about the company, and an especially important one to the military. S2 marketing even inserted a special explanatory leaflet into its military vendor profile. None of this should have been a shock to Schwager, but there he stood like Mark had just shown him a top secret weapons facility.

"What if the diesel goes out?" Schwager asked.

"We have a full backup at major centers, and temporary backups at minor centers. It's as redundant a power system as we have space for." The red light blinked dutifully.

"How do you know your own systems won't fall victim to Y2K failures?" Pritchett asked.

"Through rigid procurement requirements and testing. Because we built our organization from the start to combat Y2K problems, our own compliance has always been part of our culture. We have the luxury of not needing to fix millions of lines of code or replace expensive equipment that isn't compliant. We only purchased or made compliant equipment. We only wrote compliant code. Y2K compliance has been a mandate for our company from the first day of business."

"How many consultants do you have?"

"Around 10,000 and growing. We expect to have 15,000 at the turn of the century."

"That's a lot of growth for two years."

"Business is booming. Everybody realized too late that they need to prepare for the inevitable. They're willing to pay almost anything. Prices will continue to rise from now until 2000. We expect COBOL programmers to earn more per hour than patent attorneys before the century's out."

"It must feel strange to charge for your services when you know you can't succeed," Schwager said.

"We can't succeed in full conversion for big business. We can still prepare an entire small to midsize business in time. For the big businesses, our triage program goes a long way toward keeping the most critical operations alive. No, we can't help them all, but we can do our best. Our best is better than anybody else's best."

They walked the last stretch of hallway toward the conference room.

"What sort of security do you have on the building?" Schwager asked. "It's important for military contracting."

"We plan to install badge readers and to establish secure areas," Mark said. "That's what your preliminary contracting guidelines suggest."

"Correct," Pritchett confirmed.

"Yes," Schwager said, "but what about defending against an all out attack?"

Mark looked at him, furrowing his brow. Pritchett stared at his colleague.

"An attack?" Mark asked.

"Yes. Your brief on the potential calamity of Y2K mentions riots and looting. How can you defend against that here?"

"We haven't planned for that. I don't think this is an area prone to rioting."

"So you have no defense against an attack?"

"That's right," Mark said, watching the recorder light blink. "We currently have no defense against an attack."

"And this is your main operations headquarters. If this location crumbles, your entire organization crumbles as well."

"It doesn't crumble. The other sites communicate with each other and could continue doing so without The Keep."

"But it would be a major disruption to lose this site."

"That's true, which is why we've built redundancy into all of our critical systems. We will remain operational from a technology standpoint. But we haven't planned a way to defend against an invasion."

Schwager nodded. The red light stopped blinking on his recorder. Mark looked uneasy, as if he'd just divulged case-winning information under cross examination with the opposing attorney.

Pritchett faced Schwager for an explanation, but received nothing in return.

"Right this way to our conference room," Mark said. "How fitting for today's meeting that we sometimes call it the war room."

"Yes, how fitting," Schwager said.

Kleewein, Susan, and several managers stood to greet the two men. Mark introduced the room to Pritchett and Schwager and explained that they were going to present the status of the U.S. military.

Pritchett looked at the faces in the room and felt a twinge of nervousness. He was accustomed to presentations, but never had he felt such a concentration of intelligence and scrutiny as he felt in the company of Mark Solvang's executives. Piercing eyes from men and women of all races fastened on him. For the first time in his long career of finding defense contractors, Pritchett felt that the contractor was deciding whether to accept the Department of Defense as a client. That was unheard of. Most potential contractors fall over themselves begging for the gravy train of government money. But the group before him didn't need the government's money. They offered salvage from the worst dilemma to ever face modern society, and they chose very carefully which lucky few would receive it.

"You are all aware that the U.S. military manages more computer code than any other entity in the country," Pritchett began. "You know that we run more computing power, rely on more embedded chip systems, and suffer the worst consequences when our technology fails us."

He picked up a piece of paper from his briefcase and donned his glasses. "This is the conclusion of an official Army memo from Major Ron Spears dated 31 March 1997: 'Therefore, effective immediately, all nonessential sustainment requirements and enhancements will be postponed until systems have been analyzed, fixed, tested, and certified Y2K compliant using existing resources.'" He removed his glasses. "You can see that the military has finally come to recognize the importance of Y2K."

Schwager interrupted the presentation. "We've read your briefs regarding the potential calamity of Y2K. If the situation proves as disastrous as you've projected, then the majority of the world's operable military equipment will be World War II vintage. That was the last era in which modern militaries did not rely heavily on computer systems."

Pritchett bit his tongue. He had intended to talk about World War II equipment himself. He hated being interrupted, particularly by Schwager.

"Several trends have brought the U.S. military to a critical situation regarding potential Y2K failures," Pritchett continued. "First, with the threat of nuclear war diminished and our core values of democracy sweeping through much of the world, we are reducing our troop count. Our overall force structure is down by at least forty percent. Our procurement budget is down sixty-seven percent. Second, the reduction of our troops increases our reliance on sophisticated weapons systems. The military of the future relies less on human bodies and more on advanced equipment. Third, the leadership of our country and the sentiment of the public at large does not perceive any military threat on the horizon. There is no cold war, there are no bad guys, there is only our happy blue planet as one neighborhood."

Pritchett breathed deeply through his nose. "I would not go so far as to say that the U.S. is complacent, but we are certainly not as poised as we've been in years past."

"You seem to think there are threats," Susan said. Her inquisitive eyes sharpened the air between her and Pritchett. "If so, then what are they?"

"To be fair, we do not see or expect a regional power or a peer competitor for the next ten or fifteen years. But we need to prepare for that possibility in the years beyond, and we must always stand ready for wild card scenarios. They are of low probability, but high consequence."

"Wild card scenarios?" Mark asked.

Pritchett nodded. He looked from face to face, making full use of the aged skin around his eyes to convey the importance of what he was about to say. He passed a stack of photos in glossy covers down each side of the table.

"These are pictures of China's military equipment. China has more people than any other country in the world. It has the largest World War II vintage military. It is still a communist country, despite the recent joy in the press about Hong Kong and the country's embracing of capitalism. The nation has tremendous economic potential, and the United States is one of its chief adversaries in the competition for economic leadership. Today, China's military poses no threat to the United States. Our planes are faster, our ships are superior, our infantry uses far more sophisticated equipment. In short, the United States is capable of defending itself against any foreign power, China included. However, take away that sophistication and we are reduced to a few footsoldiers who are unused to fighting the old way."

"That's a bit of an exaggeration," Schwager interrupted. "Naturally, we don't rely entirely on technology for our fighting superiority. A quick scan of the warfighting manual from the Marine Corps will reveal that. Technology is used to complement the human element, not replace it."

Pritchett watched the intelligent eyes of the Solvang executive team switch to Schwager when he spoke. Mark's gaze told all. He looked entirely unimpressed with Schwager, so unimpressed that Pritchett feared losing the company's interest with each additional remark from his colleague. Mark's eyes did not trust Schwager and, by extension, did not trust the military. That look was a familiar one to Pritchett. He'd seen it on the faces of reporters in press conferences and students at rallies.

Kleewein's detached expression pegged Schwager as somebody who had played games to attain his position, not as somebody who'd performed brilliantly. While Pritchett watched Kleewein, the vice president glanced at the agenda in front of him. Pritchett guessed that Kleewein checked Schwager's title. Pritchett winced at how it must appear to an achiever like Kleewein. Chief information officer for the Defense Information Systems Agency. It sounded like the most political organization a bureaucracy could offer, perfect for the maneuverings of a Schwager.

Pritchett glared at his colleague, trying his best to remain professional in front of the brain trust. He resumed his presentation in restrained tones.

"Nonetheless, you can appreciate the effect of abruptly removing technology from a fighting force that relies heavily upon it. In addition, China is not the only perceived threat under a Y2K scenario. The middle east, a perennial hot spot, utilizes warehouses full of old military equipment that will still function in a world without modern technology. Take away laser-guided missiles, satellite relays, infrared targeting, and other mainstays of our military and the Gulf War would have been far different. I am confident that we would still have won, but not without a great deal of fighting and loss of life."

Pritchett could feel the resistance in the room. This was definitely a civilian firm, unused to military concepts. But he believed in S2's capabilities, regardless of Schwager's doubts. If anything, Schwager's doubts added to the company's credibility.

"We understand the importance of technology to the military," Mark said. "But there is no way we can prevent Y2K from affecting America's armed forces. As we've stated numerous times to every industry, it's too late. The time has come for—"

"Triage," Pritchett finished for him. "Yes, I know. Which is precisely why we've come to you for a specific assignment. We are looking for a firm to prepare and monitor our critical battle operations. No accounting systems, no supply databases, no recruiting literature, just the warfighting systems. We need a technology special forces unit overseeing the transition to 2000."

"What exactly would that entail?" Mark asked.

"A dedicated team that has security clearance to examine and work on all military systems. A thorough inventory and analysis of military computing systems. A comprehensive failure projection scenario with contingency plans in place. A contract that extends beyond 2000 so that maintenance of all systems is covered. We understand that preparation is not foolproof."

"More to the point," Mark said, "preparation is guaranteed to contain problems. I need to be honest with you, Mr. Pritchett. We know for certain that we cannot prepare the military or any large business in time. The years during which that was possible are behind us now. We're eager to help in any way we can, but we insist on using our own contracts that limit our liability when—not if, mind you—your systems fail in 2000."

Pritchett was not surprised. "I'm pleased to hear that. It shows that you've done your homework and know what's most likely to fail."

"It's not hard to know what's likely to fail when the answer is everything," Kleewein said.

"I believe there are competing firms that guarantee success," Schwager mentioned. He flipped through his papers, looking at cover letters from CEOs of various Y2K firms. When nobody responded, Schwager looked up. His eyes met Mark's.

"Then use those firms," Mark said coolly.

"Are you suggesting that their guarantees are hollow?"

"I'm not suggesting anything. I'm telling you that we are the most capable Y2K preparation firm in the world. If we guarantee that we cannot fully prepare the U.S. military in the two-and-a-half years remaining, then you can draw your own conclusions regarding the guarantees of other firms."

"I already have," Pritchett said.

He had watched the room very carefully as he presented the threats to the U.S. military. Nobody was shocked. This was a firm that matched its glowing praise from congressmen. Its blunt honesty showed that it could assess problems fully and provide realistic projections. That's exactly what Pritchett wanted. No promises, just results.

"I am ready to proceed under your limited liability contracts," Pritchett said, firing a satisfied look at Schwager. "How long will it take your company to form a dedicated team and get to work?"

Mark thought. "We'll need to review your specification sheets and plan from there. My guess is that we can be working around the clock within six weeks." Susan nodded her agreement.

"Six weeks seems long given our time constraints," Schwager said. Pritchett detected a last ditch tone in Schwager's voice.

"Some things can't be sped up," Mark replied. "It takes a woman nine months to create a baby, no matter how eager you are to get the child. It will take us around six weeks to fully digest your specifications and plan the most prudent approach to the problem."

Pritchett's eyes gleamed. "We will complete our preparations quickly and overnight the appropriate documents to you."

Pritchett and Schwager shook hands around the room. Mark walked them to the lobby. Pritchett thanked him for his time, then walked with Schwager down the cement pathway to the Lincoln. He took one last look at The Keep before stepping into the back seat. He still liked that diesel smokestack.

The conference room sat quietly upon Mark's return, a condition he'd come to expect after the company's increasingly gloomy meetings. All eyes watched him proceed to his chair and sit down. "Does anybody object to working with them?"

Heads shook around the room, but still nobody spoke. Kleewein's eyes projected across the table, larger than the rest.

"Is something wrong, Kleewein?"

"What if the military takes over our operations when the lights go out?"

Mark sat still. He expected to hear fears of not getting enough work done in time, of having the military hold S2 responsible for its Y2K failures.

But, take over S2?

He hadn't seen that one coming. Evidently, he was alone. Everybody else looked at him, sharing the concern in Kleewein's face. "Are you serious?" he asked at last.

"Deadly serious."

"Where did that come from?"

"From years of working with bastards and knowing one when I see him. Did you watch that Schwager? There's something fishy about that guy. Pritchett seems okay, aside from being a military pawn."

"Think about it, Mark," Susan said. "We have a company that knows more about Y2K than any other. We're the only business that can continue operating after doomsday. They know and we know that nobody can fully prepare the military by 2000. Pritchett said he's interested in contracts that extend our duties beyond the millennium to handle any problems with preparation. You pointed out that those problems are guaranteed. Pritchett then eagerly agreed to work with us. What do you think they're going to do when the lights go out and they can't function and we're sitting here happy as clams with our terminals up and our phones ringing?"

"You don't really think they'd come in and take over, do you? What would be the point? They don't know how to run our show as well as we do."

"They don't need to run the show," Kleewein said. "They only need to make sure we run the show the way they want it run."

Mark couldn't believe his ears. "What happened to last Friday's belief that we need to work with the military? We've changed sides here."

"Schwager is what happened," Susan said quietly.

Mark nodded. "There is something wrong with him. But even if the military has ulterior motives in mind, what can we do? We might as well fix them and get paid for it. They know about us whether we help them or not. We'll still be here with electricity and telephones regardless of who worked with them. Most importantly, there's nothing we can do about this worry. If they want to take us over, they'll take us over."

"You're wrong, Mark," Susan said, standing and pacing the room. "We need contingency plans. Our mission from the start was to be able to withstand the Y2K disaster so that we could help get society back on its feet. That's why you and Margaret started this place. We never confined our definition of 'disaster.' If it means a government gone awry, then we need to be prepared to deal with that. Let's stick to our mission. We didn't all join hands to build this organization only to let it be misused by a runaway bureaucracy to serve its own purposes."

"Wait a minute," Mark said. "A functional military is hardly a runaway bureaucracy. It serves an important purpose. Pritchett's explanations of threats to the United States are real."

"Maybe, then again they've used fake threats in the past to get more funding. I don't see why they wouldn't use fake threats now to—"

"To what? Fix their computers? Where's the evil in that?"

The room fell quiet once more. Susan took her seat again. Mark mulled the views of his executive team. On Friday, he wanted to turn down the military; others wanted to sign them on. Today, he signed them on; others thought it was the wrong decision.

"Hire the best security force in the country," Kleewein suggested, his voice cutting through the silence in characteristic form.

"Security force?" Mark asked. "To combat the military?"

"Yes, if necessary, and any other threat."

"I don't see how a security force could stand a chance against the military."

"I said the best security force in the country. Let them figure out the details. We have enough money to pay for the services we need. All of this is just planning for the worst. If nothing comes of it, it was a cheap insurance policy."

"What are we becoming, our own country?" Susan asked.

Mark rested on his elbows. "We might be the only country still intact two-and-a-half years from now."

4

THE COUNTDOWN

JULY 6, 1998

"It should come as no shock that S2 poses the largest job we've ever faced."

Jules Hartmire spoke plainly to Mark Solvang, the only way he ever addressed clients. They walked a cement pathway across green lawns and through hills around The Keep. They were joined by Hartmire Security lieutenants Eric Elwell, a former marine; Chris Lauer, a former FBI agent; and Todd Klepac, a former BATF agent. They had turned down drinks from the executive briefing center. It was not the style of Hartmire Security to sip beverages while discussing business.

Mark looked severe to Hartmire, who was himself a severe-looking man. Hartmire wore a dark blue business suit with no jewelry. His hair was short, his shoulders broad, and his wide-set black eyes extremely alert. Years of training taught him to observe his surroundings. When Hartmire and his lieutenants first arrived, they met Mark in his office. Photos of Mark with his wife and children hung on the walls, but they were old photos. Newer photos showed only Mark and the children, much older now. A few photos included an elderly couple Hartmire assumed to be the grandparents. There was no evidence of a new woman, leading Hartmire to conclude that the wife had not left through divorce. The wife was dead.

"S2 is an unusual business," Mark said. "We are preparing for extreme circumstance like this country has never seen. It took me six months to find your company and another four months to run background checks. I hired a private investigation firm to make sure you are free from government connections and I hired a second private investigation firm to check on the first. I think you're the right company for the job, but I want to be very honest about the nature of this assignment. You need to understand the power of our potential enemies."

Jules Hartmire nodded solemnly. He had already considered S2's needs before agreeing to an onsite visit that day. He would not have come unless he was sure that Hartmire Security could handle the job. Still, it would be a challenge. "After reading the briefings you sent, I do understand." His deep voice resonated authority.

They crested a grassy hill north of the Solvang buildings. Mark looked to be in shape, but Hartmire heard quicker breathing from their host. Neither Hartmire nor his three lieutenants, all wearing suits and walking in dress shoes, noticed climbing the hill.

Most men were intimidated by Jules Hartmire, a fact he had come to expect over the years. It fit his business and even increased the amount he could charge clients. He was no amateur. He had served his country as an Army Ranger. He received a purple heart and a silver star in Vietnam after sustaining three bullet wounds while carrying wounded soldiers to a helicopter, a bronze star for covert actions in the Middle East, and a bronze star for gathering critical intelligence in the Gulf War.

Hartmire had no regrets except one. From childhood he had been tougher than his peers. Most people weren't foolish enough to fight with Jules Hartmire, those who were served as cautionary tales for other potential rivals. He had never decided to become a tough man any more than a cheetah decides to run fast. It was built in. In a late night skirmish, he blinded a man several years older than himself in one eye by punching with his middle knuckle extended. Nobody taught him that technique. He was born knowing.

But his abilities came with a price. His combat history and aggressive nature kept him from marrying, a situation that saddened even a hard man like Hartmire. He knew that he liked Mark Solvang from their correspondence and conversations on the phone, but he couldn't say why. Sure, Mark was the picture of professionalism, knew what he wanted, and was willing to pay for extraordinary services. Those were excellent qualities in a client. But there was something even beyond those traits that made him likable.

After sitting in Mark's office and drawing conclusions from the photo history, Hartmire knew what it was. As different as his life had been from Mark Solvang's, the two shared a deep sadness. Neither man was married and neither man was happy about it.

Eric Elwell gazed across rolling grass to The Keep. "We do not hire shopping mall security guards, Mr. Solvang. Most Hartmire professionals have seen real-life combat in the field, whether military or para-military activity such as police work. Our forces consist of award-winning men and women who behave prudently under extreme circumstances."

Hartmire spoke with deadly calm. "The U.S. military is a formidable opponent on even the smallest scale. To make this absolutely clear, if the U.S. military wants to take over S2, it will take over S2. Neither my firm nor any other can prevent that. The military cannot be resisted by brute force."

Mark looked into Hartmire's black eyes. It was obvious to Hartmire that Mark understood. Nobody in his right mind would expect a security firm to resist the military. "How exactly would you defend The Keep from a takeover? It's not a military structure."

"We plan to make it one," Klepac answered. "There are four entrances to The Keep. Each will be fitted with a reinforced steel door. We will also install bulletproof glass windows around the immediate entry points."

Elwell continued the explanation. "We will station a guard at each entrance and dozens throughout the building on both preset and random patrol paths. Hartmire guards carry normal sidearms during the course of each day, but will have access to high power rifles, explosives, and riot gear at their stations. The heavy entrance doors will be powered by hydraulics. If they are rushed, our guards can retreat to their stations, push a button to force the steel doors shut, and return fire through slits in the door and surrounding wall."

Mark looked across the grass to his building. "You've got to be kidding me. This seems absurd."

"I hope so," Hartmire said quietly. "I hope we install this fancy equipment, train the best guards in the business, and wait while the equipment gathers dust and the guards never shoot at anything but a paper target. I hope at the end of 2000 you come to me and say, 'Jules, what a waste of money you were.'"

"How soon can your defense plans be fully implemented?" Mark asked.

"By early 1999. We will make the confidential nature of this assignment an integral part of our training program. Every guard working at an S2 site will understand the company's business, the threats to its operations, and its contingency plan."

"Contingency plan?" Mark asked.

"Yes. It's important to remember that we cannot resist a full attack from the military. Therefore, we recommend developing a contingency plan. We've begun working on it. You'll know more as we finalize the details. You hired us to defend your firm's ability to operate in any condition. We intend to do just that."

"I seem to have found the right firm for the job," Mark announced. "Welcome to Solvang Solutions."

"It's a pleasure to be here," Hartmire replied.

"One more thing. I assume that shooting is a last resort?"

"Mr. Solvang, we are not bloodthirsty. We do not want to shoot anybody." Hartmire clamped a hand on Mark's shoulder, drawing the intelligent green and silver eyes into his own black dots of fury. "But if the situation becomes severe enough to warrant shooting, Hartmire guards will shoot to kill. We do not warn with bullets, we do not threaten with bullets, we do not wound with bullets. If it's important enough to shoot, it's important enough to kill."

December 7, 1998

The phone call came from far across the ocean. Mark answered himself. He instantly recognized the caller's voice.

"Embedded systems are going to kill us. We can't keep up, Mark. It's beyond our control and we're going to need help."

Mark checked his watch. "Fly to San Jose immediately."

Dan Van Lan could get more excited about computers than anything else in life. He sported a full beard and chubby cheeks that obscured his mouth. His rotund figure jiggled during excited tirades in front of a computer as words spilled from somewhere deep inside his beard and cheeks. His supercilious blue eyes tracked the world from their outposts behind glasses, under bushy eyebrows, and surrounded by folds of skin.

He looked more like an ewok than a computing whiz, but he was one of S2's finest team leads. He could have joined the company's founders if he'd been old enough in 1990 when Mark and Margaret formed the company. He didn't graduate from MIT until 1991, when he joined S2 fresh from college. He was only twenty-one years old and already knew more about computers than anybody Mark had ever met.

Kleewein took Dan under his wing almost immediately. Susan thought the quick bond had to do with their shared oddness. Kleewein spoke and thought like a robot, and his enlarged cranium added to the effect. Dan slumped from room to room, hairier than many four-legged mammals. He fixed difficult problems casually, devising solutions with a brilliance that seemed entirely inappropriate for a man of his countenance.

Those who worked with Dan discovered a kindness not immediately discernible through his hairy face. He was careful to watch work schedules and balance the load between members of his team. He formed friendships for life and rarely allowed work difficulties to interfere. Mark once read a memo from Dan to a disgruntled programmer who demanded to be moved to another team because he couldn't stand a colleague. Dan's memo encouraged the worker to place more value on the human side of his job. "After all," the memo concluded, "people are all that really matters in our lives. When was the last time a computer cheered you up?"

Dan was responsible for developing the problem search routines of *Solvang2K*. After the completion of version two, Dan moved from development to consulting. His team became one of the most effective in the company. He began with only five members, then fifteen, then forty. The Van Lan group worked its way from small business information systems to insurance companies to banks to the Boeing account. Dan and his team lived full time in Seattle until Mark called them back to San Jose. Dan protested, saying that every minute counted. Mark assured him that he understood, but that minutes counted even more elsewhere. Dan flew back to San Jose and discovered that Mark wanted him to lead the Department of Defense account.

"You want me to fix the DoD?" he had said in his theatrical style only a day after Pritchett and Schwager made their presentation. "Mark, how can you ask me to do this? You know my background."

Dan grew up in a household that abhorred the military. His father served in Vietnam where he lost his two best friends. When he finally returned to the states, he met with ridicule and a military that refused to honor its promises of education money. He sat Dan on a park bench in Boston while there was still time for his son to refuse admission to the military academy at West Point.

"Dan," his father said in a mortician's voice, "I know it's exciting to get this much attention. I know everybody in school has heard about your congressional appointments. I know your test scores are among the highest in the nation. You deserve the best and the military puts on a good show. But look harder, son. It's an illusion. Your intelligence will not matter when men are dying and contracts aren't worth their paper and you realize that, in the end, the only thing your brains are good for is killing. You deserve more than that, son. Think hard. It's your life and you are a genius. Do some good for the world."

Dan listened to his father. He turned down the academy and poured his abilities into a top-flight civilian education and a slew of job offers. He accepted the offer from Solvang Solutions. It fit his father's advice to do some good for the world, advice Dan could not forget. And now, Mark was asking him to use his abilities to further the very organization that his father had taught him to hate.

"Mark, you know I can't do this. I've told you how I feel about the military. You know why I came here."

"You can do it," Mark told him. "You came here because you wanted to do some good for the world. I'm not asking you to go to war, Dan. I'm asking you to help the military protect men like your father. There are good people in uniform, Dan. They depend on computers. You are a computing genius working for the only company capable of helping. You will be doing good for the world."

After a fancy meal that night and a salary increase the next morning, Dan agreed to head the team that would repair the U.S. military. On the phone to his father, Dan explained that he was going to help the military protect its men and women. He was finally able to believe in his new mission only after his father took a deep breath and said, "Son, you made the right choice. Do your best."

Dan Van Lan took his team of fifty-one consultants and began working eighteen-hour days on the DoD account. Pritchett and Schwager overnighted every document the team needed. By the end of 1997, Dan's team had grown to 524 full time S2 consultants working in twenty-two different locations. Dan spoke to Pritchett every morning and to Kleewein every afternoon. He made trips to remote military sites to drop off two-man teams for quick three-week assignments. S2 consultants showed up on Wake Island and Pearl Harbor. The colored pins Mark used on his wall map to track S2 presence spread across the world.

On December 7, 1998, Dan placed the emergency call about embedded chips. On December 8, he arrived at The Keep with a presentation for S2's executives.

"I believe we're making good progress on the software," Dan said in his voice deep within the beard. "We've already tested targeting systems for Navy surface-to-air missiles and they check out. We're close to doing the same for Air Force plane-mounted missiles. The software is not the problem. Embedded systems are."

"Have you run a complete test on the Navy missiles, or just the software?" Susan asked.

"Just the software. The Navy has an excellent simulation environment that allows us to load the targeting software and then test it against just about any variable. When we first started, they didn't have a variable for a malfunctioning chip system. So we helped them write one with our best guesses as to how a misbehaved chip would act. The results were disastrous."

"What do Schwager and Pritchett say?" Kleewein asked.

"Schwager said everything's going to be fine. He never shows concern even though I've gone out of my way to convey that the situation is critical. I don't like him. He's an idiot."

"And Pritchett?" Mark asked, taking notes on a pad.

"He understands. He's contacting the chip manufacturers, but the progress is slow. I'm sounding the alarm now, barely one year before 2000. If those chips aren't replaced then our software fixes are worthless. We are wasting our time if the hardware can't respond to instructions."

"Have you encountered embedded systems anywhere else?" Kleewein asked. "So far you've just mentioned missiles."

"Not yet, but they're waiting for us. Specifically, radar units, communication subsystems, digital engine control, and flight navigation are exposed. Fighter plane engines are so complex and sensitive that a pilot can't tend to them while carrying out the requirements of his mission. So the military developed a system called Full Authority Digital Engine Control, or FADEC. It's a real time interface between the pilot and the aircraft flight control computer. FADEC handles the power requirements of the pilot's maneuvers by monitoring every system on the aircraft and responding appropriately in less than fifty milliseconds. It's a very sophisticated system, and one that uses embedded chips everywhere.

We're not sure which ones will fail, but I would not want to be relying on a FADEC system in 2000."

"FADEC is entirely hardware driven?" asked Susan.

"No, there's a token software system, but most of the problem lies in the chips. We hoped that FADEC chips wouldn't use date or time functions, but they do. Part of FADEC's job is to alert mechanics to maintenance schedules. Schedules require time stamps, time stamps mean dates, dates mean broken chips."

"What's the next task on your list?" Mark asked.

"We're supposed to start work on the Navy and Air Force flight navigation software next week. I'm doubtful. The signals use different receivers on different types of aircraft. Inertial Navigation Systems and Global Navigation Satellite Systems, abbreviated INS and GNSS respectively, are the same technology used for commercial purposes. So, any advancements S2 has made in oil drilling companies or back at Boeing would be greatly appreciated."

"Don't hold your breath," Kleewein said.

"I won't. Remember, I used to run the Boeing account. Navigation is at least as complicated as FADEC."

"Does anything look like it will be completely fixed by 2000?" Mark asked.

"Not at this point. The military fights with software-controlled delivery systems. The software by itself has a good chance of being fixed. But, as I said, that doesn't matter if the chips are broken. It's like repairing the engine of your car without buying tires for it."

APRIL 19, 1999

Susan spent Monday mornings checking with lead managers at The Keep. She walked from department to department, writing down pressing issues on a notepad as she went, dispensing information, keeping tabs on S2's operations. After checking in with Nikolaas Groen, the lower terminal room manager, she sat on the edge of a planter in the hallway to jot a few notes. Consultants milled around the bulletin board to read current postings. They did not notice Susan sitting behind them, obscured by leaves.

"I tell you what," a tester told a COBOL developer, "if this gets as ugly as they say it's going to get, there's no way you'll find me in here on New Year's Eve 1999."

Susan tilted her head to listen. That day's posting revealed the latest field reports from S2's world locations. Each Monday got bleaker and bleaker. The current one reported more evidence from Pacific Gas & Electric showing that California would be without power for at least two weeks, possibly longer.

"I hear you," the developer said. He read the posting headlines. "No lights, no phones, no food, no thanks. I'm sitting by a well-stocked pantry with a shotgun to protect my wife and kids. The rest of the world can fend for itself."

"We aren't the only ones who feel this way," the tester responded. "My whole department has discussed it. None of us are going to be here. This place will be a cemetery at midnight."

The two men walked down the hallway, leaving chills along Susan's neck. She hurried through the rest of her morning checkups then knocked on Mark's office door.

"What is it?" he asked.

"We won't have any employees on New Year's Eve 1999."

"What are you talking about?"

"I just overheard a discussion at the bulletin board outside the lower terminal room. Think about it. We've been telling them how bad it's going to get. We've been predicting no lights, no phones, no food, no security systems. What kind of parent or spouse is going to come to work while the world explodes around their home?"

Mark pinched the top of his nose and closed his eyes. He saw Jeremiah and Alyssa sitting with Grandpa Solvang, reading a book. He saw flames outside and shadowy figures carrying guns in the street. He saw leering grins in the window, waiting for the right moment to break through the glass and pillage the old kitchen and hurt his parents and take the children.

"You're right," he said at last, snapping his eyes open to look at Susan. "You're absolutely right. Nobody will come here unless they know their families are safe."

"Then what do we do?"

"Make sure their families are safe. Get Kleewein and our management team. I want to draft a memo."

April 21, 1999

TO: All 12,511 Solvang Solutions Employees
FROM: Mark Solvang, President
DATE: April 21, 1999
SUBJECT: Solvang Solutions Y2K Survival Kit

Our mission at Solvang Solutions is to save the world from the impending Year 2000 computer crisis. As one of S2's cherished employees, you already know that. But it is more important to you and to me that you save your family first. We can't save anybody else until we've saved those we love most.

Therefore, I am pleased to present you with seven simple steps to take toward ensuring your family's survival. By taking precautions now, you better your family's chance of a smooth adjustment to life in the first months of the Year 2000, and you also free your mind for the valuable service we are asking you to provide here at S2.

Here, then, are the seven simple steps:

Purchase a one-year supply of nonperishable foods. For each person in your home, store fifty gallons of water in deoxygenated containers.

Purchase a pistol, rifle, and 1000 rounds of ammunition for each. Become proficient with both weapons and make sure that your spouse and older children are also proficient.

If you live in a cold climate, stock enough firewood to last the entire 1999-2000 winter.

Get a complete physical and begin exercising regularly.

Purchase a one-year supply of everyday medicine such as pain killers and first aid kits, and a one-year supply of prescription medications. Purchase two pairs of spare eyeglasses for everybody who needs them. Inoculate every member of your family against major third world diseases such as cholera, tetanus, typhus, and hepatitis A, B, and C.

Keep hard copies of all 1999 financial and billing records in a fireproof box. Request stock certificates from brokers.

Obtain copies of your credit report both before and after 2000 to check for errors.

You are in better position than most of the world to know that the situation we face with Y2K is a serious one. It is impossible to be too prepared. By following these seven steps, you can be sure that you have done everything in your power to protect your family from a millennium disaster.

Please photocopy this memo and distribute it freely to your friends and extended family. The more people we prepare for Y2K, the better we'll all survive it.

Warm Regards,

Mark Solvang
President

APRIL 26, 1999

"We aren't the only people who need to know," Mark said in the conference room. The feedback from employees had been tremendous. They hung the memo in their cubicles and placed it on their refrigerators at home. It was still common to see consultants leaning against S2 bulletin boards in the hallways, committing the seven tasks to memory. Mark had gathered Kleewein, Susan, and top managers to discuss ways to get the word out to a broader audience.

"We can't just send the memo to the entire world," Susan said.

"Why not?" Mark asked. "We can buy full-page ads in major papers. We no longer need our marketing budget—we can't handle any new business. Let's use those dollars to prepare people for what's coming."

"It'll look too much like a real advertisement," Kleewein said. "People will question our intentions. We should work it into a press release instead."

Susan reworked the memo into a press release and delivered it to the publicity department. It went out that day. Phones began ringing almost immediately.

"Mark," Dana Marsh from the *San Jose Mercury News* said into the phone. Being from his home town, she was the only reporter who addressed him by his first name as if they were old friends. "Are you sure these survival suggestions are in the best interest of the public?"

"Of course they are. How could they not be?"

"People are saying S2 has failed in its work and is now creating a smoke screen of goodwill."

"We haven't failed at anything and you know it," Mark huffed into the phone. "You're an insider around here, Dana. You know how hard we work. You also know that we've been telling people for years that they need to get moving on this issue or it will be too late. When it became too late to fully solve everything, we publicly announced the fact and suggested that companies fix what they could in the time that was left. Now, we're taking the next logical step, which is to tell the people who depend on those businesses to prepare for the worst case scenario. Our suggestions were initially intended for our employees only. Then we realized the public needs to know, too."

"It's a business-building stint."

"No, it's not. We already have more business than we can handle."

"So you *have* failed in your work."

"Dana, I'm saying that we're trying our best while keeping a realistic eye on the situation. A lot of computers are going to break in 2000. Some of them are critical to the lives of ordinary people. The memo is intended to help those ordinary people survive the meltdown."

The New York Times ran a story about the decision to send the survival memo, without even printing the points of the memo. *The Chicago Tribune* printed a one-panel cartoon depicting Mark Solvang hurling a brick through a family's living room window into the monitor of their home computer. Tied to the brick was a letter titled "S2 Survival Memo." It read, "Prepare for Year 2000 computer problems now! Call Solvang Solutions at 888-REAL-BAD." The deer-eyed daughter who had been working at the computer turned to her father and said, "But Daddy, our computer was working fine a minute ago."

Internet investment sites jumped on the Y2K investment gamble. NeatMoney.com wrote extensively on Solvang Solutions. It pointed to the firm's private satellite network and diesel generators as proof that S2 believed what it wrote. The article lamented S2's choice to remain a private company.

Rush Limbaugh interviewed Mark over the phone. Limbaugh was concerned that the message of S2's memo had been lost in the media slant. "Folks, you're hearing it here first, as is so often the case. The Year 2000 has the potential to affect your lives in many ways, most of which can be lessened by following the seven suggestions on this press release. Ignore the popular media. They're wrong, which is why they're popular. This is not a publicity stint, this is a public emergency announcement."

"Thank you, Rush," Mark said from the phone in his office. "Y2K is a grave problem that we're trying hard to reduce. But there's no harm in preparing for catastrophe before the day."

"And it's not just home computers that will be affected, as I understand."

"No, in fact home computers won't be much of a concern. Macintosh computers won't be affected at all. The computers to worry about are the ones people never see. The big mainframes that run phone companies, television networks, power plants, banks, and air traffic control. The little chips that run cars, can openers, and digital watches. Your listeners calling in right now are being directed through phone company switches that might break in 2000. This radio program itself depends on the EIB network, which uses sophisticated equipment to broadcast to millions. It could all end in an instant, like flipping a light switch."

"That's it in a nutshell," Rush said, rattling papers in the background. "I'm holding in my hands the press release sent from S2 just days ago. It contains seven things to do to get your family ready for the Year 2000 computer problem. You won't read the seven points in the press. Why? Dear friends, you should know by now the answer to that question. Because the media loves buzz, not information. Calling this a marketing ploy is a better buzz than identifying it as important material. I see it for what it is and will repeat the seven points when we come back in a moment. You're listening to Rush Limbaugh, talent on loan from God."

"Rush," Mark cut in quickly before the break, "we could use some time on loan from God."

MAY 2, 1999

Tom Clausen stepped into the cool Sunday morning air to retrieve the *Los Angeles Times*. His Encino neighborhood was quiet except for the sound of birds singing. The town provided him with the best of everything. Downtown Los Angeles was only a thirty-minute drive southeast and some of the best surfing beaches were only a forty-minute drive southwest. He grabbed the paper and walked to the kitchen table.

He moved his belt and LAPD badge out of the way. It had been a long Saturday night and he wasn't able to sleep when he got home. He went straight to the kitchen for a bowl of cereal and left his equipment on the table. Very bad form. He carried the pistol, handcuffs, pepper spray, and badge to the bedroom. He quietly hung them in the closet, careful to close the door gently so he didn't wake Adelle, his wife of two years.

Back in the kitchen, he poured himself a cup of coffee and settled in front of the paper. He didn't read right away. The sun poured through the breakfast nook, capturing Tom's thoughts. He had dated Adelle for eight years, then married her. Ever since they married, things had slowly deteriorated. That's how Adelle described it to her sister over the phone one night. Nothing was tragically wrong. It was just not quite right.

Tom told Adelle that it was his fault. He wasn't the same happy-go-lucky kid she met in college. Joining the LAPD changes a man in a lot of ways. Especially a white man. Tom needed one-hundred percent on his tests just to get in. His fellow officers knew that, so they watched him to see if he could live up to the score. If he'd been a minority or a woman, he could have skated in with a seventy. But he was a young white man and he needed one-hundred and he got it. It brought a lot of pressure. When he busted a usual— shorthand for a young, black male—he was racist. When he didn't, he was patronizing. And he was always in danger of being sued, even if he was clearly upholding the law. It was hard for him and he felt it change his outlook on life and the course of his marriage. Tom's situation was common among police officers, a fact that made it harder for him to accept. He read about it in the officer's guide and listened to veterans warn him about it, but he had been unable to prevent it.

Adelle talked about getting her own apartment, but he said no. They could work through these hard times as they promised each other in their vows. They could endure hollow greetings and dreaded comings home for the greater good of their marriage. Tom needed Adelle. He couldn't imagine living without her. He loved her more than ever, and he believed she loved him.

He opened the paper to the headline, "Prepare Now for Year 2000" followed by the hook, "Year 2000 repair firm suggests seven ways to save your family." Tom remembered a department presentation about potential security breaches caused by a computer date problem. He read the story.

Tom felt Adelle's presence in the air before she arrived. She shuffled to the kitchen with doleful steps, offering a weak "good morning" as she poured a cup of coffee. She plopped into the chair opposite him, looking across the table with red eyes that had seen their last of yesterday through tears.

"How'd it go last night?" she asked.

"The way it always goes." It sounded harsh as he said it, the last feeling he wanted to convey. He quickly pointed to a present on her side of the flower centerpiece. "But I bought you something."

She opened a bottle of perfume, gave a shy look at him, and sprayed it on her wrists. "Thank you, Tom," she said, coming around the table to hug him. She smiled, and he thought it a genuine smile.

"What's news today?" she asked.

"This," he said, pointing at the headline. "Remember when I told you about the department's security concerns over the Year 2000?" She nodded. "Well, apparently we're not the only ones. This company in the Bay Area says everybody needs to be careful because the whole world's going to end. They say we should stock up on food and medicine and keep our bank statements."

"Sounds smart to me. I read something about it in *Newsweek* not too long ago. Let's go today."

"Go where?"

"Shopping for food. I need to go to the store anyway. Why don't you come with me and we'll start stocking."

He pulled her onto his lap, smelling the new perfume and feeling her silk nightgown slide across his legs. "I don't care where we go today as long as we go together." His words sounded forced.

Meanwhile, in a tiny collection of homes on a hill outside Portland, Gary Maris eyed the same story in *The Oregonian*. His wife Patricia whistled in the background as she whipped together a batch of crepes for Gary and their two daughters, Claire and Danielle, both of whom watched TV in the next room.

"Finally!" Gary yelled across the kitchen. Patricia stopped whistling. "Somebody had the guts to tell it like it is."

"Tell what like it is?" Patricia asked.

"Y2K, honey. It's all you've heard me talk about for three years. It's the reason I can't sleep at night. Chief information officers tremble in their boots at the mention of that weird little word, Y2K. Remember when you wondered if it could be as bad as I thought? Well, wonder no more. Take a look at this."

She walked over with a spatula and hot pad to peruse the headline. She was used to outbursts from her husband, a passionate sailor and part-time philosopher who never felt indifferent toward anything. He was either fanatically in favor or psychotically opposed. There was no middle ground for Gary Maris.

Particularly in this case. Gary was the information technology manager at Brysco Distributors in downtown Portland. That was his self-described "food on the table, gas in the tank" job. He would have much rather spent life lounging with his women, as he referred to Patricia and his daughters, and sailing his thirty-two-foot sloop rig in the Columbia River. But life's course is hard to steer and Gary ended up managing the computer systems at one of the West Coast's largest food distributors. He watched the clock count down to what he saw as the most severe technology dilemma to ever face his company and, as that day's article proved, the world.

Patricia returned to the stove. "I still don't see how it could be that bad, Gary. No lights, no phones, no food?"

Gary let the paper fall from his hands to the table. He stood loudly, almost bumping his head on the hanging light. "Yes, my dear! Yes! It will be that bad. I can guarantee the food part and I'm pretty darned sure about the lights and phones. It could be hell out there."

"Hell? Listen to you. We live in paradise."

From the next room, a portable phone rang. Claire answered and began speaking. Before Gary could reply, somebody's pager jingled in a remote part of the house.

"Oh, paradise, sure. Have you seen our daughters' boyfriends recently? They're minions of Hell. They dress in black, carve designs into their ankles, shave their forearms. Danielle's latest fling pinned a dead cockroach to his lapel, honey. How's that for a homecoming date? I'm so proud putting their pictures on my desk." He took a sip of orange juice. "Believe me, anything that happens to the rest of the world can happen right here in Portland too."

Patricia chuckled. Her husband never failed to amuse. "Fine,

Gary. I won't care if the world ends as long as you promise to keep your enthusiasm."

"Great to hear." He sat down and began writing furiously on a pad of paper.

"What are you doing now?"

"Making a list of the items we need from the store today. This article got me thinking. Let's beat the crowd and start filling the garage. We can't be too prepared."

He jumped from the table, trotted to the edge of the kitchen. "Claire, Danielle, up and at 'em!" he yelled through cupped hands.

"Claire's on the phone and I'm watching TV!"

Gary looked back at Patricia, who just shrugged. "Nobody ever listens to me around here."

"Try calling them on the portable phone," she suggested.

"Or I could always page one of them." He cupped his hands again. "The world's ending soon and we need to stock up on food. Let's get going, ladies! Phones down, pagers off. There's not a moment to spare!"

MAY 11, 1999

"Bank withdrawals reach their highest level in decades. Story at 11:00," said the news trailer.

All eyes glued on the television that night as heads across the country reported that withdrawals had increased by five percent in the past week. Five percent is a minor fluctuation for the banking system, but the media saw big news.

"Some speculate that America is not taking chances with possible Year 2000 bank failures," reported news anchor Jane Roman in Los Angeles. "An April 26 news release from prominent Year 2000 repair firm Solvang Solutions sparked widespread concern with the computer date problem. Worries have led many to literally take their money into their own hands. Lidia Aceves reports."

Lidia stood in front of the Glendale Wells Fargo building with a man in his thirties. "Ryan Crabtree doesn't like taking chances with his money. Today he decided that he would rather have cash in hand than numbers in a computer. Ryan, what do you find most frightening about banks today?"

She held the microphone to Ryan's mouth. "Most of all I'm just thinking about my family. I don't want to leave my money somewhere I can't get it. Banks haven't figured out their computers, so I'm keeping my money until they do."

"Were you afraid that if you waited there wouldn't be any money left?"

"Hell yes. It's all over the news. My grandparents told me about the Great Depression and I've been reading about it in the papers lately. If it happened back then it could happen today. I'm not going to get my family's dinner from a trash dumpster."

"Why today? Why did you decide on this day to withdraw your money from Wells Fargo?"

"Because I was driving to work and I heard on the radio that people were lining up at the ATMs before the lobbies opened. One guy said he could only withdraw 300 dollars a day from the machine, so he got in line for a teller. I exited the freeway and saw a line at Bank of America and I said to myself, 'that's it. I'm getting my money.' So I came over here and got it."

"Was there a long line?"

"Not a long one. But people were upset. There were a lot of old people in line and they stood very still with bank statements under their arms."

Similar news stories broke in towns everywhere. People heard 'banks,' saw lines, and jumped to conclusions. Small lines became big and big lines became huge. Within days, the number of withdrawals went from thousands to hundreds of thousands.

The five percent jump had occurred on a Tuesday. By Friday, more than two-million accounts had closed. Banks in Boston, Chicago, New York, Miami, and San Francisco put velvet ropes outside their doors to direct lines in orderly fashion. Muggings skyrocketed as burglars learned about the herd of people leaving banks with cash in hand. Police stationed themselves at major banks.

The FDIC received its first call on Friday from River Bend Bank in Hattiesburg, Mississippi. Bank President John Atkins said he'd reached his marginal limit and needed assistance. By the end of the day, Atkins was joined by 210 other small banks in the same predicament. Lines formed at 5:00 AM Saturday morning.

The FDIC could not immediately meet demand. It rationed its resources to banks the same way banks rationed resources to depositors.

The cycle quickened. People showed up at banks, the banks

couldn't redeem their account values, word spread that banks were out of money, more people panicked to get their money, the banks requested help from the FDIC, the FDIC reached its limits, word spread further that banks had busted, and even more people wanted their money.

Sunday papers and weekend news broadcasts followed the crumbling bank scenario mercilessly.

Unable to get their money out of banks, hordes of investors began selling their stocks and mutual funds on Monday morning. There were more individual investors in 1999 than ever before in U.S. history. While they had proven to be resilient during market downturns such as the October 27, 1997 drop of 554 points on the Dow, they didn't behave so calmly in the face of losing their bank accounts.

"Nobody understands!" Mark bellowed. "There's nothing wrong with banks yet. This is completely unnecessary."

"It might not be as unnecessary as you think," Susan said. "I spoke with my sister last night. She checked her bank account balance online and a blinking message said that her money is temporarily unavailable. She pays her bills electronically and her house payment is due this week. She planned to sell shares in one of her mutual funds this morning so she could transfer the money directly to her mortgage lender. That's not irrational behavior, Mark."

"No, I suppose not."

S2's mutual fund company clients called with equally grim reports. Charles Schwab & Company in San Francisco, Fidelity Investments in Boston, and T. Rowe Price in Baltimore said their stock fund managers were forced to sell holdings during the price plunge as redemptions continued pouring in. When huge firms sell into the storm, prices fall even further.

All three firms brought in backup phone representatives to handle the volume of calls. People still reached busy signals. When the NYSE closed at 10:30 AM Tuesday morning, the panic hit full steam. Phone systems at Schwab, Fidelity, and Price directed forty-eight times as many callers to automated "we're sorry" messages than to human operators.

The Internet offered little protection. People savvy with their finances, like Susan's sister, turned to their online accounts to place trades. Theoretically, the Internet could provide a backdoor entry to the trading system while others sat on hold for hours. Reality was far different. Investors at E*Trade, Ameritrade, and Datek hit busy signals when trying to log on. When they finally did log on, they encountered errors when placing trades. Fax lines were busy as well.

The market closed for the second day in a row on Wednesday morning. The Dow had dropped 637 points on Monday, 841 points on Tuesday, and another 978 points on Wednesday.

Banks operated on special schedules. Small banks required appointments. Large banks such as Wells Fargo and Bank of America operated their branches in shifts. The corporate banking assets could keep pace with measured demand, but not constant demand from every branch.

Geoff Thorne called the brain trust on Wednesday from S2 London. "Could the Euro timing have been any worse?" he wailed. "Our banks are fighting Y2K on one front, the European currency on another front, and now this latest fiasco on a third front. It's mad."

"We think this is coming to an end," Mark told him.

"What, the banking system?"

Mark managed a smile. "No, Geoff. The run on banks."

"I hope you're right. I'm not sure we can get any work done in this environment. It's a bloody mess over here."

"It's a mess over here too," Susan said.

"Let's think of better times."

President Clinton appeared on national television Wednesday night. "I have placed America's financial community on holiday for the remainder of the week. There will be no banking, no bills due, no stocks traded, and no mutual funds sold. The financial industry will freeze on Thursday and Friday while government officials work through details."

The President leaned forward on his desk in the Oval Office. He spoke calmly to the nation. "The recent banking problem arose not from a weakness in our economy. Nor did it happen because Americans have a sudden need for their money. It is nothing more than a misunderstanding. Our free press understands that Americans demand information. It has reported diligently on the so-called Y2K computing situation as it might affect banks. Even if the computer problem eventually faces us, it is not here today. I have faith in

America's technology workers to ready our great nation for the next century."

The Washington Post ran a full story on Thursday morning expanding on the President's words. It explained that the run on banks was unnecessary. If it simply stopped, everything would return to normal.

The Miami Herald wrote in a special report titled "Financial Fiasco" that the bank run was a self-fulfilling prophecy. A few people wanted money, which made a few more want money, which made even a few more want money. The money is there, but not immediately available in hard currency for everybody.

More stories and broadcasts appeared throughout Thursday and Friday, with comforting Sunday papers arriving on doorsteps everywhere. Mark retrieved *The Mercury News*. The top story headline read "Banks Safe Again." He called Susan.

"Looks like the clouds are lifting," he said. "Did you see the *Merc* this morning?"

"Yes. It gets old watching these predictable cycles."

Business resumed on Monday. People went to work instead of lining up at banks. In the four-day hiatus, banks replenished their supplies and the FDIC helped smaller banks ready themselves for another wave of demand.

But the demand never appeared. Instead, banks caught up on their backlog of withdrawal orders from depositors, most of whom turned down the withdrawals after the cooling-off period.

It turned into a picture-perfect bank run. As soon as the money was available, nobody wanted it.

The Dow posted a 1645 point rise on Monday, its largest one-day point gain ever. Bargain hunters snapped up shares of headline stocks like Intel, Coke, and McDonald's. By the end of the week, billions lost during the banking scare had magically reappeared.

It took two weeks for Mark to receive final reports from S2's financial clients. The data had been sliced and diced dozens of ways in an attempt to find trends and ways to stop them in the future.

"What's most interesting," noted Richard Ensman from Schwab, "is that people have not begun reinvesting. There's still a scare in the air. Mutual funds are sitting at half their former asset levels. Money from stock sales is sitting in cash accounts."

"People are finally aware of what Y2K means," Mark said.

An informal S2 survey of corporate 401(k) retirement plans

revealed that participation had reached its lowest level in fifteen years. John Spears at The Vanguard Group in Malvern, Pennsylvania noted that the company's popular S&P 500 index fund lost one year's worth of regular investments in just three days. The falling market combined with record redemptions left the fund reeling.

"Most of the redemptions were switches to other Vanguard funds," Spears explained. "People watched their retirement nest egg drop ten percent a day for three days and decided that bond funds aren't such a bad idea after all. We added three billion dollars to our total bond index fund."

"More than two-thirds of our participants stopped their regular investments," reported Tom Longua from IBM's tax-deferred savings plan. "The assets we manage have been radically shifted from stocks to bonds and cash. Nobody wants to live through that hell again."

"This was a case of the market getting the sneezes," wrote Alan Abelson in *Barron's*. "It did not catch the flu."

Mark shook his head as he read. "Don't get too happy, Alan," he muttered, tossing the paper in the trash. "If that was the sneezes, get ready for the Ebola virus."

JUNE 14, 1999

"This needs to be kept entirely quiet," Hartmire concluded gravely in the executive conference room. "If anybody but the core team knows, then the advantage is lost. Its secrecy is its only strength."

Mark sat alone at the head of the table, searching his thoughts for the right way to refuse. It was too late. It was too extreme. Jules Hartmire and his three lieutenants occupied the other end of the table, a collection of hard faces. Eric Elwell, Chris Lauer, and Todd Klepac sat like wood carvings as Hartmire spoke. They stared unwaveringly at Mark.

"I'm not sure there's time," Mark said.

"There is time," Hartmire replied instantly. "There is also enough money in the security budget to accomplish it. Moreover, there is no other solution. If you want to be completely secure through whatever may come, this is the only way."

Hartmire security guards had been posted at The Keep since the beginning of the year and had become a normal part of the day. Every Solvang employee used a badge to enter the building.

The installation of security doors and roving security guards raised an awareness throughout the company that times were getting serious. Everybody knew the nature of Solvang's business. Everybody knew that it might be the only company operational after New Year's Eve. Everybody knew that such a company would face enemies, and that such enemies would be formidable.

To keep the security quiet, all employees were asked to sign non-disclosure agreements. The attention started rumors of hidden email accounts, complex passwords, and encrypted file transfers. The rumors were true, as Mark and a coterie of select employees knew. Those in the know were part of the newly formed Solvang Solutions Secret Division, or S3D. They worked as usual alongside their unknowing colleagues, but they attended different meetings and checked confidential email accounts. They devised backup security systems to rival those in the Pentagon, fitting since that's who Mark most worried about. This was the tone of security preparation at Solvang Solutions in 1999.

So it came as no surprise to Mark when Hartmire said that his firm had finished drafting what it considered to be a drastic but necessary final phase in Solvang's security plan. Hartmire had requested a private meeting with Mark, highly unusual around Solvang. He presented the idea in fifteen minutes, showed location maps, displayed blueprints, and sat silently awaiting Mark's approval.

Mark liked to work closely with Kleewein and Susan. He did not like keeping plans secret from his executives. He would agree to the secrecy for now, but in his own mind he doubted he would maintain the silence. Kleewein and Susan were part of his team long before Hartmire Security.

"S3D should know," he tried.

"No. Only the few people needed to get it working."

"These are my people."

"Mark," Hartmire said carefully, "I've been in this security business longer than you've been in the computer business. Trust my judgment. You do not know where your breaks will originate. Christ was betrayed with a kiss. It will take far less to betray everything you've worked to build. Only the necessary members of S3D can know."

Mark heard the faint ticking of the wall clock behind him. He could have requested digital, but chose the ticking timepiece instead.

It was more appropriate to S2's line of work. He let his gaze wander to the nature photos hanging above the motionless heads of Hartmire Security. He especially liked the photo of a bear and her cubs at a cave entrance.

"Let's do it," he concluded abruptly, still staring at the bear cave. Hartmire nodded, no sign of emotion on his face. "We'll call it The Lair."

JULY 16, 1999

Dan Van Lan swaggered his furry bulk into the main testing facility at Pearl Harbor. The site was quickly becoming the most active of all his field locations. Dan placed his best testers in Pearl Harbor and spent most of his own time there as well.

"How's it going this morning?"

"Nothing out of the ordinary yet," replied Carl Albright, Pearl Harbor's lead tester. He sat at his terminal with a cup of coffee, watching the *Solvang2K* interface. His job was to examine code and flag potential Y2K problems. He electronically highlighted problem code inside the *Solvang2K* work environment, forwarded the file to the repair team, and followed up on the repairs afterward.

About an hour into his work, Carl noticed something for the third time that week. *Solvang2K* was showing a strange symbol in the left margin of some code lines. It appeared ghosted, meaning that he could not click on it for a result.

"Hey, Dan, check this out."

Dan walked over to Carl's workstation and peered at the symbol. "What's that?"

"I don't know. I was hoping you knew."

Dan shook his head. "I've never seen it before. Did you check the online reference?"

"Yeah. It's not listed in the symbol chart."

"That's strange. Solvang documents everything. Call The Keep on speakerphone."

Carl dialed the technical support room in San Jose. "Hi Mary Ann. It's Carl and Dan in Pearl Harbor. We found a strange symbol in the left margin of *Solvang2K's* code analyzer. It's not listed in the online reference. Can you check it for me?"

"Sure," she said. "Let me bring you up onscreen. What's your terminal code?" Every S2 terminal had a unique code to identify it on the S2 satellite network. Mary Ann could open a window on her monitor and view the contents of any S2 terminal, just by typing in its code.

"14899."

"I see it. Hmm, that is new. Hold on a second." They could hear her flipping book pages and typing on her keyboard. "I found something in the developers' notes. The symbol identifies the line as derivative code."

"Derived from what?" Dan asked.

"Here's what the note says: 'This symbol is used to identify lines of code that are derivative. A derivative line of code depends on the results of another line of code not present in the current file. The symbol appears ghosted if the file containing the line of code that resolves the dependency is not loaded into *Solvang2K*. The symbol appears active if the file resolving the dependency is loaded into *Solvang2K*. Clicking on the active symbol will open the resolving file to the line depended upon by the derivative code.'"

"Why isn't that explanation in our online reference?" Carl asked.

"Because it's an obscure feature that was used on one project internally. You are only the second inquiry on the history file. It takes three inquiries to make it into the online reference."

"Thanks, Mary Ann," Carl said. He hung up the phone and turned to Dan. "The resolving file has got to be in the system, right?"

"I would think so. It couldn't resolve otherwise. But we've loaded every working file in Pearl Harbor and every joined file from other bases. Unless it's an F-117 stealth file, we should have picked it up in the normal process."

"We have access to all systems. It's in the S2 contract."

A quiet man in uniform had been listening for several minutes. He kept his eyes pointed directly at his monitor. His fingers typed as he listened.

Dan slapped Carl on the shoulder. "Looks like we've got another long weekend ahead. We've got a file to find."

The quiet man printed the document he'd typed. He did not save the file. As soon as it rolled from his personal laser, he closed the editor to expunge the information from his computer's memory. He folded the printout into his pocket, got up, and walked past two fax machines on the way to his car. He drove to a little-known copy shop in Honolulu with self-service fax machines. He paid the cashier in advance for a fax to the mainland. He unfolded the printout, placed it in the feeder, and entered a number in Arlington, Virginia.

JULY 19, 1999

In a satellite surveillance tower in Guam, Petty Officer Pete Dubridge watched the South China Sea. Guam is the first U.S. territory to see each new day. Pete Dubridge learned that fact the moment he arrived.

"Hey Dubridge," came a woman's voice behind him. He turned to face April Pennington, the only person he'd known through every stage of his short Navy career. "Check out the path line from the Philippines to Tokyo. It's a big one."

They manned some of the military's best surveillance equipment. Dubridge and Pennington watched screens all day long to see that what happened in the Pacific Ocean is what the Navy wanted to happen in the Pacific Ocean.

Their system took a day's worth of position coordinates from the photos and created plot lines on a map of the Asia pacific region. Looking at the plot lines showed the paths of ships in the water and planes in the air. Pennington and Dubridge would end their days looking at the lines, guessing who was doing what.

"I see it," Dubridge answered. He zoomed in closer on the satellite photos. "Let's see how long they stay in Tokyo, then we can check how long the ships have stayed in other cities before. We're getting quite a file on these guys."

That's how they spotted China's expanding patrol zone. Pennington noticed that the He Zhang battle group, one of China's most capable forces, made frequent stops at non-military ports. Because the group's home port was Zhanjiang at the southern tip of China, the ships usually drove around the South China Sea, stopping at well known fishing destinations like Qui Nhon and Sibu. That was unusual, so Pennington flagged the group.

She and Dubridge then dug out a longer history of the He Zhang travel patterns. They saw that the group's normal area in the South China Sea had gradually expanded over the previous six months. Most of what they knew about the He Zhang was from much older files, as far back as three years.

By November, the He Zhang had reached Japan and then left in a wide arc that took the ships east of the Bonin islands, past Guam, around the southern tip of the Philippines, through the Sulu Sea, and back into their home waters. The route was not only a departure from the He Zhang's normally contained patterns, it created a swath through territory rarely covered by any ships in the area.

"This is no fishing trip," Dubridge concluded. He looked at Pennington. "Call Honolulu."

JULY 20, 1999

Albert Schwager drove east on I-66, away from Arlington. Once he reached cruising speed, he pulled a satellite phone from under his seat. He pressed a speed dial button.

A calm voice answered. "Zhan Qiao Chau."

"It's Schwager. You fucked up."

Mr. Chau inhaled long and carelessly. "Pardon me, Mr. Schwager?"

"You heard me." He hated Chau's permanent relaxation. Didn't the man understand what they'd gotten themselves into? Schwager couldn't contain himself. "Solvang is already looking for missing files in Pearl Harbor! If they find them, we're finished. On top of that, the whole Pacific Fleet is screaming about increased Chinese patrol zones from Japan to the Bonin Islands to the Sulu Sea. What the hell are you doing over there?"

He heard the rush of a lighter at the other end of the phone. It crackled the end of a cigarette, then clinked shut. Women giggled in the background. Mr. Chau blew smoke across the telephone receiver. "I see that there are no problems at all, Mr. Schwager. The U.S. is worried, yes?"

"Yes!"

"Good. Then the U.S. will panic and present you with two very rich opportunities. You do understand opportunity, Mr. Schwager?"

"Of course I understand opportunity, but what the fuck are you talking about?"

"I am talking about a lesson from old China. The best way to defeat your enemies is to make them fight each other."

"I don't have time for one of your goddamned—"

"You are worried about this Solvang. You did not want Solvang working on the military. Pritchett likes this Solvang. Now, you can tell Pritchett that Solvang is not performing. You need a new vendor."

"Why the hell—"

"That will result in one of two responses," Mr. Chau continued, calm as ever. "One, Pritchett will agree that Solvang is inadequate and will search for another vendor."

"Highly unlikely. He would sooner—"

"Or, two, Pritchett will open himself to the suggestion of overtaking Solvang's operations when the New Year comes. You would, of course, handle the occupation. I believe we discussed this possibility when you panicked after visiting Solvang's headquarters in California."

"We don't need Pritchett's consent to overtake Solvang."

Smoke floated almost imperceptibly across the telephone wires, tickling Schwager's inner ear. "That is unimportant, Mr. Schwager. You must plant seeds of doubt that grow into saplings of anger that bloom into a towering forest of hatred. Do you not see the value of making enemies of this Solvang and Mr. Pritchett? At their moment of greatest need, they will feel their deepest distrust." Another cloud of smoke blew around the world into Schwager's ear. "That, Mr. Schwager, is opportunity."

The phone rested silently against Schwager's head while he thought. Pritchett was indeed a wreck at the Pentagon that day. The whole place had been a wreck, even the Secretary of Defense had been called from a briefing. These were touchy times and Pritchett did not take chances in touchy times. If ever he were ripe for the suggestion of Solvang's incompetence, it was now.

"You should have told me earlier," Schwager managed in a subdued voice. Mr. Chau may have been right, but he went about it in the wrong way.

"Why? You would not have listened until your emotions demanded it."

Mr. Chau clicked the line dead. Schwager threw his phone under the seat, humiliated. He stared down the miles of freeway stretched in front of him.

He needed to clear his mind. He needed to think of what to say the next day. He needed to seize the opportunity that Chau had created.

JULY 21, 1999

Dan Van Lan wasn't sure he'd heard correctly. It was bad enough to have flown halfway around the world to meet in Pritchett's office for information that could have come over the phone, but this?

"Fire Solvang Solutions?" he asked Schwager. "What exactly do you have in mind for the millennium then?"

"Schwager, please," Pritchett said, standing from behind his desk. "That is not what we discussed. I'll do the talking."

Dan glared at Schwager, perched smugly on the edge of Pritchett's desk like a pet monkey. The son of a bitch had resisted Dan's suggestions from day one and now he had the audacity to suggest that S2 was responsible for the military's plight? Dan couldn't wait to tell this one to The Keep.

"What we are noticing," Pritchett said, sitting in the empty chair beside Dan, "is that things are not moving as quickly as we'd like."

"With all due respect, no shit."

Pritchett looked stunned.

Dan's voice climbed to its theatrical limits. He hefted his bulky frame from the seat. He backed up a pace to face both Pritchett and Schwager, chopping the air with a furry hand as he talked. "What have we been telling you from the start? It's the chips! We're doing our best on the software side and we're making good progress. But we don't do chips! I have submitted several recommendations to you for vendors who could handle the hardware while we handle the software. Every one of them has been filed away with no further action on your part."

Pritchett looked at Schwager. "I didn't know about that."

"My office handled them," Schwager said flatly. "S2 submitted a raft of recommendations, most of which we followed. We ordered new equipment, offered higher headcounts, and even opened old testing facilities for S2 usage." He looked at Dan. "Additional vendors have been contracted, Mr. Van Lan."

Dan shook his head and closed his eyes. "You hired a bunch of wire heads in Long Beach to review the specs on old missiles. You did not hire the firms we recommended, namely Mercury Systems and Atlantic Aerospace Electronics. That's who we need to work with in order to make significant progress. It's already too late to fix everything. But by working with Mercury and Atlantic, we should be able to repair critical systems in time."

Pritchett looked hard at Schwager. "Get those vendor recommendations to my office immediately."

Schwager nodded.

Pritchett turned back to Dan. "In the future, submit all critical requests through this office."

"I thought we had."

"I mean directly to me at this office. In the meantime, you need support from Solvang. There is no way that you can handle an account the size of the military on your own. Follow the military's lead on this. Do you think the Secretary of Defense knows every problem on every base every day? Hell no. There are plenty of bases he's never seen, nor should he see them."

Dan sat down again. "That's a suggestion I can agree to."

"Good, then let's call Mark Solvang immediately." Pritchett returned to his desk and dialed Mark on the speakerphone. "We need more support for the DoD account," he said.

"No," Mark replied. "We've already discussed it and decided that we can't spare any more people." Dan thought he saw Schwager's eyes brighten.

"I don't care what you've discussed," Pritchett said. "This is the U.S. military and you knew what you were getting into by signing on with us. We're not making enough progress."

Mark's voice came like a tornado through the room. "You knew what you were getting into when we signed. We said that we could not repair you in time, now you see why. I'm sure Dan has explained the hardware situation."

"He also explained the software situation," Pritchett retorted. "Your team is behind on all fronts. The latest is that they can't find a critical file in Pearl Harbor."

"As I understand it, Dan has the missing file and all other dilemmas under control. Is that correct, Dan?"

"We're doing our best, Mark, but more people would help."

A long silence followed. Dan felt like he sold out his president. He waited for word.

"How many more people do you need, Dan?"

"Not many people, but I'd like somebody to handle half the account with me. I would take the Atlantic region to continue working with the Pentagon. The new person would handle the Pacific region and tackle this missing file, among other problems."

"Who did you have in mind?"

"It's a long shot, but Billy Stamp."

"Forget it! That would place our top two guys on this one account. We are a—"

"Well, we need them, goddammit!" Pritchett roared. "Why should I expect anything less than your top two guys?"

"Because we have other commitments! Nowhere in our contracts does it say that the military will overtake S2's entire base of operations. If I say Stamp remains where he's at, then he remains where he's at."

"I understand that," Pritchett growled. "I'm asking that you tell Stamp to help Van Lan prepare the U.S. military. I'm not running your company, Mr. Solvang. I'm asking you to help me run mine. My company happens to be Uncle Sam's company."

"Let me talk to Dan alone."

Pritchett pulled the receiver from its cradle and handed it across the desk. "I'm here," Dan said.

"Why Billy?" Mark asked.

"I've worked with Billy since we were both assigned to the Boeing account. He scored higher on his entrance exam than any candidate to date, including myself. He is very bright, tenacious, and single. I mention the last because I think it's important in a job like this. Twenty-hour work days don't go over well in a family. This military account is a monster. It needs Billy. He's the brightest you've got back there. You said so yourself."

"If you say you need him—notice you, not the goddamned feds—then you'll get him. I'm going to ask one last time. You're sure you need me to pull Billy from important civilian duties to help you with the military?"

"Yes."

"Then consider it done. I'll talk with Billy tonight. Fly back here immediately so we can start planning this transition. Billy has a loyal team to bring with him."

"Thanks, Mark." Dan stood to hang up the phone. He gathered his documents, threw them in his briefcase, and stood to face Pritchett and Schwager. "I need to fly immediately to San Jose. Billy Stamp is joining my team and I want to make sure it happens smoothly. I think you'll be pleased with the results." With that, he exited the office.

"Well, that could have gone better," Schwager said, genuine concern in his voice. "I hope we didn't anger them too much." He noticed Pritchett's face, several shades redder than usual. His jaw muscles pulsed and quivered beneath the skin. "Are you all right?" he asked.

"I'm fine," Pritchett spat. "What I would like to know is why you are not fully cooperating with Solvang Solutions. Do you have some sort of interest in seeing them fail, Schwager? Is there something I don't know here?"

"Jesus!" Schwager said. He scooted from the desk to stand while he spoke. "Of course not. I don't know what happened to the vendors they recommended. My office put the files through the normal process. I'm not in the business of reviewing defense contracts. Solvang Solutions may not know the process around here, but we do. There is nothing fishy about a suggested vendor not getting picked up right away."

Pritchett cast a crimson eye on Schwager.

"I told you from the start that Solvang Solutions is not the most capable firm on the market," Schwager continued. "I saw this catastrophe coming a mile away. I tried to tell you, but you insisted on using this greenhorn firm. They have never worked with government before. You heard Mark Solvang on the phone. The man has no respect for what we do. It's this very dilemma I hoped to avoid by choosing a different firm. But now we're stuck with Solvang Solutions."

"They're going to succeed," Pritchett insisted. "I'll be damned if your vacant cries of ineptitude are going to get in their way. I have seen nothing but professionalism from S2, nothing but promises kept, nothing but progress where it is possible. So what if they can't find a file in Pearl Harbor? It's a problem they'll figure out. I just want to make damned sure that you aren't putting speed bumps in front of these people. Somebody is dropping the ball around here and it isn't me. Quit being a bureaucrat, goddammit! Place this project at top priority and grab a few throats if you have to. We are facing a century without any military capabilities, Schwager. Has any of this sunk in yet?"

"Yes it has and I fully agree. That's why I personally think we should hedge our bets."

"What the hell are you talking about?"

"I'm talking about making sure that Solvang Solutions remains committed to its promises. We can't leave anything to chance. I hope with all my heart that they succeed. But what if they don't, and the lights go out, and they start putting all their resources into civilian tasks?"

"Won't happen."

"Why not? Mark Solvang has admitted to having a bent toward civilian responsibilities. We are not top priority at S2. The sooner we accept that, the sooner we can treat this as we would any other threat."

Pritchett's face contorted into a mask of disbelief. "Threat? What in God's name are you saying, Schwager?"

"I'm saying we should be prepared to take control of S2's operations if we reach a state of critical need and they are not coming through for us."

"Invade The Keep?"

"Not invade. Station troops within and make sure that critical military work gets done. It's a last ditch plan, but one that I think would be wise to have prepared ahead of time."

Pritchett sat chewing his thumbnail. Schwager saw the old man's thoughts moving behind his watery eyes. Could it really be this easy? Would he go for it this quickly?

"Things are getting worse by the day," Schwager injected into the old brain before him. "This file business has me worried. Now, we have reports of increased Chinese patrol zones from Japan to the Sulu Sea. I'm sure it hasn't escaped your judgment that China operates the largest non-computer-dependent military in the world. The cards are quickly stacking against us. We can't leave everything to the whims of Mark Solvang, who admits to favoring civilian repairs over military. We need to be prepared to use his company's resources in time of crisis."

Pritchett closed his eyes a moment, looking very angry. Schwager had never seen the Undersecretary of Defense for Acquisition & Technology appear so furious. If he looked hard enough, Schwager swore he could see wrinkles in the air above Pritchett's head. The old man's veins bulged and his jaw muscles flexed and his eyes soldered on a point in space.

"It's not a bad plan," Pritchett said tautly at last. "This could be your chance to redeem yourself, Schwager. I'm leaving this part up to you. Make the necessary arrangements and report back to me as you put the pieces in place." He turned his pulsing head to glare at Schwager. "I want you to understand that this is entirely my call and that I'm viewing it as an eleventh hour solution. We are not to consider this the normal course of action. Am I clear?"

"Absolutely," Schwager replied with a flourish. "I'll get on it immediately." He strode from the office.

AUGUST 9, 1999

"It's unbelievable!" Billy screamed into the phone from Pearl Harbor. "I'm telling you, these bastards replaced faulty global positioning receivers with equipment that will break in 2000. How could anybody be so stupid? They took machines that were going to break on August 22 and replaced them with machines that are going to break on January 1. Why did I ever agree to this account?"

His official paperwork identified him as William Stamp, and that's how he introduced himself to coworkers and military personnel. But, inevitably, he became Billy Stamp in hallway conversations and evenings on the town.

The name had served him well as a kid delivering papers in Sunnyvale. His golden blond hair and eyelashes and eyebrows stuck cutely from beneath a baseball cap worn backwards. When he showed up at the end of each month to collect money for the paper, he received generous tips and food for the walk home.

He could even manage to look cute in front of a computer. He didn't lapse into the grease covered, pizza breath image of most computer professionals. He sat straight and looked sharp. His freckles disappeared over the years and his blond eyelashes were joined by blond whiskers, but he still wore a baseball cap. Frontwards, though.

Dan and Billy made an unlikely duo. Dan could have been the shadow to Billy's beam of light. Dan's large hairy body added an element of fear when he entered a tirade. Billy's tirades were more boyish, almost bratty. He was fiendishly intelligent and arrogant about it. He drove fast cars, wore iridescent sunglasses, and had a different date every Friday night. He worked longer hours than anybody on his team, then took longer vacations. He liked it that way. He couldn't understand for the life of him why anybody would work outside the computer industry. He was asked if he'd be interested in working on special effects in Hollywood. He said no. Not while making more than $200,000 a year solving a few simple computer problems—and now living in Hawaii on top of it all. Billy would never leave the good life of computer work.

S2 hired him on a coop program from Stanford. He began work with Dan on the Boeing account. Dan, at the ripe age of twenty-four, had been the senior member of the Boeing team. Billy graduated from Stanford in 1995 and immediately came full time to S2, with high marks from Dan. He achieved fame within the company when Dan could not solve an embedded chip interface problem. Some of Boeing's planes relied on old Flight Data Acquisition Units, or FDAUs, that used embedded chips from a manufacturer that was no longer in business.

Boeing intended to replace the FDAUs as soon as possible, but there was no guarantee that it could happen by 2000. So S2 decided to write "belt and suspender" safety code to trick the embedded system into working properly with a changed date. Dan tried unsuccessfully to doctor the data being fed into the embedded chip. It still choked on the data and spit out garbage commands on the backside.

Billy was the first consultant in S2 to work around an embedded chip by analyzing the errors it generated, then doctoring the garbage on the backside before it arrived at processing systems.

Billy's solution became S2's preferred backup plan for simple embedded chips. It proved itself on the Boeing account and ultimately landed Billy as second in command on the team handling the DoD, S2's biggest account.

"We've replaced most of the critical global positioning system equipment to preempt the breakdown on August 22," Dan said to the conference room over the phone. "Most military navigation systems will be able to make it to 2000."

"But, they won't make it any farther," Mark said.

"That's right," Billy answered from Pearl Harbor. "Pritchett is livid, naturally, and is riding the vendors to get systems in place by the new year. To our great credit, most software will be ready. We've received specifications from chip manufacturers in advance. Our software code is written with variables in place of specific information for each chip system. When the new chips are finally installed, we should be able to fill out the variable table and have the code automatically pull in the right information for each chip."

"Brilliant, as always," Susan said. "Where is most of your work being done?"

"In San Diego and Hawaii."

"On what systems?" Kleewein asked.

"Submarines, ships, planes, missiles, and torpedoes. That sums up our lives these days. Each of those systems is nothing but a collection of wires, chips, and software. Our active attack systems such as heat seeking missiles and pinging torpedoes rely on timing devices run by embedded chips."

He showed his trademark Billy Stamp smile, invisible to all in the conference room. "We've got our work cut out for us."

NOVEMBER 25, 1999

Mark needed to look happy for his children. It was Thanksgiving day and Grandma Solvang was preparing a marvelous feast. Jeremiah and Alyssa, now fourteen and twelve, showed their dad what they had been doing in school. Susan joined them and drove most of the conversation. Mark could not clear his thoughts. They were only thirty-five days away from the millennium, and he did not have time for holidays.

"Look, Dad," Alyssa said, holding up a poster she made for Thanksgiving. "Did you know that I won first place?"

Mark turned his eyes to the poster, seeing nothing but a swirl of color. Behind his eyes, a million deadlines danced. "That's great, honey," he managed.

Susan jumped in immediately. "Of course it's great, Alyssa. How many other children entered the contest?"

Their conversation became a distant chatter to Mark. He heard instead the ticking of the wall clock in the executive conference room. He hated being so distracted. These were his children at his father's home. It was Thanksgiving. Margaret would not have let her mind wander so far from family. Or would she? She cofounded the company. Maybe from her place in death, she does not condemn me, Mark thought. Maybe she understands.

"Want to see my computer program?" Jeremiah asked.

"What?" Mark asked, snapping back to the moment.

Jeremiah's green eyes looked enormous under a sandy shock of hair. He laughed at his Dad. "Did I scare you or something?"

Mark smiled. "No, I just can't concentrate, Jeremiah." He pulled his son to him, something that wasn't as easy as it used to be. "Wow, you've gotten big."

"I'm fourteen now. I'm going to be in high school next year. I have to be big."

"I guess so."

"Do you want to see my computer program or not?"

"I'd love to see it."

By late afternoon when Grandma Solvang served dinner, Mark still hadn't been able to relax. He sat beside Susan opposite his children. Grandpa and Grandma Solvang sat at the end of the redwood table in the dining room that Grandpa had built himself. Windows rose from floor to ceiling on two walls and then extended between the rafters of the ceiling. The wooden lattice splashed California sun in cheerful patterns across the floor, making the dining room feel like an outdoor picnic. His mother's jungle of flowers hung from wooden beams and rose from floor planters, adding to the intended effect.

Mark had grown up in the quaint home in Los Gatos and, aside from the dining room addition, it still looked the same. It still smelled the same. It was a retreat from the frenetic pace of his life, the one hideaway he could count on to soothe his mind with smells of fresh baked cookies from his mother's kitchen and sawdust from his father's workshop.

But not that day. Nothing could pull Mark from the realization that the world as they knew it had just thirty-five days to live. The nuclear regulatory commission confirmed that it would be shutting down all 107 plants within the next month. The FAA had failed in every one of its final tests and major airlines questioned whether they would fly in 2000. Automobile manufacturers issued statements warning against broken digital chips with unpredictable consequences. One of the main worries came with digital antilock brakes. Ironically, several models malfunctioned in test labs and locked up at seventy miles per hour. AT&T finally admitted that it would not be ready for 2000. That admission started a wave of public statements from WorldCom, Sprint, Excel, and a slew of minor carriers. Then there was the Department of Defense. Even with Dan and Billy managing hundreds of S2's finest consultants, they could not ready the military in time. Some computers would work, but most would not and the ones that would not were the critical—

"How are things going at the company?" Grandpa asked Mark and Susan after the turkey platter made its way around the table.

"As good as we can expect," Mark said dreamily.

Grandpa looked down the table with his fork and knife in midair, watching his son. Mark felt the keen observation. "And just how good is that?"

"Oh, that's enough," Grandma said. She cut at her plate in dainty motions, just enough to ripple her plump arms. "It's Thanksgiving and we don't need to worry about business."

The kids loved their grandparents. Mark was grateful that his parents were willing to help with Margaret's death by letting the kids live with them. Because Grandma and Grandpa Solvang lived just blocks from Mark's home in Los Gatos, Jeremiah and Alyssa were able to keep their same friends and attend the same schools. It was also easy to visit their father when he was available, a rare but cherished event that made him appreciate their proximity.

Everybody loved Grandpa Solvang's stories of the good old days. His good old days extended back to the country's founding. Being a history buff, he carried anecdotes about Jefferson and Hamilton and Lincoln and Roosevelt like they were old friends.

"You know, kids," Grandpa said over dessert, "during the Great Depression we used to get our dinners off the street. We had no money, so we'd wait for somebody to throw trash into a dumpster. Then we'd dig through it to find food for our families." He told his stories first person, even if they were about the Revolutionary War. To the kids, he was old enough to have seen the mountains form.

"Some people still get their food that way," Jeremiah said.

"Yes, but not like we did during the Depression. There were long lines of people waiting for scraps. And the President of the United States would talk to us on the radio every night after dinner."

"What did he say?" Alyssa asked.

"He told us that everything would be all right. He said we shouldn't be afraid. He said that other people in the world had it much harder than we did, and that we should buck up and persevere."

"What does persevere mean?" Alyssa asked.

"It means never give up."

Mark watched his father. He thought of him getting meals from a dumpster. "You've stocked up on plenty of food, right Gramps?"

Grandpa nodded, looking into Mark's face for a long moment. Mark recognized the look in Grandpa's contemplative eyes. Grandpa knew why his son's company enjoyed so much business. And he knew history. The Great Depression could happen again for any number of reasons, maybe even this computer thing his son always talked about.

Mark spent a few moments alone with his mother in the kitchen, helping her clean dishes while Susan and Grandpa played games with Jeremiah and Alyssa in the family room.

"Those kids need you, Mark," Grandma said. The front of her apron deflected soap suds away from her blouse.

"I know, Mom."

"Jeremiah was five-years-old when you and Margaret started this company, now he's fourteen. He'll be a man soon and will have never known his father. There is more to life than business."

"The company is more than business, Mom. You know that."

She rubbed the washcloth across one plate after another, looking into the suds for the right words. "Every businessman I've ever known has said the same thing about his company, Mark. But time slows down for nobody. Your son will be a man whether you are there to see it or not."

How had this happened? Mark and Margaret had wanted to solve a simple goddamned computer problem. They never set out to save the world. He didn't want to save the world. He wanted to throw a ball with his son. He wanted the presence of mind to see the picture that his daughter painted to win first place in an art contest. He wanted to work forty-hour weeks and spend weekends at the beach. He wanted a normal life. But it was not going to happen in the near future. He knew that Christmas was out of the question. Past that, who could say? If everything exploded beyond repair, maybe he'd have all the time in the world to spend with his family.

One way or another, their lives would change in just thirty-five days. He couldn't shake the number from his mind. Thirty-five days.

"I know the sacrifices I've made and I stand by them," he retorted. "You have no idea how devastating this new year will be. My work is as much for my children as it is for anybody else." He put a dish in the cabinet and let his voice drop to a softer tone. He placed an arm around his mother's shoulder. "You're right about one thing, though. Time slows for nobody."

DECEMBER 30, 1999

Mark looked at the countdown clock in the cafeteria. It showed the number of full days left until the Year 2000. He'd never seen "1" look so stark. It normally conveys first place, top dog, a job well done. Not one day until the world ends.

He wore his dark blue suit and sat in a high back chair. The camera man moved his head from the eyepiece to the side of the camera to get a clear picture of Mark. Kleewein and Susan sat around him and consultants from The Keep took seats in chairs arranged to face the event.

All Solvang employees had agreed to be back at work on December 30 for the company-wide video conference. A core team of 1,000 employees would be at work on New Year's Eve, ready for the worst. The company's remaining 11,880 employees would be on call for the entire New Year's weekend and would be back at work on Monday, January 3, 2000.

Nobody liked forgoing a long holiday vacation, but this was no standard holiday for Solvang Solutions. It was the very reason the company had existed for the previous nine-and-a-half years.

That one night, the last New Year's Eve of the twentieth century, marked the event that every countdown clock on the walls of Solvang sites had been clicking toward since the company's founding. Their new year would start on December 31 as the millennium made its way around the globe.

"Nervous?" Susan asked Mark.

"Yes," he said.

She looked surprised. "Just watch your parents and your children and remember that I'm here next to you."

"I'm not nervous about the cameras."

Out of the corner of his eye, he saw her looking at him. "I know," she said. "We're all nervous. But we did our best."

The camera man told Mark to stand by. He counted down from five and they went live across the entire Solvang company.

"Good day," Mark began. "I say good day not to be stuffy, but because our company is so big now that morning and evening apply to us all day long. Like the British Empire, the Sun never sets on Solvang."

The camera man gave a thumbs up. Everything was working fine. Mark continued from under the white lights. "I, like you, am in this through whatever comes tomorrow night. I have the luxury

of speaking truthfully in this forum, free from the equal time
nonsense that clouds Y2K in the press. The correct story gets half
the space, the incorrect story gets the other half."

He paused, looking hard into the camera. He hoped he didn't
need to add any extra gravity to the situation. Just the facts should
have been grave enough. "I believe firmly that New Year's Eve will
be catastrophic. I've watched the reports come across my desk for
nine-and-a-half years. We've worked wonders for hundreds of
companies. I'm proud that, thanks to Solvang Solutions, 534
companies are fully Y2K compliant. Thousands more are going to
be better off than if we'd never helped. But there are thousands that
will disappear altogether, and thousands that will fail and seriously
impact our daily lives. You know it, and I know it, and no matter
what the press thinks, tomorrow night is going to be a doozy."

He held his watch up for the camera. "The New Year is coming
quickly. It will hit Fiji first. That will be 4:00 AM California time
and we'll be at our stations. With computers connected around the
world, a break in Asia could affect systems in New York or Denver
or Los Angeles. California will be one of the last places in the world
to see 2000. We need to be ready for anything as it comes our way."

Heads nodded around the Solvang cafeteria. Mark rested the
watch on his lap. "By now, all of your families are prepared for the
worst. You should have plenty of food and supplies at home, a
detailed paper record of your valuables, and so on. Having taken
care of all of that, you don't need to worry about your families.
You're free to worry about saving the rest of the world."

He chanced a smile. "I want to commend all of you for the hard
work you've done so far, and for the hard work you're about to do.
The next few weeks are going to test the mettle of this company,
this country, and our global community. I look to the future with
pride at our accomplishments and faith in our abilities. Stay together,
people, and remember that your very best is what the world needs."

He let the presidential portion of his speech hang in the air a
second. He glanced at the countdown clock's ominous "1" on the
red digital readout.

He looked at the faces of his children and of the hundreds of
consultants in the cafeteria. Mary Ann from the tech support center
smiled at him. Jules Hartmire gave a thumbs up. Debbra Jeffries,
the executive secretary, clenched her fist at him in a show of strength.

He knew that Dan Van Lan watched from Virginia, Billy Stamp

from Hawaii, Geoff Thome from London, and Taka Nishida from Tokyo. S2 Japan awoke at 3:00 AM to watch the conference call. Their countdown clocks read "0." For them, it was already New Year's Eve and midnight was less than twenty-one hours away. California had thirty-eight hours to go.

Mark remembered the first meetings with Margaret and the Solvang executives. How naive they'd been. He saw Billy's face fresh out of college. He saw Dan's cheeks bursting with energy no matter how bad things got at Boeing or the DoD.

He felt all of their blood in his veins. They'd tried so hard. They'd worked so many hours in front of terminals and at press conferences and in congressional hearing rooms. They'd known for years that time was of the essence. Now, time was up.

The digital readout didn't lie. 2000 was one day away, and they weren't ready, and the world had no idea what that meant.

Mark looked into the camera. "Have a happy new year, everyone. God bless us all."

He looked past the camera to the clock on the wall. It seemed to fade before his eyes.

5

THE MILLENNIUM MELTDOWN

It was the biggest party in history. Reservations at resorts, on yachts, in country clubs, and fancy restaurants had been booked as far back as 1995. Nobody wanted to miss this New Year's, indeed this New Millennium's, unveiling.

Despite the extensive worldwide preparations, Solvang's party remained a small one. It existed only to lift the spirits of everybody forced to be at work that day and that night. Ribbons hung from the cafeteria ceiling. The caterers arranged six food tables and placed glasses of liquor and punch on a seventh table. Large screen monitors showed New Year's festivities for the handful of visitors, such as Mark's parents and children. Smaller monitors provided viewing in terminal rooms and hallways throughout The Keep.

Given the insanity of the rest of the world that New Year's Eve, Solvang's party seemed a pathetic affair. No drunks, no orgies, no fights, no vomiting in the bathroom, no lovers' quarrels, and no toasts. It was a tense because-we-need-to-act-like-normal-people-for-awhile kind of party.

Tokyo was the first major city to go dark. Japanese partyers tipped back cans of Sapporo and smoked cigars. Dancers at The Liquid Room in Shinjuku's Kabukicho provided interpreted interviews for viewers around the world. The Japanese counted down from ten seconds to midnight as televisions showed Tokyo's date and time in the lower right corner.

At midnight, the lights in Japan went dark. Screens turned black then lit up again from Tokyo's fireworks. Most viewers around the world assumed the lights went out to make the fireworks clearer onscreen. But the date and time readout betrayed what really happened.

It was a live feed from Tokyo. When midnight arrived, the computerized clock rolled to a year of 00, failed to recognize it, and displayed *1/-l/0¬ 1~:00:23.

After the fireworks stopped and the light faded onscreen, Tokyo's backdrop remained black. The camera's light provided the only illumination for viewers. A Japanese woman with ribbons around her forehead and bloodshot eyes spoke toward the camera in perfect English. "The power is out in Tokyo. We blew the fuses! Now that's a party! Happy New Year from Japan!"

2000 came darkly around the globe. S2 consultants donned headsets and began typing at keyboards during Tokyo's party. They continued monitoring screens as the new year brought darkness to Seoul, Hong Kong, Kuala Lumpur, New Delhi, Kabul, Riyadh, and Moscow. When the new year reached the heart of Europe, S2 divided its screens among several cities at once.

Mark watched sadly. "Nobody understands."

"Understands what?" Susan asked.

He pointed at the screen.

They did not understand that the woman screaming in Helsinki was not doing so out of crazy joy. She held her collapsed father while an outdoor symphony played into the freezing night. He clutched his chest, unaware that the tiny chip inside his pacemaker had stopped functioning when 2000 arrived.

An ambulance might have shown up to help, but Helsinki's emergency dispatch system was dead. Newer model ambulances would not start. Hospitals lost power. A few people gathered to help the woman and her poor father, but they could do little for a stopped pacemaker. Crowds nearby continued feasting on reindeer steaks and cloudberry daiquiris and every once in awhile somebody would enter the camera light and wish the world a happy new year.

The good times rolled to Warsaw, Stockholm, Vienna, Rome, and Berlin. In Sweden, where seventy percent of the population relies on wireless communications, Ericsson called S2 London to report that its Eripower units stopped supplying juice to telecom equipment and that its AXE digital exchange systems were down.

Amsterdam, Brussels, and Paris took their turns on the television screens. The world's love affair with Paris led people to watch that city more closely than any so far.

The banks of the Seine had been completely renovated for the new year with twelve kilometers of uninterrupted pedestrian paths and attractive lights. Every famous Parisian museum was honored during New Year's day.

"There stands one of the world's best known monuments," said the American reporter in Paris as her camera filled its view with the beauty of the tower. The Eiffel proudly displayed red and blue lights for the millennium. People surrounded its base, fireworks poised for launch. The countdown began.

The reporter said, "In just ten seconds, we'll be dazzled by the Eiffel's explosion of lights and a backdrop of fireworks. Five, four, three, two, one, Happy New—oh my goodness. The tower is completely dark."

The millennium cam found its way to The Slimelight, London's famous goth club. A crowd of fantastically dressed "millenniacs" poured around the industrial building. Music pounded from speakers on the first floor while the band Project Pitchfork made waves through the smoky groundfloor air.

"Happy fuckin' New Year!" screamed a heavily pierced woman held sideways by her friends.

The music died to a hush and the main DJ overtook the speakers to countdown to 2000. "Three, two, one, bang!" he yelled to the convulsing mob. The music raged to a loud crescendo, then died as the light faded around the rooms.

"What the hell?" came a voice from the darkness.

The Big Tree Tavern in Dublin forwent the sweaty clamor of dance clubs, instead providing a stage for local bands to play. Folks blew the froth from mugs and tossed hats across the room. At midnight, the lights blinked out and within two minutes the entire pub was relit with lantern fire. Nobody skipped a beat.

DECEMBER 31, 1999, 8:30 PM PST

The new year crept across the Atlantic ocean. Manhattan was delirious with anticipation and it oozed from Solvang's televisions like napalm. Only thirty minutes until 2000 hit the New York.

Solvang consultants manned terminals to help S2 offices around the world. Electricity and phones were dead everywhere. So far, every S2 office remained fully operational, providing at least something for Mark to be thankful about.

"I've got S2 New York on the phone," a consultant called to Mark. "Have you got a second?"

Mark took the call in the conference room with Kleewein and Susan. Harvey Patlis was in charge of S2 New York. He never chit chatted and only called when it was important. "Harv, you're on speakerphone. What's up?"

"We have teams in place at Con Edison's main sites. They're getting worried. We've been watching this thing come around the globe and we want to preempt it. I called Edison and they welcomed us with open arms. They can read the writing on the wall."

"How many consultants on site?" Susan asked.

"About twenty. We have four in Manhattan, the Bronx, Queens, and Westchester."

"Why the dispersion?" Kleewein asked. "Wouldn't it be smarter to keep them all at Con Ed headquarters?"

"I don't think so. Con Ed's got its own smart folks over there. My goal is to keep the different sites talking to each other after the lights go out."

DECEMBER 31, 1999, 8:50 PM PST

Mark and Susan turned their attention to the television screens.

Times Square 2000, the official name of the Manhattan celebration, began at 4:00 AM Pacific time for the express purpose of ushering in the new year as it started in the Fiji Islands. Enormous video screens faced Times Square. More than 100,000 people watched the new year come around the globe.

Mark looked at Manhattan's famous ball of lights perched atop its seventy-seven-foot flagpole at One Times Square. At 8:59, the ball began its descent. Its fog machine blew mist into the air, exciting the Manhattan crowd into deafening cheers. A 250,000-watt lightning simulator sliced the mist and blasted Times Square in white light. The ball began its descent, dazzling the crowd with its 10,000-watt xenon lamp, 180 halogen lamps, and 144 xenon glitter strobes. All 320 of its light-emitting ventilation holes shot beams of photons through the mist into the most watched city in the world. Everybody knew that at midnight, the ball would light up the digits 2000, crack the air with more simulated lightning, and join the display of fireworks in illuminating the city brightly enough to be seen from the moon.

"Ten, nine, eight, seven, six," screamed the crowd in New York. Every guest and consultant at S2 stared at the television screens. "Five, four, three, two, one, Happy New Year!"

The New York symphony played *Auld Lang Syne* by heart, ignoring for the moment that their music stand lights went black. The ball reached its final destination and turned into a suspended lump of wire. No lights, no digits, no lightning. It was like Cinderella at midnight, no more glamour. Fireworks temporarily lit the night.

The explosions over Central Park and around the Statue of Liberty were the biggest ever launched in New York. News cameras from all networks captured the beauty for viewers in the western three-quarters of the United States. Viewers on most of the East Coast lost power to their televisions and could no longer watch.

After the New York fireworks turned to embers and fell from the sky, everyone at S2 watched a CNN reporter come into view. "New York has lost electrical power, but the party rages on."

As if to prove his point, people hung their faces in front of the camera with peace signs and beer and incoherent yelling. The camera panned the scene in Times Square. News vans aimed their floodlights into the crowd. People turned on flashlights, car lights, and some even burned candles. The news networks continued delivering footage via satellite to the rest of the country.

"This might be a better party than ever!" said the reporter. A bottle, thrown from somewhere off camera, crashed down on his head. He crumpled to the asphalt, one hand in his bloody hair and the other still holding the microphone. The camera man continued filming.

"It's complete pandemonium," the reporter yelled. He sat up and looked into the camera, a trickle of blood running down his forehead. Legs ran behind him in the deafening roar.

"Welcome to 2000."

DECEMBER 31, 1999, 10:08 PM PST

Power didn't go out in each region of the country as cleanly as the time zones would suggest. Thanks to deregulation of the energy industry, some communities in the central time zone received their power from eastern providers. Those communities went down with the east coast.

2000 moved across the country, taking down the current time zone and parts of the next as it went. People in time zones ahead of the disaster watched their fate on television.

After watching darkness fall on Manhattan, Mark, Susan, and a crew of consultants scurried back to their terminals. Kleewein had never left, preferring to watch events unfold on the terminal room televisions. In front of him sat a display grid of six monitors. S2 had equipped the Solvang satellite network with a limited camera capability. Kleewein said it would be handy to have a bird's eye view of the world. That was five years ago. Now he wished they'd installed a better system.

"We don't have real time," he reminded everybody as they gathered around him to watch the screens. "We're seeing a time lapse of fifteen minutes, and in one minute slices at that."

The satellite photos were grainy. They looked like weather screens on the late night news. They were good for overall trends, but that was about all. The Solvang satellite network was no Hubbell. At best it could provide a pixelated view of an area the size of Los Angeles.

"That's fine," Mark said. "Regular television broadcast will work as long as we have power."

Kleewein nodded. "But even the stations with their own auxiliary power won't continue sending signals to a blackened country. There'd be no point."

"Nonetheless," Mark said, "we have real-time TV as long as they broadcast. Then we can switch to the satellites."

"Watch this," Kleewein said, pushing a button and pointing to the large screen above the six monitors. It displayed satellite footage of Japan just before midnight and then fifteen minutes after. The coverage moved its way west around the globe, showing the regions before midnight and after. Once everybody had the idea, Kleewein rewound and sped up the playback.

The footage was frightening. Earth spun its way into darkness. Like somebody going through a large house turning off lights in every room, 2000 tromped across the planet. Light, dark. Next country. Light, dark. Next country. Light, dark.

Mark groaned. "It's like somebody's pulling a black curtain around the earth."

DECEMBER 31, 1999, 11:30 PM PST

The Keep's diesel generators cranked into action. Mark placed his hand on the side of one, feeling the vibrations run up his arm and through his body. The enormous mass of steel settled into the rhythm he'd come to know so well, a rhythm providing light in the darkness. Electrical systems in the building transitioned from Pacific Gas & Electric power lines to diesel. Aside from the minute flicker seen only by those who watched for it, nobody noticed the switch.

DECEMBER 31, 1999, 11:48 PM PST

Hooper Heliport covered four acres on the roof of C. Erwin Piper Technical Center at 555 Ramirez Street, Los Angeles. From there, LAPD's Air Support Division coordinated its fleet of more than twenty helicopters. The fleet's job was to provide ASTRO—Air Support To Regular Operations. LA residents knew the copters by their intense search light beams pointed at fleeing criminals, car accidents, and stolen vehicles.

The fleet's newest addition was a Bell 407. The bird had room for six passengers in addition to the pilot. It was nimble, fuel efficient, and very sophisticated. The new Bell used an Allison 250-C47B engine with Full Authority Digital Electronic Control. FADEC, as Dan Van Lan had explained to the S2 executives, is an advanced system that keeps engines working at optimum efficiency during maneuvers. It monitors hundreds of variables and alerts mechanics to maintenance schedules. At midnight on New Year's Eve 1999, it shut down completely when its embedded chips rolled their hard coded date routines to 00.

Lieutenant John Tarman and officer Marty Selrich flew the 407 on New Year's Eve. It was a typical night. They responded to a burglary call in Torrance and tracked the bad guy past bushes and dumpsters and fire hydrants until ground units caught and cuffed him. An officer on the ground waved thanks into the search light.

LA looked pretty at night. Its tinkling splendor covered 486 square miles from beaches to mountains. Helicopters watched over the City of Angels twenty-four hours a day. Marty was still a rookie in the sky, and still loved the view.

"LA looks so innocent from this altitude," he said.

John looked out the side window. "It really does."

They passed over Hollywood. Marty watched the Sunset Strip bustling through New Year's Eve. The Marlboro Man billboard reigned over the activities, joined by laser lights from the House of Blues and a giant inflatable shamrock hovering above Dublin's.

"Murray's having a social just past midnight," John told Marty. "The usual non-alcoholic fare. He says we're all clear to stop by."

"I heard about it," Marty said. "Sounds fun to me."

Murray Teft ran the Air Support Division. He'd been the Big Kahuna as long as anybody could remember. He rarely flew anymore. He just made sure everything kept running smoothly and that his people were happy.

There's a lot to be said for a guy like Murray, especially in LA police work. Nobody was too surprised that he arranged a social gathering on New Year's Eve. It was also par for the course that he'd be there himself. He never married. The division was his family. There were no other people he'd rather spend New Year's with than his crew, even if it did mean coming in to work that night.

"Hey you two slackers," Murray's voice called over the radio. "Feeling thirsty up there?"

John smiled. "You bet. It's about that time, isn't it?"

"Yes it is."

"We're going to catch showtime at the Hollywood Bowl. Killer fireworks."

"I'm jealous. Keep an eye on the city at midnight, then come on home, boys. I've got goodies to go around."

"Roger that," Marty said, joking. They never really said "roger that" except to be dramatic. He could tell Murray was smiling when he replied.

"Ten-four, good buddy."

DECEMBER 31, 1999, 11:59 PM PST

In southern California, the biggest party of all time raged toward the finish line. Known simply as "Party 2000," the event attracted 2.5 million people to a 4,500-acre site outside of Palm Springs.

The party began on December 30 and ran twenty-four hours a day. People stayed in four campgrounds, ate from 3,900 cement barbecues, and wandered through an arena containing five of the largest stages ever built.

The mob at Party 2000 started the countdown, providing the only sound at The Keep. Other screens around the room showed parties at the Seattle Space Needle and San Francisco's Golden Gate Bridge, but they remained mute to avoid confusion. The Space Needle's lights burned brightly, just as the ones on the Eiffel Tower had done. The Golden Gate Bridge displayed an enormous red, white, and blue light sign that was supposed to shimmer into "Year 2000" at midnight while fireworks launched from Alcatraz.

"Five, four, three, two, one, Happy New Year!" screamed Party 2000. The Space Needle turned black and stood like a wraith in the glow of Seattle's fireworks. The Golden Gate Bridge became a fallen log across the water. Alcatraz burned the sky in sparks and explosions and streamers and flame tails. The bay became fire in the sky and reflections in the water, nothing more.

Party 2000 was supposed to welcome the new millennium with music from The Rolling Stones, Metallica, The Spice Girls, and a few new bands. Not a peep came from the amplifiers, not a single colored gel lit the stage. The bands stood quietly among dead wires and microphones. Drummers started banging out solos, but the sound made it only a little way into the crowd. No power, no concert.

Once the fireworks cleared the air in Seattle and San Francisco and at Party 2000, the broadcasts continued with the usual camera battery light providing illumination. The reporter at Party 2000 gestured wildly and babbled onscreen. A male voice off camera interrupted her.

"Deveera, nobody's watching."

"What do you mean?" she asked, annoyed at being interrupted in the middle of her report.

"I mean no TVs have power. Look around. You're just talking to me. Let's get out of here."

The camera view fell to the ground. Deveera started to say something, but the camera shut off and the screen went blue.

January 1, 2000, 12:00 AM PST

Just before midnight, Lieutenant John Tarman had piloted the Bell 407 over the Hollywood Bowl for an aerial view of LA's fireworks. He hovered unnoticed above Mulholland Drive. The crowd in and around the Bowl held small lights of all sizes. At ten seconds to midnight, they turned off the little lights for the countdown. John and Marty watched the clock on the Bell's instrument panel. At midnight, the crowd went crazy and the fireworks exploded. At the same instant, the endless field of LA's lights went black.

Marty sat bolt upright in his seat. "Holy Christ. Did the city plan that?"

"I doubt it. They're festive, but not that festive."

"Wow. Look at that." The instant darkness was more moving than the lights had ever been. "It's like the city's gone."

Even seasoned John stared at the blackness. He tried thinking of something appropriate to describe it, but was interrupted by a wheezing noise from the engine. He craned his neck to look and felt a vibration turn his stomach. The vibration stopped. The engine noise disappeared. The breezy spinning of the rotor grew quiet.

When a helicopter loses power, there's no hope. It can't glide to a safe landing like a plane. No power means no lift. No lift means dropping to the earth like a rock.

"John, what the—" Marty started. His voice squeezed shut when he felt the lightness of falling. From the corner of his eye, he saw John furiously flipping switches and pushing buttons. Marty watched a firework bloom for what seemed his entire life. He remembered watching the same thing as a kid. He tasted the summer hot dog with extra relish. He saw his mother's face. The firework filled the heavens.

John managed to push the distress button before impact. From a place that seemed millions of miles away, Marty heard a metallic crunch.

It was the last sound of his life.

January 1, 2000, 12:01 AM PST

Captain Murray Teft saw the distress signal and immediately got on the radio. "Gents, everything all right up there?"

No reply.

The power shut off around him. Other officers turned on flashlights. Murray pushed the radio transmit button again, but nothing happened.

"We've lost radio power," he called over his shoulder. "Get me some juice in here." He referred to a switch lever that put the Air Support HQ on special lines from Pacific Gas & Electric. An officer threw the switch. Nothing happened.

"We're still dead," the officer told Murray.

"What? The dedicated power is off too?"

"Yes. Want me to try the generators?"

"Right away. We got an alarm from John and Marty."

A crew of officers disappeared into the building, their flashlights shining ahead of them. Five minutes later, the lights in Air Support HQ pulsed faintly then reached three-quarter brightness. That's as good as it would get with the generator.

Murray pressed the transmit button again. Still dead. "We can't transmit. Somebody pull a radio and try contacting me. Let's see if the whole thing is dead."

An officer sat at the auxiliary panel and tried to radio HQ. "No signal, Murray. I think the whole dispatch is down."

"Great timing," Murray said, pounding the counter. "The town shuts off, I get an alarm from the field, and half a second later the damned dispatch dies."

He paused a moment to think, then turned to Frank Martinez. "Fire up the Euro and fly to the Hollywood Bowl. They wanted to watch the fireworks. See what's going on and fly directly back when you've found something. Don't be gone more than twenty minutes."

Martinez ran across the flight deck to the Eurocopter AStar. He flipped switches as fast as his hands would go. The building roof lights shone dimly, ghosts of their usual brightness. The helicopter wouldn't start. Martinez tried again. No response. The lighting on the instrument panel illuminated and he could hear clicking sounds as he tried starting the engine. But no power. He tried again.

The Euro's Turbomecca Arriel engine was the fastest in the fleet. But the Turbomecca Arriel is electronically controlled, known for its multifunction response and fine tuning. It was a smart engine, and smart engines use chips.

Martinez ran back to HQ. "The Euro won't start," he gasped.

"Goddammit!" Murray said. "What did it do?"

"Nothing. It sat and clicked. The instrument panel lit up but the engine is dead."

A sick feeling came over Murray. He remembered service bulletins from Textron and American Eurocopter and Boeing. Textron makes Bell helicopters and Cessna planes. The company recommended replacing certain digital systems in its newer model aircraft due to potential problems arising in the Year 2000.

Potential problems? That hadn't sounded too bad to the Air Services Division. Murray thought they could handle poor timing or failed instrument lights as needed. Aircraft companies are notorious for nickel and diming their way to profits with add-ons and luxury features.

But now Murray feared the worst for the Bell 407, and his friends John and Marty. The Euro's engine wasn't nearly as automated as the Bell's. If the engine on the Euro didn't start, what might have happened to the Bell during flight?

Murray grabbed his coat. "Martinez, come with me. The rest of you watch HQ."

"For what?" an officer asked. "Nothing is working."

"Then sit here in the dark until it starts working!" Murray roared. He didn't often lose his temper. "Get the old Motorolas out and fire them up. Martinez and I are driving to Van Nuys. If none of our new birds are flying, we'll try the old birds."

"You really want to fly those?" Martinez asked.

"I'll watch this city in the damned Hiller if I have to."

The Hiller was the division's first helicopter, flown back in 1956. Murray hoped he had been kidding about flying it. It was around for nostalgia only.

Murray and Martinez arrived at Van Nuys Airport in twenty minutes. Few people shared the road with them. Murray's old Chevy started on the first key turn. They passed enough broken new cars to convince Murray that the Year 2000 was responsible for the helicopters. Chips are chips. If they're broken in cars, they're broken in birds.

Murray and Martinez ran to the office of LA General Services, LAPD's helicopter maintenance outfit. A lone security guard stood at the door, waiting for a repair crew to turn the lights back on. He had no idea how long the wait would be.

"Our new birds won't fly," Murray blurted to the guard.

"What do you want me to do about it?"

"Nothing. We're testing our helicopters and taking one out. Just relay the message if anybody asks."

"You got it."

They ran to the LAPD helicopter lineup. "Start trying to crank them up," Murray said. "The first one that goes live is our birdie."

The first few helicopters were Bell JetRangers. No luck. They tried a couple Euros again. No luck. They worked their way down the line of useless birds, and steadily back in time. Each model was a generation older than the last.

They finally reached a joke of a helicopter: the Bell 47. It was not much of an improvement over the Hiller. The 47 looked like a dragonfly with no wings. Its cockpit was surrounded by bubble-shaped glass. The engine housing sat like a shipping crate below the rotor, the word POLICE stamped in block white letters. Its tail was a long series of braced metal tubes extending back from the bubble body to a narrow point. It could have been an electrical tower turned in its side. If anybody wanted to film a comedy about cops in helicopters, this would be their model.

But the 47 started right up.

"Here's our birdie," Murray yelled to Martinez. He put his headset on while Martinez ran over and got in the passenger side. The 47 was supposedly a two-seater. That was for small people, evidently. A one-and-a-half seater seemed more accurate.

"You've got to be kidding me," Martinez said, looking around the cockpit.

"Hey, don't argue with success. She's running, isn't she?"

"Thank God you're here," Martinez said. "I sure as hell can't fly this thing."

"Hold on, son."

Murray held the stick and eased the 47 forward. It buzzed like a locust in a wheat field. He revved it louder. Martinez laughed, reminded of mowing his lawn. The 47 shuddered, lifted slowly off the ground and started its way across the valley. Murray followed the 101 freeway back toward Los Angeles. The few cars on the road zoomed passed the aged helicopter. Martinez watched them through the glass bubble.

"Does it take this long to warm up? Let's get going full speed."

Murray turned to him. "Martinez, we *are* going full speed."

JANUARY 1, 2000, 12:05 AM PST

Consultants kissed their spouses and children goodbye, then sprinted to their stations, placed headsets, and began working.

"Happy New Year, Mom and Dad," Mark said to his parents.

"Happy New Year, son," Grandpa said. They hugged. "We'll take the children home with us now."

Jeremiah and Alyssa smiled at Mark. "Happy New Year, Dad," Jeremiah said. "Everything you told us would happen really did happen. It was cool."

Mark pulled the kids to him. "I'm glad it was cool." Grandma Solvang's fluid eyes watched them but Mark could not tell if her eyes watered more than usual. It was late and she was tired. Her tired face looked very much like her sad face.

"When are you coming home?" Alyssa asked.

"Not for awhile. You know I have to work."

"Is it going to be bad at home, like we saw on television?" Jeremiah asked.

"There won't be any electricity. But Grandpa has lanterns and a special satellite phone you can use to call me. Grandma has plenty of food to eat."

"What about you and Susan?"

"There's food here. We're going to keep working until we fix everything you saw break."

Alyssa's little body began to shake from crying. "You're never coming home, are you?"

Mark knelt down beside her. "That's not true, Alyssa. You know it's not true. I have to fix everything that broke. Remember all the scared people on the television? You don't want them to live without lights and food, do you?"

"No, but we don't have lights either. You should come with us and fix ours. I'll draw you a picture if you do."

Mark hugged her to him. He saw Grandma's eyes again, this time sure that they watered from sadness. Alyssa sobbed in his arms. She felt tiny and bony, so vulnerable to all of the world's cruelties. How could he let her go? The children came to their father's office and watched the world crumble and then their father sent them into the night without him. If only Margaret were there.

His own sadness must have been apparent on his face. Grandpa Solvang rested a hand on Mark's shoulder. "It's all right, son. We'll take good care of them until you get home. We know you have lots to do."

Mark stood. Alyssa reeled around to hug Grandma Solvang. The soft, warm old hands caressed Alyssa's bony head and back. "It's okay, now," Grandma cooed. "Everything's okay."

Grandpa slid an arm around his son. "The children will be fine, Mark. You do what you have to do. We're only a short drive away and we've got the satellite phone. Don't you worry."

Mark looked to his father, then to his son. He patted Jeremiah on the cheek. "Take care of your sister."

"I will. You take care, too."

Mark smiled. "I will. Now get on home." He stood alone in the cafeteria to watch his four family members walk slowly to the doors. They turned to wave before slipping into the Y2K night. He waved back, then stood watching the door after they'd gone. He'd never doubted his duties until that moment, looking at the door that swallowed his family, wondering when he'd see them again.

An arm slid around his waist. That was not supposed to happen at the office, but he didn't care. "They're going to be fine," Susan said gently into his ear. "Come on. I'll pour you a glass of punch."

JANUARY 1, 2000, 12:09 AM PST

Tom Clausen got New Year's Eve off. He and Adelle went to a party at a neighbor's with twenty other people from the area.

Their neighbor's home in Encino, near Los Angeles, fell completely black at midnight. The group lit candles and tried turning on a radio. Every frequency was silent. They kept partying, but Tom felt uneasy. He'd left his gun home that night. With power out everywhere, he needed to check in with the department.

His beeper displayed January 1, 1980, 12:00. When he pressed a button, the screen showed a line of blinking dashes. "My beeper's out too," he told Adelle.

"Do we need to get home?"

"I don't know why we should go home, but I should check with the department. A city-wide power outage in Los Angeles is bad news."

"Just call from here."

Tom walked to the phone. It was dead. He walked back to Adelle.

"I'm going home to try my radio. It should be working. I'll come right back."

The street was black. Tom jogged the half block to his home, fumbled with the keys at the door. He felt his way to the coat shelf where he kept a flashlight. He clicked it on and walked to the dresser in the bedroom. The radio sat next to his badge and belt.

He pushed the power switch, relieved to see the red LED light up. The radio sat quietly. He spoke into it. "Tom Clausen requesting status." He waited thirty seconds and tried again. No response. The phone on the nightstand was dead. He'd better drive to the station. He put his badge in his back pocket and slung his shoulder holster under his coat.

Back at the neighbor's, Tom found Adelle with the others near the fireplace. They all warmed their hands, joking that it was just like a big camp out.

"Adelle," Tom called to her. She walked over to him. "I need to take the car and drive to the station. My radio is out."

"Is it safe to go home?"

"Probably, but I don't see why you should skip the rest of the party. Seems cozy in here. You might as well stay."

"All right. I guess you can't call or anything. How will I know what you're up to?"

"I'll come back to tell you anything major. Given what the papers wrote about this computer problem, I'm betting the city is a mess."

"Be careful."

"I will." He kissed her on the cheek before he left. It was a quick kiss, the only kind they shared anymore.

The trusty Jeep started on the first turn of the key. Tom had always liked his old Jeep, but never as much as that night. It drove like a charm past dozens of broken-down vehicles on the road. Every light in town was out. Tom arrived at the North Hollywood station in record time. Flashlights burned in all directions as cops arrived from around the valley. The sergeant addressed everybody from the steps of the station, being that there was no light inside anyway.

"People, the dispatch system is down. So are the new cruisers. We've pulled the old Motorola walkie talkies out. They have a range of three miles. We'll have to daisy chain messages back here and daisy chain them back out. That means you should work in pairs to patrol your designated areas. We'll use the proximity cards to divvy up the town. You should wear the orange vests. The reflective strips won't do much in these conditions, but it'll be further proof that you're a cop. Let's get out there."

Tom's partner was Davis Munoz, a tough guy he liked a lot. They'd gone through the academy together. They grabbed vests, walkie talkies, and their proximity card. The cards and walkie talkies were a smart backup plan that the various Los Angeles police departments devised to deal with riots in case of equipment failure.

The card was a bright orange plastic to be easily seen with a flashlight. It contained a number on the back, and a map of the city section that the officer carrying the card was supposed to patrol. On each edge of the card were the numbers of its surrounding cards. When all cards were taken, the city was covered in its entirety. The cards divided up a department's area into proximities that were small enough to be covered by the walkie talkies. The card numbers got smaller as the proximities came closer to the department. That way, an officer knew which way to send messages.

To reach backup, an officer would speak the request into the walkie talkie and reach patrolling officers in the surrounding areas. To get word back to the department, the message would need to make its way from one proximity to the next, and the next, and the next, and so on. It was clumsy and slow, but it worked in a pinch.

Munoz drove a new Nissan, and it didn't start that night. He caught a ride to the station from a neighbor cop. Tom's Jeep became their official patrol vehicle.

They drove quickly to their proximity, just a few miles from Tom's house. They took a fast tour of the local storefronts and banks. Satisfied that all was well there, they began driving up and down residential streets.

"What's this all about, anyway?" Munoz asked.

"You really don't know?"

"No, I really don't."

"It's Y2K. That's what's going on. Computers stopped working when 2000 hit at midnight."

Munoz looked out the window. "Actually, I remember reading something in the *Times* about that. Wonder when they'll have it fixed? Probably soon."

They came to a car facing the wrong way on the side of the road just past a dark intersection. A young couple laughed and coughed in front of the open hood. Tom parked the Jeep. He and Munoz walked with their flashlights pointed toward the couple.

"Everything all right?" Tom asked.

"No," the man said drunkenly. The woman fell onto his shoulder, laughing.

"Had a bit to drink tonight," Munoz said. "Think you're in condition to drive?"

"Sure," the man said. "Except my car is dead."

"What happened?"

"I was driving along, wondering where the city went, and all of a sudden the brakes seized or something. Next thing I knew, I was pointing back the way I came." The woman burst out laughing.

Tom got the man's license, registration, and insurance for the usual round of checks. He didn't have any verification equipment in his Jeep, but a cursory look at the documents told him they were legit.

"Where you folks heading?"

"Home," the man said. "Can't you call a tow truck?"

"Not tonight," Munoz told him. "Let's just get you home. Is the address on the license correct?"

"I guess so. If the DMV didn't screw up, then that's my address." The woman guffawed, then coughed.

Munoz turned to Tom. "He lives on Lasaine. Let's just get them home."

"Sounds good to me. We're not in much of a position to be busting tipsy drivers."

They drove the couple to the man's home on Lasaine. Tom and Munoz watched the couple stumble to the front door, unlock it, and fall into the house.

"That should take care of them," Tom said.

Cruising along Ventura Boulevard turned up a few more broken cars. People complained that their portable phones didn't work and asked when power would come back on. The police couldn't tell them. After dropping off the third back seat full of stranded drivers, Tom drove along Ventura again.

"What's that?" Munoz asked, looking out the passenger window to the top of the hill. Tom pulled over. They stood next to the Jeep, looking up.

"Oh shit," he said as they both realized what it was. "You've got to be kidding."

An orange glow pulsed over the hill from Los Angeles. The

sight was every cop's worst nightmare. Fires in the city. Riots. Looting. And they didn't have a dispatch system.

The walkie talkies chirped to life. "Prox 29, this is prox 33. You there?"

"Prox 29, go ahead," Munoz replied.

"You see the hill?"

"We see it."

"All units are headed back to the station. Enough of this taxi service. We've got a riot to stop."

JANUARY 1, 2000, 12:26 AM PST

The 129 men aboard the USS *Helena* had waited a long time for sunshine. They left Seattle three months prior for a trip around the Aleutian Islands, through the Bering Sea, and under the polar icecap.

Commander Donald Brosseau knew his men needed a few weeks in Honolulu. He tried to be back by New Year's so they could enjoy the big party Hawaiian style. Leis and lays were good for morale.

No such luck. The schedule placed them back in Pearl Harbor on January 5. He had notified the executive officer—the XO—and the rest of the ward room. Word passed quickly to the men.

Brosseau filled out paperwork in his cabin. His thoughts wandered to the University of Colorado, his alma mater by way of a Naval ROTC scholarship. He was among the Navy's best and brightest, rising through the ranks from nuke school. Commanding a 688 attack sub by age thirty-eight is not bad. And he hadn't even attended the academy.

Three knocks came on the bulkhead. "Come in." It was the XO.

"Skipper, sonar is having trouble analyzing signals. The conn has lost navigation processing. I'm sorry to bother you, but I think you should see this."

Control was missing a few glowing lights when Brosseau and the XO arrived. Brosseau knew the small room by heart. He could see every part of it with his eyes closed in his bunk. The periscope, dive controls, communications, and plotting charts were all like family. The place was normally alive with glowing lines and contours and dots and pulsing buttons. Not that night. Faces turned from the too-dark room as the senior officers entered.

"What happened?" Brosseau asked.

"Sonar reported that it can't process any signals."

"*Any* signals?"

"Yes, sir."

They walked to sonar. "What's up?" he asked the chief.

"More like what's down, sir," he said, pointing to his screen. "This should be filled with contacts, as you know. I'm getting noise, but the computer can't process any of it. It doesn't know water conditions, it seems to have forgotten its entire signature file, everything. I can't even compute ranges."

This was completely unacceptable. A submarine's ears, and the ability to understand what those ears are hearing, are its only means of interacting with the ocean. A sub without sonar is like a car without windows.

The anger built inside Brosseau, far down in his gut. He would keep it there. No use rattling his crew. But the anger would not go away. Somebody would pay for this.

"Keep the headsets on and listen for big stuff," he said to the chief. "I don't want to be running into any oil tankers. You still have ears and you know the major sounds. This would be a problem in battle if we were tracking torpedoes in the water. We're not. As of this moment, we're steaming through open seas for a dry dock in Pearl Harbor."

"Aye, sir."

Back in the conn, Brosseau asked about navigation.

"We've lost computer tracking of our progress," the Nav said. "I've pulled our charts."

"Good." Brosseau looked at the ocean floor contour screen. It stared blankly at him, useless. "Rise to periscope depth," he commanded. "Prepare the antenna and GPS receivers. I want to get a fresh fix."

"Aye, sir."

Helena came to within fifty feet of the ocean surface and slowed to three knots. Her antenna poked through the water.

"Update the GPS fix," Brosseau ordered.

"Aye, sir."

The precise positioning service would reveal *Helena's* location to within twenty-two meters horizontally and twenty-eight meters vertically. Combining the GPS information with the inertial data from the ship's own systems, they would know their exact location.

"No read, sir," the petty officer said.

"Try again."

The petty officer pushed a button. That was as hard as the procedure got. He couldn't mess it up. "Again, no read, sir."

"Try the old receiver."

"Aye." The petty officer switched to the sub's old receiver. "Still no read, sir."

Brosseau gripped the rail, hearing his knuckles crack. "Prepare to transmit." He should have been able to transmit a message anywhere inside the U.S. military satellite network within ten seconds. He waited twenty seconds for confirmation. None came.

"Prepare to transmit," he repeated.

"Aye, sir," the petty officer replied. "I'm locating a primary satellite. I can't find one."

What the hell was going on?

"Try secondary, then tertiary if you need to."

"Aye."

The secondary network was comprised of old satellites left over from the 1970s. The tertiary network consisted of Sputnik vintage contraptions from the late 1950s and early 1960s, never used anymore.

"We've picked up a secondary carrier, sir."

"Good. Transmit."

Helena sent a message to Pearl Harbor. "USS HELENA. NO GPS DATA. REQUEST STATUS. REQUEST IMMEDIATE RETURN TO PEARL HARBOR."

The response transmission returned moments later. "GPS RECEIVERS DOWN. PROCEED IMMEDIATELY TO PEARL HARBOR."

Brosseau leaned to the XO. "I think we're not alone in these malfunctions."

"I agree. I'm beginning to think the entire Navy is feeling its way in the dark."

"It's the computer glitch."

"Yes, I believe so."

Brosseau looked around the conn. "Does anybody know celestial navigation?" he asked with a smile. This was taking them way back to training school, stuff they never thought they'd use.

"Yes, sir," replied the Nav.

"Take her topside," Brosseau commanded, still smiling. "Nav, get us a bearing on your favorite star. After that, XO, take her to cruising depth and proceed to Pearl Harbor at full speed."

"Aye, sir."

"And you," he said to the petty officer at the contour screen, "keep those charts handy. Let's not discover a new island the hard way."

JANUARY 1, 2000, 12:28 AM PST

Admiral Philip D. Robek stood with his arms folded. Hawaii held the last major U.S. military bases to enter the new year: Pearl Harbor, Hickham, and Camp Smith. But their interests lie in the Western Pacific, where 2000 arrived first. The new millennium reached out and grabbed Camp Smith by the throat almost a full day before its clocks turned. Guam lost satellites. Ships disappeared from radar. Regular communications stopped and hadn't started again.

Robek's blood turned to steam in his veins. His voice remained steady and his manner calm. Forty-two years of naval service taught him that emotions are not public events. They are important motivators to be directed in a prudent manner. They are powerful. They are inevitable. But they are not to be shared.

"I want Pritchett online ASAP," he told Rear Admiral Macey. "I want our civilian teams in place by 0500 hours."

"Aye, sir."

Robek graduated from the Naval Academy with distinction in 1958. His career took him from flight training in Pensacola, Florida to Attack Squadron 176 on the aircraft carrier *Shangri-La*. He served on ballistic missile subs and fast-attack subs. He oversaw advanced submarine development in San Diego, helped create the Navy's long-range planning group, and became the Commander in Chief, U.S. Pacific Fleet, in 1995. After just one year at that post, the President nominated him as Commander in Chief, U.S. Pacific Command. He assumed his duties at Camp Smith in 1996.

Robek's job as CINCPAC left little joy in his life. He was responsible for 350,000 people serving in the Army, Navy, Air Force, and Marine Corps across 103 million square miles in the Pacific and Indian Oceans—half of the Earth. When midnight hit Guam, the Pacific lost two-thirds of its surveillance capacity.

Two-fucking-thirds, Robek thought to himself. He couldn't see what was happening in a sixty-eight-million square mile area.

The global positioning system fiasco had been bad enough. He had Tomahawk missiles that couldn't find their way to a continent, fighter planes that thought north was west. Swarms of engineers came to replace the faulty GPS equipment in July and August. For all the military expertise involved in the project, it took Billy Stamp from S2 to point out that the new equipment would last only until 2000. Robek was flabbergasted. The military had spent millions of dollars on the new equipment, and it had a shelf life of four months?

Now the New Year was upon them and Stamp was right. Global navigation was defunct.

"Sir," said a lieutenant. "We've received word from the *Helena*. She's lost sonar and navigation."

"Power systems?"

"All a go. Nuclear isn't affected by the computer problem."

"We should assume the worst for all 688s." The 688 Los Angeles class attack submarine was the Navy's mainstay under water. Until the Seawolf was commissioned in 1997, the 688 was the most advanced attack sub in the fleet. The Seawolf was faster, quieter, and better armed. But the Navy had only three Seawolf attack subs. It still relied heavily on the Los Angeles subs, with more than fifty cruising the world's oceans.

"Yes, sir. The *Helena* was able to transmit with her surface antenna. I don't know why we haven't heard from any others."

"As I said, assume the worst. This situation has been anyone's guess for the past six months."

"Yes, sir. The *Helena* has requested to return to port."

"Tell her to proceed."

"Aye, sir."

Without sonar and navigation, a submarine was useless. If other subs reported the same problems as the *Helena*—which Robek was assuming they would—he would need them to return to port as well. The same went for ships. If the fighting equipment broke on every vessel, Robek would have no choice but to call them back for repairs.

The U.S. would be forced to evacuate the Pacific Ocean, the world's largest theater.

JANUARY 1, 2000, 12:30 AM PST

"We've got thousands of car accidents in every major city," a consultant reported to Mark. "S2 Los Angeles says there are heaps of new cars broken down on roadsides. Families are huddled along dark freeways like refugees. Traffic lights are dead and radio is silent."

"Is all radio silent?" Mark asked. "Somebody find out if any radio stations are working."

A consultant ran toward a far terminal.

"Why would radio be off?" Mark asked Kleewein.

"Digital broadcasting."

The consultant caught his breath and swallowed. "New Year's Eve drivers are notoriously bad. Add the fact that everything shut down tonight, including most new cars, and we've got a catastrophe. The regular news delivery systems are down, but our own people driving from site to site are reporting back to their local S2 offices. The offices are reporting to us."

"Can you give me any specific number of accidents?"

"Not really, just that it's a lot."

"Okay, let's focus on the issue at hand. We can't do anything for the people in accidents. That's up to the police."

"But the police dispatches are broken."

Mark's brow furled. "Police dispatches are broken," he called to the rest of the room huddled around terminals.

"No shock there," Kleewein replied. "Most are run by computers. They sort calls by region and notify the nearest ambulance, police cruiser, or fire truck."

"All right," Mark said to the consultant. "Do we have teams helping the emergency dispatch systems?"

"No."

"The traffic lights are probably not broken, they just don't have electricity. We have people at the power companies."

"Almost all of our people," the consultant clarified.

"Are you trying to tell me something?"

"Yes. I think we should move some of our people from power systems to emergency dispatch systems. Folks are dying out there."

"I doubt many are dying. We need to stay focused. We can't save everybody. Get me work estimates from PG&E and Con Edison and the other major power plants. Based on that, we'll reevaluate whether to pull people to work on dispatches."

Mark stood like a sculpture in the center of the room, watching everybody work, running priorities through his mind. They needed to stay on top of power and phones and food. Those were the priorities. With more people in the morning they might be able to—

"Mark!" Kleewein cried out. "Take a look at this."

Mark ran to the satellite screens in front of Kleewein. The large overhead showed a shot of the United States.

"This is the country five hours ago," Kleewein said. The map was mostly dark with bright splashes of light in major metropolitan areas like San Francisco, Los Angeles, Seattle, Denver, Chicago, Miami, New York, and so on.

Kleewein pushed a few buttons. A new map image loaded from the top of the screen to the bottom. "This is the country one hour ago." The map was completely black. If not for the digital outlines of the country and states, Mark wouldn't have known what continent he was viewing. Kleewein pushed the buttons again. "This is the country fifteen minutes ago. Notice anything?"

Mark stared, unsure what he was seeing. The country was still black, but faint glows showed in Los Angeles and Detroit. "They've got power already?"

"Fire," Kleewein said. "The looting and rioting have already started."

JANUARY 1, 2000, 12:35 AM PST

Susan watched the satellite photos. "Can't we get a closer view of LA?" she asked Kleewein.

"We can zoom a bit closer, but it won't be news footage. I'll have a better view for you in fifteen minutes."

"The time delay is awful."

"I know. It's tough to update a satellite. We're using cameras from 1995. That's generations ago in this business."

"I've got S2 Los Angeles on the line," called out a consultant. "Who wants the call?"

"Conference room," Susan announced. She ran there, joined by Mark. "What have you got?"

"All of our New Year's people are tied up at Pacific Gas & Electric. Their first estimate isn't encouraging. They say it'll take a week just to sort through the LA code. We've got embedded chip trouble, as always. It's anybody's guess when we can get those fixed."

"Any estimate on live power?" Mark asked.

"No sooner than a week. That's extremely optimistic. The problem is this deregulated power grid. Nobody's in charge. Everybody owns it and nobody owns it."

"The buck doesn't stop," Mark said, disgusted. "Tell the PG&E team to start parsing the code with *Solvang2K*. We'll have our entire lab up and running by 8:00 this morning. If they can get the code to you, you can get it to us. We want to aggregate all the power company code here at The Keep. We'll be able to reuse more of our efforts that way. Hopefully, we can send fixed code back for proprietary changes at each power site."

"You got it."

"How about the city?" Susan asked. "Our satellite map shows fires."

"Yes, there are fires in South Central. That's all I know. I haven't seen them myself."

"What about phones?" Mark asked.

"Our telecom team won't be here until later this morning. But we got a call from Pacific Bell. It's just what we expected. Routers, switches, hubs—all shot. And of course, there's no power available for interval testing."

"Keep at it," Mark said. "Things might get worse."

JANUARY 1, 2000, 12:39 AM PST

Pete Dubridge and April Pennington sat sternly at their posts in Guam. All radar was down, and two-thirds of the satellites had stopped working as well. Officers came and went much more frequently than usual. Dubridge and Pennington combed the Asia Pacific region with the satellites they had left, crippled by their reduced resources, but still able to function. Ever since they discovered the He Zhang battle group's foray past Japan, their monitoring skills went unquestioned.

"Hey, Pennington," Dubridge called out during one of their moments alone in the tower. "I think I spotted them again."

"The He Zhang?" she asked.

"That's right. I can't say for sure, but they're not hanging around China anymore. It looks like they're headed for Batan."

Pennington rolled her eyes. "Batan again. They're probably going to Japan."

JANUARY 1, 2000, 1:25 AM PST

It took Murray and Martinez thirty minutes to find the crashed Bell 407. Murray maneuvered the decrepit old 47 helicopter along Mulholland and the hillside above the Hollywood Bowl. Martinez directed the ancient searchlight, convinced that a service flashlight might have provided as much illumination. At last they saw the crumpled body of the 407 lodged among thick shrubbery. Its rotor lay broken next to it.

Murray landed the 47 at the top of the hill. It descended in jerky motions, the engine creaking and whizzing its way to the ground. Martinez held the sides of his seat for impact, but the 47 managed a soft touchdown. Murray left the rotor on a light spin while he and Martinez hiked down to the 407.

"Jesus, that looks bad," Martinez said. He slipped in the flashlight beam as they stepped from grass clumps to rocks to shrubs, trying not to fall down the hillside. Between steps, Martinez shined his light down on the wreckage.

"They probably weren't too high. Hope for the best."

They slid the final ten yards to the pile of metal. The air smelled of fuel and exposed earth. Murray shined his light inside the bent cockpit door. John and Marty lay still, blood trails glistening on their faces. Marty's eyes stared forward, already dry and wrinkled in the air.

"Take Marty's pulse," Murray commanded. He pushed his own two fingers into the side of John's neck. Martinez worked his way around the wreckage to Marty's side.

"John has no pulse," Murray reported. It had already been an hour since they wrecked. With no pulse and no breathing, there was little hope for John. Murray knew that, but he would proceed with CPR anyway. Any other officer would do the same for him.

Martinez arrived at Marty's side and stopped. A piece of metal protruded from the side of Marty's head. His hair matted in the blood and clear fluid. It was obvious to Martinez that Marty was dead, but he felt around Marty's neck for a pulse anyway. Nothing. He pushed farther into the cool tissue, desperate to find a pulse. Still nothing. He closed his friend's eyelids.

"We'll still administer CPR," Murray said.

Martinez shook his head. "There's a piece of metal through his skull. We should focus on helping John."

"Damn," Murray said under his breath. Marty had been excited to go out in the new Bell. Before that, he'd been excited to join the Air Support Division at all. Small town kid in the big city. Murray looked over at him, strapped carefully into his seat. His head rested at a crooked angle. Aside from that and the blood, he could have been napping on the job.

"God bless you, son," Murray said. He looked up at Martinez, who wasn't any older than Marty. "Come give me a hand with John."

Martinez scooted around the front of the wreck, stabilizing himself against the copter's crushed body. Murray extended a hand to him for the last few feet.

"We need to hold him very still while we pull him out," Murray said. "There's fluid in his ears. He's got a concussion and I don't want to be jerking him back and forth."

Martinez nodded. Murray unclipped John from the seat. He and Martinez pulled the body carefully out and placed it flat against the hillside. Murray listened at John's mouth to double check. There was no air.

"We need to start CPR." He cleared the airway, tilted John's head and pinched his nose. Four blows later, he listened again while John's chest fell. He blew four more times. Martinez began chest compressions between Murray's breaths. They continued for roughly ten minutes.

"This could go on all night," Murray said. "Let's get him to the 47 and off to UCLA."

They pushed their arms under John's body, careful to keep his neck straight, and began the long trip up the hill. Hard as they tried, they could not keep from slipping on loose rocks. Their flashlights shined in odd angles that changed direction with every agonizing step. It was difficult to hold their lights steady and carry John at the same time. They paused every few feet to puff breaths into John's lungs and pump his chest. It took twenty-five minutes to get him to the helicopter, and still he showed no signs of life.

Martinez continued breathing into John and compressing his

chest as Murray flew the 47. He sat John in the half-passenger seat and faced him. He pumped John's chest against the seat with one hand and held John's head straight with the other hand. The 47 lifted creakily off the ground and buzzed the trio across the hills to UCLA Medical Center.

"Oh shit," Murray said once they were in flight.

"What's the matter?"

"LA's burning."

Martinez took a quick glance out the window. He saw flames and smoke past downtown, toward Lynwood. It was going to be a long night. He turned his attention back to John, giving breaths and compressing his chest.

Murray touched down ten minutes later at UCLA. Nurses with flashlights ran to the 47, wondering where in the world it came from. They'd never seen a helicopter like it before.

"Murray Teft, LAPD," Murray announced, showing his badge. "We need a stretcher right away!"

He and Martinez helped lift John onto the stretcher and walked inside the hospital with the emergency team.

"We have no power," a nurse told them, trying to explain the flashlights and lanterns hanging in the emergency room. Heaps of people sat moaning on the floor, on couches, in chairs. She noticed Murray looking. "Mostly car accidents. There've been a ton of them tonight."

The team took John down a dark hallway. Murray and Martinez needed to get back to Hooper Heliport. With the city on fire, they couldn't afford the luxury of waiting by their friend. He would have understood.

The 47 rattled into the sky above Westwood. Murray flew over Beverly Hills to downtown. The fires toward Lynwood already burned bigger than before, supplying the only light to be seen in the city.

"I see fires closer to town, too," Martinez reported. "They're already in Maywood, maybe Vernon."

"Come on, dammit!" Murray yelled at the 47 as they inched their way to Hooper Heliport. "We've got a war to fight!"

January 1, 2000, 1:30 AM PST

Tom and Munoz listened to the sergeant address the crowd of cops outside the North Hollywood station. "People, it's looking a lot like '92. We've got fires and looting and beatings. The National Guard and the military won't be able to arrive until daytime at the soonest, I'm doubting we'll see anything until Sunday. You remember how it went last time."

They sure did. The 1992 riots left fifty-five dead, more than 2,383 injured, and 13,212 arrested. There were more than 11,000 fires. The monetary damage to LA rang up to $717 million in three days. It was the biggest urban unrest in U.S. history.

The supposed cause of the riots was the acquittal of four LA police officers in the beating of Rodney King. Anybody involved in trying to stop the mayhem knew differently. The first rock might have been thrown by somebody upset about the trial, but all the rest were people who wanted any excuse to kill, steal, and pillage a city with as many ethnicities as the world has to offer. More than half of those arrested had never heard of Rodney King.

Christ, Tom thought to himself when the sergeant announced that they would issue riot shields. After grabbing a shield, they were to return home for bullet-proof vests and report back to the North Hollywood station. From there, they would be transported to hot spots in LA for basic containment.

"This ought to be fun," Tom said to Munoz.

"The sarge said containment?" Munoz whispered. "My ass. We couldn't do squat eight years ago and that was with the city operational. What's it going to be like tonight? Look at the vehicles they have lined up for us."

"And people," the sergeant concluded in a voice slightly lower than usual. "You've all got service weapons, but let's be frank. It's not going to be pretty out there. There are rules of engagement on the one hand, and there are desperate times on the other. I would arrive fully prepared to defend good people, including yourselves. I'm sure you read me."

Old police vans lined the street, waiting for the officers to drive home in carpools and return to the station. A few would remain in the Valley to quell any unrest there.

Tom and Munoz would go to LA. They walked to the Jeep with their riot shields.

"Hey, Tom!" a voice called from the crowd. A burly black man in his thirties ran up. It was Chris Butler. He lived in Encino as well, not far from Tom. He and his partner, Ryan Woo, shot pool with Davis and Tom. "You got room for two more?"

"Sure, but hurry. We need to get back here ASAP."

"Right."

He ran back to the crowd, returning moments later with Ryan Woo, a decorated officer who made the *Times* in a dramatic photo of him carrying a kidnapped girl under one arm and holding a pistol with the other. Butler and Woo sat in the back seat of the Jeep. Tom drove to Encino. He dropped off each man before driving home.

Adelle was still at the neighbor's house, which was fine by Tom. He hated the thought of her sitting at home in the dark by herself on a night like this.

There were four riot shields in the back of his Jeep and orange glows coming over the hill. With scenes of 1992 running through his head and adrenaline coursing through his muscles, he was glad Adelle stocked plenty of food and medicine. He wondered for a split second how the rest of the country was faring. Were other cities doing as badly? How could he know? He shrugged it off. LA was enough to think about. He placed his flashlight vertically against the bedroom mirror, lighting the room so he could find his equipment.

He velcroed the Kevlar vest in place over a t-shirt. He wore blue coveralls with "LAPD" on the shoulders and back. His badge sat snugly in the breast pocket. He buckled his service belt in place, checked the laser grip on his standard Beretta, and grabbed a helmet and gloves from the back of the closet. LAPD didn't require that officers have their own riot gear, but after 1992 many purchased it anyway. They trained extensively the rest of that year, then most fell back into the normal routine.

Time dulled the memory of fires and screaming and crazed looks and motionless bodies. But a few alerted senses bring dull memories crisply back to life. The sights and sounds and smells brought a mild panic to Tom's gut. The orange glow. The sound of the riot shields piling into his Jeep. The rip of velcro. The smell of his helmet. The weight of the coveralls and boots.

His mind raced outside his bedroom over the hill to the streets of LA. He knew he would smell the smoke and the gas, and hear the screaming again. His ears prepared for helicopter blades. His body cringed, anticipating the shatter of a bottle across the shoulders. His arms felt the heaviness of a still body in them.

Tom wiped the dust from his helmet and pulled it onto his head to check the fit. Snug. His head hadn't grown any. He took the helmet off. He strapped a shoulder holster in place and checked his real gun, a Desert Eagle .44 magnum, popular among Tom's LAPD cohorts as their official unofficial weapon. It delivered far more stopping power than the 9-millimeter Beretta. The Eagle is an Israeli weapon. Israelis can't afford to shoot twice.

The Eagle felt powerful in his hand, weighing more than two Berettas. Tom's rubberized grip was custom made by a local gun shop. His thumb and palm slid firmly into place. A slight squeeze of the grip produced a red dot on the wall, precisely where the bullet would strike at a velocity of 1,470 feet per second. When Tom relaxed his grip, the dot disappeared. He hoped never to see it against anything but the paint on a wall. Tom had never shot anybody.

He reached to the back of the closet behind his suits. His hand came back clutching a Mossberg 500 shotgun. He taught Adelle to shoot the 12-gauge and she wasn't half bad. He smiled, remembering her suggestion that he put a laser dot on it so she could aim better.

"A laser on a shotgun?" he'd asked her. "Why not just tape a flashlight to the barrel? The shots scatter to a circle the size of the television."

He loaded the Mossberg from the box of shells behind his dress shoes. He left the chamber empty. Adelle would need to pump it before firing. The sound of a shotgun pump in the dark was usually enough to send intruders running. If not, the subsequent blast that followed always did the trick—regardless of whether it hit. He returned the loaded rifle to the back of the closet, and retrieved his last weapon: a SPAS Model 12.

The SPAS—special-purpose automatic shotgun—is one of the most potent close-range weapons on Earth. It holds seven 12-gauge rounds in a compact length of just twenty-eight inches. In less than two seconds, the SPAS can fire all seven rounds. Tom's hand folded around the pistol grip.

The SPAS even looked mean. He could fire it with one hand, although he discovered at the range that the one hand would remember such an event for days after. The folding butt hooked around Tom's forearm to steady his shots.

Tom left three flashlights inside the door for Adelle. He carried the SPAS and his helmet to the Jeep, locking them in the back while he walked to the neighbor's house. He stopped at the door before knocking.

What would he say to Adelle? She knew about the 1992 riots. They made her cry. They made everybody cry, everybody but the news pundits who managed to dissect the disaster into a million component motivations until the whole event seemed scholarly. It wasn't. It was war on the streets with civilian casualties. Now Tom was armed for another.

He knocked on the door. The hum from inside quieted down a moment. Knocks in the middle of a lightless night are always unnerving.

"Who is it?" asked Myra, the neighbor wife.

"Myra, it's Tom. I need to see Adelle."

Myra opened the door, a lantern in her hand. "Hi Tom. I'm glad it's you. Why are you dressed like that? Is there trouble?"

"Yes, I'm afraid. I need to go to LA to help contain some fires and such. Would you please send Adelle out?" He didn't want to go inside wearing his gear. Everybody would start firing questions and providing commentary. He didn't need it now. He just wanted to see his wife.

"Sure," Myra said. She disappeared into the dark.

Adelle came to the door. Her face fell immediately when she saw his outfit. "Oh no," she said to Tom's grim expression. "You can't be serious."

He pulled her outside, closing the door behind her. He held his wife's hands in his for the first time in months.

"Adelle, Davis and I are going to Los Angeles for the rest of the night. There are fires again. You can see the glow from Studio City."

"Tom, what's happening?"

"I don't know yet. It looks like the usual looting, maybe a bit worse. Probably nothing to worry about, though."

She let go of his hands and crossed her arms. "Nothing to worry about. Sure, Tom."

"I don't know what we'll find over there."

"How can I get hold of you?"

"You can't right now. We're using old walkie talkies. The dispatch is down. Portable phones and beepers are out. Regular phone lines are down. There's no radio yet and, of course, no TV. I don't even know if the paper will come out this morning."

"What should I do?"

"Just stay here at Myra's as long as you can. Stay until daylight. If you decide to go home, have Bill or Kevin walk you. I put flashlights right inside the door." He looked at her, not sure how to say the next part. "Adelle, if you get scared, or if anything at all goes wrong, I've loaded the shotgun for you. It's in its usual place at the back of the closet."

"Tom—"

"It's important, Adelle. I know it sounds scary, but you probably won't need it. If you do, it's there and it's loaded. Just pump it once and you're live. You know how it works. You've done it before. Remember the flashlight dot discussion?"

She smiled. "Yes."

"Well, that's all you need to remember. If anybody threatens you, just point that barrel at them and pull the trigger. The Mossberg will handle the rest."

"Nothing is going to go wrong."

"No, it won't, baby. Come here." He hugged her to his coveralls. Her slim arms clenched around his chest. He could get his entire fist around her forearm. He lowered his nose into the part on top of her head. He'd seen half a dozen hairstyles on her, even a couple different colors. He'd smelled countless shampoos in her hair. She'd worn new hats every Friday. But through it all her scalp still smelled like Adelle, the same girl he'd known since she was only twenty. The same girl he eyed across a college lecture hall, those slim limbs working double time in tight clothes. His Adelle. All these years, all their troubles. He inhaled her scalp deep into his lungs. She pulled hard into him.

"You know I love you," he said.

Her head nodded.

"I mean that. Through good times and bad, remember?"

She nodded again. If not for the Kevlar vest, he would have felt the warm moisture of a tear through his coveralls. She pushed back from him, clearing tears under each eye with her thumbs. She folded her hands again. "Be safe, Tom. I'm going to miss you the whole time. I'm going to be thinking of you, and wanting you home. I love you, Tom. Don't get hurt. Tell Davis I'm going to hold him responsible for anything that happens to you."

He smiled. "I will, baby. I'll come back to you." He kissed her without noise. They pressed their closed lips together for several seconds, the warmth spreading on their faces.

JANUARY 1, 2000, 2:10 AM PST

Tom drove the Jeep back to the North Hollywood station, the tears of his wife drying on his coveralls. Munoz sat in the passenger seat, Butler and Woo in the back. Every man loaded a helmet, a box of shotgun shells, and a SPAS in the back next to the riot shields.

"Everybody have their Eagle?" Woo asked. Everybody did.

Tom parked near the transport vans. All four men filled a pouch with extra shotgun shells and clipped the pouch to their belt. They carried the SPAS shotguns pointed down, their helmets under one arm.

They sat in the backseat of the van. Other officers filed in, similarly clad and armed. Nobody talked. The driver slid the door shut, and drove onto the 101 freeway.

"Folks," he said once they were en route. "We've been assigned to Koreatown. As you all know, it's imperative that we protect that area. It took too much of a beating in 1992 to be forsaken tonight. Ourselves included, there are only thirty-five cops in Koreatown tonight."

A groan went through the van. They passed broken-down vehicles on the side of the road. People walked along the freeway, holding their thumbs out for the few cars that came by. One man shook his fist at the van when it didn't stop.

"You don't want a ride to where we're going," Munoz said.

The officers groaned at the low number of cops in Koreatown because the area was a rioting war zone. Racial tensions existed between Koreans and blacks. Just before the 1992 riots, a Korean grocer was granted probation after she shot and killed a fifteen-year-old black girl named Latasha Harlin. The grocer accused Harlin of stealing orange juice. Fifty-five of the first fifty-seven buildings set ablaze in 1992 were owned by Koreans.

Koreatown was so invaded by rioters—and forsaken by overwhelmed police forces—that store owners took to the rooftops with hunting rifles and shotguns to defend themselves. One tearful Korean woman explained to the *Times,* "We didn't do anything wrong. We worked like slaves here. We fought to make our community. We'll fight to defend it."

And defend it they did. Mobs ran around corners to be greeted by waves of gunfire. Korean snipers picked off bottle throwers and firestarters with an accuracy that brought newfound respect from the mob. Rioting is only fun when other people are dying.

The one Korean gunned down in the attack was eighteen-year-old Edward Lee, an only son. He and his friends heard a cry for help on Radio Korea. His last words to his mother, Jung Hui Lee, were that he'd be back in ten minutes. In the haze and confusion of battle, a Korean store owner mistook Edward for a rioter and shot him dead. As late as 1997, the *Times* reported in a special issue commemorating the riots that Jung Hui Lee could not dispose of her son's items. His books still sat on the shelves in his room. His clothing still hung in the closet.

Thousands of Koreans left LA to return to South Korea after the riots. Still, more than 200,000 Koreans remained in Los Angeles County, eighty percent of them foreign-born. Many emergency workers felt a special obligation to Koreatown. They had failed the hard working community once before. They vowed that it would not happen again, yet here they were showing up with a handful of cops and a few guns. Against what? Mobs of hundreds?

The driver waited for the groans to subside, then continued talking in the van. "Hopefully backups will arrive from the National Guard and maybe the military. We don't know."

They crested the hill above Hollywood. The view silenced everybody. Los Angeles looked like a bed of coals glowing in the darkness. Flames lingered around the shapes of buildings and houses and streets. Above the glow, billows of smoke rose into the night sky. The distant city toward the beaches was obscured from view by ashes in the air.

The driver kept talking as the van drove closer to the city. They passed the Hollywood Bowl, and the normally bustling lights of Hollywood. That night, Hollywood along the freeway sat still in the darkness while fires loomed in the distance.

"You'll work in groups of four until we get further backup. Your job is not to stop riots, it's to limit damage. Protect civilians. Don't worry about looting. Merchandise is not worth losing a life over, even a bad guy's life. Your radios have a range of three miles and should hold a charge until noon. Patrol on foot in your area until you receive other instructions. Do not stray from a five-block radius of where you're dropped off unless extreme circumstances warrant it. Orders will be delivered over the radios. If you're out of range, you won't know what's going on."

"Are we to repeat orders for proximity?"

"Yes. Repeat orders you receive so that any officers within your range, but outside the range of the order, will receive it. That'll lead to a lot of repeated messages, but it's well worth it."

The van exited on Western Avenue. The streets were deserted for the moment, utterly dark and ominous. Tom could barely see the rows of furniture stores in the periphery of the van's headlights.

"There's not a lot going on here yet, hence the low numbers of cops. Most people are headed south to Lynwood and Compton. There's a lot of stirring nearby, however, and we want people on the streets of Koreatown now. We're not going to pull another '92 on these folks. So, it looks quiet. But the action is not far away. Be ready."

Tom, Munoz, Butler, and Woo got out on the corner of Third Street and Vermont, a scene of major looting and arson in 1992. They watched the van's tail lights drive down the street, then disappear around a corner.

The glow from the southern horizon chilled Tom. He could hear a distant roar, perhaps caused by the fires alone, perhaps by the fire and screaming and shooting. He couldn't tell. Tall palms stood silhouetted against the fiery horizon.

The four of them stood on the corner without moving. The parking lots of Vons and Ralphs grocery stores stood empty. The streets were completely empty. During a normal day, they'd be filled with people of all colors selling books and trinkets and magazines from wooden stands. Pregnant mothers with rough hands would get in the way of fast moving kids wearing jewelry. The sound of air brakes would occasionally rise above the chicken coop clamor of people on the sidewalks. Tonight, all the characters were home. Koreatown waited with them.

The four officers slung their SPAS shotguns on their backs. They held the riot shields on their left arms. Their right arms were free to speak into the radio and swing as they walked.

"What now?" Munoz asked.

As if to answer him, the sound of breaking glass and a shout reached their ears. They ran up Third Street toward Western. A lone gunshot and scream came next. They ran faster.

JANUARY 1, 2000, 2:20 AM PST

Mark couldn't believe his ears. "Are you telling me that the entire air traffic control system is offline?" he nearly yelled into the phone.

"Yes," the S2 consultant replied. "We're at O'Hare and they have no planes on the screen. Dozens are scheduled to land across the country in the next ten hours."

"Power is out, of course," Susan checked.

"Yes."

"What about O'Hare's backup power system?" Mark asked. "Every airport has one."

"It's not working either."

"How are they going to land the planes?"

"They do have a generator for vital systems. They've got runway lights up."

"Is that going to be enough?"

"It's all the airports can do. The bigger question is how the planes are doing. None have communications because the radio towers are down. The whole damned cockpit is computer controlled these days."

Mark hung up the phone then looked around the room. "Who handled the FAA account?"

"Nobody," Kleewein answered. "The FAA never contracted with us."

"This moves to top priority. Lives are on the line right now. Didn't our Boeing team work up best-guess procedures for this very event?"

"Only what Van Lan and Stamp put together before going to the DoD," Susan said.

"Well how good was the stuff they put together?"

"It was fine for ground-based systems. There's nothing we can do for defunct planes in the air."

"There's also nothing we can do in the next ten hours," Kleewein pointed out, his voice quiet and distant. "I don't think our priorities should change."

Everybody's eyes looked down. Mark gathered himself.

"Kleewein, I want you to handle this FAA disaster. Get the procedures Dan and Billy put together, contact the local FAA, and stay in touch with our airport teams."

JANUARY 1, 2000, 2:49 AM PST

Chicago O'Hare is the nation's busiest airport, running more than 90,000 passengers through in a typical day. Its backup power systems reached full capacity moments after midnight. Runway lights remained on. But Chicago Approach Control could not communicate with planes.

Radio was functional, but no planes responded. There were ten flights scheduled to land at O'Hare between 5:00 and 7:00 AM Central. The first two flights at 5:00 AM were international and were already in the air when 2000 hit. The other eight flights were domestic. Each was grounded at its origin when 2000's troubles became evident. The two international flights made their way to Chicago from London and Paris.

"How big are these planes?" asked Maureen Dedrick, the S2 consultant assigned to O'Hare.

Junior controller Paul Delgado stared out the window, not sure what to do. He wished the FAA would arrive. "Big enough. It takes a big plane to handle international ranges. The Paris flight is a Boeing 747 with 384 passengers. The London flight is a Douglas MD-11 with 291 onboard."

"Do the pilots still have control of their aircraft?"

"Judging from the shutdowns around here, the autopilots are probably gone, but the human pilots can fly manually. I'm more worried about navigation and collision avoidance. Modern planes are nothing but electronics and hydraulics."

The FAA duty officer from Chicago's Flight Standards Office walked in. He stuck a cold hand out to Maureen. "Richard Rand."

"Maureen Dedrick from Solvang Solutions."

Rand turned to Delgado. "What's the status?"

"No communications and only ten minutes until scheduled touchdown."

"Why can't they hear our communications?" Maureen asked. "We're able to transmit."

"I have no idea," Rand said foggily. He pushed buttons and

flipped switches to see if anything responded. Nothing did. "Probably because communications are broken. Airplanes are run by dozens of computer systems, Ms. Dedrick. Right now, we're looking at two big broken computers with wings."

"And people inside," Delgado said sadly.

"Jesus," Maureen said to Rand. "What can we do from here?"

"Watch and pray."

The auxiliary lights went black. Outside, the runway lights disappeared.

"And keep the lights on!" Rand yelled. "What the hell are they doing?"

Delgado picked up the phone, forgetting that it was dead. "Hand me that radio!"

Maureen handed it to him.

"Where are the lights?" he yelled into it.

The radio screeched. "The generator missed. We don't know why our uninterruptibles are down."

"You better figure it out quickly! We're five minutes from touchdown by planes that might not have controls of their own. Do you read me?"

"I read you. We're getting flares."

Out the window, Maureen saw an army of flashlights scatter down two runways. Along each edge, the men placed burning flares. They ran as fast as they could to cover the length of the runways.

"Where are the ambulances and fire trucks?" Delgado muttered to himself. Two old airport fire trucks idled at the end of the runways. For situations like this, there should have been dozens lined up next to twice as many ambulances.

Rand looked at Delgado. "Good question. When did you call?"

"Two hours ago. Told them to be here by 4:45."

"Most emergency vehicles can't start," Maureen said, her voice colder than she expected.

"How do you know?" Rand asked.

"Because we've studied this scenario."

"In that case, what's going to happen to my planes?"

"I don't know. The FAA is not a client. Neither are these airlines."

Rand turned back to the window. With no inside lights to create reflection in the glass, he had a clear view of the flared runways. The red torches looked pathetic stretching into the distance. He'd seen brighter lights from cigarettes. His eyes looked upward. "Here she comes."

The Boeing pierced Chicago's cloud cover. Its massive wingspan cradled pads of air as it settled its bulk toward the Earth. Beams of light shot down ahead of it, finding reflective paint on the asphalt.

"Slow down, slow down!" Rand cried into the glass.

The plane had no guidance from the tower, no proximity warning system. The flares provided little assistance. The entire city of Chicago was dark. There were no lights to tell the pilots that they were anywhere near the right place. It was a miracle that they even made it to O'Hare. But they could not see precisely where the ground was. They approached too fast. The pilot saw the runway and pulled up to avoid impact.

Too late. Maureen could not see completely through the plane's landing lights, but she saw the smooth trajectory of the Boeing suddenly jerk and twist into an explosion of sparks. Its tiny landing gear flew in all directions like children's toys. The sound of rending metal screamed through the tower glass. The Boeing's nose edged under, ripping the cockpit from the fuselage. The plane slid 150 yards on its belly. The engines had snapped from the wings and bounced end over end behind and next to the plane. The body swerved off the runway. A tip of the starboard wing caught the snowy grass edgewise and flipped the enormous mass of steel and luggage and petrified bodies. The plane flipped side over side. It took three revolutions from one wing stub to the next before the Boeing corpse came to rest in the snow next to the runway. Bits of metal and sod and asphalt rained from the air. A cloud of smoke billowed from the remains.

Maureen screamed. She'd never seen anything so horrible in her life. She leaned against the window, smearing tears on the glass. "Oh God," she groaned.

The two fire engines roared to the fuselage. They sprayed foam along the outer body while the mob of flashlights ran to the wreckage. The men poured into the yawning tip of the plane to unbelt living bodies. The smell of vomit and blood and jet fuel overwhelmed them. An arm hung from a cargo bin. One mother had crushed her baby to death trying to hug it tightly to her during the crash.

Maureen leaned against the window, Rand collapsed into a chair, Delgado stood still. After two full minutes of total emotional shutdown, Rand cleared his throat to try to overcome the pinched feeling. His voice came as a whisper.

"We should probably make sure they're still working on the lighting."

Nobody answered.

He picked up the radio. "This is the tower," he said in a husky voice. "How is the power coming?"

An equally strengthless voice responded. "We're still working on it."

"The faster, the better," he said.

"I know. Believe me, I know."

Rand dropped the radio on the desk. There was nothing he could do. There was nothing to fix, nobody to command, nothing to inspect, nothing to change, nothing to do but wait. But for what?

"So we just sit here like some sick audience to watch the next show?" Maureen blurted.

"I don't know what we can do," Rand said, not angry with her. He felt the same way.

"How long will it be?"

"Any time," Delgado answered.

Rand picked up the radio again. "Place the fire trucks at the ends of the runways. When the plane begins to descend, light them up."

"Good idea. We're lining the runways with men waving flares this time. The flares on the ground combined with others waving in the air might show them where the runway is." A voice in the background told the man something. "Right. We're also laying reflective strips on the runway."

"Sounds good. We'll keep trying to transmit."

Maureen watched Rand press the transmission button. He spoke into the microphone. No response came. She wiped the tears from under her eyes and sniffed. "I'm going out to wave flares with the others. It sounds like it might help."

"Me too," Delgado said. "It only takes one person in here."

"All right," Rand whispered. "I'll keep trying to transmit and telling them to hurry up with the power. I don't know what else there is to do."

Maureen and Delgado ran down the hall to the stairwell. They bundled in jackets and gloves and hats as they went. They ran from the building to the maintenance shack. A foreman handed them each two flares and pointed them to the clear runway on the right.

Delgado showed Maureen how to pull the rip wire that ignited the flares. "Don't do it yet, though," he shouted. "Wait until we see the plane."

A crewman directed them to a spot halfway down the runway. They stood next to each other in a line of men holding unlit flares. Their faces could have made the cover of *Newsweek* during a war.

"Here she comes!" a man yelled.

Maureen listened to the whoosh of flares igniting along the runway. She tugged the wires on her flares. The searing red flames shot out two inches from the ends, much brighter than she expected. Following the lead of those around her, she moved the two flares in a cross pattern above her head. An army of moving flames framed the runway.

The MD-11 descended through the cloud cover over the other runway, where the Boeing crashed earlier. It approached slowly as the Boeing had done, but Maureen learned that what looks smooth and gentle in the air isn't always so on the ground. The plane's lights splashed the end of the runway and floated closer to the debris-strewn landing surface.

A few men started to run to the other runway to alert the plane. Maureen stepped forward to follow.

"Stay where you stand!" a man yelled to the flare crew. "Keep waving, people! Keep waving!"

The plane's nose pulled up to provide a final slowdown before touching the asphalt. It still moved much too fast. The slats and flaps on the wings hung low to catch the air, but the ground came up quicker than the landing gear could withstand.

"Slower! Slower!" the men started yelling. "Come on, you! Slow that sucker down! Stop! Pull back! Easy, baby!"

As if it heard, the plane's engines suddenly screamed to life and the wings launched upward into the sky. The plane climbed away from O'Hare back into the clouds. The noise of a plane taking off had never sounded so soothing to Maureen. The flare crew cheered wildly.

"They know!"

"Keep waving the flares."

The plane came in slowly and far beyond the beginning of the runway. It descended to a low altitude and flew slowly toward the flared runway. It's lights began flashing.

"Great," Delgado said. "Now what?"

The lights flashed in short blinks and sustained beams. Blink, beam, blink, blink. Beam, beam, beam. Beam. Blink, blink, blink. The lights continued flashing as the plane neared. It did not descend to the runway.

"It's Morse code," the foreman yelled. "Everybody follow."

Delgado watched closely. He spoke to Maureen as the message came through. "LOTS...FUEL...WAIT...DAYLIGHT. He keeps repeating that message. Excellent plan."

The plane flew overhead, fired its engines to full force, and disappeared into the cloud cover.

"That's using your brain!" the foreman yelled. "He's waiting until daylight. Let's get back to the wreckage. Leave your flares along the edge of the runway."

Maureen did as instructed. She and Delgado followed the crew to the wreck. She braced herself for what she knew waited there.

JANUARY 1, 2000, 3:02 AM PST

A disquieting realization came over Tom as he ran with his partners along Third Street. The Koreans would not be able to see that the four of them were cops. Emotions would run high and people would start shooting. Friendly bullets were as dangerous as unfriendly. The only Korean to die in 1992 was killed accidentally by another Korean.

The four of them rounded the corner at Normandie Avenue. A crowd of roughly fifteen figures held flashlights and threw rocks through storefronts. The crowd yelled and whooped. The twirling flashlights created a confusing strobe effect. Tom could not make out any faces through the darkness.

"Flashlights!" Tom commanded. He and Woo pulled their lights and shined them directly into the crowd. That left Butler and Munoz with free hands for the bullhorn and weapons, if necessary. "Butler, on the horn!"

"Back away from the store!" Butler yelled into the bullhorn. The official crackle of his voice through the horn rolled across the night. The crowd turned in a confused tumble. Some figures ran away. Others started yelling.

"Man, who the fuck are you?"

"You better back off!"

"Get them!"

Butler yelled again. "This is the Los Angeles Police Department. Return to your homes immediately. If you do not move away from the store, you will be arrested."

"Fuck you!"

From the nest of shifting lights and dark figures came a projectile. Tom could not see where it went, but only that somebody's arm moved quickly and that an object flew through the flashlight beams.

"Down!" he commanded.

The four of them dropped instinctively to one knee, crouched behind their shields. A bottle crashed to the pavement nearby. Before they stood back up, another bottle broke behind them. Something else thudded and rolled.

"Go!" Tom blurted. They could crouch all night and yell until the bullhorn ran out of juice. People who do not respond to warnings immediately do not respond at all.

The four officers stood together and ran at the crowd. Tom and Woo replaced their flashlights on their belts and grabbed nightsticks. The swirling flashlight beams from the crowd searched the night for the cops. One beam found them, then another. The mob yelled and scattered.

Butler reached the first man and bashed him with his shield. The full power of his 250 pounds lifted the man off his feet. He let out a cry and fell to the ground. Butler pounced on him immediately, kneeling on his back. The man tried to get up, but Butler bashed down again with the shield.

"Hold still!" he yelled. He dropped the shield to unclip one pair of handcuffs from his belt. He cuffed the man and told him to remain on the ground.

Munoz cold cocked a fleeing vandal and left him cuffed on the sidewalk. Tom and Woo each had one man as well. The rest of the mob dissolved into the darkness.

They lined the four captures along the sidewalk, then radioed for assistance. The message reached another team of cops working Koreatown on Western Avenue.

"You got how many?" a cop on Western asked.

"Four," Tom repeated, still out of breath. "Cuffed and quiet. We need somebody to pick them up. We can't drag them around all night."

"Right. We're in the same boat. We have three."

"Pass our message along. We're at Fourth and Normandie. Stay in touch. Eight cops are better than four."

They stood with their captures. Tom took a deep breath. His hands shook. They always did after a skirmish. After extremely tense moments, he got tears in his eyes. They weren't crying tears, just moisture he couldn't control. It had happened twice on the job, once during a North Hollywood bank shootout where the robbers had better guns than the cops. Tom and his fellow officers raided a local gun shop for assault rifles. After they killed the robbers, the Army gave the department a load of M16s so they wouldn't be outgunned again in the future.

The other time was during a drug bust in Van Nuys. An old Mexican woman came out of nowhere with warpaint on her face and a spear in her hand. She nearly skewered him. Tom reacted too fast for his own better judgment, and cracked the woman across the face with his nightstick. He'd never felt so bad in his life.

"What's the matter with you people?" Butler asked the four cuffed bodies in a row. "What in the hell is the matter with you? The city loses power, people are scared, and the first thing that comes to your mind is causing trouble. It's shitheads like you that make LA such a hard place to raise a family."

The men said nothing.

"And don't tell me your sob story about being poor," Butler continued. "I was poor. I grew up in South Central and you don't see me breaking windows and stealing cars. Munoz there was poor, too." Munoz rolled his eyes. Butler always had a speech for the criminals. Many of them didn't even speak English. "He clawed his way out of Echo Park. You think his kids are going to be Cholos? Hell no. They're going to college."

Butler turned to Tom. "Clausen here has never hurt a good person in his life. He put his privileged self in the line of public duty just so he could save decent people like his family from scum like you. Woo put himself through school frying rice and making 3:00 AM deliveries to rich frat rats at UCLA. You think that was easy? Hell no. Nobody has it easy. So shut up about being poor and underprivileged. We've all seen empty dinner plates."

Butler took a breath. "You know something else? If I could have a dollar for every dirtbag—"

Tom patted Butler's arm. Butler looked over. A roar of flame reached into the sky from the direction of Western Avenue. Their radios crackled.

"Clausen, you still there?" came the officer's voice.

"Still here," Tom replied.

"An appliance store just exploded and we've got a serious crowd forming. I think you four should mosey this direction."

"Where are the prisoner vans?"

"Don't know. Bring the John Does with you for now."

Tom shook his head. He looked to his partners. Munoz shrugged and pulled his man to his feet. "All right," Tom said into the radio. "We'll meet you at Fourth and Western in ten minutes."

They got all four prisoners on their feet and pushed them down Fourth Street. A gunshot pierced the night, followed by several more. Tom recognized the rapid popping sound of an AK-47. His hands started to tremble again.

"Officer down!" screamed the radio. "Officer down!"

Tom pushed his prisoner into a run. "Get moving!"

JANUARY 1, 2000, 3:10 AM PST

The Bell 47 settled its decrepit frame onto the flight deck of Hooper Heliport in downtown Los Angeles. Murray and Martinez were greeted by surprised officers.

"What the hell is that?" asked one.

"It's the old Bell," Murray replied, trotting with them into the building. He pointed to two of the men. "Grab one of the new search lights and mount it on that old bird. Martinez and I need to take her out right away."

The men started in a different direction. Murray yelled after them, "and I want it lockable and controllable from the pilot seat and the passenger seat. Move!"

He turned to another officer. "Top off that fuel tank."

Inside the half-lit building, Murray continued barking orders to officers. They ran from post to post, caught up in the excitement of their usually steady captain.

"Are the old Motorolas still working?" Murray asked.

"Yes. We're following the riots from the field, but the lines of communication are slow."

"Any word from the mayor or chief?"

"Not yet."

"Good. Martinez, grab an M-16 with a laser and an ammo box. Get a dayscope and a nightscope."

Martinez disappeared down the hall. Outside, Murray saw his men rigging up the 47's new search light. Its high power beam would cut through more clutter than the weak light Martinez used to find the crashed 407.

Martinez returned with his armament. Murray glanced at it and nodded. "All right," he announced, "Martinez and I are heading out in the 47. We're taking two radios. It'll be light in a couple hours. Bad guys, like vampires, slow down in sunlight. Now, what's the latest?"

"Valley cops have already come over the hill. Most are south in Lynwood and Compton and Watts. A few are in Koreatown already."

"Good," Murray said. "Somebody remembered Koreatown. Where are the waves moving?" He referred to the trend of riot outbreaks. They move in waves, like forest fires. Neighborhood to neighborhood, home to home. The desire to riot reverberates in bigger circles as word gets out.

"Hard to say, but generally north. We've got new skirmishes breaking out all over the place."

"How far away?"

"The newest are in Vernon and Jefferson Park."

"That's just south of Koreatown," Murray said. "Come on, Martinez. We're flying to Little Pusan."

JANUARY 1, 2000, 6:35 AM PST

"According to your report, this place was ready to go," Pritchett said through clenched teeth.

Dan looked directly into his eyes. "We fixed these systems. Solvang rewrote the code to process new signals from Mercury chips and Atlantic Aerospace microelectronics." Pritchett and Schwager finally chose Mercury Systems and Atlantic Aerospace Electronics Corporation to lead the hardware side of the Y2K preparation. Mercury supplied most of the chips and digital signal processors, Atlantic Aerospace supplied most of the microelectronics to support the chips. Solvang rewrote the software to control the new hardware. "These systems are working on fresh software using fresh hardware. We tested until there was no room—"

"Then what's happening here, Dan?"

"I don't know. We turned every clock in this place—in this whole building—the same way we tested Solvang headquarters itself. These systems passed. We identified critical components in all of our triage meetings. You were there, you remember. The command center was at the top of our list."

"Fine. But it's beginning to look like we've accomplished nothing in two years."

"These systems were good to go as of two weeks ago. You read the report."

"Yes, I did. It said the command center was fully compliant. We expected to lose links with certain parts of the world due to remote system failure, but local systems would remain intact. Is all of this trouble due to remote systems?"

"You know it's not. What's different tonight? Are we on a different power supply? Is somebody wearing a new beeper? These systems were golden two weeks ago and tonight they're shot. I'd confirm it with Mercury if they were here. But they're absent."

"Have you called them?"

"Yes. Nobody's answering the regular phones or picking up the satellite phones. Every team lead has a portable regular and a portable satellite phone, so does Bertelli, Mercury's CEO. Nobody's answering. I can't reach the Atlantic team, either."

Pritchett felt the numbness creep farther up his fingertips. It tingled around his neck. If Van Lan said the systems were fully operable two weeks ago, then the systems were fully operable two weeks ago. What had changed that? What could have possibly gone wrong? S2 and Mercury had continued working the whole time. They would have seen any problems or change in system response.

"Are you fixing it?" Pritchett asked.

"I'd love to, except that it's not a software problem. We've been looking at our work all day. We need Mercury here to help find the problem."

"Keep working,' Pritchett said. "I'm going to get Mercury and Atlantic in here pronto." It was not his job to coordinate hardware vendors. It was Schwager's job.

JANUARY 1, 2000, 6:40 AM PST

The satellite phone rang at The Keep. Mark pushed buttons on his belt to wire his headset into the call. Kleewein and Susan did the same.

"Mark, the National Military Command Center has shut down," Dan reported breathlessly. "No monitors, limited communications, reduced launch capabilities."

Mark's face pulsated. "That's everything we placed on priority so this phone call would never happen!" he yelled.

"I know."

"Dan, it worked two weeks ago."

"I know, Mark! Believe me, I know. I'm at my wit's end."

"Are the hardware crews there now?"

"No, we're still trying to reach somebody."

"The Pacific isn't faring any better," Mark said. "Billy reported that Guam's satellites are almost gone. Major weapons systems, flight systems, sonar, radar."

The headsets sat silent for a moment. "You're doing all the right stuff," Mark said. "Keep doing it and keep sending code back here for us to work on. The entire crew will be here soon and we'll work this thing over."

"How's the rest of the world?" Dan asked.

"Not good," Susan replied. Her fingers clicked on a keyboard as she spoke. She read off the terminal screen. "We've got riots in Los Angeles and Detroit, power out everywhere, three planes have crashed, phones are down, and traffic is a nightmare."

"My God. I'll stay in touch."

Mark walked to his office. The hallway lights shone at half their brightness to conserve energy. The computers mattered most. He opened a file drawer and pulled several folders related to the Department of Defense account. He had one on the DoD systems, one for Mercury Computer, one for Atlantic Aerospace, one with progress reports from the Pacific team, and one with progress reports from the Atlantic team.

Systems certified compliant by S2 teams should not have been breaking. The National Military Command Center had been completely rewired and recoded for 2000. S2 and Mercury and Atlantic all confirmed that their respective pieces were ready to go, and that the pieces worked together flawlessly. Now they were broken.

Solvang knew its hot spots. It knew what was going to fail and it knew what was ready for 2000. Only the military suffered from broken systems that S2 had certified would work.

"Everything all right, Mark?"

Mark jumped in his seat. It was Jules Hartmire and two guards. "Yes, as all right as it can be at the moment."

"I saw your office door cracked and wanted to make sure it was you in here." Hartmire's face provided a reassuring calm. It was the face of somebody whose job was entirely under control.

"I'm checking on the defense account, coincidentally. We hired you because of our work with them."

Hartmire nodded. "Have they called?"

"Yes. Pritchett and Schwager are livid. I'm sure they'll be coming here."

"Why do you say that?"

"I'm guessing. If I had hired a vendor who was onsite and everything was breaking anyway and that vendor kept communicating with a headquarters that was totally functional, I'd get myself to that headquarters."

Hartmire nodded. "So would I. We'll be prepared when they get here."

"Let's not be too friendly. I don't want them overstaying their welcome."

JANUARY 1, 2000, 6:45 AM PST

"Who the fuck is responsible for this?" General Marquist demanded of a lieutenant. "I've got a Red Phone system that doesn't know where to call. I've got a billion-dollar satellite system that isn't aware of which planet it's orbiting. I've got ICBM and SLBM warning systems that don't know what a ballistic missile is. Are we still in the United States? Where are my capabilities?"

The lieutenant stood speechless, looking between the general and a blank monitor screen.

"They're broken, General," Pritchett said flatly. "I've got the best civilian software contractor on the job and the best embedded chip manufacturers on the way. All teams are working furiously to get things moving again."

"Working furiously. Do you realize what we're talking about here?"

"Yes, I do. This is the biggest freeze in our history."

"Didn't DISA know about all this? It seems to me that when a whole nation full of equipment is set to expire on the same day that our information systems agency might have known about it."

Schwager walked over. "We did, General. It's been at the top of our priority list for three years. We're still working on it."

General Marquist moved his eyes between Pritchett and Schwager. Pritchett knew his expression. It betrayed a profound loss of respect, an expression more painful than hatred to a man with Pritchett's résumé. "I hope to God you can fix it soon," was all Marquist said.

"Schwager," Pritchett said quietly, "let's talk for a second." They walked to the far side of the terminal room. "What are you planning to do here?"

"I'm planning to work through this as best we can. The same thing anybody would do."

"Yes, but where are the extra developers and where is Mercury?"

"I have no idea where Mercury is. Solvang is here. It's their fuckup, Ed, not ours."

Pritchett resisted the temptation to grab Schwager by the face and twist his mouth shut. This was clearly DISA's responsibility.

"Listen, Al, it is not Solvang's problem, it's ours. It's our job to defend the United States against all enemies foreign and domestic. That company has worked with Mercury around the clock on jobs that you assigned them. They've briefed me completely along the way and reported a lot of progress. Their report as of two weeks ago said this command center was fully prepared for 2000. You tell me why everything is breaking."

Schwager's lip snarled as he spoke. "If you're trying to put the blame for this century date change in my lap, you're out of your mind. We've all been in the same hot water for years. I'm not the one who built the world's biggest military around computers that don't understand four-digit years. I'm not the one who decided to use S2. They couldn't prevent this disaster in time. You've said so yourself. They failed. What can I say? You want me to make excuses? I don't have any. It was the biggest damned job in history and you chose a lead vendor that couldn't pull it off in time. You failed, I failed, Solvang failed, Mercury failed. We've got blank screens and broken phones and I feel like shit about it. But your riding my ass over whose fault it is does nothing to help us."

Schwager was smokescreening. Pritchett had never seen anything so obvious. Electricity shot through the nape of his neck, like he'd just seen a sniper in the window.

Schwager clutched a fistful of notes inside white knuckles. He leaned closer to Pritchett's face. "If we want this organization fixed, we need to take control of S2. Marquist is furious. Enough of this civilian bullshit! Solvang is too slow and they have not placed us at top priority. The only way we're going to get through this mess is with our own leadership. Let's militarize Solvang Solutions immediately and fix the armed forces ASAP!"

Pritchett had felt a numbness in his fingertips when the room started shutting down. Dan Van Lan had looked ready to collapse. Schwager should have been as stunned by the breakdown as any of them, but there was little surprise in his face. His response was almost rehearsed. The biggest damned job in history. Solvang failed. Couldn't pull it off in time. You've said so yourself. Militarize immediately.

Pritchett cocked his head to one side, looking at Schwager through narrowed eyes. Something was really fucking wrong here.

"Listen to me," he said, one step closer to Schwager's face. "Solvang Solutions has done everything it promised to do. The only failures I see in this room are yours. I said at the beginning that military control of Solvang was a last resort. I meant it. Your job is to make this military work. Do it!"

Schwager pointed a finger in Pritchett's face, the face of the Undersecretary of Defense. "I am doing my job, Ed. Stay out of my way while I work."

Lieutenant Mellec arrived at Pritchett's side. "Is everything all right here, sir?" he asked, eyeing Schwager intently.

Pritchett never took his gaze from Schwager's eyes. "Everything's fine, lieutenant. Thank you. But do me a favor and call every number you have for Mercury Computer Systems and Atlantic Aerospace."

"Sir?"

"You can get the listings from Van Lan. When you get hold of somebody at either company, keep them on the line and come directly to me."

"Yes sir."

"I'll help you get the job done by bringing two of your primary vendors onsite," Pritchett spit at Schwager. "They were supposed to be here already. Funny that nobody's seen them."

JANUARY 1, 2000, 7:00 AM PST

Pritchett's phone rang. It was Lieutenant Mellec.

"Sir, I have a Mercury Computer employee in Sterling and Dan Van Lan on the line. The Mercury employee is named Allen Baladad." Mellec got off the line.

"What's going on?" Pritchett asked.

"I'm at home with my family trying to adjust to life without electricity," Baladad said. "I got a satellite call from you guys saying that our Pentagon team is missing. You tell me what's going on."

"What's your job?" Dan asked.

"I'm a RACE computer engineer working with Atlantic Aerospace at the Center For Integration. We're still testing and verifying fiber channels for RACEway Interlink." He paused. "Do you need an emergency team from Sterling? I'm not sure what you fellows are putting together over there, but if it involves Mercury systems I'm sure we can help."

"Yes," Pritchett said. "Gather the best team of Mercury and Atlantic people that you can. Be at the Pentagon ASAP. Have a guard take your team to the NMCC. Tell them you're on a code Lansing by request of Edwin Pritchett. When you arrive at the NMCC, tell the guard to get Dan Van Lan—he's the other voice on the phone."

Pritchett walked to General Marquist. "General, an emergency team of contractors is on its way from the CFI in Sterling."

"Fine. At this point, I don't care who you bring in. Just get the place working."

JANUARY 1, 2000, 9:05 AM PST

Billy Stamp scurried around Pearl Harbor ever since the new year first hit Guam. He knew the trouble would start immediately, and he was right.

"Without its navigation system, the Tomahawk is just a pretty rocket," he deadpanned to the Navy's lead tester.

The Tomahawk cruise missile achieves its flight capabilities with an inertial guidance and terrain contour matching system, abbreviated TERCOM. It died at midnight. Global positioning could not find any global positions. Contour mapping chips failed. The Navy test team reported its results with clinical indifference.

"TERCOM rating zero," the lead tester reported to the Yeoman. A rating of one was fully functional. With something as critical as TERCOM, it was either working or it wasn't. There was no .5 rating for partial functionality.

"GPS rating zero."

"Contour system rating zero."

The results were the same for the next four missiles. "We have five Tomahawks that don't work," the lead tester said to Billy. "We'll keep moving on the others and provide a final report later."

"Right. I'm heading back to the terminals. Leave a copy of your report with me or Carl Albright."

Carl was standing when Billy walked back in. That was always a bad sign. Carl raised his eyebrows at Billy when he saw the usually happy face twisted with concern. "You go first," he said.

"Tomahawks are completely useless," Billy told him. "The navigation system is broken."

Carl shook his head. "Submarines and ships are reporting on the secondary satellite wires. Phalanx mounts are broken on the *Nimitz* because of the radar, sonar computers are down on every submarine so far, fighter planes can't fly, and even helicopters are grounded. Other than that, we're sitting strong."

"Even Phalanx is down," Billy said to himself, shaking his head. "That means the big systems are down as well." Carl nodded. He had arrived at the same conclusion.

Phalanx is a close-in weapons system whose only job is to shred missiles and aircraft that penetrate outer defenses. It's a ship's last hope if anti-missile missiles and chaff rockets fail. When an enemy missile or plane comes within 2,000 yards of a ship, the Phalanx activates its own self-contained engagement system. The smooth white cylinder of the Phalanx brain sits above an M-61 Gatling gun. The radar cylinder searches, detects, evaluates incoming threats, acquires its targets, tracks them, fires the Gatling, and assesses the kill. The Gatling uses a pneumatic gun drive to fire 4,500 rounds per minute. When one of the first Phalanx systems accidentally locked onto a sailor running across deck, all they found were his boots—feet still inside.

Because the Phalanx is a microcosm of every automated defense onboard a ship, its failure did not bode well for the Navy. If the small radars were down, so were the big. If the small tracking devices failed, so did the big. If a machine gun didn't work, what hope could there be for a fighter plane?

"Have we heard back from any missile cruisers?" Billy asked. Cruisers use the legendary Aegis combat system. Aegis is similar to the Phalanx in that it's a completely automated defense, but far more sophisticated. Instead of controlling a single machine gun, it controls the complete missile capabilities of the ship. Its computer can defend against planes, ships, and submarines—all at the same time. It deals with trouble in piecemeal fashion, killing the most pressing threats first. Tracking the progress of threats means time stamps and sophisticated computing. That was the wrong mixture in 2000.

"We don't need to," Carl said. He looked at Billy. "Aegis is dead in the water."

Billy closed his eyes.

"Everything's dead in the water."

6

TRIAGE

The Maris neighborhood was a quiet collection of homes sprinkled around a cul de sac on the side of a hill. Rivers ran through meadows in the distance, pine trees etched jagged shapes across every horizon.

Gary loaded the woodstove. Patricia had moved cold food from the refrigerator and freezer to the back porch. Her cooking pans sat beside the woodstove, which had become her new kitchen.

The Maris family had adjusted well to Y2K. Gary and Patricia followed the S2 survival memo and had plenty of water and food. After loading the woodstove that Monday morning, Gary inventoried the food stored in his garage and pantry. Over the weekend he'd given some away to his neighbors, most of whom had not prepared for 2000. Gary was careful to go to the food storage alone so as not to allow any of them a look at what his garage had to offer. The last thing Gary wanted was word getting around the neighborhood that the Maris home had become a crisis grocery store.

Neighbors talked in the living room during daylight. Most of the talk focused on how ridiculous the situation seemed and that it shouldn't be much longer until everything was back to normal. Then a neighbor would casually mention how amazed they were at what just a few days without modern conveniences can do to a household.

"How are you folks coming on food?" Rob Hansen had asked on Sunday. His family lived directly across the cul de sac.

"Fine for now," Gary answered. "If this thing doesn't last too long we should all be fine."

"You would think so."

"What are you saying, Rob?"

"We were due for a grocery run just before all of this. We bought some New Year's party type of food but didn't use the same trip to buy standard household groceries."

"You running low?"

Rob nodded. He was the fourth neighbor who'd visited over the weekend. Gary was afraid that word was already getting around. There were eight homes in the cul de sac. Four of the seven other homes had already stopped by for food.

"What do you need?" Gary asked.

"The basics. Would you mind lending me a few cans of vegetables and some cuts of meat?"

"Not at all. Wait here while I go round up a bag of groceries for you."

Patricia, by then familiar with the scene, began talking to Rob while Gary went to the garage. From the wooden shelves, he grabbed cans of corn, peas, mixed vegetables, fruit cocktail, and beans. He tossed in a box of Pop Tarts for the kids and a box of Wheat Thins. From the freezer, he chose a package of pork chops and two pounds of ground beef. Every home in the neighborhood had a woodstove and was able to cook. Lastly, he grabbed one gallon of water from the shelves against the far wall.

Rob took the bag and the water, a mixed look of embarrassment and appreciation on his face. "I'll be sure to return two bags of groceries when the lights come back on."

After the Monday morning inventory of the food shelves, Gary walked back into the house. Patricia and the girls huddled around the woodstove, warming themselves while a pot of water came to a boil.

"How's it look?" Patricia asked.

"We're fine for now. We've given away a week's worth of food."

"How many weeks are left in there?" Claire asked.

"We've got enough for another few months."

Danielle rolled her eyes. "I think that should do it, Dad. I mean how long could this last?"

"I don't know and neither do you. I think it will be enough food, but that doesn't mean I want to throw caution to the wind and start setting it out on the street. It'll last our family three months. It'll last the neighborhood three weeks."

"I need to get more candles," Patricia said. "We might as well get more food for the neighbors. We should all go."

"I haven't showered," Claire said.

"I'm warming a pot of water," Patricia told her. "We can wash up in the sink again."

Gary decided to take their old minivan. He wanted to keep gas in the GMC truck as long as he could. It was a tougher vehicle than the minivan, better in a pinch.

The grocery store parking lot was a zoo. Cars ignored lines on the pavement and arranged themselves in clusters of old metal and bald tires. Everybody drove their ancient vehicles that would still run. A long line stretched its way back from the store's front entrance. Workers in red overalls walked up and down the line, trying to keep people calm. The doors were shut tight.

"Holy shit," Danielle said, pressed against the glass.

"Normally, I'd reprimand you," Gary said. "But on this occasion I have to agree. Holy shit."

Gary parked at the far end of the lot, away from the bustle. He hated crowds and he hated waiting in line. The whole grocery store scene tensed his jaw muscles. But the neighbors needed food and Patricia wanted candles. His normally good-natured girls were not having much fun these days. They showered in the sink. They walked across frozen grass with a roll of toilet paper in their hands to relieve themselves over a bucket. Afterwards, they sprinkled lime powder on top of the fresh waste to tame the smell. If candles would lift their spirits, candles they would get.

The school of people shifted among themselves, swirling in front of the glass like fish at the top of an aquarium when the food hatch swings open. Even without food falling into the water, they would swirl and bite each other and keep eyeing the surface for a tiny flake of parchment.

"Open the damned doors!" a man yelled.

"I need food for my children," wailed a woman with a baby.

An overalled man stood on a chair, addressing the crowd through a cone. "We do not have power. Our lights are off. It's dark inside and we can't operate our registers. Please take a number and—"

"Then let us in to get the food before it spoils!"

The crowd yelled. The Maris family worked their way forward, then stopped. Gary didn't want to be in front of too many people when the doors opened. If they opened.

"Screw your checkout system! We need the food!"

"Our distributors should be here by the end of the week," the overalled man yelled. His voice was getting lost among the shouts. "We can't open our doors until power is back on. Please take a number and come back later in the week."

A man jumped on a car hood and tore up his number. He waved a tire iron in the air. "Open those goddamned doors or we'll open them for you!"

The mob roared. Somebody threw a rock at the doors. It bounced off. Another rock and then another flew through the air.

"Come on!" Gary yelled to Patricia and the girls. "We've got to get away from this."

They backtracked through the crowd. People continued yelling and shaking their fists. Every man's cheeks and chin were covered in raggedy stubble. Greasy heads framed angry faces, screaming past the Maris family as they worked their way against the flow. Gary reached the edge of the mob just as the man with the tire iron let out a berserker scream and leapt from the car hood.

"Storm the doors!" the man screamed. "Storm the doors! Storm the doors! Storm the doors!"

The mob picked up the chant. Rocks darkened Gary's view of the store. The workers in red overalls moved away from the doors, covering their heads with their arms.

A wall of people pressed against the glass. The man with the tire iron wormed through the mob, screaming the whole time. He stuck the flat edge of the iron between the doors and pried them inches apart. Hundreds of fingers grasped the edges, jerking the doors open one inch at a time.

Another wave of screaming washed across the mob and the mass of bodies surged forward, pressing the front line of people against the doors. A man cried out and fell to the ground. Somebody stepped on him, then he disappeared beneath the feet around him.

The doors jammed. The man with the tire iron yelled again. He raised the iron above his head and smashed the glass of the left door. He raised it to smash the other door but the crowd surged forward too soon. A solid mass of people forced the front line through the jagged glass of the left door like meat through a grinder. People screamed as their bodies scraped across the broken edges. Each person broke more of the glass away until there was little left to cut the others. The left door broke through entirely. The mob ripped the right door from its tracks and poured inside the grocery store.

"Dad, are we even going to try getting in there?" Claire asked.

"Nope, not now. We can wait to see what goes on. When the fuss dies down, maybe we'll get inside for some candles. But I'd rather not risk our lives to do it."

After forty minutes, most of the people had left with armfuls of groceries. The workers in red overalls tried stopping the first few, but quickly gave up. Fights broke out and several bodies lay motionless in front of the doors. A few had been trampled, one guy was knocked out by a fist, another woman just sat and cried.

"Come on," Gary said. "Let's at least pull them out of the way. I can't believe people."

The Maris foursome walked to the fallen bodies and pulled them to the side. Patricia talked to the crying woman, trying to find out what was wrong. The woman couldn't say clearly.

"Do you need food?" Patricia asked.

The woman nodded.

"We'll try to get you some food after the store has calmed down. There will be something left."

"You can't go in there for food," a worker said to her. "It's illegal and we won't allow it."

"Give us a break," Gary said. "Did you just arrive or something? Take a look around. Most of the food is already gone and your store is in ruins. The damage is done. Giving a little food to a hungry lady isn't going to change anything."

The man stood a moment, then helped Danielle and Claire with the last body. "Where are the cops when you need them?" he said to nobody in particular.

"I imagine they're busy," Gary said. "You're not the only store in town, and these aren't the only hungry people."

Gary looked around at the clamoring parking lot and the packs of angry people running from the store with food. Why did they bother to run? "I'm going inside for some candles and whatever food I can grab."

The worker nodded. "Here," he said, holding a flashlight toward Gary. "You'll need this."

"Thanks. You and the girls stay here with him," he said to Patricia. "I'll be right back."

"One of us should go with you," Danielle said. "We can carry twice as much food that way."

"I'm glad you've got your mother's brains. Danielle, come with me. We'll be back soon."

Gary and Danielle walked to the darkened grocery store. They edged around the side of the broken doors to avoid being hit by somebody hurtling out of the frenzy. Light from the doorway and windows gradually gave way to darkness. Looking into the store revealed movement everywhere, but nowhere. It was hard to identify any single person's activities. The crowd became a colony of insects clamoring over themselves at an abandoned picnic.

A sour smell wafted around Gary and Danielle as they walked through the check stands toward the end of the light. It smelled like somebody had taken every piece of food from every shelf, blended it together in a processor, then spilled it across the floor.

Gary clicked on the flashlight. Food displays at the end of each aisle were toppled. Loaves of bread had fallen to the floor and been trampled into flat dough. He shone the light down the cereal aisle. The floor was covered in spilled cereal, the shelves almost entirely empty. A few people felt along the shelves in the darkness. Others sat on the floor holding their bloody heads, apparently the losers of skirmishes over a bottle of juice or a can of soup.

An occasional cry and yelling pierced the general bustle, but nobody spoke. Standing still at the shelves, Gary listened to the crinkling of packages, the thudding of feet on the floor, the tapping of metallic shelves, and heavy breathing. It came from everywhere. When he shone the light across people, they turned their backs toward him and used the beam to see what they could grab before somebody else beat them to it.

Gary held Danielle's hand. They walked quickly along the ends of the aisles. Determined as he was to stay above the mob mentality, Gary couldn't help the feeling of urgency that overcame him. This was a food store and his neighborhood needed food. The noise around him acted like the steady clicking of a timer toward the end of a round. When the round was up, the food would be gone and that would be that. He shone the light down each aisle, looking for a missed pocket of food in the confusion.

They found half-full shelves of condiments. They pulled bottles of ketchup and mustard and barbecue sauce down until they couldn't carry any more. "This is silly," Gary said, putting the bottles back again. He grabbed Danielle's hand and trotted back to the checkout counters. He ripped two handfuls of plastic bags from the end of the counter.

"Take half of these," he said to Danielle as they trotted back to the condiment aisle. He shone the light down the aisle again. People had found the condiments and were cleaning the shelf. Gary walked to the next aisle and found empty shelves.

"Let's get to the meat."

The meat counter was empty and the glass smashed. They walked behind into the butcher area. Past the grinding and slicing machines, they pushed through two large black flaps into the main storage freezer. Gary pulled the silver metal handle and shone the flashlight onto shelves full of uncut beef. Pools of blood and water had collected in the bottom of the freezer as the temperature warmed and the ice melted.

"Bingo." He put one plastic bag inside another. "Hold this." Danielle held the bags while her dad half filled them with meat.

"Is it getting too heavy?" he asked her.

"Yes, that's probably enough."

"Set it down and let's do it again."

She double lined two more bags and he half filled them with meat. "Don't you want any chicken?" she asked.

"No, just beef."

They each carried a bag of meat into the main grocery store. The first aisle they approached was empty. The next aisle had a few bags of chips and cans of dip. They put them into plastic bags. The next aisle displayed party supplies, none of which had been touched.

"Candles, Dad," Danielle said. They found boxes of party candles and scooped the lot of them into a bag of chips and dip. They found a few medium-sized candles in the shape of numbers, but most of the candles were small for a cake. Gary pulled a dozen boxes of matches into the bag, then moved on.

They bagged boxes of crackers, flour, a few bags of candybars, and some cans of tomato paste. The ready-to-eat sections of the store were almost entirely empty. Danielle did find cans of ravioli and spaghetti. At the back of the same shelf was a bundle of noodles that somebody had missed. She grabbed it too.

Gary reached across her for a bottle of Ragu on its side. Somebody seized the bag of meat in his other hand and tried pulling it away. He fell back from the shelf. The flashlight clattered to the ground.

"Dad!" Danielle screamed.

Gary regained his balance quickly. He couldn't see who held the bag. He pulled back on it and felt the plastic stretch thin in his hand. A fist hit him in the arm.

Danielle retrieved the flashlight and pointed it at Gary and the attacker. It was a young man with blond hair. She directed the beam into his eyes, blinding him. Gary clenched the fist of his free hand and swung into the man's face. He hadn't felt the squash of a nose beneath his knuckles since high school. He punched again. The man cried out and let go of the bag. The second punch brought a splatter of blood across Gary's hand and forearm. The man fell backward onto the floor. He held his nose with both hands, cursing Gary.

"Dad, look out!"

Three more people ran from the back of the store up the aisle toward them. The grocery bags attracted attention. Gary grabbed the Ragu and ran with Danielle away from their pursuers. He couldn't defend their bags against three people. Even if he won the fight, the food would be lost and the entire expedition into the store would have been for nothing.

They rounded the end of the aisle, Danielle slightly in the lead with the flashlight to guide them. She ran into a woman.

"Watch out!" the woman screeched. She grabbed for Danielle's bag. Danielle elbowed her in the side of the head. Gary heard the footsteps of their pursuers coming up the aisle. He pushed Danielle forward.

"Over here!" he said, ducking into the next aisle. "Turn off the light!"

Danielle clicked the flashlight off. They backed against the shelf. Gary set his bags down, ready to fight. They watched the three people silhouetted against the storefront windows. It looked like two men and a woman. The three of them walked past the woman holding her head after Danielle's elbow smash, then along the ends of the aisles. They went to a checkout counter for their own bags and began walking to the far end of the store. Gary watched them until they disappeared from the window light.

"Let's get out of here," Danielle said.

"Give me the light." Gary clicked it on and pointed down the aisle. He picked up his bags with his bloody hand and walked down the shelves. He grabbed a six-pack of Coke and a two-liter bottle of Orange Crush.

"I hate that stuff," Danielle said.

"I'm not working off a list, Danielle. Now we can get out of here." He clicked the light off.

They walked carefully toward the front doors. People continued streaming in and out. Everyone leaving held as much food in their arms as they could carry. As Gary and Danielle neared the doors and the light from outside, Gary felt people's eyes on the bags of food.

"Let's get moving!" he barked at Danielle.

They ran into the light, through the doorway, and onto the parking lot. Patricia and Claire saw them.

"We've got to get this to the car!" Gary yelled. He and Danielle kept running. They passed the shopping carts, weaved through the chaotic parking lot, and arrived at the minivan. Gary set his bags down, turning to see if anybody ran at them. It was only Patricia and Claire.

"What happened to you?" Patricia asked, looking at his bloody hand and sleeve. His hair was messed up and food clung to his back where he'd fallen on the grocery floor.

"We were attacked," he said, unlocking the rear liftgate.

They loaded the groceries. Claire lifted the last bag, peering inside it. "Ugh," she said to Danielle. "I hate Orange Crush." Danielle nodded.

Gary drove out the back of the parking lot. He was still out of breath. He looked in the rearview mirror at his daughters. Danielle's eyes were open wide and watery. A smear of dirt covered her nose and left cheek. Her hair had come out of its clip. It hung in blond clumps across her sweaty forehead.

He glanced at the gas gauge. The minivan had a quarter tank.

JANUARY 2, 2000

"Radio is trickling back onto the scene," Kleewein announced over the headsets. "Backup power systems are filling in for the time being. According to the satellite footage, radio has brought an unforeseen side effect."

"What could that be?" Mark asked.

"Word has spread about the rioting and looting. Radio was as much a starting gun as anything. People in major cities heard about the mess in LA and Detroit and the rioting has spread."

The Keep was already a real life experiment in sleep deprivation. Around the terminal room sat piles of food containers from storage. Quick trips to the bathroom allowed people to run water over their hands and fingers through their hair. Half-eaten packages of breath mints lay on tables and office equipment around terminal rooms. Eating a mint was faster than brushing teeth.

"How far?" Susan asked.

"Miami, Chicago, New York, Philadelphia, Denver, St. Louis, and San Diego. It's the opportunity of a lifetime. Cops don't have dispatch systems, alarms are out, everything's free. It's the great Y2K shopping spree."

"What about LA and Detroit?" Mark asked.

"LA seems to be picking up steam. The early morning satellite photo shows more fires there than before. Detroit is falling off a bit."

"It's colder there," Susan said. "People can't have as much fun when they're freezing."

Mark and Susan walked to Kleewein's satellite station.

"How bad is LA?" Mark asked.

Kleewein pulled the latest photo onscreen. "This is LA at 5:00 AM this morning. You can see fires all over the downtown area. Some up here now, too. They weren't there before."

Susan's mouth went dry. Kleewein didn't know LA like she did. To him, the fires simply started "here" and were now burning in new places "up here" and "over here." But she knew the names behind the "heres."

"The fires have spread from South Central to downtown," she started, pointing at the screen with a pen. "They've even moved to the beaches. That's Santa Monica."

"Then there's all this mess down here," Kleewein added.

"That's Orange County. I can't believe it. Even conservative Orange County is looting. That's around Newport and this up here is near Buena Park."

"And up here?"

"Those are fires in Hollywood, and these," she said, moving her pen farther up the screen, "are in Studio City and Burbank. There are fires all over the valley. These are Encino and Sherman Oaks. My God."

"What's the matter?"

"Most of the trouble is in residential areas."

JANUARY 5, 2000

Pete Dubridge could now confirm his earlier suspicions. He had speculated to Pennington that a new crew of ships was coming down from the Yellow Sea. Now he could prove it.

"Pennington," he called across the room. "Look what I've got." She came over. He pointed to six hours of plot lines. "Tell me where those originated."

"The Yellow Sea," she answered.

"Where are they heading?"

"Down past Shanghai."

It was a lot of movement for six hours. Due to the reduced satellite capability, Dubridge would lose tracking on the group for the next six hours.

"Do you think they have anything to do with the He Zhang?" Pennington asked.

"Yes, that's exactly what I think. You've been tracking the He Zhang. Where are they these days?"

"They steamed right past Batan and into the Philippine Sea. They've slowed down considerably."

Dubridge grew serious. "You think they're going to Japan again? That whole loop that caused such a fuss last time started in Japan. Remember?"

"Of course I remember. I wish our damned satellites were working. Losing our plots every six hours is like watching the world through a strobe light."

"I know, but we're good at projecting."

"So far. One slight course change and our contacts will appear anywhere."

"Not anywhere." He held a compass up for her to see. "Once we know their speed and heading, we can use this to see the maximum distance they could cover in the six hour interval. Then we just open this thing to that distance, place one point on the contact and draw a circle around them. That shows us where they have to be when the lights go back on six hours from now."

"And since few of these big boys ever change heading by more than a few degrees, we can reduce the circle down to a fairly narrow arc in the direction of their current heading."

"Exactly," he said with a smile.

"You're a genius, Petey. When do the two groups meet up?"

"This new group won't even reach Okinawa until Friday. How much of a hurry is the He Zhang showing?"

"Not much, actually. They've slowed way down from their fast tracks last Saturday. They raced from the South China Sea to Batan, then started crawling from Batan into the Philippine Sea."

Dubridge looked fiercely at the plot lines. "This is really starting to worry me."

JANUARY 1, 2000

"I can't see a damned thing," Tom whispered. He crouched between stores in a Koreatown strip mall. Butler and Woo crouched beside him, Munoz slightly behind. Each man clutched his Beretta.

A fire raged across the street and Tom heard a woman screaming. They would have run to help her except that a mob of roughly fifty people occupied the mall area, throwing rocks through windows. A gun fired. People yelled and scattered.

"Did the shot come from the crowd or a rooftop?" Woo asked. The Koreans had already taken to defending their businesses. It heightened the danger. Bodies were bodies to a crazed store owner, especially in the dark.

"The crowd," Munoz answered. "I'm almost sure."

It was Saturday night. Tom and his three partners patrolled all of Friday night after helping get the wounded officer from Western Avenue into a van with their four prisoners. Daylight brought some peace, but not much. Looters sacked every grocery store in Koreatown, sometimes running right past the owner as he boarded up the entrance.

Another shot rang out across the parking lot.

"Where was that?" Butler asked.

"Behind the dumpster," Tom answered. "He's firing at the rooftop across the street."

"Are you sure?" Munoz asked.

"No."

Flickering light from the fire gleamed across eyes in the

darkness. People peered around broken cars and signs and furniture in the street.

The boom of a shotgun blasted through the scene. Tom heard pellets bouncing off the dumpster. They would do little damage at that range. Still, a man yelped and ran from behind the dumpster. He held something in his hand.

"Should we nail him?" Woo asked.

"We don't know if that's a gun," Munoz answered.

The man cursed and stumbled along the street. He held himself in agony. In the firelight, they could not see the object in his hand.

"He's going to disappear down the street," Butler said.

"We'll go before he gets away," Woo hissed.

The man paused to hold his arm. Another shotgun blast broke through the sound of crackling fire and yelling. The pellets scattered across the parking lot.

"Goddammit," Woo said. "That Korean is going to kill us all."

The man started jogging up the street.

"Go!" Tom yelled.

The four of them rose in unison and sprinted across the parking lot. The man saw them coming and began firing wildly into the night. Two shots rang out before Woo pulled the trigger of his Beretta. The man fell back off his feet onto the cement. His pistol clattered across the sidewalk into the grass.

They were on him in seconds. Munoz shined a light on the fallen body. Blood poured from the man's chest and gurgled from his mouth. His eyes opened and closed, then locked shut with his hands clutching his chest. He arched upward and rolled onto his side where he would stay until the dead wagon picked him up at 2:00 PM the next day. Woo stared at the motionless body.

"Oh my God," he said.

Butler started to say something but was interrupted by another shotgun blast. "Ah!" he cried out.

Tom, Woo, and Munoz screamed as the pellets tore through their shirt sleeves and pants. Other pellets rattled against their helmets and shields. They felt impact vibrations through their Kevlar.

Tom grabbed Munoz and shoved him around the corner of a building. Butler and Woo dove after them. They huddled against the cinder block wall, holding their arms the way the dead man had done two minutes ago.

"Shit, shit, shit!" Tom cried, his face crunched in agony. He felt heat searing his arm as the nerves sent a million signals to his brain. The blood soaked his sleeve.

Tom looked at his partners. Munoz caught a pellet in the neck. He looked the worst of the four. Munoz pressed his fist hard into his neck to stop the bleeding. Tom shone his light on the wound, breathing a sigh of relief when he saw that the pellet hadn't opened his partner's aorta.

"It's just the flesh, Davis," he said. "It's not an artery. Can you think clearly?"

Munoz nodded. He recited his name, badge number, and date of birth even before Tom asked for it. He knew the routine.

Woo radioed for help. The only officers in range said they were in the middle of a firefight on Western Avenue.

"Get on the bullhorn to that son of a bitch with the shotgun," Tom said to Butler. The pain in his arm and leg subsided to a hot pulse of blood. His temper ran even hotter, and he was the coolest head of the bunch.

Butler scooted to the edge of the building. "This is the Los Angeles Police Department," he yelled into the horn. "You are shooting at the Police. Drop your weapon and come down from the building with your hands up. I repeat. Drop your weapon and come down from the building with your hands up."

"They're burning our stores!" a man yelled down.

"Drop your weapon and come down from the building with your hands up."

"You're after the wrong people! They are the criminals!"

"If we need to come up there, you are the criminal and our guns will be drawn. Now drop your weapon and come down from the building with your hands up."

"Don't shoot!" a woman screamed.

Two people walked around the building with their hands in the air. Tom stood, joined by his three partners. The four of them limped across the street, noticing for the first time that the Koreans defended a joined building with a general store and a small restaurant. They probably lived upstairs.

In the area surrounding the strip mall parking lot, the mob of fifty reemerged from the shadows and charged the two people standing with their hands up. A flaming bottle flew overhead, joined by dozens of projectiles.

"Back away!" Butler screamed into the bullhorn. A stick

clattered against his shield. The mob ran at the four officers and the two people on the sidewalk.

Tom had holstered his Beretta to help Munoz. With his free hand, he pulled a can of crowd mace from his belt and emptied it into the wall of running people. They tumbled over themselves as the burning spray hit their faces and fumed up noses and into mouths. The first ten collapsed into a heap of snot and tears and saliva. The rest of the crowd dispersed in all directions.

The flaming bottle had crashed against the storefront, igniting its fuel. The two people who had come from the building now tried frantically to put out the fire. They smacked at it with palm branches from the sidewalk. Others came from the back of the building with blankets and a pot of water.

They doused the flames and yelled at each other in Korean. The four officers limped over.

"I told you!" a kid yelled at them. Butler recognized the voice. "They won't stop! They're crazy."

An old Korean woman stood nearby holding a shotgun. Two men with blankets over their arms held pistols.

"We know they're the bad guys," Butler said in a loud voice. "But you shot us. We shot the man shooting at you from behind the dumpster, then caught shotgun pellets in the arms and legs."

"We work hard," the old woman said. "Protect family."

"We know," Tom nearly yelled. "But protecting your family doesn't mean killing everybody who walks past your store."

As if to rebut that thought, another flaming bottle smashed against the storefront. The Koreans covered the burning liquid with their blankets while the four officers turned to face the mob. Nobody was in sight.

"Fucking Koreans!" yelled a man.

Butler raised the bullhorn to his lips. "This is the Los Angeles Police Department—"

"Fucking pigs!" came a teenager's voice. "I hate pigs!"

"Yo, it's a motherfuckin' pig roast in Korean barbecue sauce!"

Another flaming bottle flew through the air from behind a parked car. It broke on the sidewalk. The pool of gasoline burned itself out quickly. Munoz saw an orange glow behind the car.

"They're lighting another one!" he yelled. "Go!"

They ran at the car, shields out front. The lit bottle flew over their heads and people started yelling and running from behind the car. Munoz bashed one of the men with his shield. The man didn't go down easily. He rolled across his back onto his feet. He pulled a knife from his back pocket and flipped it open. Munoz didn't hesitate. He fired his Beretta into the man's chest.

People scattered in all directions. One man huddled against the car, his face pressed into his hands. Butler kicked him in the back. The man cried out and collapsed.

"Police brutality!" he said into the pavement.

Butler pulled the last pair of cuffs from his belt and secured the man's hands behind his back.

"Did you hear me?" the man said. "This is police brut—"

"Shut up!" Woo screamed into the man's face. "One peep out of your ugly mug and I'm spraying pepper directly up your nose into your brain. Then you'll know brutality."

They walked back across the street to the Koreans, who had already extinguished the fire from the thrown bottle. Butler pushed the prisoner in front of him. The old woman bashed the cuffed man across the face.

"Enough!" Tom shouted. His hands shook badly. He could taste adrenaline in his throat. He wanted to kill somebody. He hadn't felt this seething, bloody fury since the North Hollywood shootout. How dare these worthless scum destroy Korean businesses and threaten the lives of his friends.

A single rifle shot shattered the night. The young Korean recoiled from the bullet in his stomach and fell backward against the store. His face contorted into a still life image like photos Tom had seen of prisoners in North Korean death camps. Blood smeared on the wall as the young man fell to the ground. The old woman ran over to him.

Tom was hardly aware of moving forward. He threw the shot man across his shoulder and pushed the old woman around the side of the building. Munoz, Butler, and Woo pushed the rest of the Koreans.

Tom failed to see the rock flying quietly through the air toward him. It cracked against his helmet, causing no damage but startling him almost into hysteria. In a very uncharacteristic moment for Tom, he turned and fired randomly in the direction of the rock's impact. The bullet shattered a car windshield.

He heard laughter in the night. Laughter. Adrenaline and blood raced each other through his body. He holstered the Beretta and ran with the wounded Korean.

January 2, 2000

Grandma and Grandpa Solvang took Jeremiah and Alyssa to church on Sunday.

"They probably won't even have church today," Jeremiah said in the old Plymouth.

"Yeah, Grandpa," Alyssa added. "All the lights are out."

"No, kids. You'll learn as you get older that churches never close. It wouldn't matter if hostile forces occupied San Jose and shot people on sight. We could still find a place to worship."

"Even with no lights?" Jeremiah asked.

Grandpa nodded. "Even with no lights. The church has windows and candles."

The church was packed. Candles burned at the end of each pew and along the altar. A band and choir stood at attention. One member strummed gentle tunes on his guitar while the greatly expanded congregation gathered. The Solvangs took seats as close to the front as they could get. Grandpa looked around him. "The going gets tough and the tough get religion," he grumbled to Grandma. They knelt and motioned for the kids to do likewise. All four of them folded their hands and bowed their heads.

The darkness inside the church was a pleasant darkness, not a depressing one. Sunlight filtered through twenty-foot stained glass windows depicting Christ's journey to the cross. Voices came as whispers in the stillness. Hundreds of people sat reverently, thinking, praying, hoping.

Father Davidson walked to the altar while the congregation sang "How Great Thou Art." Two servers flanked him in beige robes. He kissed the altar and sang the rest of the song.

"Please be seated," he thundered. The microphones did not work. His lungs filled the church, reverberating his words between stained glass. "We gather today in these most difficult of times. Our routines have been shattered. We find our loved ones and ourselves in great peril. We are uncertain about our jobs. We are uncertain about our next meal."

He gazed across the ocean of faces, most of which he had never seen before. "Indeed, we are being forced for the first time in a long while to examine our place in the world. Our place as a people unto ourselves. Our place living as our ancestors lived for millions of years. Our place without the diversions of modern life."

To Father Davidson's surprise, heads nodded. His usual congregation of Silicon Valley technology experts had long challenged him to prove that God still mattered. Nobody seemed to question it that day.

"We know this opportunity won't last forever, perhaps not even for much longer. The lights will come on, the televisions will blare again, the freeways will jam, the ambitions of career will obscure the nurturing of family. These dark, quiet days at home will be forgotten. Nothing will have changed. The question before us today is whether we will have changed."

Heads nodded again. People listened. Father Davidson bellowed to the end of his introductory remarks. "Times like these bring us closer together, closer to our families, and closer to God."

He let his words disappear into the congregation. Nobody made a sound. Father Davidson raised his hands, palms to the sky. "Let us pray."

JANUARY 3, 2000

The USS *Helena* arrived in Pearl Harbor with little fanfare. Brosseau looked through binoculars as his submarine neared the dock. He saw that the *Helena* wasn't the only boat invited to the party. He'd never seen so many ships in Pearl Harbor at one time. Who the hell was watching the water? Through the binoculars he saw the *Olympia* at dock. The *Olympia* was commanded by his old college roommate, Morris Ferdelle.

"Morey," Brosseau said to himself, the first genuine smile of the day crossing his lips. "I still owe you a beer." It was a tradition of theirs. Morey had introduced Brosseau to the Navy in college. Now, Brosseau was forever indebted to his former roommate and lifelong friend. He showed his appreciation by perpetually owing Morey a beer.

It seemed to Brosseau that half the fleet had convened in Pearl Harbor. "I thought we stopped doing that fifty-nine years ago," he said to the XO.

Through the binoculars he saw the aircraft carriers *Nimitz*, *George Washington*, and *Carl Vinson* all in one place. That was unheard of. Aircraft carriers are the nucleus of the modern fleet. They are supposed to be at sea, not in a port with dozens of other ships, and certainly not three of them in the same port at the same time.

Brosseau and his executive officer walked into the Pearl Harbor briefing room, already filled with people. Morey was there with his XO, beaming from ear to ear as Brosseau entered.

"Sir!" Morey saluted with great respect. He and Brosseau shared an identical rate and time in service.

"Sir!" Brosseau returned. Then he relaxed and gave a firm hug to his best friend. "Good to see you."

"Too bad it couldn't be under better circumstances."

Admiral Robek and Rear Admiral Macey walked into the front of the room. A team of civilians followed them. The roomful of officers stood respectfully. Robek was the Commander in Chief of the U.S. Pacific Command. They would not have been more attentive if the President himself had walked into the room.

"Have a seat," Robek ordered. The room rumbled with the sound of officers sitting firmly in place. "The Year 2000 computer problem has greatly affected the U.S. military. This briefing is about the breakdown and what we are doing to solve it."

He walked a few steps, hands clasped behind his back. "The Pacific Command has lost two-thirds of its satellite monitoring capabilities. Our communications are equally crippled. Our primary lines of communication have been rendered useless." He turned to Rear Admiral Macey. "Mr. Macey will provide a fleet overview."

Macey flipped the switch on a battery operated overhead projector. The overhead showed black silhouettes of ships. It started at the top with an aircraft carrier then worked its way down the page with gradually smaller vessels: cruiser, destroyer, frigate, submarine. Next to each silhouette was a bullet list of crippled or useless systems.

"Ladies and gentlemen, this is the state of our fleet. I can't mince words. I have never seen the United States Navy in such poor condition. I will summarize the major failures."

He pointed a laser dot at the aircraft carrier, then circled the entire list. "Cross platform failures include sonar, radar, navigation, and common weapons systems. The Global Positioning System, even after last August's upgrade, has failed. That means the navigation of our ships and planes is being done manually, as everybody present in this room knows firsthand.

"Not only does the loss of radar, sonar, and navigation affect our vessels, it impairs our weapons systems. Self-guided missile platforms such as the Tomahawk are incapable of tracking their location and therefore incapable of flying to their targets.

"Radar-dependent weapons such as the Phalanx and the entire Aegis system cannot find or monitor hostile contacts.

"Sonar-dependent weapons such as the Mk 48 torpedo are similarly handicapped."

He pointed the laser dot at the cruiser. "Without the Aegis system, these are little more devastating than a cargo barge."

The red dot settled on the submarine. "Perhaps most affected are our subs. Submarines are critical to our superiority at sea. When fully operational, they are fast, unseen, and deadly. Today, they are useless."

He replaced the overhead with one showing silhouettes of aircraft. "Our aircraft have also been severely impaired. The most devastating failure is the FADEC and related flight systems. Our computer systems are not just unresponsive, they are misperforming. We lost two F-14s from the *Nimitz*. They were in flight when their systems rolled to 2000. The engines shut down, but not before each aircraft performed an uncommanded dive at Mach two."

The briefing could have been held in a grave. Eyes cast down at the latest report. "As you can see, the Year 2000 problem is a deadly one to our national defense capabilities."

Rear Admiral Macey waved his hand at Billy Stamp. "I'd like to introduce William Stamp from Solvang Solutions, a Year 2000 computer consultancy in San Jose, California. Mr. Stamp will outline the repair process for you."

"You can appreciate the enormity of the task before us," Billy said quickly. "It will take years to repair the entire fleet of complex systems such as Aegis. Because we recognize that such a time frame is not acceptable, we have suggested breaking the fleet into component battle groups and prioritizing them. We should be able to restore basic fighting capabilities to a single battle group fairly quickly and then focus on its advanced systems.

"The goal is to have at least one battle group fully functional as soon as possible. A tight collection of capable ships and planes beats an ocean full of sitting ducks."

Macey walked forward again. "The *George Washington* battle group is top priority. Joining the *Washington* is the cruiser *Chosin;* the destroyers *Ingersoll, John Young,* and *Harry Hill;* and the submarine *Olympia.*"

Brosseau liked the battle group idea. His only complaint—voiced to no one—was that he would not be in the top priority *Washington* group. If any trouble arose in the water, he wanted to be there.

JANUARY 2, 2000

"It's sabotage," Dan Van Lan said to Pritchett, Schwager, and Marquist. He was joined by Allen Baladad, the Mercury Computer team lead, and Matthew Reynolds, the Atlantic Aerospace team lead.

All around them, the National Military Command Center looked like a mad scientist laboratory. Computer boxes sat on their sides, wires pulled across desks and hooked to testing equipment from Mercury Computer and Atlantic Aerospace.

Dan held a chip, some wire, and a computer printout. Baladad pushed a work cart with two computer boxes and a monitor on it. The six men walked from the ant hill that used to be the world's most advanced military command center. Marquist felt like the captain of the Titanic. Reynolds shut the conference room door behind them.

"Something on these local systems is broken," Dan said to his morose audience. "It can't be the chips, wires, or circuit boards because we just found the identical models working perfectly upstairs. The only part of the NMCC's system that might not be identical is the software."

"So S2 screwed up," Schwager said. He raised his voice. "Your software blew apart and that's why nothing's working."

Dan let his hands drop to his sides. His eyes and cheeks fiercened. "I know that's a tempting conclusion for you, Mr. Schwager. However, the code I installed on these systems is the identical golden master code that we used throughout the Pentagon and other military centers."

Pritchett waved his hand impatiently. "Then what's the problem and how can we fix it?"

"The problem is that these NMCC systems are no longer running the golden master code that we installed. The code has been modified."

"By whom?" Marquist asked.

"If we knew that we'd have drawn guns," Pritchett replied.

Marquist turned to Pritchett and Schwager. "Who the hell had access to these systems?"

"Only these three vendors and our own work teams," Pritchett said.

Schwager nodded gravely. "That's right. The NMCC has been under constant surveillance during the preparations. Maybe this was a mistake by a crew member. Dan, can you show us how the code was modified and when?"

"I could, except that it has all been encrypted with a matrix algorithm that we can't break."

Pritchett felt the numbness in his fingertips. This could not be happening. He thought he felt his teeth come unrooted from his gums and fall clattering to the center of his mouth. "What?" was all he could manage.

Marquist looked stunned. "You're sure that these systems were deliberately sabotaged?"

"Yes."

"Son of a bitch!" Marquist screamed. "So none of this has anything to do with the goddamned date change."

"That's not true," Dan said. "The alteration in the code relied on the date rollover to break the systems. Somebody knew what they were doing. They made it look like a Y2K breakdown."

"Somebody on the inside," Schwager rumbled. He looked at Pritchett. "Somebody who has complete access to the NMCC and understands how the systems work."

"Dan," Pritchett said, ignoring Schwager's surmising. "What are the options from here?"

"We can't break this encryption in a timely manner. We need to install new hard drives with fresh golden code and reinstall the flash chips."

"Do we have the equipment we need?" Pritchett asked.

"Not for a wholesale conversion," Baladad answered. "We have enough to get a few critical systems working."

"Plus," Dan added, "the teams who are best equipped to convert these systems are still missing."

"Can't your teams handle it?" Pritchett asked Baladad and Reynolds.

"Yes," Baladad answered, "but we don't have as much equipment on hand and it's not what we normally do. It will go slower than if our core teams were present."

General Marquist looked like he'd joined a wax museum. "We still have the problem of not knowing who is responsible for this."

"We'll have full time supervision and only these core personnel working around the clock," Pritchett replied. "Dan, we're going to need more people from S2. It's the software that was sabotaged. We need to fix it and prevent other occurrences. I want your people working on this like God himself put you to it. I am talking about twenty-four hours a day until this is solved. I don't care about the cost or the fact that private industry will need to wait."

"I don't make those decisions, Mr. Pritchett. You know that. I have my team here and we're doing the best we can. You'll need to call Solvang about additional manpower."

"I'll do that."

"In the meantime," Marquist commanded, "start working on satellite communications and monitoring."

"That takes precedence over weapons launching capabilities?" Dan asked.

"Yes. Seeing your enemy is more important than the capability to shoot blindly. Restore our eyes first."

"We will," Dan said.

Marquist turned to Pritchett, a low growl in his throat and death in his eyes. "I will call the Secretary of Defense. He will call the President."

Pritchett nodded. "They need to know."

Marquist raised a finger in the air. "I want those other teams found."

JANUARY 5, 2000

Admiral Robek stood with a fleet roster. As crowded as Pearl Harbor had become, he still didn't have all his ships in place. Several were at sea, neither seen nor heard from.

"Admiral," a lieutenant said. "We have reports from Guam of increased naval activity in the Yellow Sea, the South China Sea, and the Philippine Sea. Large battle groups are sailing to new locations. According to Guam, the groups have deviated from their routine patrols."

"Can we identify the groups?"

"One has a positive ID. It's the He Zhang battle group from China. The others are nothing but wakes in the water so far."

"Any sign of our own vessels out there?"

"Not yet."

"Tell Guam to continue watching the new movement and to search specifically for our stray ships." He looked back at the chart. "Lord knows there are enough of them out there."

JANUARY 2, 2000

Murray saw flames burst fifty feet into the air. He guided the aged Bell 47 helicopter over heaps of rubble and bodies and burning cars to the scene on Western Avenue. An appliance store was the fuel for the spire of flame. Hundreds of people gathered in the glow of the fire. To Murray's sickened realization, four officers stood their ground between the burning building and the mob. The officers held their shields in their left hands and their Berettas in their right.

The mob continued throwing flaming bottles and rocks and sticks at the building and at the officers. One officer yelled into a bullhorn, but Murray couldn't understand a word of it. The mob couldn't either, or they simply ignored him. Murray swooped down to assist.

"Martinez, spotlight the crowd!"

The powerful beam of light splashed across the clamoring pile of people. Most shielded their eyes. A few threw projectiles at the light.

"This is the Los Angeles Police Department," Murray's voice echoed through the street. The helicopter's bullhorn was more than twenty times louder than the handheld bullhorns used by the ground patrol. "Turn and walk away from the building immediately. Your continued aggression will result in deadly force. I repeat, walk away from the building."

Murray had seen riots before, and he knew the mob was ready to run. The people seemed to pulsate. They had reached their limit of restraint and would break into a million particles flowing. He could not tell if the people would disperse through the streets in all directions—as he hoped to God they would do—or if they would roll over the four officers.

He had one last chance to try to push them away. He buzzed the helicopter down nearly on top of the crowd. A few people fell to the ground. One person leapt at the Bell, another threw a rock. Murray heard it clink against his door. He pulled up and leveled out. When he looked down again, it was too late.

The mob broke toward the four officers. Martinez followed the front edge with the search light, hoping to help the officers see what was coming. It didn't matter. They fired a few times each with their Berettas and people fell. But the crowd wasn't a collection of individuals anymore. It was a moving, seething creature of its own. Gunfire came from the mob of people and one officer fell.

"Back away!" Murray screamed into the bullhorn. "Back away!"

The intense white light from the helicopter moved forward with the mob and enveloped the officers. A quick cry for help came across the radios. The officer dropped the radio and redrew his pistol just as the first bodies arrived.

Murray and Martinez watched the bodies crash into the officers. Their pistol shots were lost in the yelling and running and helicopter rotors. Martinez continued shining the light where the officers had stood.

The mob collected on that one point, raising clubs time and again into the air. The gunfire stopped. Knives flashed in the helicopter light, first silver and then crimson. A riot shield flew through the air, landing on the heads of the mob and quickly disappearing. A helmet came next. More people accreted in a hot concentration of all the fury society feels toward police officers.

There were four fewer of them in less than forty-five seconds.

JANUARY 2, 2000

Sunday, Bloody Sunday. The Koreatown Massacre. History books would use both names to describe the events of January 2, 2000.

Over Tom's radio an officer cried for help.

"Give me your location," Tom replied. His radio was fading out. He wondered if the officer ever heard him.

Tom had placed the young Korean on a counter inside the back door of the building. The old woman cried over the expanding blood on the young man's stomach. Others bustled about the storage room with lanterns, pulling supplies from shelves and chattering back and forth in Korean. Tom assumed they were preparing a treatment for the young man, something all four officers could see was futile. The man would be dead within thirty minutes.

A strange sounding helicopter flew slowly overhead. Tom wondered if it was LAPD. He hadn't seen any copters yet. He assumed they were all broken.

The young Korean died. The old woman sobbed over him in the lantern light. The front of her store was charred and its glass window shattered. Her grandson was dead from a bullet shot by somebody who didn't care who died. The murderer saw moving bodies in front of a Korean store and fired. He never knew if his shot connected or not.

Tom felt sick. The smell of blood hung in the air. Adrenaline drained from the bodies of the four officers, relaxing their muscles and exhausting them. They hadn't slept in nearly two days.

"How old was he?" Tom asked one of the Korean men.

"Twenty-two. He would have graduated from UCLA this spring. We are very proud of him and his brothers."

"Where are his brothers?"

"Upstairs. Loading more guns."

"Take us up there," Butler said.

The man led them down a dingy hallway to a small staircase. They creaked their way to the loft above the store and restaurant. Two Korean boys sat at a window overlooking the street where their brother was shot less than half an hour earlier.

"How's Andrew?" asked one round-faced boy holding a hunting rifle.

The man shook his head. What could he say?

"Dad, how's Andrew?" the boy repeated in a high voice, the shine of tears already in his eyes.

"Andrew died," the father said.

Both boys fell forward across their own laps, crying profusely. The rifles thudded to the floor. Bullets rolled across the room. The older boy, the one who asked about Andrew, kept wailing something in Korean. The old woman and two younger women hurried up the stairs to cradle the two brothers.

The wailing of the boys was joined by sobbing from the women.

The father knelt beside his family. Tom saw the lines of tears that had silently appeared on the father's cheeks.

The four officers collapsed. The urgency of battle leaked from Tom's limbs. He looked at his partners. Butler bit his lower lip. Woo's head hung on his chest. Munoz sat quietly beside Tom on the couch. All four officers fell asleep in the home of the boy they failed to save.

The father awakened them at 8:00 AM. Tom's eyes cracked open to a hazy day, the sun obscured by dark clouds and smoke from the still-burning city. The rifles and bullets lay where the boys dropped them earlier that morning. The boys and women were nowhere to be seen.

"This will help you," the father said. He gestured toward a small table with four bowls of steaming broth. Each officer took one and sipped. It tasted like chicken noodle soup, Tom thought.

"Campbell's," the father said.

Tom smiled. "You were afraid we wouldn't like Korean."

"You don't need spicy, you need mild."

"That's for sure," Butler said.

Tom walked to the window above the rifles and bullets. Outside, Los Angeles struggled under the ominous cloud cover. People ran past the storefront. He saw the car the mob hid behind to throw flaming bottles. He saw two bodies. Woo shot the one on the sidewalk. Munoz shot the one on the grass. The man's knife still lay near his open hand.

Tom cradled his forearm. The shotgun pellet wounds had swelled in the few hours they'd slept. Munoz's neck looked like hell. A blue ring stretched both directions from the black, bloody crater where the pellet was still lodged under his skin. It ruined Tom's soup to look at it.

"Davis, how are you feeling?"

"Better than my neck looks, I'm sure. Pellets always make ugly wounds. I can feel it. It's swollen and tender, but I'm fine."

"How are you two?" Tom asked Butler and Woo. Both nodded. "We should radio in those two bodies. They're still lying out there."

Woo pulled his radio and pressed the button. No indicator light. "Mine's dead."

All three other officers checked theirs, and all were dead. "Great," Munoz said. "It's not like we could use any help out here or anything. It's just the whole city attacking us."

"I don't think we're alone," Tom said.

"I know we're not alone," Butler answered. "The last thing we heard on these radios was a request for help. Remember?"

"I remember," Tom replied. "I hope those guys made it."

Nobody said anything for several minutes. The room sat silently except for the sound of an occasional sip of soup. "How are your two sons?" Woo asked finally.

"They are sleeping. They are very sad about Andrew."

"So are we," Woo said. "I'm sorry."

Butler nodded. "Yes, I'm sorry too."

Tom and Munoz added their own apologies. The father nodded. "I don't understand what is happening," he said. "America keeps the world at peace while its own people are at war."

Nobody replied. The old woman hobbled up the stairs with a tray full of items. One was a bowl of hot water. Around it sat pieces of cloth and tweezers and bottles with Korean writing on the outside. The two younger women followed behind her.

"For your wounds," the father said.

"Oh no," Munoz replied. "We'll be fine."

"You'll be better with treatment. Let them help you."

Tom rolled up his sleeve. One of the younger women sponged his arm with the hot water. The old woman tended to Munoz's neck while the third woman sat Butler down in his chair and began cleaning his arms.

The woman sponged Tom's arm until there were no flakes of blood left clinging to his hair, no pieces of skin hanging roughly from the wounds. She dabbed each pellet hole with cotton soaked in a brown fluid from one of the Korean bottles. She dipped the tweezers into a tiny dish of liquid, then plucked a pellet from each hole. He winced and clutched at his knee to hold his arm in place. She never wavered. The folds of her eyelids remained on his arm. She paused when he pulled away, but never moved the tweezer more than a few inches from his wounds.

Tom, Butler, and Woo removed their belts and dropped their trousers to expose the wounds on their legs. The purplish, black holes made ugly patterns on their thighs. The women worked diligently from their tray of liquids, salves, and hot water. A dish filled with misshapen metal pellets taken from their bodies.

When the last pellets were removed, the women dabbed ointment across the flaps of skin surrounding each hole. They covered the men in bandages. The officers redressed themselves and strapped their equipment into place. All four of them thanked the women.

"Thank you," the father said.

"I wish we could have saved Andrew," Munoz told him.

Before anybody could respond, a rock crashed through the window onto the floor. It rolled into the table leg holding the tray of medical supplies. The small table shuddered, then fell over. The water poured across the floor. The small bottles of healing fluids and ointments bounced and the dish spilled bloody pellets.

The women leapt back from the couches and chairs. They ran to the back rooms. The father picked up one of the hunting rifles and crammed bullets into its side.

"No!" Tom cried, pulling him away from the window. "Let us handle it."

The four officers flanked the window, peering out front. People bobbed their heads from behind the car across the street. More flooded around the strip mall buildings, picking up rocks and lighting pieces of cloth hanging from bottles. The low buildings of Koreatown disappeared into the hazy morning, and shapes of people emerged from the gray cover to join the fray.

"Son of a bitch!" Butler said. "It's daylight for Christ's sake. Who's heard of this going on in broad daylight?"

"This isn't normal," Munoz said. "Why do they keep coming back to this store?"

"Because they found resistance at this store," Tom said. He remembered the laughter from the night before.

"But mobs usually run when you shoot at them," Butler said. "They're cowardly at heart."

"I don't know what the hell's going on," Tom replied, still looking at the assembling crowd. "But we need to do something fast."

They turned from the window and ran down the stairs. They passed Andrew's body, covered with a sheet on the counter where Tom placed him. The blood from his stomach turned the sheet dark purple overnight. They ran out the back door. Tom heard the rabble noise at the front of the building. People yelled obscenities. Bottles broke. Glass shattered.

The four officers gripped their shields in their left hands. Butler pulled the bullhorn. Munoz and Woo looked at Tom. His body picked up where it had left off the night before. The pleasures of chicken soup and soft bandages disappeared. All he could remember were the screams from last night, the flames, gunfire, Andrew collapsing against his family's building, the frothy mixture of adrenaline and blood in his own body. Enough was enough. Tom didn't care about protocol.

He reached his free hand inside his coat to the shoulder holster below. The thick Kevlar pressed against his bones. The Desert Eagle slid from the shoulder holster. Its massive .44 magnum barrel came into the hazy day like something a train would drive through.

"I don't want to shoot anybody twice," Tom said. Without a word, Munoz and Woo reached inside their own coats and pulled their Eagles.

Four-hundred miles north of Koreatown, Grandma and Grandpa Solvang sat with Jeremiah and Alyssa in Father Davidson's church. The pews were packed to the bursting point with more Catholics than Grandpa Solvang knew existed in Silicon Valley.

"Before I present my homily," Father Davidson said, "let us sing the wise words of Longfellow."

He held his hands wide before him. "It's still the spirit of Christmas. The spirit of Christmas is of a family that needed shelter on a cold night when there was none. The son of God came into our world on a bed of straw in a barn full of animals. Stars guided the wise men to him that night. It was a world without electricity, a world without modern convenience of any kind. In the same world long before, young David killed Goliath with a single stone from his sling. In the same world long before that, a carpenter named Noah built an Ark of gopher wood to save every animal on earth. My brothers and my sisters, humanity's finest hours have blossomed from the simplest of times."

He picked up his hymnal. "Please turn to song 435 in your hymnal and join with me and the choir in singing 'I Heard the Bells on Christmas Day.'"

The choir hummed an introduction. Grandpa Solvang held the hymnal for his family to sing along. The hundreds of people gathered their voices in praise of the struggle for peace.

> *I heard the bells on Christmas day*
> *Their old familiar carols play*
> *And wild and sweet the words repeat*
> *Of peace on earth, goodwill to men*

The four officers leaned against the building to peer around the corner. People continued running from hazy morning distance to viewable foreground. They yelled back and forth to each other. Some yelled obscenities across the street to the Korean restaurant and general store. The first bottle flew threw the air and broke on the sidewalk. Its fluid burst into flame.

Tom considered fighting from the side of the building where he and his partners would be somewhat protected. Two young men with flaming bottles ran to the storefront, dispelling that idea. The officers would need to be where they could be seen. That was the dilemma. Remaining behind cover would offer protection, but little show of force to deter the mob. Moving into the open would allow them to better protect the Korean family, but would leave them wide open for attack. In the seconds he had to think, Tom decided that moving into the open was a risk they would need to take. Their whole purpose in coming to Koreatown was to protect it.

"Let's move," Tom said. The four of them walked as a unit from the corner of the building onto the small area of grass in front of the restaurant. They could see the well-tended flower bed trampled into pieces of color in the dirt. Andrew's blood stained the building above it, his last footprints in the soft soil.

The four officers stood shoulder to shoulder in front of the flower bed. To an ordinary citizen on an average day, they would have been very intimidating. Each carried a clear shield, wore a helmet, and held a pistol in his right hand. Butler held the bullhorn, something that added to the effect. But they didn't face ordinary citizens on an average day. They faced a crazed mob, delirious with its own need for violence and locked on that building as one to be destroyed and on those men as cops to be killed.

They weren't civic minded folk who filled their calendars with school events and town meetings. They were the underside of LA who dreamed of their first cop kill and joined organizations with initiation rites of drive-by shootings, drug running, and rape. The sight of four cops in full riot gear in front of a damaged Korean building moved the excitement up several notches. This was real. This was blood in the water. This was reputation-making time.

The officers sensed it. All four of them had seen unruly crowds before, had seen riots before. This crowd was not a loose gathering of students that would disperse at the first sound of a bullhorn voice. The crowd was losing its status as a collection of individuals. It was becoming a creature of its own, seething, roiling from buildings to bushes to cars, reaching the tidal point where it would flow over anything in its path.

Rocks and bottles flew overhead. Plumes of fire exploded around the four officers and against the building. The Koreans dumped water from their roof and high windows, extinguishing the flames. The water came from tanks of purified drinking water for the restaurant. Tom had seen the tanks in the room with Andrew's body. The water couldn't last forever.

"Get on the horn," Tom said.

"This is the Los Angeles Police Department," Butler announced in the surreal voice. "Turn and walk away immediately. We are prepared to use deadly force. I repeat. Turn and walk away immediately. We are prepared to use deadly force."

"Prepare to die, sucker!"

"You ain't the only one with deadly force."

"Get out of our town!"

"Fucking pigs!"

The mob creature moved closer to its tidal breaking point. Tom felt his hand shaking and pulled his firing elbow tight against his ribs. He didn't want his partners to see him shaking. He swallowed dryly. He moved his feet farther apart, bracing himself for whatever might come.

Murray flew at moped speed over Koreatown. The hazy morning prevented him and Martinez from getting much of a bird's eye view of the city. They wanted to follow up on the night before. Neither could shake the image of the four officers being swallowed alive by the mob. With fires burning in all directions and radios going dead, they feared the worst for other officers in Koreatown.

"It had to have been around here," Martinez said, referring to Tom's response to the officer's cry for help. He and Murray both heard it just before the mob closed on the four men. With the limited range of the radios, they knew the responding officers had to be close to the scene.

The Bell 47 flew low to the ground. The hazy, smoky air above the city gave the impression of flying through a dream, seeing the pieces of life fade into and out of existence. A furniture store here, a restaurant there, a group of kids walking, a car on fire, palm trees disappearing into the gray wall that surrounded the city in every direction.

"There!" Martinez said, pointing out his side of the helicopter. An enormous crowd popped and fizzed and boiled in a strip mall. His heart sank. It was the same scene, but bigger this time. People dove over bushes and threw objects across the street at a duplex building. Standing in front of the building were four officers, looking as vulnerable as the four from the night before.

"Oh no," Murray answered. "Those guys don't have a chance."

Father Davidson's robes hung from his arms as he directed the singing. The choir's voice lifted above the congregation, blending with hundreds in striking harmony.

> *I thought how, as the day had come*
> *The belfries of all Christendom*
> *Had rolled along th' unbroken song*
> *Of peace on earth, goodwill to men*

Tom saw the helicopter out of the corner of his eye. It looked like something out of a World War II picture book. But it said POLICE on the side, and at the moment that was prettier than tropical shores. With a bird in the air, they might have a fighting chance.

"Clip the bullhorn," Tom said to Butler. "Let the bird do the talking. Get your Eagle ready."

"This is the Los Angeles Police Department," came the screaming bullhorn from within the rotor noise. "Disperse and return to your homes immediately or you will be shot. I repeat, return to your homes immediately or you will be shot."

"Damn right," Munoz said. It was unusual to hear such blunt language on a public bullhorn. All four officers were glad to hear that the helicopter understood their situation.

A wave of flaming bottles came across the street. Tom, Butler, Woo, and Munoz raised their shields. The bottles crashed against them, igniting the clear plastic and burning in front of the men. They stood their ground.

They looked like paladins on a battlefield, invincible in their plate mail armor, walking through flames to continue the fight. The fuel burned on their shields in orange and blue sheets twining together in and out of their faces. The men opened their arms to move the heat away from their bodies.

Through the fire, Tom saw the crowd reach its tidal breaking point. It flowed around bushes, cars, and buildings. The street filled with angry voices and raised weapons. The already hazy air obscured even more with specks of thrown debris and whirling bottles of fire. The mob creature's hundreds of legs ran its hulking mass toward the four men in flames.

"We are not going to hover while four more officers die in Koreatown!" Murray yelled inside the helicopter. "Look at this scene. There must be two hundred people in sight, God knows how many others hiding in the haze. Martinez, fasten your safety line and get the M-16 ready. The time for talking is over."

Martinez strapped himself into the passenger seat of the Bell 47 and threw open the door. He held the M-16 with its dayscope into the hazy morning air. He looked through the scope steadily.

"Here it goes!" Murray screamed when the crowd surged forward. "Hold your fire until my command."

Grandpa Solvang felt the words flow from him. Jeremiah and Alyssa sang in loud voices.

> And in despair I bowed my head:
> "There is no peace on earth," I said
> "For hate is strong, and mocks the song
> Of peace on earth, goodwill to men"

The mob creature rushed its bulk across the street to the sidewalk and accelerated toward Tom, Butler, Woo, and Munoz. The creature had hundreds of faces and twice as many legs to carry it and arms to wield weapons.

"Turn back!" Tom screamed, his hands shaking uncontrollably. He didn't care anymore. "Turn back, dammit! Turn back!"

"Do you want to die?" Butler yelled in his deep voice.

"Turn back!" Tom cried one last time.

The mob creature poured itself over the sidewalk at the four men. Tom squeezed his hand around the Eagle's grip and a red dot appeared on a man's chest. In a distant part of his body he felt the recoil of a manstopping bullet leave the pistol. Before his arm returned to firing position, the man flipped backward off his feet as the bullet ripped through his rib cage and blew a hole out his back. Red dots appeared on bodies as the other officers fired with Tom. Another man flew backward into the mob, then another, then a fourth.

The mob creature stopped in its tracks, roaring in confusion. It retreated back across the sidewalk in an overlapping mixture of bodies and weapons. Something moved like a wave from the back of the mob creature in the haze. Tom could not see what it was, but he knew the mob creature was not finished. It retreated not to get away, but to gather itself for a bigger push. Deadly snakes draw themselves back before they strike. This mob, unlike any Tom had ever seen, appeared to follow the same pattern.

Through the haze, the four officers could see people running to join the mob creature. Instead of losing four faces and eight weapon-wielding arms in the shooting, it gained an untold number.

"The whole city is here!" Munoz yelled.

"Back up to the wall!" Tom said. "They're going to charge again. We can't let them get behind us or we're dead."

They backed in lockstep to the front wall of the restaurant. Their feet pushed into the flower bed soil, obscuring the footprints left by Andrew before his death. Tom's jacket wiped across the boy's dried blood. He felt something hard scraping against the wall. The SPAS 12 on his back.

"Change weapons!" he screamed. The other three shot quick glances at him. He placed the Eagle in its holster and reached over his shoulder with a trembling hand. The pistol grip filled his palm and steadied his nerves. The Beretta was a pea shooter, the Eagle a bazooka, the SPAS 12 a gunship. They could use a few gunships.

Tom pulled the combat shotgun across his shoulder. He steadied its wicked barrel with his shield hand while he wound his arm through the hook.

In the interminable seconds before the second charge, Tom's eyes saw minute details and smelled odors irrelevant to the conflict. The scent of ointment from Munoz's neck mixed with scorched grass and wood.

The helicopter rotor seemed to have only one blade and Tom could see it revolving in slow arcs around the ancient Bell. It created a sound like wind in the palms of Malibu, where Tom took Adelle surfing during better times. The man hanging out the open door of the helicopter reminded Tom of Munoz. He didn't stare down an M-16, ready to kill citizens of Los Angeles. He looked the length of a pool cue, ready to win a free beer from his buddy.

The morning haze and smoke hid LA's skies, bluer than they'd been in decades before. Tom wanted to be in Malibu with his wife while dolphins coursed through the water next to them, an ocean wave all that let him and Adelle keep pace.

Butler, Woo, and Munoz readied their shotguns. Tom heard the metallic clicks and adjustments. Between the four of them, twenty-eight 12-gauge rounds sat ready to fire a storm of heavy pellets, oddly shaped pieces of metal edges and points that would tear through bone like it was baby hair.

The Koreans took their places in the building. The father hung a hunting rifle out the broken window. The two young women lay on the roof with their rifles trained on the mob creature. The old woman sat in front of another window, her gnarled hands gripping a .22 rifle.

The crowd beast roiled on the street. The picture became clearer to Tom. The commotion from the back of the growing mob was a contingent trying to get through. He saw arms in the air and the unmistakable shape of guns. The mob creature was moving its deadliest tentacles forward.

Murray saw the officers pull SPAS shotguns from their backs. He looked at the four men pushed wisely against the wall of the building. They knew what they were doing. He saw their new weapons and didn't know what to feel. Their chances of survival were low, lower than they knew. From the helicopter he could see the terrifying size of the mob. He saw it extending into the gray haze and growing bigger. The officers made the right choice in moving to more powerful weapons.

But the mob creature was made up of citizens, some of whom worked in video stores and gas stations and fast food joints on freeway exits. They were nobody's pride and joy, but they were human beings and they were caught up in emotions without the mental capacity to see their way out of them. For less time than it takes to blink an eye, he felt sorry for the mob creature.

Murray had seen what SPAS weapons could do. He looked down at four of them held grimly toward the mob. A SPAS firing on a closely packed crowd of people was like a lawnmower in tall grass. It would sound almost the same, too.

Above the four men, Murray saw two Korean women on the roof with rifles. Martinez trained the M-16 on the mob creature.

Murray grabbed the microphone. "There are four dead already! Turn back immediately or you will be shot. You are outgunned and you will die if you do not turn back. I repeat. Turn back immediately or you will be shot."

He looked down at the mob. A group of young men worked their way through the crowd of people, all of whom vibrated out of control. Faces didn't look human anymore. The group of men carried guns through the crowd.

"Martinez! Do you see the guns?"

"I see them."

"Those men are your targets."

"I understand."

The choir surrounded Father Davidson's voice in words that he first sang as an altar boy. The congregation closed its eyes to savor the beauty of the music.

> *Then pealed the bells more loud and deep:*
> *"God is not dead, nor doth He sleep;*
> *The wrong shall fail, the right prevail*
> *With peace on earth, goodwill to men"*

The gunmen reached the front of the mob creature and the beast surged forward again. It reached full speed by the time its hundreds of feet pounded the sidewalk again. The gunmen fired.

The corner of Tom's shield shattered from the shots. Bits of the wall at his back burst into his helmet. His right hand squeezed the SPAS. All four shotguns exploded together, the recoil pressing all four elbows into the wall of the restaurant. A storm of deadly pellets melted the front lines of the mob creature.

The rifleman in the helicopter fired several shots and more men with guns fell to the ground. Tom heard booming and a crackle above him as the Koreans fired their hunting rifles and the .22.

The mob creature was bewildered, but suffered from its own momentum. It continued rushing forward.

Tom's mind disconnected. He became an observer at his own funeral, a season ticket holder at the gladiator pit. His eyes shrouded behind cataracts of disbelief. His adrenaline did its job, activating tendons to pull the trigger.

Tom, Butler, Woo, and Munoz fired again and again and again into the mob creature. The pellets spread into a Cuisinart of death, exposing flesh, ripping eyeballs, shattering teeth on their way to brain tissue and internal organs. Bodies piled on top of each other. The officers fired again and again. They emptied seven shells each into the screaming crowd of people who did not know what they were doing. The mob creature disintegrated into its components, the individual actions of people becoming evident again. Gunfire from the Koreans dropped bodies farther back from the front. Gunfire from the air dropped bodies not yet in retreat.

The four officers pulled their Desert Eagle pistols and continued firing. Red laser dots appeared on chests and stomachs and foreheads just before a manstopping bullet burst through each glow and erupted the body behind it. The strip mall returned the furious sound of four .44 magnum pistols, one M-16, three hunting rifles, and a .22 rodent gun.

Jeremiah and Alyssa read the words from Grandpa Solvang's hymnal. Their tinny voices mixed with the rich tone of the choir and the overpowering sound of hundreds rejoicing in song.

> *Till, ringing, singing on its way,*
> *The world revolved from night to day,*
> *A voice, a chime, a chant sublime,*
> *Of peace on earth, goodwill to men!*

The crowd finally ran from the Korean restaurant and general store. The screaming took on a new tone as the hundreds of rioters fled into the hazy morning. They jumped across car hoods, dove through bushes, leapt into open doorways, and ran as fast as they could.

But the cops were nowhere near the fleeing crowd. They leaned motionless against a bullet-pocked wall.

Bodies lay in heaps on the sidewalk and in the street. Groaning sounds of death were lost in the whir of the helicopter rotor. Most were already dead. Those hit by the .22 had survived and run away. The other weapons were too potent on a direct hit to leave time for dying words. A few bodies crawled in the blood, injured, scared, already in shock.

It was a scene from a horror film. The SPAS pellets obliterated the fronts of their victims. Bodies lay like open packages of ground beef, faceless and riddled with metal. The hunting rifles and M-16 and Desert Eagles bore massive, funnel-shaped holes through their targets.

In less than one minute, forty-three people died in the Koreatown Massacre. The officers responsible were never identified. The Koreans said they didn't see who had done the shooting. The coroner's report contained a paragraph about M-16 bullets being fired from above the victims, but it was never investigated.

The dead wagon came at 2:00 PM and took away as many as it could carry. It made eight trips to that section of Koreatown.

The four police officers fell to the soft soil of the flower bed. Adrenaline drained away, leaving them weak and empty. Every hand shook. Tom couldn't control the tenor of his voice. "Why wouldn't they turn back?" he asked the world. "Why wouldn't they turn back?"

Murray dropped low to the ground and Martinez jumped out of the helicopter. He ran to the four officers.

"Are you all right?"

Tom managed to nod. Martinez did not know what to do. "We're going to get you guys out of here. Radios are down, so we need to fly for help." The men didn't acknowledge anything he said. They sat against and on top of each other, looking too much like the bodies on the street. None of them would speak. Their eyes stared, their hands shook.

"We need blankets for these men!" Martinez screamed up at the windows. The father and one of the women came downstairs and scurried around the building. They covered the incapacitated officers.

"We're going for help," Martinez said. "Take care of them until we get back here." He ran to the helicopter.

The Bell wheezed into the haze and an unsettling peace filled the space left behind by its rotors. Only the fast breathing from the blankets and the groans of bodies on the street pierced the quiet. The Koreans looked at Andrew's blood on the wall and the bodies around them and the four catatonic officers and their own hands.

There was nothing to do but cry.

JANUARY 7, 2000, 1:55 PM PST

A transmission left Guam on the secondary satellite network. It traveled 3,300 miles to Camp Smith and Pearl Harbor. It continued around one third of the planet before descending to the Pentagon.

The transmission entered the hands of a lieutenant in the National Military Command Center. The lieutenant walked through a field of circuit boards and detached monitors, past teams of Mercury and S2 and Atlantic consultants to General Marquist who stood with Edwin Pritchett. The lieutenant handed the transmission to General Marquist.

General Marquist steadied his hand. He gave the transmission to Pritchett, then turned to the lieutenant. "Get me the President," he said.

Pritchett finished reading the transmission. "I'm calling S2," he told Marquist.

"You damned well better. I don't care if it takes every one of their people including the janitor, this needs to be fixed."

Pritchett walked to the satellite phone.

JANUARY 7, 2000, 2:08 PM PST

Mark called his crew into the conference room. The formerly proud Solvang management team sat emaciated in the chairs around the table. Nobody wore headsets. Their ears were raw from the grip of the pads. People wore hats to conceal their unwashed hair.

"We need to reinstate electricity right away. I don't think any of us saw the ripple effect being quite this severe."

"Just needing to reinstate electricity doesn't give us the magic ability to do it," Kleewein said. "We have stretched our resources to the limits."

"I know. But we are moving backwards as far as I can tell. Rioting and looting have moved to neighborhoods. Police have given up their attempts at protecting businesses. Food is gone from grocery stores. Even old cars are useless now that most gasoline is used up. The military is a disaster, worse than we anticipated. Everything depends on electricity. We need to pull teams from other industries to get the power grid fixed. We need electricity in this country before all hell breaks loose."

"All hell has broken loose," Kleewein said. "I don't think it's a good idea to switch horses in the middle of the stream. We're going to lose two weeks just getting people acclimatized to their new jobs."

"Power is absolutely top priority. Every basic part of America's infrastructure depends on it. We need to take people from other industries and put them to work on power."

"From what other industries?" Susan asked. "We don't have people to spare anywhere."

The conference room phone rang. Mark pushed the speaker button. "Solvang."

"This is urgent." Pritchett didn't waste time.

The room fell quiet. Nothing could quell spirits faster than a high-ranking military official beginning a conversation by announcing that it's urgent.

"Two U.S. destroyers were sunk earlier today in the South China Sea near Hong Kong. There's no confirmation on the identity of the enemy ships. The destroyers failed on all counts. Their missiles did not launch, their radar could not track enemy targets. We're the United States, for Christ's sake! We were attacked and couldn't do a goddamned thing about it."

"I thought the fleet had returned to ports for repair," Mark said.

"Most have. But we have limited global satellite coverage. To communicate with certain ships we need to wait until they steam to an area of coverage. Our information suggests that these two destroyers were doing just that. They had been on northbound courses and just reached the coverage zone. They were able to transmit a small amount of information to Guam before going down."

"Why couldn't Guam see the enemy?"

"Because the battle occurred in one of the six-hour blocks of satellite darkness." Pritchett took a breath. "We do not have the capabilities to defend ourselves. We were attacked and miserably defeated. Folks, enough planning and strategizing. We need fast-moving teams in place to fix the fleet."

Mark looked among his executives. "We have teams in place," he said. "We have a solid strategy in place as well. Stamp's people are already working on the top priority *Washington* battle group in Pearl Harbor. When that's completed—"

"We need more of your people! I want work to begin on the *Nimitz* battle group before work on the *Washington* group is complete. I don't want any delays. Do you understand what's happening here?"

"Mr. Pritchett," Mark said, "what do you have in mind?"

"Your work teams are now the most critical component of military preparedness. The Keep is best in control of your work teams. I'm flying out there on an old military transport with a core team to manage the repairs from your facility. Van Lan and others will stay here to continue working. But I need better control over the prioritization and progress of these repairs."

"When will you fly into San Jose?"

"We will be there tomorrow morning."

"Fine. How many will there be?"

"I don't know yet. I'll send those details as well."

"We will get the latest information from Van Lan and Stamp and work through the night to come up with a plan of attack."

"That's what I wanted to hear. I'll see you tomorrow."

The hissing satellite connection clicked out. All faces turned to Mark.

"What the hell are you doing?" Kleewein asked.

"I'm doing the right thing."

"You're buckling under pressure, that's what you're doing." Kleewein's eyes, weary from a week of non-stop work, blazed through their bloodshot hue. "You just invited the Pentagon to storm in here and take over our operation. Every last S2 consultant is going to be flown off to remote military bases while the country collapses. We planned to avoid that."

"Kleewein, this is top priority."

"Top priority? We just finished a discussion concluding that the power grid was top priority. Has the lack of sleep gone to your head?"

"Did you just hear what the man said?," Mark asked. "We're being attacked. Not only is the National Military Command Center not working, it was sabotaged. There's something worse than Y2K at work here. Pritchett knows it. He's exercising the only option that will improve his ability to prepare his fleet for battle.

"What recourse will we have once the DoD has control of our facilities?"

"They're not taking control of our facilities!" Mark yelled down the table. "They're coming here to get a better handle on the repair of our nation's military. Pritchett is justified in his frustration at being apart from the day-to-day progress."

"Bullshit," Kleewein said. "He's got one of our top guys by his side, another on the scene at Pearl Harbor. I don't see why he needs to be at our headquarters to keep things moving."

"Because they're not moving fast enough. I would have done the same thing if I were in his shoes."

"He's at his own control center!"

"The center is not working," Susan told him. Her softer voice came boldly through the male yelling.

Kleewein sat back in his chair, a ferocious look on his face. "We will lose the ability to take care of our priorities."

"This is top priority," Mark answered. He looked at faces around the room. "I want everybody in here to know that. If the United States is invaded at a vulnerable time like this, all is lost. We will be saving a country that is no longer ours. Forget electricity, TVs, microwaves, new BMWs, traffic lights, banks, and phones. We need to defend the country."

7

AMBUSH

JANUARY 2, 2000

The driver that picked up Tom, Butler, Woo, and Munoz thought for a moment that he'd gotten his signals crossed. Dead bodies littered the ground in all directions. He steered the van around them as he found the address given to him by the helicopter pilot. He didn't drive the dead wagon. He ferried officers from one place to another.

But the men he found under a blanket against the Korean restaurant could have passed for dead.

"What the hell happened here?" he asked them. Nobody replied and he didn't ask a second time.

Tom walked like a zombie to the van. The stone faces of his partners followed. The driver loaded their shields and guns into the back.

As the van passed Universal Studios on the 101 freeway, the driver looked into the rearview mirror. "One of you has a vehicle at the North Hollywood station. Do you feel up to driving it or would you rather I take you home?"

Tom cleared his throat. "I'll drive my Jeep from the station," he said in a tired voice.

"Not many people about," the driver noted. "Cars aren't running. Hell, the department itself is almost out of gasoline. Who knows how long this is going to last."

Nobody replied. They arrived at the station. The four officers filed from the van.

"Wait a second," the driver said. "Don't any of you want a ride home?"

"We'll all go in my Jeep," Tom said.

The driver looked at their eyes. Whatever had happened in Koreatown would be with those men a long time, he decided. "Let me get your equipment from the van."

He carried the weapons and shields to Tom's Jeep. One shield was missing a corner, all were rough and blackened from burning oil. "Do you fellows need anything else?"

Tom shook his head and got into the Jeep. Butler and Woo crawled into the back, Munoz sat in the passenger seat.

"Listen," the driver said through Tom's window. "Be careful over here. We're starting to get reports of burning and looting in neighborhoods. So don't relax too much just because you're home in the valley."

Once Tom dropped off Butler and Woo, he drove Munoz home. Aside from empty wishes of good luck, nobody had spoken during the drive. Tom stopped in front of Munoz's home.

"Are we finished?" Munoz asked.

"I don't know. We're finished for now. I might be finished forever. If anything happens, I'll come over to get you. That's about the best we can do."

Munoz nodded. He reached a fist across the seat and punched his partner in the shoulder. Tom patted Munoz on the leg, then drove the last five minutes to his own street.

The neighborhood sat quiet and still. The morning haze was breaking up and shafts of sunlight beamed onto winter green lawns. Tom parked the Jeep in his driveway.

He sat for a long time in the stillness, staring at his steering wheel. After a normal shift, he often rested in the Jeep with the radio playing. Adelle knew to leave him alone to settle his thoughts. He used the time as a decompression period, to flush LA police work from his system and let home life trickle in. Then he was ready to greet his wife and hopefully do something to make her happy.

But on that day, Adelle didn't wait. She ran from the house to her husband and pulled the Jeep door open.

"Tom, I'm so glad you're home. I was so worried." She looked at him. "What happened?"

Adelle's high voice and the touch of her hand on his cheek finally broke the reservoir inside him. The troubles in their marriage seemed so petty. His head fell forward onto his hands gripping the steering wheel. His rib cage heaved and sucked air. His lips peeled back from his teeth in a shameless torrent of sadness.

"Tom, my God," Adelle said through her own tears. "Come in the house with me. We're together now, baby."

He stumbled from the Jeep toward their house. Inside, familiar smells and familiar furniture caressed him. He fell onto the couch in a pile of uniform and Kevlar.

"Tom, drink this." She held a glass of orange juice to him.

He drank the warm fluid. "Why didn't they turn back?" he asked her. "Why didn't they just turn back?"

"What happened? Is Davis okay?"

"Yes. We're all fine." He put the glass down. "Except that they just kept coming, Adelle. We told them to stop but they kept coming. We had shotguns and Eagles and Berettas and a copter in the air. We killed them all."

He held his face in his hands, shaking his head back and forth. "Why, Adelle? Why didn't they turn back?"

"I don't know, Tom. Why are there any bad people in the world?"

He let her help him back to their bedroom. He shed the uniform and Kevlar and belt. He curled into a ball on his side of the bed. He trembled, staring out the window to the brightening sky and the trees where the birds kept singing the praises of a new year, a new millennium.

Adelle cuddled gently against his back. His hair clung to the pillow like coral to the seafloor.

His body creaked air in and out of his lungs. "Why didn't they just turn back?" he said under his breath.

JANUARY 9, 2000

Gary Maris opened the woodstove. He stirred the coals and blew across them. He chose two pieces of split wood from their shrinking stack. The wood smoked for a time, filling the room with the aroma of hot pine sap. Gary closed the stove to the sound of crackling.

"We're going to need more wood within a few days," he said.

"Where can we get it?" Danielle asked.

"Down the hill across the creek. Rob Hansen has a chainsaw."

"I didn't even know Rob had a workbench. How many CPAs do you know who keep chainsaws?"

Gary walked to the front window. A freezing wind blew through the neighborhood. Steel clouds covered the sky, threatening to snow. The thermometer showed twenty-eight degrees. He looked across the cul de sac to the Hansen house. "I wonder how they're coming along? It's been a week since we gave them that bag of food."

"A week already?" Claire asked.

"Yes. We haven't seen or heard from anybody. I hope it's because they don't need anything, not because they're afraid of offending us. I wasn't too friendly about doling out the food."

"Now that you need a chainsaw, you're looking pretty friendly," Patricia said.

"I know. I did give food, though, so maybe Rob will reciprocate with the chainsaw. I could even use his help."

"Better him than me," Claire said.

"You can help too," Gary snapped. "The more the merrier, right?"

"That goes for this place, too," Patricia said. "We might be able to pass the time better with a few friends around."

"Here?" Gary asked, turning quickly from the window to face her. "We'd be out of food in no time."

"Oh, Gary. We have enough food to last two families for a year. Let's trade some of our necessities for a little fun."

"What are you talking about?"

"Pictionary," Danielle said.

"Taboo," Claire offered.

"Or," Patricia said slowly, drama in her voice, "poker. How long has it been since we've pulled those chips out of the attic?"

"Years. Since Danielle was born, I think."

"You were always good at poker."

"Yes, I was." He turned back to the window. "I think I could give old Hansen a run for his money. Not that his money would be worth anything these days. But I could give him a run for his chips. I'm going over there."

"Take more food," Patricia said.

Gary stepped into the cold air. He set down the bag of food to button his jacket. He walked across the cul de sac to Rob Hansen's home. If not for the quiet line of smoke rising from the chimney, Gary would have thought the place deserted. He knocked on the front door. Rebecca answered.

"Good morning," Gary said.

"Hi Gary. Come on in." She showed him past the shadowy living room to the family room. Her husband and two children sat around the woodstove in wrinkled shirts and sweat pants. "Look who's here," she told them.

Rob stood to shake hands. "I never expected company on a day like this. What have you got there?"

"Just a bit of food for you folks. Figured you might be able to use some."

The children ran over and grabbed the bag from Gary's hands. "More Pop Tarts?" the little girl asked.

Rob laughed. "Those were a real hit last time."

"Gary, in case you've forgotten," Rebecca said, "this is Bobby and Allison."

The children did find a box of Pop Tarts, along with licorice and cans of juice. They chewed and drank by the woodstove. It looked to Gary like a scene from National Geographic.

"My goodness, are you that hungry?" Gary asked Rob and Rebecca. "Why didn't you ask for more food from us?"

"It didn't feel right," Rob said. "We already borrowed from you once. Also, I never expected this situation to last so long. We thought we could get by on the little we had until the stores opened again." Rebecca eyed him viciously. "Well, all right," he continued. "*I* thought we could get by. Rebecca said to ask the neighbors for help."

Gary felt terrible. He and Danielle had taken food from the grocery store with the intention of giving some of it to the Hansens. When he got back to his home and surveyed his own family's shelves, Gary had decided against it for the time being. He didn't want to take any chances. "I should have come sooner. I'm sorry I wasn't more neighborly."

"Oh no," Rebecca said. "It isn't your fault. How could you have known? We're just thankful that you brought this."

"I'll do your taxes free when this is all over," Rob added.

"How are you coming on wood?" Gary asked.

Rob looked at their pile by the stove. "We have enough for another few days. After that I figured I could cut more down by the creek. There are a few dead trees."

"How are you doing on firewood?" Rebecca asked Gary.

"We can last about the same amount of time."

Rob's face livened. "Say, we could cut wood together. We'd get a lot more that way."

"Sounds like a good plan to me. Maybe we can go one better." Rob cocked his head.

"I was talking with Patricia and the girls. It doesn't make sense for us to hole up in our separate homes with our separate piles of firewood and our separate stashes of food. We could heat both families in one home if we stay together. We have plenty of food and a big woodstove. Why don't you come stay with us until this blows over?"

Rob looked at Rebecca. "I don't know, Gary. That's asking a lot of you."

"What are you talking about? I just invited you over. I'm being selfish, in all honesty. It's getting boring by ourselves. We want people to talk with and play cards and Taboo."

"Still," Rob began, looking at his children. "I'm not—"

"Don't be ridiculous," Rebecca told him. She turned to Gary. "Of course we'll come. The children are getting bored here too. It makes sense to conserve what little firewood we have. It's also very kind of you to offer your food."

"Then it's a deal," Gary said. "I'll get Danielle and Claire to help carry your stuff over. Let's get this party started!"

He walked to the front door and opened it. "Oh, and Hansen," he called back. Rob turned. "I hope you're a decent poker player. I don't want to own your home when this is all said and done."

JANUARY 8, 2000

Hartmire's eyes recorded each movement, each tone of voice, each glance from the visitors. What were they looking at? Who were they looking for? When did they expect to leave? He could tell somebody's intentions by how quickly they settled into a place. He'd learned that trick when he guarded courtrooms. Lawyers expecting a quick resolution don't bother opening their briefcases. Lawyers who come for a long fight open two or three briefcases and carry snacks and throat lozenges.

The six military representatives carried two suitcases each, not one of which looked like it contained clothing. Pritchett and Schwager introduced their companions as a satellite control specialist from Space Command at Peterson Air Force Base, a Pacific military strategist, an Army lieutenant colonel, and a Navy captain.

Hartmire watched Schwager the closest. He noticed that Schwager looked at The Keep's entrance guards for a long time, particularly Marty Shore. The two established eye contact and then Schwager looked quickly away.

"Mr. Schwager," Hartmire said as they walked toward the conference room.

"Yes."

"When did you meet Marty?"

"Excuse me?" Schwager said, watching his own feet step through the hallway on their way to the conference room.

"I asked when you met Marty."

"Marty who?"

"The security guard at our front entrance. You two know each other?"

"No. Who are you talking about? I don't think I know any of your guards."

"Just curious. I thought you two knew each other. Have a good visit." He stopped and watched the procession continue down the hall to the stairway. He walked back to the front desk. Marty sat alone.

"Boy, that Schwager is a real character," Hartmire said in a conversational tone.

"Who?" Marty said quickly.

"Schwager, the guy from DISA."

"Oh. I don't know him," he said. He looked down at papers on the desk. He looked up a second later. "I don't know any Schwager."

Hartmire watched Marty closely. "How long have you been at this desk today?"

"Since the morning shift."

"That's a haul. I think things are going to stay quiet the rest of the day, probably the rest of this ordeal. Why don't you head home for a bit. Enjoy the quiet of the city. I'll get somebody else to man the desk."

Marty looked unsure. "Thanks, Jules, really. That's nice of you, but I'd rather finish my shift."

"Why?"

"I'm already here and I could use the money."

"Yeah, I guess we could all use the money eventually. I'll at least get you patrolling a hallway somewhere so you can get a change of scenery."

"That's nice of you, but I'm fine here."

"Expecting somebody?"

"No. What are you talking about?"

"Are you expecting somebody?" The conversational tone was gone. "You don't seem eager to leave the front desk."

"I'm not supposed to be eager to leave the front desk. It's my assigned duty."

"I'm unassigning you."

"To go where?"

"Home until we call you."

"I still don't understand, Jules."

"You don't need to understand, Marty. I'm just being careful. It's nothing against you."

Marty gathered his belongings and left. Hartmire sat behind the desk himself. He stared at the useless door monitors. The security cameras were S2's only equipment to break from Y2K. He waited alone. For what, he couldn't say. A call, a knock, a voice from behind him. He radioed Lauer and Klepac. They arrived within a minute.

"We've got trouble," Hartmire told them.

A satellite phone rang on the groundfloor terminal room. A middle-aged consultant named Sal Platt answered.

"The front entrance is off. Go to plan B."

Sal walked quickly to the rear parking lot door. The Hartmire guard saw him coming and stood straight.

"I've got to get to my car!" Sal said. He tried pushing past the guard.

"Wait a second," the guard said, blocking the door. "You know you have to come in and out the front entrance."

"Listen, my wife just called on a satellite phone and my kid is dying from an asthma attack! I need to get home. My car is out that door. I don't have time to go around front and sign out. My manager cleared this!" He pushed against the guard, who stood his ground.

"I'm sorry, but I can't let anybody in or out of this door."

"Are you fucking nuts?" Sal yelled. "My kid is dying! Can you understand that? Get out of my way!"

The young guard let his arm get knocked aside. Sal pushed on the door, but it wouldn't budge.

The guard had grown bored with defending the quiet workplace of S2. Nothing ever happened. It was a building full of geeks. The upset man seemed sincere. What could a single use of the door hurt? He lifted the metal hinge and pushed the hydraulic button. The heavy steel door began to open.

Daylight was still a sliver between the door and wall when a bullet shot from a silenced pistol into the guard's neck. Shock crossed the young man's face as his hand instinctively grabbed at the blood. His eyes rolled into his head and he fell to the floor.

Sal was already walking back to his workstation.

The door opened completely. Strong hands grabbed the dead guard and pulled him from the building. They quickly cleaned the blood from the floor.

The remote hallway of The Keep filled with men dressed as Hartmire guards. They carried silencers on their guns. Once inside, they were only two minutes from the conference room.

Pritchett's audience watched him through red-veined eyes. Mark Solvang's black hair was combed neatly despite the showerless work days. David Kleewein wore a hat to cover his unwashed hair. Their voices didn't modulate when they spoke. Pritchett had been working long hours himself, but the S2 executives made him feel fresh off a pleasure cruise.

"I can see that you've both been working very hard and I appreciate your dedication."

Neither replied. Schwager wiped his shirtsleeve across his sweaty forehead. He checked his watch.

"You both know the technical details from Van Lan and Stamp," Pritchett continued. "The NMCC is down. We are here because we cannot monitor progress quickly enough from the NMCC. Your systems are best plugged into the fixes taking place and the fixes are the activity most critical to our national security. We cannot afford to be polite about this by keeping our distance. It's too important. You have operable systems, you are fixing our systems, we need to be by your side to get the latest developments in real time and make decisions accordingly. The sinking of our two destroyers changes the urgency with which you need to regard this project."

"Which means what?" Mark asked. His green and silver eyes dared Pritchett to accuse his company of inactivity.

"Which means a rethinking of priorities and a strategy expansion. We continue repairing new systems only. We need to simultaneously reactivate older weapons and defense systems for immediate protection."

"We don't have enough people to simultaneously reactivate old systems and repair new ones," Mark said. "There's a finite supply of this talent."

"And we're requesting more of it," Pritchett replied harshly. "The military has programmers, but they are not as skilled as yours. This is absolute top priority. You need to pull teams from private industry to help the military."

Mark's expression remained unchanged. "How many did you have in mind?"

"6,000 full-time consultants."

Mark and Kleewein gasped. The reaction did not surprise Pritchett. Schwager checked his watch again.

"That's half our company," Mark pointed out. "We appreciate the urgency of the military's situation, but I can't justify giving up that much to one project. The people we do have are already defecting. Power is still down, the FAA is still down, phones are dead, and so on. In short, we have a hell of a lot of work to do outside the military."

"You'll have the same amount of work ahead and the same people to do it with," Pritchett told him. There was no room for discussion. The rules had changed and the Pentagon and the CIA and the State Department had reason to fear the worst. "The only difference is that you'll be doing most of the work for the military first, who badly needs your help."

Mark and Kleewein looked at each other, but neither offered any support. Mark stared silently back at Pritchett.

Pritchett's face reddened and his voice rose. "I'm disappointed that you can't appreciate the importance of this situation. Two U.S. warships sank yesterday. Does that mean anything to you? It means a hell of a lot to me. It means that your brothers and sisters died in a watery grave trying to use equipment that we promised would work. We promised indirectly by placing it onboard those ships. Somebody is killing your family at sea, and you're talking to me about dead phone lines?"

The doors swung open. Hartmire guards filed into the conference room without a sound. They carried their weapons drawn. Some of the guards were Chinese, some were black, some were white, some were olive skinned with black hair. Pritchett looked at Mark for an explanation, but saw that he was just as surprised.

"Who are you?" Mark asked. "Where's Jules Hartmire?"

The guards continued filing inside the room. They surrounded the table with stone faces and drawn weapons.

"What the hell are you doing?" Mark demanded. "We're in the middle of a meeting here."

Schwager stood up. "The meeting is over, Mr. Solvang."

"Al, have a seat!" Pritchett yelled.

Schwager glared across the table, sweat glistening on his brow and in the deep cut ravines of his cheeks. "Everybody walk calmly from the room. One word, one attempt to flee, and you will be shot. Proceed."

The numbness returned to Pritchett's fingertips. Albert Schwager had somehow cleared a military takeover of Solvang Solutions without Pritchett's authorization. But who were these men? The military doesn't dress in civilian guard uniforms.

"Who the hell authorized—" began the Pacific strategist. Three muzzles turned on him and issued three crisp chirps. The man flew across the conference room table onto the floor. His back left a swath of blood on the wood. The red flow continued from three holes in his uniform. His mouth opened and closed twice, then froze gaping at the carpet, a river of saliva and blood pouring from his throat.

"If everybody is finished," Schwager said in a voice too calm to be human, "we can get going." He looked at Pritchett as he spoke, visually baiting him to say something. Pritchett clenched his teeth.

They all walked from the room.

Jules Hartmire thought long about Schwager and Marty. Klepac and Lauer stood with him at the front desk. Elwell waited at The Lair, the alternate control site that Mark authorized at Hartmire's suggestion. It was the ultimate backup plan. If The Keep were destroyed or overtaken by hostile forces, a core team from Solvang could continue running operations from the secret site. Elwell remained on standby at The Lair in case anything went wrong, something that Hartmire had genuinely doubted until that day's interplay between Schwager and Marty. Now he had a horrible feeling he'd missed something.

With his security camera system broken by Y2K, he worried about people slipping in and out of The Keep. There were no cameras watching the doors. Even the single guard he placed at every door wasn't foolproof. People could be bought. People could be killed. The wrong people could fake their way through even the most rigorous employment screening.

"Radio the guards on patrol," he said to Klepac. "Have them check and secure every door immediately. You stay here and keep this door closed. Lauer and I will check the conference room."

He and Lauer started to walk down the hallway. Hartmire turned back to Klepac. "Also, radio Elwell at The Lair. Let him know that something's fishy over here and that his people should stay alert for the next few hours."

Klepac nodded and began speaking into his lapel microphone. Listening to their earpieces as they walked, Hartmire and Lauer heard his message to patrolling guards.

"This is Klepac at the front desk. Guards on patrol, proceed at once to your nearest exit door. Check for tampering and insure that the door is securely shut. Report back to me immediately."

Hartmire and Lauer walked briskly through the executive center of The Keep. Even in the dim illumination of the lights on diesel power, wood shone richly on desktops and on the walls behind photos of Big Sur, the Golden Gate Bridge, Wine Country, and Yosemite.

They walked to the door of the conference room. Hartmire pressed his ear to the wood and listened.

Nothing. He listened a few seconds longer. No voices, no hum of machinery, no shuffling. He tapped his middle knuckle on the door.

Nothing.

He opened the door. "Oh hell."

He saw the dead body and strewn chairs. He ran with Lauer straight to the dead man. He felt his neck. No pulse, skin still warm and soft. He felt the seat of a chair. Still warm.

"They just left," he said.

"This is a military man," Lauer observed. "Why would the

military kill its own people? It wouldn't. We're up against another group."

"We don't know that. We don't know a thing."

Hartmire stood. He needed to react quicker than his adversaries to keep the situation from deteriorating even further.

"Klepac, this is Hartmire," he spoke into his lapel.

"Go ahead," Klepac replied.

"The Keep is compromised. One of the military delegation is dead in the conference room, everybody else is missing. The seats are still warm so they can't be far. What's the word on the doors?"

"All secured, but one guard missing."

"Which door?"

"Rear parking lot entrance."

"That's the penetration point. Instruct half of the patrol guards to stake out critical areas of The Keep, including the doors. I don't want anybody getting out of here with Mark Solvang and David Kleewein. Assemble a unit for yourself to lead an investigation of the rear parking area. Instruct the remaining patrol guards to come to the conference room immediately. We will meet them here."

"Roger."

"Be careful outside. We don't know who these people are or what they look like. Have your weapons ready."

He listened to Klepac's instructions to patrol guards, then waited with Lauer. "My guess is that they look like Solvang workers or they look like us."

"Probably like us."

"Yes, because then guns would be a natural accompaniment. Nobody would notice. This could get confusing in a hurry."

"Our guards know each other pretty well. We should be able to detect strangers."

"In peaceful contact, yes. I'm worried about a firefight with dozens of emotional guards shooting at people who look the same. I hope we don't shoot any friendlies."

They heard people running toward them from two hallways. Their hands rested on their pistols, still holstered but unsnapped and ready to be drawn. Two familiar faces rounded the corner. The guards froze when they saw the corpse against the opulent backdrop of the executive conference room.

"I'm guessing the hostiles are dressed like us," Hartmire told the two men. "They have Mark Solvang and the military delegation.

They can't be out of the building yet. We need to find them, kill the hostiles, and get our people back. Let's move."

They ran down the hallway toward the terminal room, Hartmire in the lead. He stuck his head inside. "Anybody seen Mark Solvang?" Nobody had.

They continued to the next room and the next and the next. Nobody had seen Mark or any of the others. It would take forever to search every room in the building. But as long as every exit door was closely watched, they had forever to keep looking. Hartmire's immediate concern was keeping Mark on site. If he was taken from the building, all was lost.

The group stopped at the end of the hallway. "Okay, they didn't take them in this direction. We don't need to continue searching rooms on this side of the building. They wouldn't keep them in any of them, but they might have walked them past. We've eliminated that possibility. Everybody think. What's down the other hallway that would be of interest?"

"No terminal rooms," offered a guard. "They aren't putting them at gunpoint and forcing them to issue commands."

"Not yet," Lauer replied.

"But of course they couldn't yet," Hartmire said. "They need to worry about us. If I were taking over this place, I'd do it exactly as they're doing it. Wait until the bigshots are in the same room, sneak a small force inside the building and capture them. Then what?"

"The bigshots are critical to everything," Lauer thought aloud. "I'd get them to a secure area and keep them on ice while I took out the guards."

"That's what I'd do as well. Where's the best secure area down the other hallway?"

"None of the terminal rooms," a guard offered. "Too many people in there know the bigshots."

"Some sort of windowless room where nobody goes," said the other. "There are dozens of those."

"Right," Hartmire said. "What other criteria would I have for storing my prisoners?"

"A quiet room," Lauer said. "So nobody could hear them."

Hartmire shook his head. "Sleeping gas could take care of that. Throw them in a confined space and put them all to sleep. No problem of noise."

"There'd be a problem of smell."

"Possibly. So I'd want them somewhere off the beaten path."

"The lower levels are off the beaten path," a guard pointed out. "Few people go down there."

"There are a lot of lower levels," Lauer said.

"If it were me I'd choose one that was close," the other guard added. "I'd be looking over my shoulder and would be in a panic to get the prisoners stowed ASAP. I wouldn't want to be running through stairwells all afternoon."

"Good point," Hartmire said. "Let's narrow our search to floors A and B. What are on floors A and B?"

"Diesel power is on A, shipping and receiving is on B," a guard said. "There's also some food storage on B."

"There's a huge terminal room on A," Lauer remembered. "It's near the diesel generators."

Hartmire thought a second. "I would lock them in the diesel supply room."

"Yes," Lauer concluded at the same instant. The guards both nodded. "Its noisy there and it smells like diesel."

"Few people walk by there."

"It's nearby."

"Nobody ever goes into the supply room."

Klepac's urgent voice came across their earpieces. "Hartmire and Lauer! The rear parking area is clear, but seven pickup trucks just pulled into the front area. There are roughly fifty troops jumping off the backs of the trucks. They're dressed like us. They're running to the front entrance."

"This changes everything," Hartmire said. "Who's at the front entrance?"

Three guards responded. "We see them coming," one said. "Should we fire through the slits?"

"Yes," Hartmire said. "Use the rifles. Klepac, get our trucks to the loading dock immediately. Radio Elwell at The Lair. We need to get Solvang out of here!"

"Roger."

Hartmire, Lauer, and the two guards ran down the hallway past the rooms of consultants at terminals. A few heads turned in their direction, but most didn't notice. They ran through the executive center, past the conference room, down the hallway to the stairwell. Their earpieces crackled to life with the sound of gunfire and yelling.

"We can't hold these guys forever!"

"They're going to rocket the front entrance!"

"I suggest we—"

The booming gunfire stopped suddenly. The voice activated microphones had no voices to activate them.

"What happened?" a guard asked as they continued running down the stairwell.

"They were killed from the inside," Hartmire answered. He switched on his lapel microphone as they ran from the stairwell past the glass of the lower terminal room where consultants worked feverishly on code from around the country.

"The hostiles are going to throw open the front doors and let the troops rush inside The Keep," he said into the microphone. "They'll disperse in all directions looking for Hartmire guards. They will not harm consultants. That's who they want alive and functional. Everybody proceed immediately to the rear loading dock! Everything depends on us responding faster than they expect. This is exactly why we built The Lair. Move out!"

They arrived at a corner in the hallway and stopped. Hartmire stuck a dentist's mirror around the corner and breathed a mixed reaction. The four guards standing in front of the door to the diesel supply room confirmed that his team had correctly figured the location of Mark, Kleewein, and the DoD contingent. It also meant they would need to kill the four men.

"Four of them," he whispered to his team. "Keep an eye back where we came. We need to kill them before they can radio anybody." He lay on his belly, pistol drawn. Lauer crouched above him, pistol drawn. A guard stood above Lauer, pistol drawn.

"On three," Hartmire whispered. "Keep firing until all men are down. One, two, three!"

Three sets of heads, arms, and pistols emerged around the corner. The pistols opened a flurry of shots that echoed and roared down the hallway. The four guards contorted and gulped and danced on their feet, never firing a single shot in return. All four fell still. Hartmire's team ran around the corner, pistols pointed at the fallen guards.

Hartmire saw blood on the hallway floor. There must have been a skirmish. He hoped Mark was all right.

They arrived at the four dead guards outside the diesel supply room. Lauer selected a master key from his ring and unlocked the door.

"Careful of gas," he said.

He pushed the door open. Nothing visible poured from the dark supply room, but the air smelled sweet. A can still hissed gas near the door.

"They haven't been in here long. The can isn't even empty."

He shone a flashlight inside. The six bodies lay on top of each other like members of a rabbit warren.

"Hold your breath," Lauer said.

They entered, checked pulses, exited.

Hartmire spoke into his lapel. "Klepac, have the trucks running. We have six drugged bodies to carry from the diesel supply room. There are only four of us. Send additional guards."

"Roger."

"Also, Susan Levin is not in the room. Send guards into the building to find her."

"Roger."

Lauer and the guards had already pulled the dead men from the hallway into the storage room. A guard mopped the blood from the floor with diesel work rags.

"Hold your breath." Hartmire walked into the supply room. He found Mark and Kleewein. He threw Mark over his shoulder and gestured for Lauer to take Kleewein. They exited the room.

"We need to get these two immediately to the shipping docks. They are critical. Lauer, give Kleewein to a guard. I want you to stay behind and make sure everything goes right here. When the others arrive, run the bodies out and close and lock the door."

Lauer nodded. He pushed Kleewein to a guard's shoulder. Hartmire and the guard ran awkwardly toward the stairwell. They heard troops running.

"Turn back!" Hartmire screamed at the guard. "Those aren't ours!" They wheeled around and sprinted back through the hallway. Lauer saw them coming and knew what was wrong.

"Hold them," Hartmire commanded as he and the guard ran past the storage room. The bodies of Mark and Kleewein bounced on their shoulders. Hartmire hoped to God that the other stairwell was still clear. They could not resist heavy troops for long. He yelled into his lapel as he ran.

"Klepac, send ten additional men through stairwell three ASAP! Stairwell two is occupied and hostiles are closing in on the diesel supply room."

"The first four are already coming through stairwell two. I'll notify them."

"Tell them to flank the hostiles."

"I just sent a party to find Susan Levin. I'll notify them as well."

"There's no time to find her anymore! Call them back."

Lauer knew that he and the guard would need to blast the incoming troops with enough firepower to stop them at the corner. Extreme force confuses even the best trained troops. But if they saw how small a contingent guarded the supply room, the hostiles would rush forward and overtake Lauer's position.

"Strike with all we've got," he said. "Remember to hold your breath. Don't breath the gas." He lay on his belly just inside the supply room. The guard knelt above him.

The hostiles ran into view. Lauer and the guard opened fire immediately. The first few men went down and the rest retreated back around the corner.

Lauer and the guard could not hold their breath inside the supply room forever. They scooted their heads into the hallway for air. The hostiles fired from around the corner. The guard fell to the floor, blood pouring from his forehead. He never made a sound.

"Oh no," Lauer said. He pulled the man into the supply room.

Lauer returned fire without hitting anybody. He spoke into his lapel. "I have them stopped at the corner of the terminal room."

The additional guards from the shipping dock ran from the stairwell, their latest report fresh in mind. They heard a crowd running farther up the stairwell. It had to be additional support for the hostiles. They would be sandwiched between two groups.

The lead guard spoke into his lapel. "We're approaching the hostiles at the terminal room. More coming behind us. We need to shoot our way past the first group, grab our guys, and go."

"Roger," Klepac said from the dock. "We're keeping stairway three clear for escape."

"Roger," Lauer said. "Grab and go. I'll keep firing from here to keep them occupied."

The friendly guard team ran around the first corner of the hallway without a pause. They fired their pistols as they ran past the terminal room windows.

Workers watched from inside. The muffled sound of gunfire penetrated the walls and glass. Susan looked up from her terminal near the back of the room. She stood to address her consultants. "Everybody stay put!" she yelled.

All work screeched to a halt.

"Send notes to the other rooms," Susan commanded. Everybody turned back to their keyboards, frantically typing reports to their colleagues upstairs and across the world.

The guard team killed half of the hostile force before taking any hits. The hostiles turned to face their running attackers and shot three of them dead. The remaining six men killed the other hostiles and leapt over the pile of their bodies. They kept running toward the supply room.

All but one, that is. One guard turned to check his fallen friend. The lead guard heard the man weeping, even through the adrenaline.

"Come on, Rob!" the leader yelled back. The others kept running toward Lauer as planned.

"Rob!" he yelled again. Rob tried pulling his dead friend down the hallway by one arm. "Rob, they're coming! Let's go!"

The next group of hostiles rounded the corner and shot Rob before he could even raise his pistol. The leader turned and ran to Lauer. He saw that the second wave of guards from the dock had arrived and were already carrying bodies from the supply room.

"Hold them at the far corner!" Lauer yelled. He sent three men back with the lead guard. They took positions around the opposite side of the corner where the dead hostiles lay in a pile. They shot at the approaching troops, who continued running. There must have been twenty of them. They could lose a few on their way to the supply room and still take the position.

The lead guard looked at the head of a fallen hostile around the corner. "They have earpieces!" he yelled into his lapel. "They're reporting to each other."

"They can't hear our communications," Hartmire said. "But they can report to each other what they see us doing."

"Correct," Klepac replied from the dock. "They're coming around the outside of the building. If we're not out of here in thirty seconds, we're never leaving."

"Come on!" Lauer yelled from the supply room. The lead guard and his three men turned and ran from the corner. "Everybody's out! Go, go, go!"

The remaining guards ran to stairwell three, turning to fire at their pursuers. The hostiles shot madly down the hall, dropping two guards as they ran. Nobody stopped to help. Adrenaline clouded emotions. All anybody could hear in their minds was the urgent "go, go, go!" in Lauer's voice.

The guards carrying drugged bodies from the supply room streamed from the loading docks into the beds of the awaiting trucks. They were normal pickups with no identifying marks. The men dropped the bodies violently, closed the liftgates, and crouched with their pistols drawn.

The bodies were placed in one pickup with several guards. The remaining guards packed into six additional pickups. Hartmire rode in the cab of the truck carrying the drugged bodies. The gas was beginning to wear off the prisoners. They hadn't been in the supply room long enough for the gas to permeate their systems.

The seven trucks tore from the loading dock as hostiles ran around the sides of the building and from the stairwells.

"Fire!" Klepac yelled into his lapel. The guards opened fire from the beds of the pickups. They drove from the docks into the rear parking lot.

Hostile trucks at the front of The Keep blocked the exit. Klepac expected it and already instructed drivers to take the trucks through a field behind The Keep. They bounced over the curb and threw chunks of grass from the tires. The trucks roared across the field. Three pickups pursued their escape party. Klepac did not expect that.

"They're pursuing!" he reported into his lapel.

Hartmire turned. "Keep driving and we'll lose them."

A stream of white smoke shot from one of the pursuing pickups.

It reached the rear pickup full of guards and detonated on impact. The truck disintegrated.

"Son of a bitch!" Lauer yelled.

Hartmire thought fast. He could not lose their pursuers. He had too large a party and was too closely followed. That meant he could not drive directly to The Lair. Its secrecy was its only hope. He needed to kill the hostiles.

"Elwell!" he yelled into his lapel.

"Go ahead," Elwell replied from The Lair.

"Get high power rifles and troops into the two pickups from The Lair. I'm going to lead these bastards into east San Jose. I'll coordinate with you to flank them. It worked in the hallways, maybe it'll work out here."

"Roger."

Hartmire's six remaining pickups wheeled suddenly to the right. They accelerated to the edge of the field, trading the grass and dirt for pavement in a cloud of debris from their tires. Engines revved the six trucks to top speed. They hurtled through streets to east San Jose.

Another stream of white smoke shot from the hostile trucks. It missed Hartmire's escape party, crashed into a home, and exploded. The home collapsed in a pile of dust.

"Keep turning at corners!" Hartmire yelled to the drivers. "Snake your way through the city. No straight lines of fire. Keep them turning and dodging." The empty streets provided plenty of room for maneuvering. "Guards, fire at them every chance you get. Let them know we're not helpless."

Mark, Kleewein, and the DoD contingent slowly awoke. Mark vomited in the bed of the pickup. The others wheezed and coughed the gas from their systems. It didn't take long for them to realize the situation.

"Where are we going?" Pritchett asked a guard over the sound of gunfire and rushing air.

"Away from The Keep! That's all I can tell you."

Hartmire radioed to Elwell, whose team was already driving at ninety miles per hour on highway 17 toward San Jose. "Elwell, we're moving east on Trimble."

"East on Trimble, got it. We'll take 280 until it turns to 680, then exit on McKee. Head to that general area and I'll give details as we find a suitable place. How many are there?"

"Three. They've got rockets and heavy firepower."

"Rockets." Elwell paused. "I'll work that into the equation."

Hartmire's six pickups wound their way circuitously through the city. They left Trimble, crossed through neighborhoods, rounded office buildings, drove through parking lots, across medians, and back onto Trimble. Their three pursuers did not know the city as well and there were a few times that Hartmire thought they might lose them. But they didn't. The pursuers were tenacious. The gunfire dropped to a minimum. Both sides realized that clear shots were out of the question.

Trimble turned into the Montague Expressway, one long piece of road.

"Wind back and forth," Hartmire instructed. The trucks weaved from one side of the road to the other. "Keep firing at them!" It was nearly impossible to shoot while the trucks drove so violently. But they avoided straight lines of fire and no rockets came.

They drove over 880 and continued past 680. There, Hartmire turned onto surface streets again.

"Elwell, we're heading south on Morrill Avenue."

"I don't know where that is," Elwell replied, looking at his map.

"Neither do I, but it should run into Berryessa."

"Okay, now I follow. You're already east of 680."

"Yes."

"Here's the new plan. We're going to take Alum Rock up toward Hamilton Observatory."

"I follow," Hartmire said.

"We'll find a little side road off Mount Hamilton Road. They won't be able to drive quickly. We'll ambush them there."

"Got it," Hartmire said. "We'll work our way down to Mount Hamilton Road. Keep me informed."

Mark turned to Kleewein. They both looked sicker than they'd ever been. Little sleep, high stress, and now gas inhalation left them breathing in small puffs. "Where are we going?"

Kleewein shook his head. "Beats me. I think our guys are figuring it out as they go along."

Elwell found a perfect little road in the hills of San Jose. He parked his two trucks on an even smaller road behind a blue house with a tire swing in front. He would have Hartmire stop just past the side road so the three pursuing vehicles would park in front of it. Then he could ram them and attack in the confusion.

An old man came out of the blue house to Elwell. "It's about damned time the power company arrived. Where the hell have you people been?"

"We're not the power company."

The old man didn't hear. "Jesus, you brought enough boys to get the job done. Thank goodness. Do you know how long the lights have been off around here? Even the damned grocery store is closed and—"

"Sir!" Elwell yelled. "Go back inside immediately and stay put."

"What?"

Elwell pointed his pistol at the old man's face. "Get back in your home and shut up! We are going to shoot."

The man looked confused, but got the message. He turned back toward his home.

Hartmire's trucks drove madly through the neighborhoods of east San Jose. Nobody bothered firing anymore. Hartmire worried that helicopters would appear in the sky at any moment, or additional vehicles with rocket launchers would cut them off. The hostiles had radios too. Surely they'd thought of the possibility of escape and had made more sophisticated plans than a car chase. But maybe not. Even the best prepared teams overlook something.

At last they screeched onto Alum Rock. "Elwell, we're heading east on Alum Rock."

"Good. Turn on Mount Hamilton Road. Turn right on Olive

Drive. Move as fast as you can to the bend in the road at Olive Place. There's a big blue house on the corner with a tire swing in front. It'll be on your left. You can't miss it. We're on the other side of that house. Go past it and stay on Olive Drive. Stop just past the side road so they are forced to slow down. We'll ram them from the side."

"We'll be ready to fire."

"Same here."

Hartmire relayed the plan to his guards across the six trucks. "Tell Mark and the others to lie down. Cover them through it all."

The trucks turned the corner onto Mount Hamilton. Hartmire saw the little sign for Olive and they turned sharply onto it. The hostiles followed fifty yards behind. Thick trees and rolling green hills surrounded them. The small drive narrowed.

"They'll think we're trying to lose them," Hartmire told Klepac and Lauer. "This is a smart plan."

He saw the blue house. "There's our contact," he said. "Pull past and leave the side road exposed." They rolled past the blue house. He saw Elwell's two trucks side by side, ready to ram. Elwell gave a sharp wave.

Hartmire's group stopped. The guards in the front trucks lay across the brain trust. The guards in the rear trucks crouched, ready for battle.

"Out!" Hartmire yelled.

The guards in the rear trucks leapt from the beds, guns drawn, ready to fight. They scattered into the bushes and houses and parked cars on the same side of the street as Elwell's trucks. Attacking from the same side would leave little chance of accidentally shooting one of their own.

Moments later, the three hostile vehicles drove along Olive.

They slowed at the alley, watching the trucks stopped in front of them. By focusing on their quarry, they failed to see Elwell's party lurking behind the blue house.

Just before the hostiles came to a complete stop and could charge out to fight, Elwell's trucks drove forward, ramming the side of the front two hostile vehicles.

Hartmire guards opened fire immediately, not giving the hostiles any time to adjust to the sudden impact. Elwell's men stood from the beds of their trucks with rifles and pistols riddling the three vehicles. Guards from the escape party fired from their positions in the bushes and behind parked cars and trees.

The gunfire lasted fifteen seconds. Not a single Hartmire guard was shot during the assault. The hostiles were muddled by the impact of Elwell's trucks and the swift attack that followed. The sound of gunfire dissipated into the neighborhood, replaced by the heavy breathing of men drowning in adrenaline.

Hartmire inhaled deeply. Faces peeked from homes on the street. The old man in the blue house watched through his front window. Every hostile lay dead in or around their trucks. The tires on the side of the attack were flat, the glass shot out, the metal peppered with bullet holes. Elwell's engines still idled.

"Will those drive?" Hartmire asked.

The drivers backed the trucks away from the hostiles. "Yes," Elwell replied. "We're good to go."

Hartmire nodded. He holstered his pistol. "Grab the missile launchers," he told Klepac. He crouched by a dead man to check for identification. The man wore no dog tags, carried no wallet. He was a stiff in a Hartmire uniform. Same with the others.

"They're nobodies," Lauer said.

Hartmire ripped the shirt from one man. No identifying tattoos. Some of the men were Chinese, some white, some middle eastern. Hartmire motioned Pritchett over. "Who are these men?"

"I don't know."

"Are they U.S. military?"

"I don't know."

"Do you have any idea what's going on here?"

"No."

"All right, back to the truck."

Klepac walked up. "They used all their missiles."

Lauer, Elwell, and Klepac surrounded Hartmire. "We need to get out of here," he told them. "Take one of their radios and load up. We'll drive north into neighborhoods. I don't know who we're dealing with or who's on whose side. We'll wait until nightfall, blindfold the DoD contingent, then drive separate routes to The Lair."

January 9, 2000

Billy Stamp wasn't sure what Carl Albright was trying to say. "What do you mean there's a pattern?"

"I mean just that," Albright said, standing with a screen printout of a *Solvang2K* work panel. "I finally found the file we've been looking for ever since we came across that derivative code months ago."

"Where was it?"

"On some obscure admin server."

"And?"

"And look at this." Carl handed the screen printout to Billy.

"These are subroutines set up to be deactivated or overridden with a software switch," Billy said, still looking at the print. "None of this is old stuff, either. It's new code, but it would break from Y2K. It's got hard coded dates and all."

"Exactly. This is new material that was coded to break. However, it can be overridden with a separate file. One we haven't found yet."

Billy frowned. "That file must change this code's behavior. And this code determines what the front line code does. We're talking three layers of dependency, the first two of which were changed in the last few years."

"That's what I meant when I said there's a pattern. This is deliberately structured to look broken when it really works."

"Sabotage?" Stamp asked himself. "At this level? No way. Who would have the resources to create a completely separate software structure at a facility like Pearl Harbor? Nobody. You'd have to be the military itself."

Carl tilted his head in puzzlement. "Why is that out of the question?"

Billy remembered the state of affairs at the NMCC. He looked at Albright. "It's not. Look for the third software layer."

January 8, 2000

Hartmire drove into east San Jose neighborhoods, finally settling along a tiny street near the hills. The trucks parked under rows of trees.

"Search the DoD," Hartmire commanded.

The guards searched the DoD contingent for radios and weapons. They confiscated beepers and satellite phones, leaving the DoD with nothing to contact the outside world.

"Are you feeling better?" Hartmire asked Mark.

He nodded. "I'll be fine. We need to get to The Lair immediately. They might be destroying our operations. Who knows how many consultants we lost from all this."

"Or if they're dead," Kleewein added.

"The plan is to trickle our way to The Lair under cover of darkness," Hartmire said. "We'll have everybody there by midnight. Our guards at The Lair have contacted backup consultants to join the ones who already worked from The Lair. It will be fully operational the moment you walk in the doors. A team of roughly twenty consultants is waiting for you. That's the best we can do."

"I just hope we have an organization left," Mark said.

"You will," Hartmire answered. He thought a moment, then continued. "There's a good chance they know about The Lair, and maybe even where it's located."

"Can we get consultants out of The Keep?" Kleewein asked.

"No. Whomever we're up against is too well organized and too powerful. We don't have the resources to pull off a rescue."

"It doesn't take many people at The Lair to continue running this operation," Mark said. "We can communicate with other sites and even control their equipment from The Lair."

"Fine," Hartmire answered. "However, the hostiles inside The Keep will see the communications coming from The Lair."

Mark shook his head. "Our communications will take place over S3D channels. Unless one of our core managers sold us out, then we should have secure lines of communication into each site."

"Excellent. However, don't be too sure that a core manager didn't sell out."

"The Lair is set up to see every communication that occurs on Solvang lines. If somebody is coordinating this takeover on our equipment, we'll know about it."

"Nonetheless, after what I saw today, I'm assuming these people know everything about S2. Let's not get cocky. We escaped by the grace of God. We were never more than seconds ahead of them, and that worries me."

"Do you think they're military?" Kleewein asked.

"We can't be sure that the military delegation with us right now isn't part of it. Consider how easy it would be to find the location of The Lair by having us take them to it."

"Pritchett isn't one of them," Mark said.

"You don't know that," Hartmire told him. "We'll blindfold them for the drive over tonight. Once inside, we can't let them use the equipment unless they're supervised."

Mark cracked his knuckles. "We've got to get over there. I'm dying out here. My whole organization is in limbo and I'm stuck in east San Jose." He looked at the darkening sky.

The Lair looked smaller than Mark remembered. He and Kleewein arrived with Hartmire an hour before Lauer brought the DoD contingent. The consultants already in place eagerly showed them to every working terminal, updated them on progress, and followed orders to continue gathering status from remote sites.

Mark donned a headset and sat at a terminal. He logged onto an S3D account, called up an email list of core S2 managers around the world, and drafted a note. All were briefed on this scenario. Any note arriving from S3D meant trouble. It also meant secrecy. Mark typed sparingly, just relaying the facts.

> This is Mark Solvang on S3D. You know what that means. We are safely at The Lair, getting up to speed, awaiting the arrival of our DoD client contacts. The Keep is occupied by hostile forces, the identity of whom is still unknown. They are dressed as Hartmire guards. All true Hartmire guards have evacuated The Keep to protect The Lair. We believe that consultants at The Keep are not in danger. Keep your work teams progressing as normal. Do not alert anybody to your knowledge of the situation. Reply to this note to acknowledge secure receipt. Await further instruction. Update us quickly with any pertinent information.

The note arrived at its destinations within ten seconds. It appeared in management email readers with a subject line that read "S3D Communications Initiated" from an unknown sender. When trying to read the note, each manager would be prompted for a password that only managers were supposed to know.

The Lair would track replies. Managers who did not reply would be considered a security risk.

Pritchett and the DoD contingent arrived around 12:30 AM.

Elwell and guards led the blindfolded group of men to a windowless conference room near the brain trust terminal area. The room was set up like the conference room at The Keep, but smaller. Elwell allowed the DoD contingent to remove its blindfolds. Hartmire guards stood watch in the room.

"Mark, The DoD is here."

"We'll meet with them now. I'd like you there, Jules. Security has become a major part of our decision-making process."

Mark and Kleewein filed into their new conference room. There weren't enough chairs for everybody. Mark stood at the head of the table. "Gentlemen, we need to know what you know. Let's start with Albert Schwager."

"I know that Albert Schwager is chief information officer of the Defense Information Systems Agency," Pritchett said. "You saw as well as I did that he is somehow involved with what occurred less than twelve hours ago."

"What privileges does his title give him?" Kleewein asked.

"As CIO of DISA, he oversaw a huge part of our Y2K preparations. It's his job to maintain information systems that provide command, control, and communications, abbreviated C3."

"What does all of that mean?" Mark asked.

"It means there would be nobody better to oversee the meltdown of the U.S. military information systems. The breaking computers at the NMCC, the loss of satellite communications, the deterioration of global positioning systems, all of that is related to Schwager's job. It is now more important than ever that we get your consultants to military responsibilities. Our own men were shot dead in the conference room. I need access to phones immediately. I need to call the Pentagon and inform the President. We have a traitor on our hands and this changes everything."

"You can't call out of here," Hartmire said.

Pritchett stood. "You people listen to me," he yelled. "The U.S. military is under siege. We need to inform the President. This is national priority."

Hartmire stepped forward to the table. "You listen to me. Solvang people are dead. If not for the actions of my guards, we might all be dead. None of us can trust you."

"If you think for a moment that I could not have requested a far more capable force than the one we saw today, then you don't understand the U.S. military. This is not a military action. If the

U.S. military wanted Solvang Solutions stopped, there would be nothing left of The Keep but a crater. I am the only connection you've got to the U.S. military and we are in serious jeopardy around the world. Time is wasting and you're playing games with phone access."

Mark nodded. "You can make your calls with Hartmire present."

Pritchett breathed deeply. "We still need 6,000 consultants flown to strategic command centers. We can coordinate military supply planes to take them. Hawaii is in serious need."

"We'll try our best."

"Get me a phone and let's get moving."

Mark nodded. Hartmire slid the satellite phone down the table. Pritchett dialed. He shot pieces of information to S2 consultants who ran off to act on it.

A consultant stuck his head into the conference room. "We've established a real-time link with the U.S. Strategic Command Center. There's something you should see."

Mark, Kleewein, and Pritchett followed the consultant to his terminal. Hartmire kept the remaining DoD contingent locked in the conference room.

The consultant showed Mark a paragraph in the middle of a screen of text reports. "Guam reports a fleet of ships moving southeast from the Yellow Sea to the Philippine Sea. Satellite footage."

"Where's the footage?" Pritchett demanded.

"It should be coming onto our satellite screens any minute now."

Mark and Pritchett trotted to the satellite screens.

"The report didn't say how many ships, did it?" Pritchett asked Mark.

"No. It just said a fleet."

"A fleet. I don't like the sound of that."

The satellite screens filled from the top down with grainy photos. Pritchett recognized the gray hulls and piles of older equipment on deck. The forward ship sported an eight-bay launch rack on a huge pivot. Eight missiles sat ready to fire from the Thomson Crotale octuple launcher, as identifiable to military experts as the Statue of Liberty is to New York tourists. The forward ship was a Chinese Luhu class destroyer. Behind it, disappearing into the watery horizon, came Luda destroyers and Jiangwei frigates.

The saliva drained from Pritchett's mouth. Nothing he'd seen in the past day had affected him as forcefully as viewing the photos. A realization snapped into his mind.

The U.S. maintains the world's largest advanced military. China maintains the largest old-world military. The Chinese still utilize weapons left over from World War II. They rely largely on analog radar processing. They operate weapons that would not break from a computer glitch.

"My God," Pritchett gasped. His eyes fused to the hull of the Luhu destroyer. "China is invading."

8

SILVER BULLET,
WRONG GUN

JANUARY 9, 2000

Grandpa Solvang sat at the table. He watched the lantern wick flare and subside. Jeremiah and Alyssa banged around downstairs while Grandma bustled about upstairs. For a split second, he thought of younger days. Jeremiah could have been Mark. The solitude of the evening fit. It was dark in the home. Firelight jogs the memory.

He hoped his son knew what he was doing. This was a hell of a time to be away from the family. Margaret's death left the kids devastated. Being left behind by one parent is bad enough. Being left behind by two can ruin a life. He hoped Mark wouldn't leave them behind after Y2K. It wasn't that Y2K would kill any of them, but it sure had managed to keep them apart.

"What are you thinking about?" Grandma asked suddenly. He hadn't heard her coming.

"Our family, mostly. I heard the kids below and you above and it reminded me of raising Mark."

She sat at the side of the table, holding his rough-knuckled hands. "These are lonely times, aren't they?"

He nodded. They both stared at the lantern flickering with the slightest bit of hiss. Their faces emerged from the darkness to reflect in the window, two artistic renditions of themselves. No lights outside confused the images. Only their faces, made soft and ruddy by the firelight, filled the window glass.

"It's been more than a week since the children spoke with Mark," she said. "Jeremiah has tried calling in the past few days. No return calls. No sign of his Dad."

"The kids worry about him. Heck, I worry about him. He's too focused on this work. It's going to kill him. He might save the country, but he's sacrificing his family to do it."

"Let's try calling right now." She called the children upstairs. Grandpa picked up the satellite phone.

He dialed the direct line to Mark's headset exchange. The line rang far too long. Eventually, a strange voice answered. "Yes, I'm trying to reach Mark. Is he there?"

"Mark who?" the voice asked.

"Mark Solvang, the president of the company. Who is this?"

"Just a moment, please."

He looked at Grandma. "They've got something new going on with their phone system. That clown didn't even know who Mark was." Grandma shook her head.

Another voice came on the line. "Sir, where are you calling from?"

"Why does that matter?"

"We've had some security troubles here and we want check the origination of this call. It's for everybody's good."

For a reason he couldn't say, Grandpa felt chills on the back of his neck. His eyes met Grandma's.

"What's wrong?" she whispered across the table. "Are they all right?"

"Sir, are you still there?"

"Yes, I'm here. I would like to speak to Mark first. I'll tell him where I'm calling from."

"He's away for the moment. They're testing in the lower terminal room. I'll take a message for him if you'd like."

"Who is this?"

"This is Sal Platt. I'm a Solvang consultant."

"I'll call back later." He disconnected quickly.

"What happened?" Grandma asked.

"Mark wasn't there."

"But why are you so upset?"

"Because he's always there. Even if Mark doesn't answer, somebody else I know does. It's Kleewein or Susan. I've never heard any of tonight's voices before."

Grandpa knew about the secret alternate site, though he wasn't allowed to know where it was. He didn't have a phone number, either. But Mark had explained that S2 was worried about military intervention when Y2K brought everything grinding to a halt. Could that have happened?

Grandma bit into her knuckle, tears welling in her eyes. "They might be dead, for all we know." Jeremiah and Alyssa looked ashen.

"What's going on?" Jeremiah asked.

"Now hold on," Grandpa said, scooting around the table to his wife. "We're jumping the gun a bit here. There are hundreds of consultants working at that place. Everybody's busy, and they're probably moving from one room to the next just to keep on top of everything. The chances of a strange voice answering are good."

"No," Grandma said defiantly. "They all know Mark Solvang. The damned company is named Solvang Solutions for crying out loud! Something is wrong, Grandpa." Her tears were gone, but the worry was not. "I'm going to drive over there."

"No you're not. If things are fine, we'll know soon enough. If they're not, you going over there is only going to make it worse. Think of the children. Their Dad's been gone for a week. If something happens to you, the only thing they've got is me. And I snore!"

She managed a smile. "I'm going to boil some water for tea. Would you like some?"

"Yes I would. I'll be back before it's hot."

"Where are you going?"

"To get Mark's gun loaded and set by my bed. This is not the time to take chances. History favors a loaded gun over a prayer. Although it wouldn't hurt to have both."

"Oh no," Dan said. He stared at his computer monitor in the National Military Command Center.

At the top of his email list was a note from an unknown sender. The subject line read "S3D Communications Initiated" in bold type.

He clicked open the note. It prompted him for the password, which he entered. The note was from Mark. Dan read the summary and replied immediately to register his secure clearance.

His eyes darted around the NMCC. General Marquist stood with a group of officers near the first functional computers. He didn't know what was happening. Or did he?

Dan needed information. He wanted to type a note to Mark, but wasn't sure if he should risk it. Were the traitors around him at that moment, watching his every move, reading his notes on secret systems, loading bullets with his name on them?

Mercury and Atlantic teams worked over computers in all parts of the room, as did the S2 teams. But somebody had managed to sneak around them before to sabotage the computers. Somebody on the inside. That disturbing thought remained in Dan's mind.

If they could pull the plug on something as secure as the NMCC, how hard would it be to intercept email? "Forget the term 'secure system,'" he muttered to himself. "That definition has ended as we knew it."

But he couldn't work in the dark. He would take the risk.

He typed a note to Mark under his S3D secure login. His fingers moved so fast that the keyboard sounded like an old dot matrix printer in action.

> NMCC is almost finished. How's Pritchett? I'm worried about Pearl Harbor. Haven't heard back from Billy. Guam China photos indicate severe trouble on the way. Awaiting further instructions.

Mark typed a frantic note to Susan.

> Are you all right? What's the status at your location? Are there any people behaving strangely? All is fine here at The Lair. Reply ASAP.

She replied within two minutes.

> Mark, this place is a mess. The doors are locked tight. Men dressed as Hartmire guards are patrolling the hallways and have now started patrolling the terminal rooms. Work has all but stopped. People pretend to work when the guards come through, but I haven't seen any decent progress in hours. How can there be? Guards on the way. G2G, Susan.

G2G meant "got to go." Abbreviated that way it meant she had to go immediately.

Schwager stood above Susan. His dark hair was parted neatly on the left. Two deep creases cut down his cheeks to the corners of his mouth, like levers to control the operation of his jaw.

"Susan," he said in grave tones. "I need your help."

She began to sweat. The guards around Schwager looked inhuman, ugly, like monsters in uniform. She didn't reply. Schwager pulled a chair beside her.

"This facility controls the entire Solvang organization, right?"

"Yes."

"Good. We have been sent here to keep S2 focused on its civilian tasks. The President of the United States has declared this situation a national emergency."

Susan, of course, knew differently. She gathered her voice. "We are working on civilian tasks around the clock. Our main objective is national power, followed by telecommunications and—"

"Fine," Schwager interrupted, "but there are still far too many S2 resources being wasted on the military. Am I correct?"

"We have military teams, of course. That's why you are our biggest client."

"The President wants to redirect those resources from the military to civilian matters. Can you help coordinate that?"

There was only one answer to give him. "Yes, if that's what you need."

"These four men will assist you. I will communicate with them, they will communicate with you."

Four grim-faced men in plain clothes stepped forward from the guards.

Schwager glared down the ravines in his cheeks. "They will also watch your communications to make sure that everything is carried out precisely as instructed. Furthermore, I will need ten terminals freed up for more of my men. We need to communicate outside of this building. Can you take care of that?"

"Yes."

"Good. Welcome aboard, Ms. Levin."

Schwager turned and walked out with a group of guards. The four men in plain clothes pulled chairs around Susan. They donned headsets and tested the connections.

"Our first order of business is to free up these ten terminals directly in front of you," said one of the men.

Susan nodded. "Guys," she called to the consultants, all of whom had overheard Schwager's conversation and understood their manager's need to cooperate. "Please go to the free terminals at the back of the room and have Nikolaas Groen log you into S3D accounts."

The ten consultants walked to the back of the lower terminal room, escorted by two men in plain clothes. Ten clean-cut young men walked into the room and took their positions at the front terminals.

"Who are they?" Susan asked.

"Government workers."

"What are they going to do?"

"Communicate with the government and other interested parties. They will operate independently."

Susan watched the ten young men to see how much they knew about the Solvang systems. They would need accounts. Creating accounts required management authorization.

Each man opened a briefcase and began working immediately. All ten wore headsets. Susan watched them enter the management authorization panels, create accounts for themselves, create management IDs, and test the email connections in less than five minutes.

They knew what they were doing. They understood the Solvang system as well as any consultant, better than most. How they got passwords, Susan would never know.

Nikolaas Groen watched the ten consultants take their places at free terminals. The two men in plain clothes stood quietly nearby, watching the men get situated and resume their work.

Nikolaas was the lower terminal room team lead for power grid code conversion. His job was important enough that he had management authority. He had an S3D account. He read Mark's email. He knew what was happening.

One consultant signaled Nikolaas. "We need S3D accounts."

Nikolaas looked from one face to the next. They knew he couldn't create S3D accounts for them. S3D accounts were frozen, controllable only from The Lair as of 12:00:00 AM January 1. "Did you say you need S3D accounts?"

"Yes, right away." The consultant's eyes burned at Nikolaas. "We'll be working from back here now."

"I see. Is Susan working with the new fellows?"

"Yes, she is. They're from DISA."

"That's probably enough information," said one of the plain clothes men. "Just create new accounts for these men so they can get back to work."

"Absolutely," Nikolaas answered.

He returned to his terminal and immediately logged onto his S3D account. He typed a note to Mark, copying every S2 manager in the company.

> DISA workers are commanding Susan Levin and a full team of consultants. Men are patrolling the terminal rooms. Armed guards are standing nearby.

He sent the note. "Okay," he called to the ten consultants. "Your accounts are good to go."

He saw them log onto their standard S2 accounts. The men in plain clothes watched as the ten consultants brought up *Solvang2K* and resumed work as usual.

Mark's throat went dry as he read the note from Nikolaas Groen. Schwager had Susan. Mark closed his eyes. He hoped Schwager didn't know of any personal connection. As an S2 manager, she was mildly useful to Schwager. As Mark's lover, she was a much more powerful playing piece, second only to controlling Mark's children or Mark himself. That son of a bitch better not touch her, he thought.

He spun his chair around. "They're going to start issuing commands," he informed Kleewein and the consultants at The Lair, all of whom also saw the note. "Let's get the word out. This is going as we expected. Let's do what we planned to do all along."

That was to send a simple note to all S3D account holders from the collective user ID at The Lair. Mark drafted the note.

> The hostile forces have overtaken Susan Levin's work team at The Keep and will probably begin sending commands from The Keep. You are to respond back to The Keep as though you are carrying out the commands. However, from here forward, you are to follow only those

instructions coming to you from this ID. For the time being, maintain your assigned duties and your normal work schedule. We will keep you informed.

Mark turned from the screen. "I'm ready for your signatures." He, Kleewein, and Hartmire typed them in quickly.

To send a note from the collective user ID at The Lair, three digital signatures were required. With only one signature, notes never left the building. This precaution further protected against a hostile force overtaking The Lair and issuing commands.

The note zipped from The Lair into S3D secure readers across the world.

"Mark, I need my three men from the conference room to help run these terminals," Pritchett said. "One of them is a satellite control specialist. The others know military affairs."

Mark looked to a skeptical Hartmire. "We could use more people, Jules." They walked to the conference room.

Hartmire addressed the four military men. "None of you are allowed to communicate outside this building unmonitored. If you are caught doing so, you will be immediately returned to the conference room where you'll stay for the rest of this ordeal. Is that clear?" He assigned a Hartmire guard to each man.

There were plenty of free terminals for the DoD contingent. They proved a valuable asset in helping Pritchett coordinate the massive effort under way.

"The military does not have enough operable planes to make the move," Pritchett announced late in the day. "Too many pilots are missing, too many planes are simply not working. We have the cargo capacity to carry 6,000 people, but there are just too many sites."

"We've already requested assistance from our Boeing team in Seattle," Mark replied.

Pritchett raised his eyebrows. Before he had a chance to say anything, Kleewein's voice came over the headset. "It's going to be closer to 5,000 consultants. Right now, we've got 4,943 ready to leave their S2 locations. We tried for the requested 6,000 but couldn't pull it off. Too many people have already defected, others don't want to be far from home during times like these."

"5,000 will have to be enough," Pritchett said.

"Where do they go?" Mark asked.

Pritchett spoke into the headset. "I'll have to call the Secretary of Defense on the satellite phone to get base locations."

Mark, Kleewein, and Hartmire walked over to monitor Pritchett's remarks.

"Mr. Secretary, Pritchett. We have consultants ready. Civilian jets will be taking a portion of them, military will pick up the remainder. We need final base destinations for the consultants. We should be clear for Operation Pacific Plunge."

He hung up. "STRATCOM will have the final list to us within half an hour."

"STRATCOM?" Mark asked.

"The Strategic Command Center at Offut Air Force Base. It's in Nebraska."

"Strategic. Doesn't that usually refer to nuclear capabilities?" Mark asked in a low voice.

"Yes."

"And what is Operation Pacific Plunge?"

Pritchett licked his lips. "Pacific Plunge is a backup plan only. It was conceived by STRATCOM and the specifics were put in place by the Joint Coordination Center in Fort Ritchie, Maryland. A team of your consultants will fly to Barksdale Air Force Base to help prepare it."

"But what is it?"

"As you know, missile guidance systems are severely handicapped or rendered useless by Y2K. Many of the military's modern planes are behaving erratically as well. Therefore, STRATCOM decided that the U.S. needs a low-tech defense against the Chinese threat. The B-52 bomber has been in flight since 1955. Its basic flight capabilities are not harmed by Y2K. Its global position systems, electronic countermeasures, and other advanced features are not functional, but its ability to deliver a payload is still intact."

Mark felt his throat tighten. "What payload might that be?"

"A B-53 bomb."

"What the hell is that?"

"The oldest nuclear weapon in the U.S. arsenal. It was developed in the 1950s to destroy underground targets. There is nothing at all sophisticated about the B-53. It's just a huge, ugly nuclear bomb. It's thirteen feet long and weighs almost 9,000 pounds. Precision destruction is not its game. Brute, kill everything force is its entire strength."

"How big an explosion are we talking about?" Kleewein asked. "One-hundred kilotons?"

Pritchett swallowed before answering. "Nine megatons."

"What?" Mark nearly yelled. "Nine megatons! Isn't that a little excessive? How big were the bombs on Hiroshima and Nagasaki?"

"Ten kilotons and twenty kilotons."

"And you want to drop nine megatons on a few boats?"

"Listen to me," Pritchett growled. His face and neck turned deep red. "Nobody knows their intentions. We can take no chances. We need a bomb that can simultaneously kill subs down deep and ships scattered wide. Because this is an encounter at sea, the risk to civilian life is nil. The B-53 will penetrate 1,000 feet below the ocean surface to a radius of three miles. It is a backup plan with teeth, and that's exactly what we need right now."

"Where do our consultants fit in?" Mark asked.

"Their only job is to help our airmen reconfigure the communications onboard the plane. Milsat coverage in the Pacific is spotty. With a payload as devastating as this, we want absolutely clear communications. No mistakes. We're not going to drop this bomb unless it becomes the only option. Therefore, the B-52 needs to be able to communicate with the Solvang satellite network."

"You don't need a dedicated team of consultants for that."

"We're taking no chances."

"In other words," Kleewein pointed out, "you want our people there to reprogram cruise missile warheads and other nuclear weapons."

"Yes, we want your people on hand for every possible contingency." He looked from face to face. "The military is not a horde of bloodthirsty warmongers. We would like nothing more than several peaceful years with which to fix these computer problems. But we don't have that luxury. Believe me when I tell you that the B-53 is a backup plan."

"What other plans are in the works?" Mark asked.

"We're moving additional marines from San Diego to Hawaii in case the Chinese have an amphibious landing in mind. We want plenty of our own soldiers waiting on the island."

JANUARY 12, 2000

"How are things coming over here?" Commander Brosseau asked. He stood inside the *Olympia,* looking at the repairs.

Morey shook his head. "I think my ship is in worse shape than she was before these teams came aboard."

Civilians crawled among the *Olympia's* wires and holes, holding tools in their teeth, carrying crates full of circuit boards and wires and testing equipment.

"That's hard to believe."

"How about the *Helena?*"

"She's ready to be repaired, but she has to wait her turn." He looked away. "After all, I'm not in the top priority battle group."

Billy Stamp approached. "Have you had a chance to test any of the installations yet?" he asked them.

"Test, are you kidding me?" Morey asked in a stern voice. "My boat has looked like Swiss cheese for a week. Your people keep running around but nothing's happening."

"It isn't easy," Billy replied in an equally stern voice. "It's better to spend all this time on your sub and get it right than it is to spend all this time for nothing. I'm sure you would agree."

"Yes, but this is a damned slow process."

"I know. And the military isn't the worst of it. You should see the mainland."

"We've heard," Morey said. "As far as I'm concerned, the military is the worst of it. We matter the most."

Billy stood his ground. "You have no idea. People have sacked grocery stores for food. Nobody cares about money. People are dying. I don't know if that matters to you or not."

"Listen," Morey said, stepping closer to Billy. "*You* have no idea. We're prowling these waters every day and every night listening for the enemy."

Brosseau nodded. "He's right about that. This is a big problem, Mr. Stamp. I don't know if you can move any faster, but it would certainly be in the nation's interest."

"I know we have enemies," Billy said. "I know that the end of the cold war created more tension than it erased. You'll both be pleased to hear that we have 1,100 additional consultants on the way."

"What?" Brosseau said, surprised. "From where?"

"From all over the country. They'll be here in the morning."

The color ran from Morey's face.

"You all right?" Brosseau asked.

Morey ignored him. He locked onto Billy's eyes. "Does this have anything to do with the briefing tomorrow?"

"I'm sure it does."

Morey turned to Brosseau. "There's a reason that 1,100 more of these eggheads are on the way. It can't be good."

"Do you know?" Brosseau asked Billy.

"You'll find out everything at the briefing."

Brosseau watched him talk quickly with the team lead, a sweaty man in coveralls behind an electronics panel. The blond-haired Stamp stepped around loose equipment on his way back to the ladder. Morey moved in his way.

"What's this all about?" he demanded.

"I don't know anything more than you do. Just be glad we have 1,100 people on the way to help."

"Has there been some kind of threat? Because if there has, I want my boat back together pronto!"

Billy whirled around to face Morey. "It's exactly that kind of idiotic response that will get people killed! You do your part. Go to the briefing. I'm doing my part. We're on the same side, Commander."

JANUARY 16, 2000

Susan saw the red dot on her menu bar, indicating to those in the know that new mail had arrived over the secure account. Clicking on the dot would bring a password prompt that read "Please enter password to configure mail reader."

The false prompt command was to keep from giving away the true use of the dot to any non-manager who happened by a manager's computer and clicked on the dot out of curiosity. The person wouldn't know the password and would click cancel without ever realizing that a separate basket of notes waited between the bits and bytes.

The plain clothes men sat stiffly behind Susan at all times, listening to their headsets, speaking quietly into the microphones, occasionally giving her an instruction. She could not view the mail in her S3D account without them seeing.

The ten men at terminals in front of her worked incessantly. They wore headsets and typed a constant stream of information into the terminals. At first, Susan thought the typing was a deluge of email to other teams—if there were other teams—and maybe other S2 sites. For all Susan knew, these men occupied every part of Solvang Solutions except The Lair. By now, they might even occupy that.

Unknown to the men in plain clothes or the guards patrolling the terminal rooms, most of The Keep's consultants were now parsing military code sent to them by the more than 5,000 S2 workers on bases. The Keep still hosted the most advanced code parsing facility and the largest database of problems and solutions that *Solvang2K* could search as it processed batches of code.

The guards in The Keep did not understand Y2K work well enough to know the difference between a computer screen full of civilian work and a screen full of military work. The S2 consultants realized that fact early on, and exploited it to make short work of as much military code as possible. When a plain clothes man would come by, or one of their terminal operators, the consultants would quickly switch to a screen of civilian work without so much as blinking an eye. The terminal rooms remained quietly focused on work, and nobody could tell what work was being done or when.

Susan watched the ten men working in front of her. The instructions given her were simple enough that she could complete the tasks while keeping a watchful eye on the screens facing her between the shoulders of the ten men. They understood computers. They knew Unix, they knew networking, they knew code, they knew everything. They would have passed a Solvang interview with flying colors.

But they weren't the only ones in The Keep who understood computers. Susan watched their screens carefully. She saw a familiar interface appear in front of them. They consulted files from their briefcases and spoke to each other quietly across the headsets. Susan recognized a coordinated matrix process occurring in front of her.

She needed to warn all of S3D and The Lair. She looked over her shoulder and nodded to the plain clothes men.

"Is everything all right?" one asked her.

"Yes, I'm fine. I just need to stretch a bit."

"Okay, let's take a walk."

They stood and walked around the terminal room. Susan caught

Nikolaas Groen's eye. She tried to mouth the word "hack," but it can't be recognized without sound. It just looks like a mouth opening and closing. Nikolaas did not understand.

Back at her terminal, Susan watched the ten men switching from their screens to their briefcase reports. She didn't understand what they were doing, but it couldn't have been good. She was convinced that they could inflict serious damage on Solvang's computers.

Susan brought a note form on her screen and quickly hid it behind other material. She worked in the foreground. The men said nothing to her.

In the middle of a note to a power grid work team, she typed "They are hacking S3D." She highlighted the text and cut it to memory with a split second keyboard command. The men still said nothing. She completed the note to the work team.

She stacked several completed notes around her screen. As she toggled between them, acting as if she were proofreading them, she brought the S3D blank note to the foreground, pasted the sentence "They are hacking S3D," and sent it. It disappeared. The men said nothing to her.

The S3D password prompt appeared onscreen. "What's that for?" one of the men asked.

"It's a password prompt to send the notes."

"I haven't seen that before."

"I've batched ten messages together. It's an internal security measure."

"For what?"

"Batches of notes tie up the network, so managers are required to identify themselves. S2 doesn't want ordinary workers sending batches of notes."

The man nodded. Susan smiled inside. The terminal men in front of her might have been computer experts, but the ones beside her were not. Anybody who spent time with computers knew that batched email doesn't strain a network. If it did, a company would improve its network. A password prompt for batched email made no sense at all.

Thank God for newbies, Susan thought. She entered the combination of letters and numbers. Hidden among ten normal emails, her S3D note shot across wires to every manager in The Keep. In her mind, she saw Mark reading the note at The Lair.

Kleewein would see it. Then these men would see the kind of company they were dealing with.

JANUARY 12, 2000

Mark dialed the number to his home. The phone rang five times before Alyssa answered. "Hello?"

"Alyssa, guess who?"

"Dad!"

"I'm glad you still remember me."

"When are you coming home to see us?"

"Soon, I hope. We're working harder than ever."

"Do you like it there?"

"Not especially. It's dark with a lot of computers and grouchy people. How about you? Do you like it there?"

"Actually, I do. Grandma and Grandpa light candles and lanterns every night. We don't have to go to school, either. There's one thing I don't like here."

"What's that?"

"Our toilets don't work. We have to go to the bathroom in a hole in our backyard. Jeremiah is worried that his friends from school are going to see him."

Mark laughed. "I don't think they'll see him. Why don't you let me talk to him?"

Jeremiah got on the line and reaffirmed that he didn't enjoy using the "outhole," as Grandpa had come to call it. He said everything was fine, then put Grandpa on the line.

"How's the world coming, son?"

"Not so good, I'm afraid."

"What's the latest?"

"We're not at The Keep anymore, Dad. The Keep was attacked and we needed to evacuate. We're working from our alternate site."

"Is everybody okay?"

"Everybody that you know. Hundreds of our consultants are still at The Keep, trying to continue working. Susan is there."

"Who attacked you?"

"We don't know. There's a lot of speculation."

"So what can you do now? Still try to get the power up, I assume."

Mark paused, not sure whether to tell his father about the real situation. Years of trust and a desire to share his strain with somebody he loved made the decision for him.

"Actually, Dad, we've changed our direction. We're working heavily on military projects. The military is broken. People are worried about an invasion."

"Invasion? From where?"

"China."

"Oh boy," Grandpa said regretfully. "I suppose all their muscle flexing with Taiwan boosted their confidence."

"I hadn't thought about Taiwan."

"It's the first thing that came to my mind. The Chinese launched missiles into the Taiwan Straight and sailed around the island. Beijing thinks Taiwan is getting too independent. Don't you remember any of this?"

"A little. I doubt it has much to do with them attacking us. This seems to be another matter altogether."

"Keep it in mind," Grandpa said. "It's all in history. The tiniest things can start wars. The United States sailed to Taiwan with all that trouble going on. It was a few years ago, but I'm sure the Chinese haven't forgotten. They told us to stay away, to respect their sovereignty, but we sailed into town anyway."

"Dad, I don't see how a minor dispute over an island would turn into a full scale invasion."

"What do you mean full scale invasion? They don't have a full enough scale to invade. They don't even have aircraft carriers. How could they mount a full scale invasion?"

"How do you know so much about China?"

"I read everything. When you're old and you have enough money to do what you want, you sail around the world on pleasure cruises and read the news and history books. You should try it sometime."

"Well, you happen to be right about China. This doesn't look like the country going to war."

"Of course not. Their military is made up of a bunch of little business men. You probably didn't know that, either. One of them probably broke from the pack to prove himself. I'm sure this is not going to be a major problem for the U.S. We're the strongest military on the planet."

"When we're working."

"Is it that bad?"

"It's that bad. Planes don't fly, subs can't hear, missiles won't find their targets."

Grandpa exhaled long and low. "We shouldn't have scrapped all that fine World War II equipment. No computer glitches would have broken that stuff. Send a few B-29s and the battleship *Missouri* into the Pacific. I'm sure Mighty Mo could teach those Chinese a few things about U.S. military power. She certainly taught the Japanese."

"Funny you should mention teaching the Japanese. Remember the way we really taught them?"

"Hiroshima and Nagasaki, I suppose."

"Like you always say, Dad, the lessons are in history."

Grandpa breathed into the receiver. His voice came quieter than before. "Are we already resorting to that? How bad could this renegade group of Chinese be? For Christ's sake, Mark, what can a few boats do to us?"

"It's worse than a few boats, Dad. It may not be what you consider a full scale invasion. It's not D-Day. But it's pretty damned scary when we can't even fire a missile in response. The U.S. does not mess around with this kind of threat. I've got to get back to work."

"Mark, do your best. I know you're ready for all of this. Our prayers are with you, son."

"Thanks, Dad. We'll need them."

January 16, 2000

"They're stupid to try hacking their way in," Kleewein said. "It would be much faster to threaten one of our managers into giving them access."

"That's what I figured," Mark said. "The question is, how long will they wait to arrive at that conclusion?"

"Not long, and when they figure it out, they won't announce it. They'll quietly watch everything we're doing."

"We might know anyway. The manager could send a note when they're not looking. If they try sending a note on the manager's account, they'll press the wrong button."

The S3D interface was purposely designed to confuse uneducated users. The button boldly labeled "Send" would paste a line of text at the top of the note listing the sender's node and user ID with a warning that the note was sent improperly. The correct way to send notes was to press a red area on the menu bar. Thus, if anybody forced their way onto an S3D enabled terminal and pressed the "Send" button, they would warn every recipient that an unauthorized user sat at the node identified in the note.

"We hope," Kleewein said. "There's no guarantee on any of this. They might figure it out, or force a manager at gunpoint to explain how it all works. We need to assume that every communication is being monitored. So far, they haven't sent anything out of The Keep. We're monitoring every email gateway."

"What are they up to?" Mark asked anybody.

JANUARY 18, 2000

"If there is another communication network, then get on it and see what they're doing!" Schwager yelled.

Schwager's people had found Sal Platt the old fashioned way. Platt was a middle aged work horse. He never rose in S2's ranks because the competition was too fierce. In a company full of men like Van Lan and Stamp, Platt didn't stand a chance. He had always been reliable with the work given to him, but nothing more than that. He had little initiative and no trace of the exemplary mind for computer solutions that was required to shine at S2. He was not a happy man. His career was not satisfying to him.

When the DoD began working with S2, Schwager suspected the worst. As the company progressed farther and faster than he or Pritchett expected, Schwager began to worry that S2 might actually have the U.S. battle-ready by 2000. He needed an inside connection, but could not risk his identity nor risk alerting Solvang or the DoD to his search. Years of preparation left him with an extensive network of military contacts, but S2 was a new player on the scene. It instituted strict security clearance to become a defense contractor. A representative from the DoD could not simply approach S2 consultants and ask if any were interested in helping to subvert military preparations.

Instead, a fictional defense contractor sent a series of mailings to S2 workers at The Keep. They began with a solicitation for Y2K work on the side, emphasizing current career disappointment.

The first mailer read: "Is your Y2K employer underestimating your skills? Call now for a company that will appreciate your crucial abilities and finally provide the compensation you deserve."

Only a handful of S2 consultants replied, as Schwager expected. The Solvang organization was well compensated and made a point of hiring outstanding candidates. S2 consultants, as a whole, were satisfied employees. But he knew that even the thinnest of employment screening cracks admits an occasional loose cannon.

The next mailer to the handful of respondents was a glossy packet of material about the fictional company. It showed a huge headquarters in Boston, a top secret basement project, and outlined a compensation plan three times larger than S2's. The mailer specified that employees would work in a nontraditional, secure environment that would require unconventional work hours and time away from family. That mailer narrowed the list of interested respondents down to nine.

The last nine were interviewed in person. Schwager came to Silicon Valley with a team of interviewers. He and a team of psychologists watched through one-way glass at a customer focus center rented in Sunnyvale. Platt and a man named Clark Mills were the only two selected.

With the choices narrowed to two, Schwager could reveal the entire plan with little risk. If one or both men balked or showed signs of shock, they would simply disappear. There would be no chance of them alerting S2 or the DoD of what they now knew.

Mills was shocked. He said he would never participate in such a plan and felt mislead by the entire process beginning with the first mailer. Mills went home that night, tried to make a phone call, discovered a dead line, and was never heard from again.

Platt listened carefully. He asked questions about his compensation, was assured by stern faces that he would be wealthy from his participation, and agreed to assist. He would never need to work again. Nor, if everything worked properly, would anybody be hurt. No participants would need to suffer from guilt as they enjoyed a lifetime of wealth.

Thus, Sal Platt began sending nightly reports to the east coast from his home email account. He became the S2 consultant who tricked the Hartmire guard into opening the rear door to The Keep. Now that The Keep was occupied and the plan was officially in full swing, he became the consultant who helped with all matters related to the inner workings of S2.

Platt is how Schwager and his team found out about a secret email network called S3D. Then he told them about The Lair. Then he said that military work could still be taking place throughout The Keep.

Schwager paced the executive briefing center. The body of the military strategist had long since been removed. The ravines in Schwager's face deepened and lengthened in the diesel half-light. None of this was going as planned.

As if to complicate things even more, Mr. Chau had arrived with his men, calm as ever. Schwager hated the self-assured little Chinese bastard. He resented needing to work with him.

"We can't get on S3D," the consultant said. He was one of the ten men who worked in front of Susan. "The only way to get on it is through an authorized account."

"Yes, but there must be authorized accounts in this building. It's their headquarters!"

Mr. Chau, the quiet figure near the corner of the table, spoke in his melodic Chinese accent. "The simple solution is to find somebody with access to this alternate communication channel and invite them to show us how it works."

"Every manager in this building has access to S3D," Sal Platt said. "You can have your pick."

"Good. We need to find Mark Solvang and this alternate site. Pritchett is with them and they still have communications with this place and every other S2 site.

"Why the hell haven't we heard from Dubrow?" asked a thin man in military uniform.

"Probably because they have him locked up over there," Schwager said. "After seeing me change sides in this room, they won't take any chances. Even if Dubrow is a captain, they won't let him look out a window or make a single call. They won't let him use a terminal without surveillance. I'm sure it's the same with Pritchett."

"This company is unusual," another military uniform said. "And big. I'm astounded at the number of workers they have."

Schwager closed his fists. "There are thousands of them crawling around the fleet at Pearl Harbor. Those Chinese ships are in for a hell of a surprise if the U.S. fleet is operational before we even have a chance to scare them. A hell of a surprise."

Mr. Chau spoke again. "I think the surprise will be all theirs. Yes, the work crews in Hawaii are big. But their progress is little. You read the reports."

"I know this company, Chau. If you're not afraid of a firm that has the prescience to establish an alternate control site and a secure communications channel and a private police force that ran circles around us, then you're not paying attention."

"I am paying attention, Mr. Schwager. You have been in the American professional world too long. Think like primitives thought. If you want somebody in your hand, then you grasp what is important to them."

"That's what we're doing. Hawaii, remember?"

Mr. Chau shook his head. "That is not the immediate concern. You want the founder of this company here under your control. That was the plan."

"Yes, and he got away."

"Then take something important to him. He will come back." He let his narrow eyes rest on Schwager. There was no hint of emotion. "He lives in this town. He must have family. The addresses are on the secretary's desk. Take the family members and bring them here. Tell this Solvang to come in person or you will kill his family. Very old trick. Very simple."

JANUARY 13, 2000

Pearl Harbor became an anthill. Just over 1,100 S2 consultants landed in a steady stream of commercial and military jets from across the United States. Most carried between twenty and thirty consultants along with additional testing equipment. Engineers from leading digital signal processing companies joined the frenzy.

When the marines arrived from San Diego, the whole island burst with people. Vehicles full of crew cut men zoomed from building to building. Old helicopters buzzed overhead while old planes took off and landed. C-130s and C-5s brought additional equipment from the mainland.

The briefing was about to begin. Billy Stamp and S2 team leads, Mercury managers, and Atlantic engineers all packed into the briefing room with ship captains and junior officers. Billy saw Brosseau and Morey near the middle of the room. Neither looked pleased.

Admiral Robek and Rear Admiral Macey entered the front of the room. Robek wasted no time with charts. He stood before the quiet gathering, hands clasped behind his back.

"Ladies and gentlemen, we are modifying our plans. Further photos from Guam indicate that the Chinese fleet is considerably larger than we thought, and might include troop transports suitable to an amphibious landing. Hence, we welcome the Marines to Hawaii."

A murmur washed across the room. Robek looked sternly forward until it subsided.

"We need to address this threat immediately. The President of the United States, along with his cabinet members, and the Joint Chiefs, have tried repeatedly to reach Chinese officials. With communications down across the world, they have been unsuccessful. The United States is left, therefore, with no choice but to treat this as an invasion. There has been no declaration of war, but for all practical purposes that's what we're planning."

He took a few steps to let his words sink in. The silence in the room hung like a pendulum, ready to swing in the other direction from the tension.

"We cannot prepare the *George Washington's* airwing in time. Therefore, we will not be sending the carrier to meet the Chinese. We do not currently have any fully operable ships. The ships farthest along in their repairs are those from the *GW* battle group: a cruiser, three destroyers, and a submarine. The cruiser is the *Chosin*. The destroyers are the *Ingersoll,* the *John Young,* and the *Harry Hill.* The submarine is the *Olympia.* Special civilian work teams have been assigned to each of the ships, lead by S2 manager William Stamp. The work teams will not have time to fully test repairs in port. They will accompany the battle group to sea and continue repairs and testing while en route. The remaining work teams will remain in port to repair the initial battle groups. The work teams are on rotating eight-hour schedules to keep the repairs continuing twenty-four hours a day."

He faced the room. "Following this briefing, each of you is to return to your ship and help with the repairs in every way possible. Skippers in the *GW* battle group, you will be receiving battle orders within the hour."

JANUARY 14, 2000

The S2 team lead for Operation Pacific Plunge called The Lair. It was late at Barksdale Air Force Base, where the S2 team toiled in Louisiana's humidity. "Mark, things are going slower than expected. We've rigged two B-52s with communications that use the Solvang satellite network."

"Why two planes?" Mark asked. Kleewein and Pritchett joined him at the conference room speakerphone. "Are they hooking up two of the bombs?"

"Looks that way. Each B-52 can carry two of these B-53 bombs. I guess they want backups to the backup plan."

"That's correct," Pritchett said.

"So we've got four nukes ready to fly out of Barksdale?" Mark asked.

"Not ready to go yet. The slowdown comes from the weapons delivery subsystem. B-53 bombs weigh almost 9,000 pounds. It's not like a couple of airmen can climb into the bomb bay and push them out the door. Dropping them properly requires the weapons delivery systems. The electronic and hydraulic weapons delivery systems don't work. The bomb bay doors don't open and the bomb clips don't move right."

"How hard can it be to rig up some sort of hydraulic arm to tip a tin can out the door?" Kleewein asked.

"Harder than you think. The weapons delivery system needs to open the bay doors, slide the bomb clips into place, then release the B-53 and activate its timers at the same instant. It's a lot to have happen without a single error."

"Will it work?"

"It's got to," Pritchett blurted. "The progress in Pearl Harbor is pathetically slow."

"Keep at it," Mark said to the team lead. He pushed the speakerphone button, then sat back to think. He pulled at his stubbly chin. "Something is wrong with this whole situation. Why would a Navy as primitive as China's choose to fight the United States?"

"Because they know we can't fight back right now."

"But nukes have been around since World War II. So have planes. Surely it crossed their minds that the most potent weapon in our arsenal would work without computers."

"Maybe the Chinese want something. Maybe they're trying to make a point. Maybe they're bluffing. We don't know and can't enjoy the luxury of speculating. They are a threat. The United States kills threats."

"But maybe they aren't the real threat. Where the hell does Schwager fit into all this? If they wanted to neutralize the military, they would simply destroy The Keep. They haven't. We're missing something."

JANUARY 15, 2000

Billy Stamp stood impatiently in Pearl Harbor's main Y2K terminal room, converted overnight from its normal duties as a sea traffic command center.

"This confirms what we found on land," Carl Albright said. He held a printout of a *Solvang2K* work screen. "The onboard computers turn up the same results. It's derivative code."

"Yes, I know. The subroutines are set up to be deactivated by a software switch. This is the same stuff we've been looking at for weeks."

"Right. It's positively incriminating. Somebody has tweaked this code."

"But to do what?"

"To get input from a masterfile. It's a perfect setup for a silver bullet." He referred to the industry term for a software solution that would magically fix Y2K. The silver bullet was a myth perpetuated by corporate managers in denial of Y2K's harsh realities. Rather than fix their company problems, they waited for a silver bullet. It didn't exist. But software could be cleverly designed to look like it was fixed by a silver bullet.

"Where's the third file?"

"Right here." He handed a thick printout across the terminal desk to Billy. "This is the third layer for the command terminal at Pearl." He pulled another from his briefcase. "This one is from Hickham. They're identical and they both refer to yet another file."

"And the final file is where?"

"Nowhere."

"What do you mean?"

"Look closely at the code."

Billy looked. Each line needing dates or times referred to the fourth file, then provided a piece of data to use in case the fourth file was not present. The data to use instead was "01/01/00" in all cases.

"Forced Y2K shutdown," Billy said aloud.

Carl nodded. "Yes. This is ready for a silver bullet. Somebody has the silver bullet solution to this software."

"Unbelievable."

"Believe it. And let's take a wild ass guess as to who has the silver bullet."

"Unbelievable!" Pritchett screamed in the conference room. "Sabotage across the entire military."

"Mr. Pritchett," Billy resumed, "there is no other reason for so many software layers. They're so well disguised that *Solvang2K,* our Y2K repair software, could not automatically pull in the files from the servers."

A consultant handed printouts around the room. Mark flipped through several pages, instantly seeing the pointers to the fourth file. He circled a piece of code and slid the printout to Pritchett.

"We have the file, Billy," Mark said. "I'm going to show Mr. Pritchett what you've been explaining."

He turned to Pritchett. "The circled part is called contingency code. It tells the software to get input from another file. If the software can't find that file—which it can't—then the line of code is supposed to use the results of the contingency. In this case, all the contingencies are zero zero dates." He pointed to the "01/01/00" on the printout. "That should look familiar. It's what a lot of failed code produces in a Y2K environment."

"It's the same here," Dan Van Lan said on the speakerphone. He was looking at his own printout from the NMCC. "Anybody coding this deeply into the military could have simply fixed the time and date functions to be Y2K compliant. Instead, they coded an elaborate failure structure that is custom built for a silver bullet solution."

Pritchett slammed his fist onto the printout. "Then where the hell is that silver bullet?"

"Given the current state of affairs, my guess would be with Schwager," Mark said.

"Can't Solvang fix it?"

"Not anytime soon," Billy said. "We're encountering code that we don't even understand."

"Like what?" Kleewein asked.

"Ancient stuff like CS-1, CMS-2, JOVIAL, TACPOL, and NELIAC. The military developers are helping us navigate it, but it's slow going. *Solvang2K* doesn't understand any of it."

"Son of a bitch!" Pritchett yelled.

"Have you checked the ships yet?" Dan asked Billy.

"Not yet. We're going to check them immediately after this conference."

"Good plan," Mark said.

"We need the silver bullet," Pritchett thought aloud.

"The strange thing about all of this is that we don't," Billy said. Nobody responded. "I mean it. This code just controls basic communications between satellites and boats and bases. It doesn't have anything to do with launching missiles or guiding torpedoes. Those weapons still rely on their own subsystems, which aren't software dependent. Remember, it's all chips and wires inside a rocket. There's no hard drive, no screen, no processing taking place."

"So what are you saying?"

"I'm saying that whomever arranged this meltdown couldn't have a plan in place for fixing the fighting capabilities of our fleet. The communications capabilities, somewhat. But the attack capabilities, not at all."

"It's not a true silver bullet," Pritchett said.

"Nothing ever is," Kleewein told him.

"Then, to be frank," Pritchett said, "I don't know what to make of this. Somebody engineered programs in Hawaii to look like they were breaking from Y2K. They set those programs to be fixed by a silver bullet solution. But that solution will fix only the tiny piece of the military affected by the code. None of this adds up to anything."

"Not yet," Billy answered. "But we're not done looking."

JANUARY 17, 2000

Commander Morey Ferdelle leaned against the bulkhead in the forward section of the conn. The *Olympia* was expected to cruise open waters toward a known hostile fleet of enemy warships. Nothing Morey saw happening around him instilled confidence. S2 consultants sat with laptops in front of the sub's onboard computers. Most of the work taking place happened behind electronic panels where teams from Mercury, Atlantic, and now Texas Instruments, Analog Devices, and Lucent Technologies swapped wires and chips. They carried racks of testing equipment. Men in heavy glasses peered at readouts, then shook their heads in frustration.

Morey checked his watch. They had eleven days if the incoming Chinese maintained their current speed and bearing. If they changed course or slowed down, the U.S. battle group would have extra time. If they sped up, the preparations would be cut short. Morey took little comfort in the fact that the civilian work crews would be accompanying his sub on the operation. At this rate, that only meant more dead bodies in the water.

"Commander," a technician said. "It doesn't look as though the Mk 48 torpedoes will have use of their search routines. We can't get their guidewires to work, either."

"There's no way to fix them?"

"We don't see how. The best solution we can come up with is an extended guidewire on old Mk 44 torpedoes. It would allow the sub to manually steer the torpedoes directly into an enemy target."

"That's ridiculous. The Mk 44 is battery powered. It's slow and weak. Besides, the risk of detection and depth bombs at that range would kill us in no time. We might as well fight from the surface."

"We realize that it's less than perfect."

"Less than perfect? I don't think you understand. You don't tell somebody that they're jumping out of a plane with a parachute that won't open, then offer them a plain backpack with the explanation that you realize it's less than perfect. Yeah, it's less than perfect. In fact, it's downright unacceptable. Keep working on the Mk 48 torpedoes until they work. I'm not joking when I say that we might as well fire sight rockets from the surface."

"Commander," the technician said forcefully, "I'm telling you that there are no options. You don't have sight rockets available. You know that Tomahawks have no guidance. You can't brush off what I'm reporting and tell me to make it better. We're trying to make it better, but these are the realities."

Morey looked at the tech. His eyes were strong, but weary. It was clear that he'd spent many hours crawling with his men through electronic compartments and torpedo tubes. "Fine. How long can you make the guidewire on the Mk 44?"

"3,000 feet."

"Let's go with that. But keep working on the 48s."

JANUARY 18, 2000

Susan saw Schwager walk into the terminal room. He was with the same group of men that accompanied him last time, and a group of guards. Schwager looked directly at Susan and marched to her.

"You are a manager here," Schwager said.

"Yes, you know that. I'm already—"

One of the men in plain clothes pulled a pistol and jammed its cold barrel into the base of Susan's skull. Schwager leaned the jagged edges of his face in front of her eyes.

"We know about S3D. You will show us everything in your secure reader and all subsequent messages or you will die now. Choose."

"I'll show you the messages." With shaking hands, Susan moved the mouse pointer over the red dot in her main reader. She clicked, bringing up the password prompt. She entered the letters and numbers and watched her screen fill with a list of S3D email messages.

"I want every one of them printed out immediately," Schwager said. "Leave this screen open. You will no longer send anything from this terminal."

He waved at one of his terminal operators in front of Susan's workstation. "You need to watch this screen with Ms. Levin. She is not to send a single communication from here or anywhere else. If she does, signal these guards and she will be killed immediately. Do you understand?"

The operator nodded. The assigned guards drew their weapons to underscore Schwager's message.

"Who else has access to this system?" Schwager asked Susan.

"I'm not sure," she lied. "Just top managers, I think."

Schwager turned to one of the men in plain clothes. "Bring the printouts to us immediately. Keep me informed of new messages on the screen."

Susan looked at the list of S3D messages. A new one appeared at the top. Schwager nodded. "Print that one too."

Nikolaas Groen watched the scene at the front of the terminal room. He guessed that they knew about S3D. They must have forced Susan to show her reader.

"Gee," he said quietly to himself, "we never thought of that. You guys really have us now."

He logged into his S3D account and emailed a short message to everybody on the network except Susan.

> They have forced Susan at gunpoint to show her S3D mail reader. They are now monitoring it. DO NOT INCLUDE SUSAN IN REGULAR COMMUNICATIONS.

"We have our first email!" a consultant yelled into his headset. "They just sent a message to computers not on our network. It went somewhere overseas, I can't tell where."

"What's the message?"

"I'm retrieving it now."

Mark and Kleewein ran to the consultant's terminal. A download bar appeared at the bottom of the screen, then a terse note popped into a window. The consultant read it aloud.

> Must find escape party with Mark Solvang and U.S. military. Solvang has family in area. Will find family and bring to base.

"Shit!" Mark yelled. "Where's Hartmire?"

"Right here!" Hartmire yelled back, sprinting through the terminal room doors. "What's the problem?"

"Look," Mark said, pointing to the screen.

Hartmire eyed the screen. "When was this sent?" Hartmire asked.

"An hour ago."

Hartmire's eyes closed for a split second, then reopened. "Is your family still in town?"

"Yes," Mark said painfully. His face was already pasty with fear. "My two children are staying with my parents."

"Get one of the maps and mark exactly where the home is."

Mark ran off. Hartmire turned to his lieutenants.

"Lauer and Klepac, take two of the trucks full of guards and high tail it to the Solvang residence. I will have the people move to an alternate location and radio the location to you. Get the people out immediately. Drive to east San Jose again and wait until you're sure you weren't followed. Keep radio contact with us at all times."

Lauer and Klepac ran from the room, already barking orders to guards. Mark handed them the map. He ran back to the terminal room, chest heaving. "If anything happens to my family, I won't be able to continue."

"I understand. Your family has a satellite phone?"

"Yes."

"Good. Call them and explain that they are in danger. They should wait in the backyard of a different home on the street. You specify the home and tell me the address so I can tell Lauer and Klepac."

Mark dialed the phone. It rang for what seemed an eternity. It kept ringing. His face turned a darker gray. "They might already be gone."

JANUARY 18, 2000, 11:00 PM PST

Grandpa Solvang listened at the stairs. He didn't hear a thing. Finally, the kids had gone to sleep. He walked back to the table. "That's it," he told Grandma. "Nothing but peace and quiet."

She smiled. His cup of tea waited for him in front of his chair. She sipped hers. "All things considered, I could live like this a long time. Only thing missing is our son. If we could get him home for a few weeks of this kind of living..." She let her voice trail off.

"I know what you mean," Grandpa said. He sat with his tea. "It does make you wonder in a way."

"What?"

"Why they're all working so hard. Of course, I don't really wonder. I know that we need all the modern conveniences and zip zip, beep beep gadgets that make the world go 'round. But sitting here sipping tea with you makes me wonder what they're fighting for. I haven't paid bills in two weeks and I'm not planning to pay anytime soon. We haven't received a Social Security check and I couldn't care less whether it's there. The banks are closed and the phones are down. For the first time in our lives we're able to ask why we would need the money anyway!"

She laughed. "Mark is working ungodly hours so he can return the world to a state of chaos."

"You're right. Supposedly, this world we're sitting in here at the table is the chaos they were trying to avoid for ten years. I remember Mark's talks about credit cards failing, and banks going belly up, and cars, and phones, and so on. He described a maelstrom of a world. But I'm sitting in it, and I find it sort of relaxing. Sipping tea by lantern light doesn't put people on therapy couches. Talking into a cordless phone, beepers on our belts, listening to background noise from a television and video games, and seeing the glow of a home computer being used to access accounts at work? Now that can lead to a therapy couch."

"It sure can."

They talked about the good times. They finished their tea and their eyes grew tired.

"You still know how to show a girl a good time," Grandma said. She carried their mugs to the doormat. They'd sit there until she or Grandpa rinsed them out on the back lawn in the morning. He started toward the phone on the endtable in the living room, but stopped when Grandma called to him. He usually placed it beside his bed each night in case Mark needed to reach him.

"Look," she said. "The kids left all the toilet paper outside. I don't have my slippers on. Would you mind getting that?"

"No, I'll take care of it."

He walked outside, grabbed the paper, and returned to the kitchen. She locked the door behind him. They walked upstairs.

He never thought about the phone again.

He checked the .38 revolver in the nightstand drawer on his side of the bed. Fully loaded, ready to go. He twisted the lantern into darkness and they fell asleep.

Grandpa awoke. He heard banging downstairs. He listened a moment, hoping to hear the sounds of a child crying or playing. He heard a bang at the front door.

He swung his feet out of bed. His heart pounded into a running sprint from its quiet sleeping pace. He pulled his glasses onto his nose and squinted into the night. He could make out the shapes of furniture and doorways, but little else. He reached into the nightstand drawer for the .38.

"What are you doing?" Grandma asked.

"There's somebody at the front door."

The banging had stopped by the time he reached the stairs. He heard muffled sliding noises on the door frame and knew that somebody was breaking in.

"Maybe they just want food," he muttered to himself. He peeked his head around the bottom of the staircase. Men held flashlights at the door. They fumbled with the three deadbolts and solid redwood. No wonder they started banging. They'd probably been there for half an hour already.

While Grandpa looked, somebody yelled outside the door and it burst open with a crash. "The kids first!" a voice commanded. "Get the kids first!"

Grandpa's heart pumped so hard he could feel the blood tapping against his ankles and elbows and fingertips and eyeballs.

Get the kids first? These people hadn't come for food. He remembered the phone conversation with Mark, the invasion of The Keep, the hideout called The Lair. These were desperate times. Against his son, Grandpa knew that someone might need to resort to more desperate measures. And here they were.

He swung around the corner of the staircase and aimed the .38 while pulling the hammer with his thumb. The men had stepped onto the parquet entrance and stood silhouetted against the flashlight glow. He squeezed the trigger. The gunshot permeated the house in rolling cushions of sound.

"Fire!" yelled a voice. "Fire!"

Guns exploded from the front door, breaking mirrors and bookshelves. Bullets tore through the piano, past pictures on the wall into the kitchen where they bore holes through the microwave and refrigerator. Grandpa stepped back up onto the staircase. He tripped on the steps, knocking the glasses from his face. The gunfire continued past the bottom of the staircase, riddling the living room into a mess of dust and broken decorations.

Grandpa felt the stairs for his glasses. The gunfire stopped.

"Are they dead?" asked a Chinese voice.

Grandpa snaked his hand around the corner and squeezed off another shot. Framed by tense silence, the single boom of the .38 seemed louder than the chorus of gunfire from the hostiles. A man yelped and the gunfire resumed for another ten seconds, ripping the Solvang living room into piles of debris.

Grandpa felt the stairs. He picked up the glasses and pushed them onto his nose, now sweaty.

"Gramps?" Grandma whispered from the hallway behind him. He could tell she was crying. "Gramps? Are you there?"

"Yes."

"Where are the children?"

He couldn't answer. A man ran past the bottom of the staircase and fired upward into the darkness. The bullet zoomed past Grandpa's head into the ceiling above Grandma.

Grandpa fired the .38 at where the man had been an instant earlier. An interminable silence followed.

In the basement, Alyssa cried. That's all Grandpa heard from the children. Men started running across the parquet and he had to move around the corner of the stairs to shoot.

He fired two rounds into the moving shapes. Bodies fell to the floor. A shot rang out behind him where the single man ran moments before.

Grandpa turned to fire.

He felt something bore into his soft flesh and explode out his back. He was falling. His eyes saw darkness then bright lights.

He hit the ground, warmth spreading across his back. A storm of gunfire broke over his body. Most of it came from outside.

"The kids!" came an American voice from downstairs. "We have two kids!"

"Out the back! We're being attacked from the front lawn."

Grandpa craned his head to see through the spinning flashlights and running boots. He lifted his arm and fired the .38 into the running men. A body fell, knocking several others off their feet.

The man in the kitchen shined his flashlight across the bottom of the stairs. Members of his team fired out the door while others ran to the basement. His flashlight beam illuminated an old man on the floor in a pool of blood.

He walked to him.

The old man squinted into the light through cracked glasses. He moved a wrinkled hand to point a revolver, and before the man could react he heard the click of a firing hammer falling on nothing.

The old man's hand thumped to the floor, heavy with the weight of his empty gun. The man raised his own pistol and put a bullet through the old man's forehead.

The old man went instantly limp.

The attacker jumped over the body, down the stairs. He needed to join his team before they drove away. They had the kids. That's all they needed.

January 19, 2000, 12:15 AM PST

"They're retreating into the house!" Lauer yelled into his microphone. "Flank the house immediately!"

Klepac's group leapt over wooden fences to get into Grandpa Solvang's back yard. Men streamed from a basement door, firing as they came. Klepac's team crouched in the bushes. They couldn't get a clear shot. They needed to assume the hostiles had the family. "Get a light on them!"

Three flashlights penetrated the backyard. A group of men turned immediately toward the light and fired. Gunshot echoes rolled across the suburban neighborhood. Bullets sent bits of fence flying in all directions.

"Clear shot, fire!" Klepac commanded. His men watched. The hostiles continued running past the back line of bushes. They pushed two children with them. When the children cleared the line of bushes, the Hartmire guards opened fire on the remaining hostiles, killing every one.

"Hostiles out the backyard heading east!" Klepac yelled into his headset. "Drive one block over to intercept."

"Copy," Lauer said.

"Let's go!" Klepac called to his men. They rose from the fence and charged across the backyard. They stepped over the bodies through the bushes. Behind them, Klepac heard engines starting and a truck driving madly up the street to come around the next block.

The hostiles had disappeared. In the few seconds it took Klepac's men to make it across the backyard, the hostiles managed to slip between homes and wait. For what, Klepac couldn't say. But the disadvantages to his men were overwhelming.

The hostiles held two children and waited in darkness with guns pointed. Klepac's team was open season. They would need to peek around dark corners directly into gun barrels.

"To the street," he decided. They walked past the home in front of them to look both directions up the street. Lauer's truck came around the corner and revved to the driveway. "We'll go back to the bush line," Klepac told him. "You patrol over here for any signs. We'll pinch them in."

The truck rolled down the street. Klepac retreated to the bush line, not realizing that the hostiles had already moved one house up the road. They were far enough away to continue moving undetected. Klepac's men crouched in the bush line, scanning the night for any signs of movement, any sound of children. Nothing came. Klepac heard an engine on the street. "Any signs?" he asked Lauer over the headset.

"Nothing. We're turning around and coming back."

"What do you mean? Isn't that you on the street now?"

"We're down a block."

"Shit! It's their vehicle. They're making a go for it!"

Klepac's men sprinted from the bush line to the street. They saw the kidnappers pouring into the bed of a truck. The hostiles began firing, hitting two of Klepac's guards.

Klepac's team could not return fire. The risk of hitting a child was too great. The two men crumpled onto the asphalt while their comrades dove behind fences for cover. Lauer's truck roared up the street after the hostile vehicle. He gave chase into the Los Gatos night.

"We can't shoot," Lauer said into the microphone. "We can't see where they have the kids. At this speed with these bumps, we're bound to kill one of the children."

"Keep on them anyway," Klepac said between breaths. "I'm calling Hartmire to give him the update."

JANUARY 19, 2000, 12:30 AM PST

Hartmire's headset buzzed to life. He heard the crackling noise that preceded all communications from the field, then Klepac's voice. "Jules, this is Klepac."

"Go ahead."

"We're in the Solvang house now. Lauer is chasing the getaway vehicle, but cannot fire. We were too late. They captured the two children."

"The mother and father?"

"We have the mother. I'm afraid the father is dead."

Hartmire closed his eyes. At least the call came private to his headset. This is not the kind of news to have delivered in a conference room setting. "How'd he die?"

"He has a .38 revolver in his hand and dead bodies around him. He fought hard. The gun is empty. Looks like he took a bullet to the stomach, then was shot point blank in the head. He needed one more round. Those cowardly sons of bitches."

Hartmire didn't speak right away. Klepac waited. "That was Mark Solvang's father."

"Yes, I know."

"Have Lauer confirm that the children are taken to The Keep. No engagement, only reconnaissance."

"Only reconnaissance."

"Return to The Lair carefully, separate from Lauer."

"Got it."

Mark and Kleewein walked over. Pritchett and the DoD contingent followed closely behind. "What is it?" Mark asked.

"Let's go to the conference room," Hartmire said.

"Forget the conference room! What is it?"

Hartmire took a deep breath. "They beat us to the house. There was a fire fight. Mark, your father died defending his wife and your children."

"What?" Mark said, his face contorting. "That can't be right!"

"He fired every last round in his revolver. The home is littered with enemy bodies. He died a hero."

"My father is dead." Mark collapsed into a chair. "This can't be right. Are you sure, Jules?" Hartmire nodded. "This can't be right. He's probably just injured. Have them check him again. He's a fighter. He wouldn't die from a gunshot wound. Check again."

Hartmire put his hand on Mark's shoulder. Mark hit it away. "Don't touch me! Check again, I said!"

Hartmire spoke into the headset. "Klepac, this is Hartmire. Please double check Mr. Solvang."

Klepac knew what was happening. "He's dead, Jules."

Hartmire let the headset click out. "He's dead, Mark. He died defending your family."

"So everybody else is fine?" Kleewein asked.

"No. The two children were kidnapped. Only Mrs. Solvang is with our men."

"The children were kidnapped?" Mark screeched. He leapt from the chair at Hartmire. "You stupid idiots!"

Hartmire deflected the blows at his face, standing firm and waiting for the outburst to subside.

"I can't stand this!" Mark yelled. He jumped around, tearing at his clothing, pulling his hair. "What the hell was I thinking?" he screamed. "How stupid of me! My family should have been brought here the instant we arrived. How stupid of us all!"

Hartmire saw the DoD men turn away. Kleewein walked to Mark and touched his shoulder. "Get away from me!" Mark yelled. He hit Kleewein's hand away and pushed him back. He lunged at Kleewein, knocking him off his feet. "Everybody stay away from me! Every goddamned one of you idiots!"

He fell into his chair. He held his head between his knees, racked with sadness and pain. At last, he looked up. "Hartmire, I need those children and my mother brought here immediately. I'm going to win this fucking thing if it's the last gift I ever give my father."

A consultant answered the satellite phone on his headset. Hartmire overheard. "This is not a good time. I don't care what's going on, this is not a good—what? Oh hell. Just a moment."

The consultant approached the scene at the center of the terminal room. "Excuse me," he said to the group. "Mark, I'm terribly sorry, but Billy Stamp is on a phone from the *Chosin*. He says it's urgent."

"Tell Billy that my father was just murdered," he took a choppy breath and continued in a steadily louder voice, "and my kids were kidnapped and that this phone call better be really fucking important!"

The consultant paused. "It is really fucking important. I'll put him over the speaker."

"What the hell is it?" Mark screamed.

"We've finished examining the code on the *Chosin*. It's the same pattern, Mark. This is an across-the-board sabotage. It uses the same three-file layer system with pointers to results functions. If the results aren't there, the code produces Y2K-like errors. I have our team lead on the line from a middle electronics deck on the *Chosin*."

"Hello everybody," the consultant began.

"Cut the shit," Mark said. "What is it?"

"We've found that the software side of the *Chosin's* communications was altered the same as Pearl Harbor's code. It's set up to be fixed with a software key of some sort."

Mark clicked off the speaker. "I need to take care of my children," he said ferociously. "Hartmire, get your guards and come with me. Get the trucks and guns. We're going to The Keep."

"Mark, that's exactly what they want you to do," Hartmire said. "They'll capture you too. Fight them from here."

"I can't fight very well knowing that my children are held at gunpoint!"

"Then this is a state of national emergency," Pritchett said. "I need to call out of here now."

His appointed guard stepped forward, blocking his way. "Now!" Pritchett yelled into the man's face. The guard looked to Hartmire, who nodded. A consultant tossed a handset to Pritchett. He removed his headset and dialed.

"Mr. Secretary, this is Edwin Pritchett. The hostiles have murdered the father of Mark Solvang and kidnapped his children. Yes, the president of the company. The private police force is very good, but the situation has moved beyond their scope of operations." He looked at Hartmire while he listened to the response. "That's what I was hoping for, sir. I'll expect a call from Coronado within thirty minutes." He hung up the phone.

"Did you say you'd expect a call from Coronado?" Hartmire asked.

Pritchett nodded. Hartmire allowed himself to smile.

"What's Coronado?" Mark asked him.

"Home of the Navy SEALs."

9

RECLUSE

"We're talking about my family," Mark said. "I couldn't save my wife. I couldn't save my father. I won't be able to live with myself if I fail to save my children."

Pritchett saw the pain in Mark's face. He wished he could do more. "The SEALs are coming, Mark."

Mark strained to keep his composure. "If they're coming, I want two things. First, I want my children back. Second, I want Susan back. She's in there with that psycho son of a bitch." He looked from Pritchett's face to Hartmire's. "She's family, too."

Pritchett answered his headset.

"This is lieutenant commander Ken McCrostie with the Navy SEALs. I understand the children are being held hostage at Solvang Solutions headquarters."

"That's correct. You are to recover the children." He watched Mark's pained expression. "The children and a key manager named Susan Levin. You will hand them off to the head of Solvang's private police force in a quiet part of San Jose. Solvang does not want to reveal the location of its alternate control site to anybody, not even the SEAL rescue team."

The line was quiet as McCrostie wrote the information in the margin of his orders. "That will be fine. However, you should know that our op calls for us to remain in town through the remainder of this situation. Between you and me, Mr. Pritchett, we'll know the location very quickly."

"I understand."

"Can Solvang have a vehicle waiting for us at the airport?"

"How many of you will there be?"

"Four."

"Four? That's all?"

"That's all."

"We can have a pickup truck waiting for you."

"Good. We will fly into the old terminal of San Jose airport at 0530 hours. Leave the truck near fuel tank three, keys in the front bumper. In the next twenty minutes, you need to fax us the floorplans for Solvang's headquarters. Identify possible holding areas where the children might be kept and where we can find Susan Levin. Circle entrances to the building and list the advantages and disadvantages associated with each. Also fax a map of the meeting point in San Jose where the children and Susan Levin are to be delivered. They will be handed over only if those making the pickup know this code: XPR742SS."

Pritchett wrote it down.

"Finally, I need the radio frequency of your ongoing communications."

Pritchett told him.

"Your call sign is 'Lair,' ours is 'Recluse.' We will spend the day monitoring the Solvang headquarters for work routines, several escape routes, and general terrain features. If we need further supplies, you'll be hearing from us."

"What type of supplies might you need?"

"I can't say, Mr. Pritchett. Every op is different for us. Our main strength is our ability to adapt. If we all roll with it, we might be able to save these people."

Pritchett relayed the call's information to Mark and Hartmire.

"We received a note from Nikolaas Groen," Hartmire said. "We know the children are not near the lower terminal room. The managers there would have seen them. I'll mark the maps."

"We can't get any notes to Susan," Mark said. "They're watching her reader. She won't know any of this is happening. I need to go. She'll recognize me and understand that she's being rescued. Otherwise she won't—"

"Don't be insane," Pritchett told him. "You can't go, Mark. This is a military operation. You'll be in the way."

"Listen to what I'm saying."

"No! You are not going. The SEALs will do their best at The Keep. You do your best from here."

JANUARY 18, 2000

The Bell 47 was now a familiar site to cops on the ground. Murray and Martinez had seen all parts of the city since the disaster began. It had evolved from a downtown inferno, to an outlying series of battles, to spotty guerrilla warfare, and now to neighborhood crimes, the most insidious of all urban conflict.

Murray flew over Beverly Hills on his way to Brentwood and from there down to the beaches. With only one copter in the air, they had plenty of fuel. A single bird could fly for months on the department's fuel reserves.

"I'm not sure I like the quiet as much as I thought I would," Murray said.

"I know what you mean. Finding nothing does not mean that nothing is going on."

"Helicopters don't have a lot of use in this environment. The crimes are taking place inside homes, not on the street."

The radio crackled. That meant somebody on the ground was trying to communicate. The voice came in and out of range.

"...requesting assistance...Beverly Hills...armed robbery with intent to kill..."

Murray looked out the windows and hoped that the officers were all right. There was nothing he and Martinez could do. They'd had dozens of similar calls in the past week. Without a specific location they couldn't respond, and they wouldn't hear anything else. They'd come to rely almost entirely on their own observations and radio transmissions to cops nearby.

"How's your family coping?" he asked Martinez.

"My wife and kids are living with her mother now. I went over there last night and found half the Martinez clan from here to Chula Vista holed up in the place. They had fires burning in the back yard, a pig on a spit, and tequila. Lots of tequila."

"Where'd they get all that?"

"Tequila is considered an emergency ration in my family."

"And the pig?"

"Some cousin in Tujunga. Lots of people have pigs and other animals out there. What about your family?"

"Uncle Ben's rice and Coke."

Martinez shook his head. "I'd hate to be white in all this. You people are too used to eating out. That's the problem. Mexicans and Asians and Blacks—we eat at home."

"Don't get started. There's nothing wrong with rice and Coke."

The radio crackled again. "...Rodeo Drive with no backup. I repeat...six usuals."

That one they could respond to. Murray banked the 47 hard to his left toward Rodeo Drive. Five minutes later, Murray and Martinez looked out their windows to the demolished shops on either side of the street. The formerly opulent store fronts hung in ruins. Shattered glass lay on the sidewalks, parking meters had been broken from their posts and left in the streets.

Murray looked down the street. He saw nothing. "I'm putting down. We're never going to get anybody this way."

The Bell touched down on the parking structure along Santa Monica Boulevard. Murray kept the engine at a low idle. They locked both doors and ran down the parking ramp. They took opposite sides of the street and walked briskly into the rubble.

Murray knew in his mind that Rodeo must have been destroyed, but he didn't expect what he saw. Jewelry cases were not just broken, they were decimated. Velvet strips clung to glass shards where the looters had ripped the goods from the cases before somebody else could grab them. Underneath a pile of glass and metal, he saw a decaying arm. There was one criminal who didn't make out like a bandit.

Murray realized that much of the stuff was smashed, but little was actually taken. Diamond rings sparkled in the window displays, a high-end Bang & Olufsen stereo leaned against the bent door frame, expensive furniture still sat on showroom floors. Bookstores were ruined, but the entire inventory of titles was left strewn across the floors. Glittery dresses still hung on mannequins. A Jaguar's windows were smashed and its body dented, but nobody bothered hot wiring it.

After three blocks, Martinez yelled across the street. "This is stupid. There's nobody here."

"Can you believe all this stuff?" Murray called back. Martinez ran across the street. "There's probably a million bucks worth of stuff here."

"I know," Martinez said. "Think we should take some of it?" He was only half joking.

"I couldn't care less what you do on your own time. Maybe I'll come back here myself later on, but I doubt it."

He looked in the open window of a cosmetics shop, its packaged sets of colors scattered across the floor. He could see the price tag on a small package near the door: $239. "I don't know why, but none of this is all that appealing to me right now."

Martinez nodded. "I need food for my family. Not makeup and stereos and books and evening gowns."

"A juicy steak and some corn on the cob, maybe. But not jewelry." Murray holstered his pistol and started walking back. "Evidently we're not the only ones who feel that way. Funny how the most expensive stuff is the first to become worthless."

JANUARY 19, 2000

The flight from San Diego to San Jose took just over one hour. Lieutenant commander Ken McCrostie looked over his three men and their sea bags of equipment. SEALs travel light. They bring lots of water, little food, and only enough ammunition to get the job done.

That's under normal circumstances. In the Y2K environment, far from any support, they needed to be ready for a long stay in the field. They would have use of a pickup truck, which would make transportation easy. Those two factors led McCrostie to bring extra weapons, extra ammunition, extra radios, extra food, five Stinger missiles, and five Dragon missiles.

The report sent to him from a CIA Chinese Affairs Specialist named Andrew Chen warned him that anything was possible. The CIA was convinced that the hostile force occupying The Keep was supported by China's PLA and by traitors inside the United States. They could have old helicopters and armored vehicles in the vicinity, transported from overseas by plane or ship, or even drawn from U.S. military installations. Little was known about the hostile force, thus all precautions were good precautions. They were dealing with an unpredictable enemy backed into a corner. That was the worst enemy of all.

The plane touched down at San Jose before sunrise. The sky turned orange as the SEALs transferred their cargo from the plane to the pickup truck left by Lauer. McCrostie walked to their plane's pilot.

"Do me a favor," he said. "I need to know if there are any military transports parked either here or in San Francisco. It's getting light now. Why don't you do a fly-by and scope out each airport. We'll be spending the rest of this morning less than two miles from here. When you fly by, we can pick you up on radio."

"No problem," the pilot said. The plane flew from San Jose before its tires had a chance to cool.

The five-foot Stinger missiles weighed only twenty-two pounds each; the three-foot Dragons only twenty-five pounds. Archer and Dietz sat in the bed of the truck to hold the missiles in place during the drive. They stacked sea bags against them to eliminate rattling. Sweeny sat in the cab with McCrostie.

The Stinger is a shoulder-launched guided missile used to destroy low-altitude aircraft. It's a "fire and forget" system that uses an infrared seeker to find its target. The person who fired the missile can duck behind cover after launch, confident that the missile will take care of itself. The Stinger's predecessors required the soldier to remain in place, guiding the missile manually, fully exposed to enemy fire.

The Dragon is a shoulder-launched guided missile used to destroy tanks and other ground vehicles. It is older and less sophisticated than the Stinger, requiring the gunner to remain exposed for about sixteen seconds while steering the missile to its target.

It was not by accident that the SEALs carried Stingers and Dragons. In 1989, improved Stingers were developed around a reprogrammable microprocessor. Like most other microprocessors, it broke from Y2K. However, unlike an embedded chip, the Stinger's processor was able to be reprogrammed. It did not need to be replaced. Thus, technicians at Coronado were able to repair the five Stingers in time for the SEAL op to San Jose.

The Dragons did not break from Y2K because they are old missiles. The Dragon is not America's preferred antitank missile. That distinction goes to the Javelin—the latest breed—which utilizes a powerful infrared "fire and forget" guidance system even better than the Stinger's. The guidance chips broke in Y2K, rendering the mighty Javelin useless. Thus, McCrostie's SEAL team carried Dragons to San Jose.

It took only ten minutes to reach The Keep from the airport. McCrostie parked their truck at the bottom of a small hill beside the building.

Each man wore jeans and a button-up work shirt. The public

image of SEALs assumes that they always wear camo face paint with bandannas around their heads. A complete outfit of camo field gear and gloved hands holding an M-16 with Rambo-like determination completes the locker room poster of a SEAL.

But they're not always like that.

McCrostie learned from his father, a SEAL who served in Vietnam, that a SEAL's best weapon is surprise. You do not surprise anybody when you walk up to them in special forces fatigues. You might as well send planes ahead to announce, "the SEALs are coming! The SEALs are coming!"

McCrostie remembered a story told by his father about the time his platoon needed to get upriver in the U Minh forest of Vietnam. They were supposed to drive upstream in a boat called a Medium SEAL Support Craft. Instead, the platoon leader bought a sampan from a Vietnamese fisherman. It was the same boat used by almost all of the Vietnamese, stained, well used, and this one had bullet holes on one side. It didn't just look local, it *was* local. That was McCrostie's first lesson from his father. To achieve surprise, look like the enemy, act like the enemy, and think like the enemy.

Which is why this was an unusual op for McCrostie's team, almost too simple to be true. They needed to infiltrate a civilian target on American soil. They wouldn't need diving gear, wouldn't use boats, wouldn't even get wet. Their insertion vehicle was an American pickup truck, not a Light or Medium SEAL Support Craft. Their area of operation was an American city. The critical part of their op, what's called the "actions at the objective," would take place inside a modern office building, not a jungle or a desert or the Panama Canal.

It seemed ironic to McCrostie that an op in his own country among his own people would be the most unusual he could have drawn. It meant dressing and acting like Americans—not much of a stretch for four men from San Diego. Yet at the same time, their usual preparations were for overseas ops, not up-the-street ops. In its own way, this was a challenge.

They settled behind a clump of bushes at the top of the hill. Each man carried binoculars, a radio, a sheath knife on one leg, and a pistol on the other.

"Let's see what we have here," McCrostie said. All four men looked through their binoculars. "It's a big office building with diesel exhaust coming out the top. That's their source of electricity. There

are enough cars in the parking lot to have hundreds of people inside."
He kept looking. "Not much more from here." He put the glasses
down.

They heard a plane approaching. It was their own transport. The
pilot flew low above San Jose airport and radioed McCrostie. "We
have a C-130 parked at San Francisco airport. Its tail bears China's
colors."

"Any ground vehicles surrounding it?" McCrostie asked.

"Not that we saw. The rear cargo ramp is fully open, however.
It looks like something rolled out of there."

"Ten-four. Thanks for the report."

The plane's engine noise dissipated as it flew south, gradually
gaining altitude for the return flight to San Diego. The report was
not good news. A C-130 transport is big enough to carry around
one-hundred men and several vehicles, depending on the type. The
Chinese could have brought armored personnel carriers, or even a
tank. With air detection systems down, they would have been able
to fly into San Francisco as easily as a passenger jet.

"Fan around the building. Dietz, I want you to check the front.
Stay in touch on the radios."

The men dropped below the edge of the hill, then walked
casually to places around the building. They wouldn't be seen, but
even if they were, they looked no more dangerous than guys
wandering around a town with no bars open. Each called back to
McCrostie as they gradually encircled The Keep. Sweeny, the last
man out, confirmed that he'd arrived at his observation point.

"All right, starting with Archer, tell me what you've got."

"I've got the side of an office building with grass."

"I've got the front entrance," Dietz said. "There are four pickup
trucks here. In the back are tarps covering something, could be
weapons. I can go check. Other than that, it's just the front of a
quiet office building."

"Dietz, check on the tarps," McCrostie told him. "Sweeny,
you're the last one. What have you got?"

"A side of the building with dead bodies piled in the weeds.
They look like casualties of the infiltration."

Dietz walked below the horizon line of the hill. He made his way out of sight, then walked back to The Keep on the driveway. It wouldn't look like he was sneaking up on the building.

The morning was quiet except for the birds. The light across The Keep made a dim understatement of a day. Dietz reached the truck breathing cool air and hearing birds. Without hesitation, he reached inside the bed and peeled back a corner of the tarp.

AK-47 rifles. Typical these days. He moved to the next truck. More AK-47s. It was consistent with the CIA's terrorist theories on this situation. But they could be terrorists from anywhere. Everybody uses AK-47s, even extremist American militia groups. It didn't have to be China. Still, he thought, the Chinese love AK-47s.

"Hey!" a voice yelled from The Keep.

Dietz froze. He gulped and counted to three in his head. His hands relaxed against his legs. He waved. "Good morning!" he called back to the voice.

"Who are you?" Dietz could detect a middle eastern accent, but he couldn't tell which country.

"Dave Dietz, and you?"

"Walk over here."

"Okay. Oops, dropped my wallet." He bent behind the pickup to talk into the radio. "Dietz here. I've been sighted at the front entrance. I'm about to enter conversation." He set his pistol, radio, and binoculars on the truck tire. He stood and walked to the front entrance.

"I'm surprised there's anybody here," he said to the guard. He noticed the uniform. The outfit looked like typical private security force attire.

"Why are you here?" the guard demanded. His eyes were dark and serious, his hair black.

"Oh I'm just out on a walk."

"Early in morning for walk."

"I suppose, but I'm getting bored with all this. I can't even go to work or to a ball game, nothing. Nobody's around. I'm glad I found you here. Anything fun happening inside?"

"We working very hard."

"Yeah? On what?"

"Computers."

"I'm not much of a computer guy. More of a beer and pretzel guy."

The guard didn't smile. He held a rifle sling around his shoulder.

Dietz could tell by the barrel behind the guard's shoulder that it was an AK-47. "Turn around."

"What for?"

"I will search you. We are government company. Very serious business. No visitors."

"Okay." Dietz turned and faced the morning. The guard felt clumsily along Dietz's sides and legs. He paused at the sheath knife.

"What's this?"

"Hunting knife. Doesn't get in my way down there."

The guard lifted the jeans for a quick look. Satisfied, he released the jeans and stood. "You must go."

"Hey, I hear you. I'll just walk somewhere else tomorrow."

The guard nodded, still not cracking a smile. Dietz turned and walked from the entrance back to the truck. He looked at the guard. The man had turned to go inside the building. Dietz darted quickly to the tire to retrieve his radio, pistol, and binoculars, then kept walking up the driveway. He walked out of view.

"Dietz here. I'm heading back now. No problems."

"Don't head back," McCrostie said. "Resume your observation post. We need to watch for a few hours. What did you find?"

"AK-47s. The guard was middle eastern wearing a private security uniform. Seemed nervous and new on the job. He carried an AK-47 as well."

"Did you see any other guards?"

"No."

McCrostie thought a moment. "We need to look like them when we go inside tonight. We'll get uniforms from The Lair. That's where the private security firm is now."

"We'll need AK-47s."

"Possibly. We know where to get them if needed. Internal patrols probably carry pistols. I'm more worried about the middle eastern accent and appearance."

McCrostie radioed The Keep. "Recluse to Lair, come in."

"This is Jules Hartmire. Go ahead."

"We're at Solvang headquarters. Do you know the nationality of the hostile guards?"

"American, middle eastern, Chinese, and a few Africans."

"Good. Second item: we need uniforms. We want to blend when we infiltrate tonight."

"We have uniforms for you. What sizes?"

"Bring four medium and four large. We'll figure which is best for each man when we have them."

"Okay."

"Finally, bring us four copies of the skeleton key to all storage rooms, and any other master keys you have."

"We have a key that opens all doors except the outer entrances."

"That will be perfect. Meet us at the rendezvous point in east San Jose at 1300 hours. That gives us enough time to continue surveillance. We'll have more questions for you when we meet."

JANUARY 20, 2000

Pete Dubridge and April Pennington found the Chinese ships steaming around Asia, moving from one port to the next, then out to open sea. From their posts in Guam, they tracked every movement to the best of their capabilities.

"Hey, Pennington, take a look at this." He sat at a wide table, examining a paper map of the Pacific. Tracer lines indicated satellite paths and zones of coverage.

Pennington walked over. She pulled a chair next to his. "Look at these satellite lines," he said. He grabbed three colored pencils. "I'm going to put the working lines in blue."

He traced a few lines over the Philippine Sea into the North Pacific. "Those are useful every other six-hour period. Look what happens if I black out all the dead lines." He used the black pencil to darken the network of dead satellite lines.

"Look at that," Pennington said.

"Yes, look at that." The blackened lines formed a near perfect swath of non-coverage extending from the Mariana Islands toward Wake Island and then toward Hawaii. "The Chinese ships are directly in that black zone. We can only see them every six hours and for a quick snap at that. If they were a few hundred miles north or south, we could get long hard looks at them. Then we'd see what we're up against. But as it is, they are directly in our blind spot."

"Coincidence?"

"Are you kidding me? Somebody knows the exact pattern of our satellite coverage and they're using it superbly."

JANUARY 19, 2000

Hartmire and Lauer arrived in east San Jose at 12:45. One of their own pickups drove up to the street corner just before 1:00. A sturdy man with short blond hair stepped from the driver's seat. Three ordinary-looking men joined. They wore jeans and button-up shirts.

"Code, please," the blond man said.

"XPR742SS."

Hartmire showed them to the bed of the truck, where four medium and four large Hartmire uniforms were stacked in plastic bags. One man with McCrostie carried the bags to their pickup.

Hartmire handed four keys to McCrostie. "Here are the skeleton keys. How are things coming along?"

"It's hard to tell. We'll wait for nightfall. The security doors you installed are heavy steel, so we've decided against entering through one. It would take too much C-4 to blow the hinges. They'd hear us coming."

"How will you get in?"

"Cement prongs to a second story window. Cut the glass, get inside, throw a rope to the team."

"Simple enough."

"That's how we like it. If all goes well, we'll never fire a shot. From what we saw this morning, most of the guards carry pistols. The entrance guards carry AK-47s. We'll need to carry pistols only."

"Do you need anything else?"

"No. Just wait for our radio signal. We'll see you back here with the children and Susan Levin before sunrise."

The SEALs drove back to the hill beside The Keep. McCrostie gave each man a copy of the master key. They spent the afternoon familiarizing themselves with the areas surrounding the building.

They selected the uniforms that fit them best. The Hartmire holsters weren't long enough to accommodate the silencers on their pistols. They got around it by carrying one pistol without silencer in the holster, and another with silencer on their ankle. Archer would be the man through the window. He would carry the weapons belt in a backpack while he climbed the building and cut the glass.

Dressed and ready to go, they waited at the edge of the hill. Night fell around them, silent. There were no planes overhead, no cars driving by, no sound of music and dancing. It was a dead city. McCrostie wasn't sure he liked that. Noise was good for disappearing. Silence was like a smooth sandy beach. It revealed everything except more silence.

McCrostie's adrenaline would not subside. They could infiltrate at any time. The darkness would mask their entry and exit from the building.

"Everybody has the E&E?" McCrostie asked. It stood for escape and evasion plan, the actions they would take if they were separated and needed to get away quickly. If they could get out of the building, their chance of survival increased exponentially. This was open, friendly territory. An American city. They didn't need to flee behind enemy lines.

"Yes." They all had it.

"Good. Let's go."

They walked across the field to a side of the building with no door. Archer pulled two thick metal spikes with finger grips at the dull end. He felt the surface of the building, then jammed one spike into it. He pulled down. A solid grip. Using spikes strapped to his toes and the spikes in his hands, he climbed to the row of second story windows. All were dark.

He removed a small glass cutter from his shirt pocket and cut an arc the size of a watermelon slice in the corner. He reached inside to grip the wall of the building, straining his legs and wrists. He snaked a hook inside the window and jammed it under the sill. He clipped the short rope to his harness and exhaled as the rope bore most of his weight.

Thus secured, he withdrew the big glass cutter from his backpack. Working in rainbow arcs, he cut more of the window away from his initial slice. Several small slices were easier to handle than a slice half the size of the glass pane. He dropped each of the moon shapes to the grass below. The other men carried the slices away so subsequent drops wouldn't create noise. After eight slices, the opening was large enough for Archer to climb inside. He reached across the window sill and pulled himself into the dark office.

He stepped onto carpeted floor beside a desk. He clicked on a flashlight to examine the place. It hadn't been used in awhile. The door was shut and it was quiet. From inside the office, he cut away several additional slices of the window. The larger opening would make it easier to get everybody inside and, more importantly, to get the people out.

Archer pulled sturdier hooks and climbing ropes from his pack and wrapped them around the steel desk legs, then dropped both coils out the window.

Dietz attached two jumar clips to the ropes. Jumars slide up, but don't slide down. With one hand on each of the two ropes, the men walked up the side of the building in no time. Once inside the window, they flipped the switch on the jumars and slid them down the ropes to the last man. All four men stood inside the office five minutes after Archer dropped the ropes.

They pulled the ropes inside the window and coiled them under the desk. Archer hid his backpack in the same location. He fastened the Hartmire weapons belt around his waist.

They split into two groups. They would be less conspicuous that way and would also be able to cover a wide area in little time. McCrostie teamed with Dietz, Archer with Sweeny. McCrostie and Dietz left the office first to proceed to their designated floors.

The hallway was empty. They walked quickly to the main corridor toward the stairwell. They descended to the ground level and walked to a storage room. They passed windows of consultants at terminals. McCrostie watched a man's face look at him and then away. Good. It meant they blended.

There were no guards at the storage room door. Diez used his master key to open it. He shined a light inside. "Clear," he said. McCrostie crossed the room off their list.

They walked down the hall to the next one. Dietz opened the door and shined a light inside. "Clear," he said.

They walked around the corner past another terminal room. More faces turned toward them, then away. So far, so good.

They completed the ground floor. McCrostie was not surprised that they did not find the children. The SEAL team expected to find the children in the executive suites on the second floor.

But looking there first would alert the hostiles to their presence. It was important to search easy areas first. Ruling them out left the difficult areas to be dealt with only if necessary. Conflict was not a problem if it meant getting the captives and getting away alive.

They encountered their first guards on the basement level. McCrostie felt chills as they approached. The rising panic that SEALs work so hard to control during training never goes completely away. His heart pumped wildly. He could feel Dietz's unease through the air. The other guards looked at them, but walked by. McCrostie nodded as they passed. They nodded back.

The supply rooms on the basement level were empty. They walked past the windows of the lower terminal room.

"Oh shit," McCrostie said. Workers sat terrified at their terminals. Six guards surrounded a woman at the front of the room. Her face was drawn and shiny, like she'd been crying. As McCrostie watched, one of the guards held a pistol to the woman's head and yelled at her. She cringed, then typed frantically.

"That's got to be Susan Levin," McCrostie said.

"We're going to have a tough time getting her out of there alive. There are a lot of innocent people to get shot."

McCrostie pressed the button on his radio. He spoke quietly while he and Dietz continued walking. "No children on first floor or basement level. Susan Levin is heavily guarded in the lower terminal room."

"Floors three and four are clear."

"Check five and six. We'll check two and meet you there."

The second floor was quieter than the first floor and basement. There were only small terminal rooms with few people working, nothing like the farms on the lower levels. All supply rooms were clear. McCrostie and Dietz rounded the corner of the hallway with the drinking fountain and restrooms. That was the contact point. Archer and Sweeny walked past without a glance.

McCrostie pushed the button on his radio. "McCrostie and Dietz entering the executive suite. Stand by."

The glass doors pushed open easily. They heard talking in the conference room. They walked past the photos of Big Sur and Yosemite. Wood paneling created a cozy feeling in the half-light of diesel power. Past the conference room, they neared a corner into the hallway of executive offices. They heard bantering in Chinese.

"Chinese," McCrostie spoke into his radio. There was a greater chance of detection now. He flipped the switch on the radio. It became a listening device for Archer and Sweeny. They would be able to hear everything.

The two SEALs rounded the corner at a casual pace. The Chinese instantly stopped talking.

There were four of them, all smoking cigarettes. Each carried an AK-47 slung on his shoulder. They eyed the two newcomers with deadpan expressions. McCrostie and Dietz proceeded straight past the men to the offices in the hallway, nodding a greeting as they passed. The Chinese nodded back.

McCrostie hoped the ferocious beating of his heart wouldn't reach their ears.

The Chinese watched the two men open several doors and shine lights inside. They didn't move toward them, didn't radio anybody, didn't react whatsoever. The last door was locked.

McCrostie called back to the Chinese. "Are the children in here now?" His voice sounded like a workman on the job.

The Chinese men walked over. The front man shrugged. "Na, na," was all he could say. They didn't speak any English.

McCrostie held his hands at his waist level. "Children," he said.

The men reacted at once. They dropped their cigarettes and started chattering in Chinese. One held up his hand at McCrostie and reached for a radio. McCrostie shook his head.

"No," he commanded boldly. He held up his key. The men stared at it, confused. He stuck the key in the lock and opened the door. A teenage boy and a girl with tear lines on her face sat inside the office on a small couch. They didn't say a word.

Dietz pointed at the children. "These are the ones," he said matter-of-factly, pointing at them. He and McCrostie nodded at each other, normal as could be. "Last office on the left."

McCrostie gestured for everybody to follow him into the office. The Chinese, still looking confused, followed behind him toward the children.

Archer and Sweeny heard everything over the radios. They walked briskly through the glass doors of the executive suite, past the paintings and shining wood, around the corner, past the closed office doors. They removed their silencer pistols from their ankles in mid stride. They reached the only open office, the last one on the left.

McCrostie spoke in a loud voice to the Chinese, all of whose backs were turned toward the door. "Yes, these are the children. Now, we need to know a few things from you. First—"

While they faced him, confused expressions on their faces, two silenced pistols aimed at the backs of their necks and fired. The sounds, like quick rushes of air suddenly cut off, dropped the first two men in a pile. The last two fell an instant later.

McCrostie turned immediately to the children, finger over his lips. Their eyes were glued on the bodies. "Keep quiet. We're taking you to your father."

Archer and Sweeny placed their pistols back on their ankles. They walked out of the room and proceeded back through the executive suite the way they'd come. Their job was to clear a path, if necessary.

McCrostie and Dietz grabbed the children. "Walk with us," Dietz said. "Walk quickly."

The two men and two children walked from the office. McCrostie locked the door solidly behind them and continued down the corridor. They reached the hallway where they'd first entered The Keep.

Archer and Sweeny held the door open. Everybody walked into the small office. They shut the door. Archer had already removed the backpack from the coiled ropes. They threw the ropes out the open window. They set the jumar clips to a firm resistance, enough to slide down the ropes at a controlled speed. Archer took Alyssa in his left arm, gripped the jumar with his right, and slid to the ground. He unclipped the jumar.

Sweeny clipped another jumar on the empty rope. Jeremiah was too big to carry under an arm. Instead, the boy hung on to Sweeny's back while Sweeny used jumars on both ropes to slide to the ground.

McCrostie and Dietz walked to the lower terminal room, hearts pounding. They rounded the bend in the hallway and approached the windows.

Susan Levin was not there.

"Fuck," McCrostie spit. He spoke into his radio. "Susan Levin is missing. We're searching the area."

A group of guards ran up the hallway toward them. McCrostie and Dietz rested their hands near their pistols, ready.

"Hurry!" an American guard screamed at them. "To the executive center. Didn't you get the call?"

"No," McCrostie managed. He and Dietz fell into the back of the procession. They streamed up the stairwell to the second floor and ran down the hallway toward the glass doors. Dozens of guards packed the executive suite in a frenzy.

McCrostie and Dietz broke from the pack down the hallway to their escape room. McCrostie could hear pounding feet around the corner as guards responded to the emergency call.

He slipped the key into the door and they darted inside, quickly locking the door behind them. Dietz pulled two jumars and descended out the window.

McCrostie shone his light around the room to check for any loose equipment. None. He tossed the backpack to the grass, clipped his jumars to the ropes, and slid to the ground. He unclipped the jumars and flipped the ropes into the open window. They could keep them.

The two men walked quickly across the field. McCrostie paused at the hilltop to check behind for any sign of followers. Nobody came. He walked over the hilltop down to the pickup.

Jeremiah and Alyssa rode in the cab with McCrostie and Dietz. Archer and Sweeny rode in the bed of the truck.

"What happened?" Archer asked.

"They found the Chinese. We couldn't risk looking for her."

Dietz opened the glove box and took out two Snickers bars. He gave them to the children.

"Thank you," Alyssa said in a quavering voice.

"You're welcome, honey," Dietz told her. He smoothed her braided hair, still tight from her grandmother's handiwork.

McCrostie picked up the radio. "Recluse to Lair, come in."

"This is Lair."

"Code, please."

"XPR742SS."

"We have the children, all safe, eating Snickers bars."

"They have the children!" Hartmire yelled. A roomful of people cheered. McCrostie couldn't help smiling. Hartmire came back on the radio. "And Susan Levin?"

"No."

"I see. Are you driving to the meeting point?"

"Yes. We will be there in twenty minutes."

"So will we. See you there."

McCrostie parked the truck one block away. Archer and Sweeny walked to the meeting point and waited for a truck from The Lair. Hartmire and Lauer stepped from the vehicle.

"Code, please," Sweeny demanded, even though he recognized each man from their earlier meeting.

"XPR742SS."

Sweeny spoke into his radio. "The private police force has arrived." Moments later, McCrostie drove to the curb in the pickup. The children poured from the cab.

"Thank you," Hartmire said. "You don't know what this means to Mark Solvang. What it means to all of us." He extended a hand to McCrostie, then to each of the other three men. Lauer did the same.

"Susan Levin is being held at gunpoint," McCrostie said. "They are intimidating her, maybe even hurting her. She looked weary and scared. She'd been crying. We went for her after getting the children, but she was gone. The alarm sounded and we needed to get out. A rescue at this point would be almost impossible."

"I'll tell the others," Hartmire said. He looked to each of the men in his uniforms. "You look good in them. If you ever need a job."

The SEALs laughed. "We'll keep it in mind," McCrostie said.

"Are you planning on sticking around?"

"Yes," McCrostie said. "We'll be on call. Where is The Lair?"

"I can't say," Hartmire told him. "You know that."

"You're going to make us find it?"

"I have to. I've got children and the company to protect."

"Understood. Drive safely, Mr. Hartmire."

McCrostie waited until Hartmire sat in the driver seat and Lauer moved into the passenger seat. Alyssa and Jeremiah sat in the middle. McCrostie caught the door before it closed. In his left hand, he held a small radio signal transmitter. He leaned inside the cab.

"Just wanted to say goodbye to you two," he said. "We didn't get a chance to know you very well, but you seem like good kids. Give your dad a hug for us."

"We will," Alyssa said.

McCrostie set the transmitter on the floor behind the seat while he spoke. As a backup, Archer slipped another transmitter inside the truck's rear bumper. He pressed the adhesive firmly against the metal.

"Okay," McCrostie concluded. "Goodnight everybody." He shut the door. Hartmire drove away. McCrostie and Archer ran to their pickup truck.

"How are they working?" McCrostie asked Sweeny, who operated the receiver panel.

"Fine. Both are sending strong signals."

"Good. Our backup plan's in place. Now we follow."

He started the truck and drove down the street with the headlights off. It was easy to follow Hartmire in the dim light of evening. There were no other cars on the road, and Hartmire's lights looked like a parade. They drove onto the freeway, toward Los Gatos, exited, drove into Saratoga. McCrostie pulled to a side street shortly after exiting the freeway. They were close enough to find it from there, and he didn't want to risk detection.

McCrostie drove into the hills above Saratoga and pulled onto a dirt road. They pulled ground covers and sleeping bags from the truck and arranged them in a clearing of grass. Branches formed a canopy around them.

"Think Hartmire knows we'll find them?" Archer asked.

"Yes," McCrostie answered. "He knows."

"He's glad we're in town," Dietz added. "You could do worse than to have a SEAL team on your side."

Hartmire pulled to the side of the road before reaching The Lair. "We need to search you before we take you to your parents," he told the two children. "People are looking for your dad and we want to make sure they don't find him. Okay?"

"Okay," Alyssa said.

They stepped from the truck. Hartmire checked them thoroughly, shining the flashlight in their ears, looking inside their mouths, feeling along their arms, legs, and torsos. "Did anybody tape anything to you?"

"No."

"Were you forced to swallow anything?"

"No."

"Did they do anything embarrassing to you?"

"What do you mean?"

"Did they make you take off your clothes and put something inside yourselves?"

"No."

"Okay. I think it's safe to get you to your dad."

They loaded into the truck and completed the final drive to The Lair. Everybody waited on the main floor. Hartmire, Lauer, and the children walked up the stairwell. Lauer flung open the door to a roomful of smiling faces. Mark threw his hands toward them.

Jeremiah and Alyssa ran to their dad and grandma. Mark put an arm around each of them, smelling their hair, kissing them on the cheeks and foreheads. "I'm so sorry," he said. "I'm so sorry I left you there."

Grandma Solvang draped her arms around her son and grandchildren, tears running down her cheeks.

"It's okay, Dad," Alyssa cried into his shirt.

The whole room smiled and cried. "You guys finally get to see where we've been hiding."

Jeremiah was one of the few people in the room to keep his composure. He had a lot of practice playing it cool for his friends. Even being kidnapped by gunmen couldn't make him cry.

"Where's Grandpa?" Jeremiah asked.

Mark looked at him. "You don't know? Didn't you see?"

"See what?" Jeremiah's face dropped. His mouth quivered. "See what, Dad?"

"Grandpa is dead."

"What?" he asked, tears welling in his eyes. "He can't be. We heard guns and I saw him shooting the men. He was winning, Dad. They grabbed us and ran out of the house, but Grandpa was winning. They didn't kill him! He was killing them."

"I know, son," Mark replied. "He tried to keep them from getting you. He died trying."

Jeremiah couldn't hold back any longer. His face contorted with grief. Tears poured from the corners of his dark eyes. His breath came in gasps.

"Poor Grandpa," Alyssa cried.

Mark shut his eyes tight, pulling the children to his chest. Grandma Solvang sobbed against his back. "I know, Alyssa. Poor Grandpa. We miss him so much."

"Nobody will tell us about the old days anymore," Jeremiah

cried. "I wish I listened to more of Grandpa's stories. I wasn't bored with his stories, Dad. I was never bored."

"I know," Mark said. "Grandpa knows too."

Alyssa's tears fell onto Mark's shirt and pants, soaking dark spots into the fabric. Her rib cage expanded and contracted with each sob. "I miss Grandpa so much."

Hartmire stepped forward. "Mark, there's something I need to tell you about Susan."

10

THE HE ZHANG

JANUARY 19, 2000

"What the fuck do you know about this rescue?" Schwager asked Susan. A guard pushed her shoulders down into the chair, another held a pistol against her head.

"I don't know anything," she cried. Her nerves were shredded. She hadn't slept in days. They kept her working, typing, digging for information. She tried to keep them out of secure files, but they threatened her life. They now knew as much about Solvang Solutions as anybody outside the company had ever learned. She was ashamed at giving so much away. But even the little resistance she had managed was waning. She was so exhausted.

"Nothing?" Schwager screamed.

"Nothing!" she screamed in return. Hot tears flooded her eyes. "I've been sitting in this goddamned terminal room for days without rest. Your men have yelled at me and pushed guns against my head. How the hell could I know anything? They've read everything that's come across my computer. They've been with me twenty-four hours a day!"

Schwager slapped her face. Her tears splashed across his hand and onto the computer screen. "And they'll keep watching you twenty-four hours a day!"

JANUARY 21, 2000

Billy Stamp and Dan Van Lan joined the conference room on its satellite speaker phone. Mark, Kleewein, and consultants packed around one end of the table, the DoD on the other. Hartmire and guards stood against the walls of the confined room.

"A few of the pieces of this puzzle are coming together," Pritchett said. "You have in front of you the latest reports from the Pentagon, courtesy of Van Lan's overtime efforts. I'll get to those in a minute. First, I want to discuss Schwager."

Pritchett pointed to the papers in front of him. "This is a summary of Schwager. I've worked with him for years and never liked him. But he is not stupid. He grew up in and around Boston, then began his military career as a systems analyst in the Army. He received his electrical engineering degree from MIT and was subsequently promoted to computer specialist. He served in that capacity until the late 1970s. Then his career took an interesting twist. Schwager entered the Ph.D. program at Boston University. He studied international relations and foreign policy with a special emphasis on Asia, military relations, and arms control. His dissertation was entitled *Back Pedaling: Why Superior Technology will be the Downfall of America's Military*. In it, Schwager traced in excruciating detail the progress of U.S. military technology, how it has always been one step ahead of its nearest competitor and decades ahead of lesser nations. He then constructed a scenario in which all of the U.S. technology depended on the success of an advanced microchip he called the Omega. He projected that with the rate of progress, eventually—he didn't say when—a chip would appear that could handle every military requirement. It would be fast enough for sophisticated surveillance, yet cheap enough for basic terrain crunching like that used in Tomahawk missiles."

Pritchett took a drink of water. "He described the way military procurement happens in the United States and argued convincingly that such a chip would become the U.S. standard almost overnight. The chip manufacturer would negotiate a cheap price given the volume of demand represented by the military. Because all of its equipment would use the same chip, the military would be able to standardize training programs and save millions per year. Finally, in exchange for the entire business of the U.S. military, the chip manufacturer would be willing to sign exclusive contracts, thereby limiting the use of the superchip to the U.S. military.

"Having established that such an occurrence was possible, Schwager then showed that a single problem in the chip could bring the U.S. military to its knees. Meanwhile, less developed but large militaries—particularly that of China—would remain fully functional. The U.S. would break, and opportunistic adversaries would overrun the country with older technology.

"He successfully defended the dissertation to a committee of five faculty members, one of whom was the Chair of the Political Science department. The Chair wrote, 'Rarely, if ever, have I seen such a thorough understanding of a complex topic. Mr. Schwager's research bears out his conclusions, convincingly enough, I might add, to send shivers through this examination committee.' Schwager then went on to manage military computer systems, earning honors and awards at the Defense Logistics Agency, the Defense Automation Resources Information Center, and the Information Systems Authority at Peterson Air Force Base in Colorado Springs. Peterson houses the majority of the military's space forces. Schwager then took positions at the Defense Information Systems Agency and became the chief information officer in 1995. That is the career path of one of the nation's highest ranking military computer specialists."

"Where does that get us?" Mark asked.

"That gets us to several important points. First, we see that Schwager understands technology. Y2K did not catch him off guard, nor did he fail to consider the fact that other militaries would not be as affected as ours. Second, he has held some of the most influential computer positions within the U.S. military. Combined with his current post as CIO of DISA, Schwager could easily pull off a code heist during the last five years. Given the right people in the right places and plenty of time, he could very well have devised a manipulated breakdown of communication software, which is what appears to be in front of us at Pearl Harbor. Now for the clincher. I'll let Dan take it from here."

Dan's high voice crackled across the speaker. "The military software was modified on purpose. There may be a silver bullet solution somewhere, but that solution fixes only communications and satellite surveillance. Plus, it fixes them only in the Pacific region. This is a repair intended specifically for the Chinese threat."

"That addresses what has been my concern all along," Kleewein said. "Nobody could have fixed the entire military in time, much less created a complex breakdown like we're finding in Pearl Harbor."

"Correct," Billy said. "This has to be localized, and we've found the location. Schwager's predictions were accurate. He foresaw the off chance that something like this could happen."

"It wasn't an off chance at all," Pritchett said. "Nobody in the world knew of the U.S. vulnerability better than Schwager. Instead of asking who could possibly know that this situation was coming, ask yourself if anybody was in a better position to take advantage of it. I can't come up with a soul."

"But," Kleewein said, "why would he do it? It doesn't make sense."

"It does if you want to make money," Mark said. "This isn't a military question. It's a business question." He looked to Pritchett. "How much would the military pay for the silver bullet that would restore communications to Pearl Harbor and the Pacific?"

"Any price."

"Exactly. Any price sounds like a lot of business potential to me."

Kleewein stared at Mark. "It couldn't be that simple, could it?"

JANUARY 20, 2000

Schwager hung his head. On top of everything else gone wrong, somebody had snatched the kids from under his nose and disappeared out a second story window on a couple of ropes. Solvang and Pritchett knew who he was and they were still hidden. This was going from bad to worse. Their plan was slipping into the mud. And he still hadn't heard from Dubrow.

He looked at Chau. The quiet Chinese man didn't seem to be bothered. He never seemed bothered. Chau sat smoking his thin cigarettes, almost amused. It was as if he didn't understand the events happening around him.

"There's no way a private corporation can work anymore," Schwager blurted. "Nothing can mask our intentions. Nothing can conceal my identity."

The plan had never been to take over The Keep. Schwager had established a Delaware corporation called Legacy Conversions. It was comprised of legitimate civilian developers who coded the silver bullet to fix the modified military software.

The plan was for Schwager to work with Pritchett and Solvang until the breaking point, then to "discover" a company with a product that would fix military communications. Legacy Conversions would work with S2 to install the fix, and the military would pay Legacy when Y2K was fixed, just as it would eventually pay S2. There would be no whiff of criminal wrong doing, no need to launder money, no need to run from anybody.

But it didn't work out that way. Solvang was even better at its job than Schwager anticipated. He knew that the company would not be fooled by Legacy's silver bullet code.

So Schwager and his people devised a backup plan.

They would take The Keep by force and hold S2 captive during the announcement and implementation of the Legacy code. Pritchett's agreement to create a military takeover plan gave Schwager the out he would need to avoid incrimination later. Solvang's executives and the members of the DoD would be the only ones who knew that the code was a bogus solution. They would be monitored at all times during the occupation, never allowed to communicate outside their working quarters.

Once the DoD contracts were signed with Legacy, the solution would be implemented, the U.S. would see that what looked like a Chinese invasion was a much smaller ordeal. To everyone's surprise, the Chinese would turn back. There would be no danger to the Chinese nor to the Americans. Legacy would make billions. The handful of S2 executives and DoD members would be quietly disposed of. It was a messier backup plan than Schwager would have liked, but the only option.

Then that plan disintegrated around them. Solvang got away, along with the DoD. They still communicated with The Keep, they knew about Schwager, and they might already know about the modified code.

It was now impossible for Schwager to get away unidentified. He had already accepted that. He was concerned now with figuring out how to take a lifetime of money with him. Otherwise he'd be a wanted man with nothing to show for it. Being paranoid and rich would be bad enough. Being paranoid and poor was out of the question.

None of it bothered Chau. "That is true," he said in his quiet voice. "The corporation will not be able to disguise you anymore. The U.S. military knows too much. Your only option is to have the corporation deliver the code and get the money the old fashioned way."

"We can't get money in this environment. Banks aren't working. Wire transfers won't go through. We can't wait for payment either. If they know this is treason, they'll have my head before anybody gets paid anything."

Chau sucked on his cigarette. He held the smoke in his lungs a moment, then exhaled without a care in the world. "I said the old fashioned way."

"What, cash?"

"Gold."

"Request payment in the form of gold?" Schwager asked, incredulous. "I know a low-tech world leads to low-tech answers, but we're starting to sound like pirates."

"Consider it more carefully. How was money transferred two hundred years ago? There were no wires, no computers, no international bank networks. That is the world we have reentered. Gold is always valuable and it is easy to exchange anywhere in the world. It is even easier to disguise than cash because its point of origin remains a mystery. It is a soft metal, easily melted and formed to new shapes, new coins, new bars, new jewelry, or anything necessary. You are working with people who know how to accomplish quiet wealth. Gold is an extremely private medium."

Schwager thought. It might work. "We need the gold divided among several ships. The ships would depart from different U.S. ports for different destinations. We will need smaller boats to intercept the ships, transfer the cargo, and disappear."

"That could be arranged."

"But will it be enough money?"

"It will not be what we had intended, but it will be worth our while. You will not be able to return to the United States."

Schwager nodded. "I know that. I've known that part from the moment they escaped. This plan derailed less than thirty minutes after we arrived here."

Chau's thin eyes showed nothing. "It derailed the moment you allowed Solvang to become the primary contractor."

JANUARY 21, 2000

Mark looked around the room. "If this modified code has a pattern to it, we should be able to change *Solvang2K* to understand the pattern. It's what we've done in every other unique situation. There's no reason it won't work here."

The door to the conference room opened. A consultant stepped inside. "We've received a communiqué from a company in Boston called Legacy Conversions. It was sent to the Pentagon and hundreds of military bases."

"What does it say?" Pritchett asked.

"The company has developed a computer solution to the military problems. It is willing to sell the solution to the U.S. in exchange for gold bars delivered to ships in various ports." The consultant looked up. "It then details which ships and how much gold and further instructions."

"They got around the banking problem," Kleewein said.

"What's Legacy Conversions?" Pritchett asked.

"Sounds like a Y2K firm, but I've never heard of the company."

"Neither have I," Mark said. "If we haven't heard of it, it's not much of a firm. It's probably just a front company. I think Schwager intended for things to go much differently than they're going. Had it not been for our expertise, Legacy Conversions could have marched in like a hero, sold the solution to the military, and received payment in the future. Nobody would have known of Schwager's involvement."

"You're right about that," Pritchett said.

"I believe we're the monkey wrench in all this," a consultant added smugly.

"We're not buying their ridiculous silver bullet," Mark said.

"Of course we're not," Pritchett said gruffly. "Hand me the phone. I need to talk to some friends in the J. Edgar Hoover Building."

JANUARY 22, 2000

It was Pennington who first noticed the slowing of the He Zhang battle group. Dubridge had plotted the group's projected path of approach to Hawaii, complete with estimated arrival points that he monitored in the six-hour observation windows of the crippled satellite network. While Dubridge busily ran the satellites, Pennington watched the data feed.

"Pete, they've slowed to a crawl."

He walked over. "How slow?"

"Look." She pointed to their map. The He Zhang should have been to Wake Island by then. "They're still a day this side of Wake."

"What the hell are they doing? If you want to get somebody when they're down, you don't stop and wait for them to get up."

Pennington looked at the progress patterns. "They went full steam out of the South China Sea. They flew past Batan."

She traced her finger across the progress dots. In the Yellow Sea and near Batan they moved at high speeds. In the middle of the Pacific, they slowed. "That was back when we first noticed and everybody was in a panic."

She moved her finger along the dots to the area past Batan where they started slowing down. "Right about here was when we all knew they were coming. Just when we took everything seriously and cranked our wheels into motion, they started slowing down."

"But not enough for us to notice."

"Not then. But over here," she said, sliding her finger farther along the dots to the middle of the Pacific west of Wake Island, "the slowdown has become so dramatic that we can't miss it. We can also see that it started a ways back."

Dubridge looked at her. "Are they giving up?"

"I don't think so. It's like they're waiting."

"For what?"

"For us to get our act together?"

"That doesn't make any sense at all."

"It does if you think about the communiqué from Legacy."

Dubridge nodded. "The computer company that says it can fix our satellite systems."

"Yeah, and it also demanded to be paid in boats full of gold. That's not legit. You and I have come up with some pretty accurate theories in the past. I think we can do it again."

"So what's the theory now?"

"My theory is that Legacy Conversion is in cahoots with this battle group. The He Zhang went full force to get everybody's attention. They got it. Then the U.S. was given an ultimatum: pay this company in Boston with boats of gold or be overrun by the Chinese. Now, the Chinese have slowed down to give the U.S. time to coordinate the gold delivery."

"We're not going to pay, though."

"Doesn't matter. The only point I'm making is that some of our own people have got to be working with this Chinese group. They're going to split the money. I'd bet anything."

Dubridge thought a moment. "You know something even more interesting?"

"What?"

"I've received orders to switch most of my surveillance on this next satellite pass to Taiwan and the Spratly Islands."

Pennington's eyes sizzled. "You're kidding me. Why would they redirect surveillance at a time like this?"

JANUARY 23, 2000

Pritchett spent several hours on the phone. Nobody else knew who he spoke with, but he used titles like "Mr. Secretary," "Sir," and "General." At one point, he said "Mr. President."

The latest satellite photos came from Guam. As always, they weren't much. The resolution was grainy and some were pure black. But this batch broke new ground in their efforts. They revealed an enormous fleet of ships. Still no firm count, but enough for Pritchett to be very concerned.

"Every one of these ships carries the symbol of the He Zhang," Pritchett said. "That's a division of the People's Liberation Army. Very aggressive and opportunistic. China itself has had trouble controlling them in the past."

He made several more phone calls and forwarded copies of the photos to CIA headquarters in Langley, Virginia. Less than twenty minutes later, a satellite call came from the CIA.

"Mr. Pritchett," a consultant said, "Mr. Andrew Chen is on the line."

"Pritchett."

"Hello Mr. Pritchett, this is Andrew Chen, Chinese affairs specialist at the CIA. We've received the latest photos. This confirms an earlier suspicion."

"Oh? I didn't know you had any suspicions about this."

"We've been following it all along."

"Can you add anything to the story? We still don't have a clear picture as to what's going on."

"I believe I can add a lot to the story. I'm meeting with the President, Joint Chiefs, and national security advisors. Following that, I would like to brief you and the defense contractor. I'll call back in two hours."

"Can you hear us, Mr. Chen?" Mark turned the volume of the speaker phone to its highest level, compensating for a weak satellite connection. Everyone at The Lair circled the table.

"Yes, thank you. My name is Andrew Chen, Chinese Affairs Specialist at the CIA. I have received a full report of the military situation and all photos taken by Guam. I've also been able to conduct additional research on my own using hard copy files here in Langley and central databases researched over the phone, with hard copies faxed to me via satellite. I've assembled what I believe to be a likely explanation for the current events."

The line fell silent for a moment while Chen organized his papers. The weak satellite connection hissed and popped in the foreground. "China's military is a self-funded organization. The People's Liberation Army sponsors small enterprises, most of which sprang from the country's economic reforms. We think there are more than 20,000 of these businesses, some of them very profitable. The officers controlling certain of these businesses have established mini empires for themselves. With a strong leader in control, powerful military capabilities at hand, extensive contacts among terrorist nations, and plenty of income, these empires are very influential in directing Chinese policy."

He took a breath. "The He Zhang is one of the largest and most aggressive of these empires. It is lead by Zhan Qiao Chau and an ever-shifting list of underlings. The CIA updates its records every three months and his list of advisors is almost completely overhauled each time. Working for Chau appears to be a very short career path. Chau comes from a long line of Chinese businessmen. It was expected that he would continue the family's real estate dynasty— known as the Chau Group—which maintains property in Beijing, Shanghai, Guangzhou, Tianjin, Xiamen, and Hong Kong. Hong Kong is the Chau Group's most profitable city."

He turned a piece of paper. "Chau predicted the rise of China's power through the 1980s and 1990s, with the potential to position the nation as a superpower in the early twenty-first century. He worked his way through the ranks of the PLA, not to defend his country, but to further his own financial interests, both personal and on behalf of the Chau Group. He has been very successful. He managed to work closely with the Poly Group, one of the Chau Group's peers. The He Zhang and the Poly Group have cooperated on several business projects. Many of the profits have flowed through the He Zhang into Chau's own pocket and into the coffers of the Chau Group. The combined enterprises turned a profit large enough to build the Poly Plaza, a seventy-million dollar hotel and business complex in Beijing."

"How did they make all their money?" Pritchett asked.

"Arms smuggling and undisclosed imports of goods. I could show you photos of He Zhang soldiers providing protection for arms smugglers. It's big business in China, particularly since the country has an established nuclear program. We're convinced that the He Zhang conducts arms trading with a number of terrorist groups. But that's not all they do. In the Hainan fiasco of 1993, more than 500 million dollars worth of Japanese cars were imported duty free and resold on the mainland for enormous profit. The He Zhang was a major player in the Hainan fiasco, if not the main driving force behind it."

Navy captain Vince Dubrow stared at the speakerphone. "Yes," he said suddenly, "but we have no proof that the Chinese battle group is comprised only of He Zhang ships. The He Zhang is, after all, still part of the PLA. It would make sense to see their ships in a large battle group."

"True, but we don't see any other ships in these photos. In addition, there's further evidence to suggest a connection between the He Zhang and the troubles with our fleet."

He turned a page. "Chau has his eyes set on Taiwan and the Spratly Islands. Taiwan is an area of immense economic opportunity. It's the ninth most important American trading partner. It maintains the world's largest foreign-exchange reserves. It is located in the middle of the sea lines of communication that supply oil and raw materials to Japan, our most important Asian ally. The United States cannot allow China to completely reunify Taiwan. Chau knows this, and he has been one of the most outspoken advocates of direct military conflict with the United States."

He shuffled his papers. "In March, 1996, China conducted military exercises in the Taiwan Strait using the He Zhang division of the PLA. It was a powerful show of force, intended to scare voters

during Taiwan's presidential election. The United States responded
by sending two carrier battle groups. Not one carrier battle group,
mind you, but two. The United States does not consider conflict
with China to be a trivial affair. The Taiwan incident disappeared
from the press in a hurry, forgotten almost overnight by the general
public. But we have not forgotten, nor has China and, more
specifically, nor has Chau. It has set the stage for our nations to
collide militarily and, in my opinion, has ushered in an era of tension
that will culminate in an all-out war."

"Perhaps it has," Pritchett said.

"Yes, perhaps."

Chen turned a page and took a deep breath. It was obvious by
his voice that he felt strongly about China's threat to the United
States. He didn't speak of the nation as one speaks of Iraq or North
Africa, like mosquitoes buzzing around the head of the United States,
needing a swat now and then. Andrew Chen spoke of China the way
people who live below dams speak of torrential rain.

"Everybody is familiar with Taiwan, but the Spratly Islands are
less known. They are located in the South China Sea and don't
support any permanent population. They are claimed by Vietnam,
the Philippines, Malaysia, Taiwan, and China. The islands provide
valuable fishing but, much more importantly, vast oil reserves.
Natural resources have interested the Chau Group for several years.
China is currently an exporter of oil, but with its population
continuing to grow and demand modern conveniences that require
energy, China is destined to become an importer of oil and gas within
a decade. The country must find substantial new resources. The
Chau Group wants to control those resources."

"And the U.S. is hindering them?" Mark asked.

"Yes. Exxon, an American company, has teamed with Indonesia
to develop the nearby Natuna island oil field. The cooperation has
caught the attention of everybody trying to handle the Spratly Island
claims fairly. Diplomats around the region are suggesting strongly
that joint development of Spratly is the way to settle the many claims
on its oil and fishing proceeds. As you can imagine by now, that is
entirely unacceptable to both the He Zhang and the Chau Group.
But to the United States and other interested parties, it's the only
solution."

He turned a page. "In 1995, we discovered a series of meetings
between Chau and a U.S. company called Legacy Conversions. There

appeared to be nothing unusual about the meetings. Chau meets with companies all the time. In this case, he was discussing computer software to fix broken military systems. There was nothing suspicious, so we stopped monitoring those meetings. That was a mistake. We now know from your information and from the communiqué sent from Legacy that the company was involved in developing a solution to the Y2K problem."

"A staged Y2K problem," Mark clarified. "They did not develop a genuine fix."

Pritchett shook his head impatiently. "Are you saying that the Chinese knew about this Legacy company?"

"Not just knew, Mr. Pritchett. The He Zhang funded Legacy Conversions."

"What?" Mark asked. "The group that is invading the U.S. paid to develop a military solution to counter the invasion? Why would they do that?"

"Because the invasion is a decoy to distract the U.S. while China reclaims Taiwan and takes Spratly."

"Then why the demand for money?"

"To trick Schwager into making the distraction a big one. Chau needed an inside connection, somebody motivated to make the invasion as frightening to the U.S. as possible. Chau found Schwager and convinced him that he could get rich this way."

"What a stupid plan," Kleewein said.

"It was actually a superbly conceived plan. The He Zhang military division received legitimate work from Legacy Conversions. That explains their meetings and raises no suspicion against the Chinese. The attack on the U.S. can also be explained."

"How?" Pritchett asked, looking angrier every moment.

"The global positioning system on our two destroyers broke from Y2K. That led them to wander inadvertently into Chinese waters. Thus, the He Zhang can explain their attack."

Mark shook his head. "But their plans have been wrecked. We know about the ties to Legacy and Schwager, we know about their intent to occupy Taiwan and Spratly. Let's tell them we know the story and that they should call off the ships."

"No communications," Kleewein reminded him.

"Even if we could communicate with them, it wouldn't be that easy," Chen said. "Regardless of their motivations, they are still a fully armed hostile force heading to our shores. We need to defend against that. Furthermore, it's to Chau's benefit for the He Zhang to fight. They can still point to the breach of their waters as justification. If they make it to U.S. soil, it elevates the He Zhang's reputation in its own military and among its criminal partners. Both are important to future business."

"They will not make it to U.S. soil," Pritchett swore. "We're going to sink every last one of those ships."

"Mr. Pritchett, you don't understand Chau. He doesn't care if the ships sink. Turning back now would indicate more knowledge than he is supposed to have."

"Plus," Mark added, "the man has nothing to lose. The ships are a small price to pay for Taiwan and Spratly."

"True. There is also a remote chance that the U.S. will comply with the demands and that Chau will profit handsomely from the boats of gold bullion. He knows it's a slim chance, but better than the zero chance he'll have if his ships turn back."

The room sat quietly. Everybody found it hard to accept that the country had been duped by a Chinese terrorist.

"What are Chau's plans now?" Pritchett asked.

"I believe he will justify the He Zhang attack with the U.S. breach of Chinese waters. He will then claim ignorance of any wrongdoing on the part of Legacy Conversions. His division did receive legitimate work from Legacy. He'll say that his funding of the company was to get the work done."

"So he will get away," Kleewein said.

"Most likely. We don't know where he is now, but you can be sure he's not on one of the ships. He will make a clean break."

"And Schwager?" Mark asked.

"Not a chance for him. We know of his involvement. If he escapes to China, the He Zhang will kill him. If he escapes to somewhere else, he'll have the U.S. government and the He Zhang looking for him. Most people would rather be dead."

"Our plans don't change," Mark said. "We still prepare the military to deal with the He Zhang. It looks like they will attack and probably attack hard."

"Yes," Chen replied. He took a breath. When he spoke again, his words came heavily. "This discussion is just now reaching the most important part."

"What could that be?" Pritchett asked, worried.

"Please listen very carefully. You understand the immediate

threat of the Chinese ships. However, the CIA is more concerned about the bigger picture. We believe that Chau is not acting alone. China is insistent on becoming the leading Asian superpower. The United States is insistent that no single country can be allowed to dominate Asia. Our policies place the two countries on a collision course. Our military is inoperable at the moment, for all intents and purposes. Theirs is not. We believe that when the smoke clears, China will occupy Taiwan and the Spratly Islands with heavy firepower. If so, the United States must be prepared to act."

"Jesus Christ," Pritchett said. "You're talking about World War III."

"If what I just described comes to pass, then that's exactly what I'm talking about. This would not be a policing action. This would not be a five o'clock news brief. This would be a war."

"One that we're not prepared to fight," Pritchett said weakly. "This could be the end of our Asian policy."

"Yes it could. And that means the end of our superpower status. The United States would become irrelevant."

An eerie silence hung in the conference room after Andrew Chen's briefing. Pritchett remained in his chair, glasses off, rubbing his eyes. "My God." That was all he said.

People walked from the conference room, back to their terminals to try working. Vince Dubrow needed to use the restroom.

He and his assigned guard walked down the hallway and through the men's room door. Dubrow splashed water on his face from one of the buckets.

"That's something about China, isn't it?" he asked the guard.

"Yeah, it's amazing. I hope it isn't all true."

"What do you think?"

"Well, I don't know much about China. I trust the CIA guy, though. He seemed to know what he was talking about."

Dubrow leaned down close to the water bucket. "What in the world is that?"

The guard came over. "What?"

"That." He leaned even closer, peering into the water.

The guard leaned over to see. Dubrow clutched the man's hair and slammed his head against the sink. The guard tried pulling away, but Dubrow brought his knee into the man's face. He felt hard teeth and the crunch of a nose. He smashed the guard's head into his knee again, and again, and again. He threw him against the tile wall. The guard tried reaching for his pistol, but Dubrow caught his arm. He punched the guard four times in the face. The man's neck went limp and he slid down the wall.

Dubrow picked up the guard by his armpits and dragged him into a stall. He unfastened the man's pants and dropped them to his knees, then set him on the toilet, leaning against the divider. The guard was unconscious, but breathed in shallow mouthfuls.

Dubrow pulled a thin wire from his pocket and wrapped it around the guard's neck. He tightened it until it disappeared into the folds of skin. The sound of breathing stopped. The man's face turned purple, then blue. His lips fattened and his eyeballs pushed hard against the lids. Dubrow tightened the wire. The guard's arms jerked a few times. Dubrow released the wire and checked for a pulse. None.

He tucked the guard's pistol into his pants. He locked the stall door and crawled underneath. He glanced back at the stall. The guard's pants were rumpled around his ankles. It looked normal. Just a guy relieving himself. Dubrow wet a paper towel to mop the small amount of blood on the floor and tile wall. He walked quietly out the bathroom.

The briefing sent Dubrow off the edge. He had no idea it was this big. Schwager didn't know either. It made Dubrow furious to be a pawn in Chau's bigger plan. But he didn't see any way out. He would proceed with his instructions. He hoped he got his money and got away. He'd been through too much to back out now.

In the time he'd spent at The Lair, Dubrow had seen smaller terminal rooms on floors above and below the main control center. He walked upstairs to a cluster of four computers in a corner office. It was a network control room. He knew that The Lair monitored every communication on its networks, but he didn't care. They'd entered a do-or-die stage of operations. Schwager, Dubrow, Platt, and everybody else had risked too much of their careers to let everything disappear because of a roomful of smart people.

He logged into a standard S2 account using a password he saw a consultant use over and over again. He watched the keys as the consultant typed. After three times, he knew the password. His only hope was that the consultant wasn't currently logged on. There was a good chance after the briefing they'd just experienced. Meetings usually follow such a heavy load.

Dubrow breathed with relief. The consultant was not logged on. Dubrow entered the system and opened a note panel. He needed to send it and hide.

He didn't know where he'd hide. If they found him, they would kill him. They rescued the Solvang executives. They managed to get the kids out of The Keep. Dubrow swallowed. He typed desperately.

Dubrow from DoD party. At alternate control site. Escaped to remote terminal. Site location still unknown. (Blindfolded transfer). CIA knows about Legacy, code, Zhang, entire plan. Only hope is destruction of alternate site and all personnel. Will send signaling information ASAP.

11

ASSAULT

"Finally!" Kleewein said. "Some good news. Check this out everybody!" It was early in the morning as they entered the fourth week of the Year 2000.

Mark and consultants ran to his terminal. They could use some good news. It was a note from the power grid team in Nebraska. "They have completed localized testing of grid capacity in New Mexico. Pacific Gas & Electric teams estimate that power in California will be back up within a few days. The Con Edison teams think they can have power to the northeast within one week. The rest of the country should follow shortly thereafter. We're going to have electricity!"

The room erupted into applause. "Excellent!" Mark said to anybody near him. "Excellent news!"

"Now," Kleewein said, "aren't you glad we didn't move everybody to the military effort?"

"Yes I am."

He returned to his work terminal to send a note to Nikolaas Groen at The Keep. Nikolaas lead code conversion efforts for the power grid team, and had expressed concern that when they completed their grid work, they'd need to move immediately onto another project. Partly because there was so much to do, but partly because consultants could not afford to appear idle with the hostile force peering over their shoulders.

On the S3D network, Mark typed a note to Nikolaas and copied other power grid managers and military managers.

Nikolaas, congratulations on your success with the power grid! Finally,
light is on the way. To fill your time, I want to allocate your code
conversion team to the military effort. It is critical and an enormous
task. I'll let you know details as they develop.

"That's not the only team popping champagne!" a consultant
announced. Everybody looked at him. "I just received a note from
the telecom team at The Keep."

Mark and Kleewein ran across the room for another batch of
hope. The consultant continued. "The Lucent, Nortel, and Siemens
teams have revived several major networks of electronic switching
systems. They've tested them with auxiliary power and say the
results are promising. The other teams are not far behind. AT&T
thinks its entire network can be ready to go on a limited call basis
within three days."

Again, the room thundered with applause.

Mark's voice rose above the clamor of smiles and back slapping.
"If we can get electricity and telecommunications back up, we can
get gasoline into the transportation system and start delivering food
to people. We might have the big three back on track by the end of
January."

Another cheer sounded across the room. Even Pritchett and the
DoD party got caught in the commotion. Hartmire allowed a smile,
though he remained staunchly at his post near the terminal room
door.

Lauer walked in, a grim look on his face. He spoke loudly into
Hartmire's ear, barely communicating above the festivity. Hartmire
raised his hands into the air. "May I have your attention," he said.

A few people in front heard him and told a few others who told
a few more until the room stared at Hartmire, laughter reduced to
smiles.

"Vince Dubrow's guard was found slain in the men's room.
Dubrow is missing. We need to check the email logs to make sure
he hasn't communicated our location outside this building. If he
alerts them to our location, then we've got to fight a battle right
here. How many fronts do we want in this war?"

The smiles disappeared. Pritchett's face froze on his skull, looks
of disbelief and rage competing for dominance.

Hartmire continued talking. "We are beginning a complete site
search for Dubrow. When we find him, and we will, we'll bring
him here for questioning."

"Good," Pritchett barked. He turned to Mark. "How soon can we have those power grid and telecommunications work teams transferred to the military?"

"The power grid code conversion team can transfer right away. Their job is finished. Nikolaas Groen leads that effort from The Keep and, unfortunately, work conditions aren't the greatest over there."

"No, of course not. But the extra resources will help."

"Absolutely. The Keep is the fastest code processing facility in the country. As long as Schwager doesn't make a move, they will accelerate the military preparations."

"Thank God. They need all the acceleration they can get."

JANUARY 23, 2000

After sending his initial note to The Keep, Vince Dubrow had set up a timed delivery for a note to leave The Lair early the next morning. He knew Solvang would quickly catch on to his escape, and then watch every email leaving the building. He needed a way to trick them so he could make his escape, and he thought he found it. The timed email delivery read:

> Dubrow at alternate site. Will launch flare from rooftop at 1200 hours. Proceed with attack.

He saved the email in a file on one of The Lair's servers, where it would wait until its delivery the next morning.

Then he fled the room. He needed to find flares and a suitable place to hide. Schwager discussed this possibility with him long in advance. Schwager had known something about an alternate site, but not its location or its capabilities. Dubrow was to be a plant to learn about the alternate site. Dubrow thought he would eventually overhear the location from Mark and Kleewein. He had no idea that they would all be swept from The Keep to the alternate site. He should have reported its location long before now, but he could not get away from his assigned guard to go to the restroom, much less send email or talk on the phone.

To prepare for the possible interception of his email, Dubrow had already planned with Schwager that any communications indicating a time of alert were to be preceded by two hours. Thus, by 1200, Dubrow would have already fired flares two hours prior. The forces would already be in place for an assault on The Lair. Surprise leads to wonderful advantages.

Dubrow walked to the emergency supply closet on the first floor. It was near the entrance from the parking structure, a place empty nearly all the time during Y2K. Only Hartmire guards coming and going from the trucks passed by. The closet was unlocked for quick access to the emergency supplies. Dubrow opened the door and searched for flares.

In a heavy plastic carrying case, he found a gun and ten flares. He closed the case. He grabbed a coil of rope, a flashlight, and a toolbox. He closed the door and walked quickly up the stairwell to the top floor of the building.

He knew he could not escape the building as the situation stood. Hartmire had the place locked up tight as an airdrum. Lower windows were screened so nobody could see in or out. Dubrow's only chance was to wait for the attack on The Lair, and get away after the building was wrecked. If he could survive the assault, he might live through the whole ordeal. He had the rope. If he got trapped on a high floor, he would climb down.

He could see out the windows on the top floor. He saw a small town, nothing at all like the area around the main headquarters. There were little shops out one side of the building, a field on the other, and green hills turning to mountains out the remaining two sides.

He wondered if he was anywhere near The Keep. The drive hadn't seemed long enough to go too far, but he feared that the Chinese would not be able to drive to The Lair in time. They would be coming from San Francisco airport if they hadn't moved the vehicles. Maybe even further if they had. With only a two-hour time slot to work with, they might be cutting it close.

There was nothing he could do about it. Chau flew in the firepower and expected to use it.

Dubrow found an electrical room past some empty offices. He entered it and closed the door behind him. The flashlight revealed thick cables running to the ceiling, where they disappeared behind a metal panel. He used the electrical rack as a ladder to climb to the panel. It was held in place by six screws.

He held the flashlight in his mouth while he worked the screwdriver from the toolbox. He took all six screws out and gently lowered the panel. He stuck his head into the hole. There was a crawl space of roughly two feet. The room was near the edge of the building, so there was a solid edge for him to rest on.

He pushed the toolbox, rope coil, and flare case into the ceiling hole. He pulled himself up, careful to avoid knocking too much dust and debris into the room below. Once inside the ceiling, he braced his legs on two support beams. He reached through the hole for the panel and pulled it up the electrical cables until it neared the ceiling. He reached one hand under the panel to hold it at a small angle while he fed two screws through the ceiling holes into metal. They would come through in the wrong direction, but would look fine with a casual glance in the dark.

He scooted to the solid edge, stirring dust as he went. It invaded his nose and throat, choking him, causing him to sneeze. He buried his face in the crook of his elbow to muffle the sound. When the dust settled, he scooted the last few feet to the edge, then settled in for the night.

He illuminated his analog watch. The alarm would go off at 0900 hours. That would give him one hour to get into place and fire the flares at 1000 hours. The watch set, he settled against the wall.

He would not be able to sleep, but he would be as quiet as a dead man.

JANUARY 24, 2000

The terminal operators in front of Susan received the notes from Dubrow. Only they would see them. Only they monitored the special account they had managed to establish at The Keep. They printed the notes and carried them upstairs to Schwager and Chau.

Schwager looked over the notes. "Finally," Schwager said, relief crossing his face. "Now we can get moving again." He turned to Chau. "Call San Francisco immediately. Give them the information."

Chau blandly watched Schwager's optimism. The man had no idea. Chau spoke Chinese into the radio. A response came back in Chinese. Chau spoke again, and that was all.

"What did you say?" Schwager asked.

"I told them to get in the air by 9:30 AM and look for a flare at 10:00. They will mark the location and radio back to the ground crew. The ground crew will drive the tank to meet our trucks at the alternate site and destroy it."

McCrostie found a cozy place to park the truck above Saratoga. He and the SEAL team could watch everything around The Lair, and enjoy an idyllic view of the town at the same time.

The first day, they watched intently. Nothing happened. The building sat, the sun moved across the sky, it got dark. Nobody came and nobody went. Same with the second day, third, and fourth.

Such was the life of a SEAL. A lot of waiting for something to happen. When it does happen, it usually happens big. Either the SEAL has an adventure to tell, or he's dead.

"Think anything will happen today?" Archer asked on the fifth morning. They sat on lush grass with their binoculars. They didn't need binoculars to see the building, but the extra detail didn't hurt anything.

"No," McCrostie said, staring across the valley. "But I think we're going to get wet. Look at those clouds."

Archer and the others had already noticed. "It's that time of year," Dietz said. "That's the reason it's so green now."

McCrostie felt a blade of grass. He looked back at The Lair through his binoculars. Nothing moved. Nobody made any noise. "I'm hungry. Somebody pass me an MRE. Let's get this picnic underway."

"We've got two notes from Dubrow," the consultant announced. "One was sent last night just after the CIA briefing. The other left this morning at 6:00 AM. Both went to an address not in our records. It's located at The Keep. They must have established their own account."

He scrolled to the next note in the gateway archive. "He said he's going to launch flares from the rooftop at noon."

"Where were the notes sent from?" Hartmire asked.

"Last night's came from the network control room upstairs. This morning's came from the same place, but it wasn't sent at that time. Hold on a second." He clicked a few buttons and scrolled through a text file. "Aha, this was a timed delivery. He saved it to be sent this morning. It was actually written just after the one last night."

"Allowing him to be far from any terminals when we detected it."

"Yes. He hasn't been near a computer since last night."

Hartmire contained his anger at not being able to find Dubrow. He was somewhere in the building, but they had already looked everywhere.

"Elwell," he said. "Take your guards and head immediately to the rooftop. Shoot Dubrow on site when he arrives. We can't let him launch those flares."

Elwell ran from the terminal room.

JANUARY 23, 2000

Dan Van Lan didn't expect FBI agents to look as normal as they did. They flew Dan to Boston, then rushed to a plain building in an industrial complex east of the city. There was no name on the outside.

"This is Legacy Solutions?" Dan asked.

"This is it," the driver said. "Not much of a place to make such a fuss over."

"I guess not."

The front door was held open by FBI agents in blue jackets. Dan and the team were escorted by the lead agent down an empty white hallway to a terminal room filled with more agents and several engineers who looked like they'd been plucked off their couches while eating popcorn during a football game. The engineers sat in the center of the room, handcuffed, and bewildered. Portable generators ran loudly near the windows, their exhaust hoses flowing outside. Computers behind the engineers were plugged into the generator power strip.

"Your job is just to get what you need," the lead agent told Dan. "We'll deal with any criminal wrongdoing later. So don't waste time asking if they knew what kind of trouble they were causing and so on. It's irrelevant to your purpose. Then we'll get you out of here. A lot of important people want you in other places."

Dan sat across from the engineers. He removed the code printouts from his briefcase. "We know about this," he said. "We know that there is a fourth file or an application that supplies the necessary parameters. Where is the code we need to make this work?"

"The code we wrote is right here. I have no idea what you mean by fourth file or application. They brought us the problem and we fixed it. Why are you accusing—"

"Quiet!" an agent yelled. "Just answer the man's questions."

Dan looked at the agent fiercely. He believed the engineer. "I understand," Dan said. "All I need is the file that will make this software work." He rattled the printout.

"If you uncuff me, I can run the computers to show you what I have. I'll cooperate. Like I said, I didn't even know there was trouble here."

Dan nodded. "Uncuff him, please." The agents uncuffed the engineer. "Now, let's move quickly."

The engineer turned around to his computer and typed commands into the system. A development environment appeared onscreen, similar to what Dan had seen at other corporations. "This is where we worked—"

"Spare me the tour," Dan said. "Get to the code."

"Fine."

The man clicked his way through several windows showing the same information on Dan's printouts. "Those screens contained everything supplied to us by the military. We were supposed to write code that took satellite data and returned it to the software in a useable format."

"Stop," Dan said. He looked at the code onscreen. It wasn't everything they'd found at Pearl Harbor, just the third layer. Whomever organized this did a thorough job. Legacy had no idea what they were developing. The second and first layers were never shown to Legacy. "Do you have any idea what this software is supposed to do?"

"No," the man said. "It was a defense contract and we weren't supposed to know anything more than that. It was the old 'we could tell you but then we'd have to kill you.' Evidently it wasn't a joke."

"No, and it wasn't the military. Show me what you wrote."

The man brought up a listing of files. "These files are the same program written in a bunch of different languages. Old languages that nobody uses anymore, except us."

"Like what?" Dan asked. "NELIAC, TACPOL, and so on?"

"Yes," the engineer said, surprised. "All the software does is take inputs from the satellite communication network and massage it to work with the software they supplied to us. That's it. There's nothing cloak and dagger about it. It's a bunch of numbers and dates and times. Big deal."

"Look around you," Dan said. "Dates and times have become a very big deal."

"I see that now."

"Show me the code."

The man switched to a different view on his screen. A window opened, filled with gibberish to a casual observer. "Each file is about two million lines of code."

"Jesus," Dan said, glad they found it instead of needing to rewrite it on their own. "Have you tested it?"

"Of course. Every file works perfectly against the files they supplied us."

Dan pulled a data tape from his briefcase. "This is the third layer from Pearl, the same code you were given. I want to run the files against this code, straight from Pearl."

He handed over the tape. The man slid it into the tape drive, loaded it onto the computer, then opened two windows side by side.

The test ran error free. "Excellent," Dan said. "Now I need every one of those files copied onto two tapes."

"Fine." The man pulled two blank tapes from his desk drawer, copied the files onto them, and handed them to Dan. "You have everything we worked on. Can we go home now?"

"That's not my department," Dan said, standing. He gestured to the agents. "That's their department. I've got to get to the Pentagon."

JANUARY 24, 2000

Dubrow did not need his alarm. He was awake the entire night, checking his watch every hour. He turned the alarm off just before 9:00, and crawled back to the metal panel. Part of him recoiled from it, wondering if he'd unscrew his way into a room full of Hartmire guards waiting to kill him. He worked the screws out. He edged his feet through the hole to the electrical rack. He retrieved the flare and rope. He wouldn't need the toolbox anymore. He left the panel off as well.

He moved quickly to the window facing the town of Saratoga.

It was the window closest to San Jose, where the Chinese would be looking from.

At 10:00, he used the flare case to break the window. The glass was sturdy. It took three smashes with the case to finally send shards into the fresh air, falling like water to the grass below. He listened for the running feet of guards. None came.

He loaded a flare into the gun. He reached his hand out the window and pointed the gun toward the sky. He pulled the trigger. A puff of air rushed over his hand and the flare shot skyward like a model rocket. He pressed his cheek to the glass to watch its trajectory. It rose for ten seconds, then exploded in a plume of fire and debris.

He loaded another flare and fired it, then a third, then a fourth. He stuffed the gun into its case and retreated back to the electrical room. He didn't hear guards. Nobody knew he'd fired the flares. Dubrow smiled to himself.

The C-130 is an enormous plane, not the sort usually taken into the air on a recon mission. But the Chinese had little choice. They couldn't fit helicopters inside the C-130, and they didn't have enough time to send smaller aircraft on boats. Schwager had arranged for the seven American pickups to be waiting for them at the airport.

The C-130 flew out of San Francisco airport at 9:25. The pilot circled high above Silicon Valley, his crew watching in all directions. Chau could not tell them where the flare would come from. They were high enough to see it fired from just about anywhere in the valley. If it was fired outside the valley, they would miss it and experience the unfortunate duty of calling Chau with bad news.

At 10:00 AM, eyes watched in every direction. The pilot saw the first flare. It exploded near the green hills on the west side of the valley. He angled the plane and dove toward the flare.

A second flare exploded, confirming that they had the right vicinity. He leveled out, circling with a strong angle, allowing maximum viewing through the side window. He instructed the navigator and flight engineer to use binoculars for a better view.

A third flare exploded, eliciting chatter from the men watching through the windows. They were almost sure it came from the office building near the field and green hills. It seemed unlikely, given the small town around it, but that's what they'd seen. The fourth explosion made up their minds.

The pilot turned north, heading back to San Francisco Airport. He radioed Chau, happy to be the one to deliver the news.

McCrostie saw the rain clouds coming closer across the valley. It didn't bother him. They were trained from day one to work best in and around water.

"What's that noise?" Sweeny asked.

All four of them tensed, ears alert and muscles ready for anything. In the distance, they heard a rumble.

"An aircraft."

"It's a big one."

The SEAL team scattered instinctively under the trees. The truck was hidden under a thick stand of pine.

They listened. They could not see a plane. McCrostie pointed his binoculars through the branches at the sky. Something exploded above The Lair.

"Signal flare," Archer reported immediately.

The rumble of the plane came closer. "It's the C-130 from San Francisco," McCrostie said. He watched it in his binoculars. Another flare exploded above The Lair.

"Sweeny, get on a Stinger."

Sweeny scrambled to the Stinger missile launcher.

"I'd be real surprised if they attack with that thing," McCrostie said, "but let's be ready for anything."

Two more flares exploded and the plane turned back north toward San Francisco. Sweeny crouched tensely behind the loaded Stinger.

"The picnic's over, gentlemen," McCrostie said, taking the binoculars from his eyes. "Sweeny, stay on that Stinger. Archer, take the other launcher, load another Stinger. Dietz, man the loaded Dragon. I'll load the other Dragon."

Pritchett was the only one to hear Recluse calling over the milsat radio. He grabbed it up quickly, not wanting to alert Mark. Recluse was not to establish radio contact except for dire emergencies. Just hearing the call weakened Pritchett's joints.

"Lair," he said. His Hartmire guard listened carefully.

"Recluse," McCrostie said. "A C-130 just buzzed your location and saw four signal flares. We have a bad feeling."

"We can't evacuate. There's too much work to do."

"Then be prepared for trouble. We're watching, but have no idea what's on the way. We'll keep you posted."

Pritchett's guard began to say something, when a radio beat him to it. Elwell's voice came through the main terminal room to Hartmire, Lauer, and Klepac.

"We just saw four flares!" he blurted. "They were launched from the side of the building."

The brain trust turned from their terminals at the commotion. All ears listened to the report.

"Already?" Hartmire asked. "It's not supposed to happen for another two hours. Launched from the side of the building, too. The whole note was a decoy."

"There's more. A plane flew overhead. We couldn't see what kind of plane, but it sounded big. I'm sure it saw the flares."

"Goddammit!" Hartmire yelled, flipping the switch on his hip pack. He spoke to Klepac, Lauer, and into the headset microphone simultaneously. He wanted every guard to hear what was happening.

"The flares have already been launched! Dubrow still has not been found. Lauer, take your guards and fan out across the grounds surrounding The Lair. Elwell, remain on the rooftop to watch for Dubrow and keep an eye out for airplanes. Klepac, commence another search inside the building for Dubrow."

Guards ran in all directions. The consultants looked back and forth at each other. Evacuation crossed everybody's mind but it would be just as dangerous outside. As a whole, they turned back to their terminals. There was work to be done.

Elwell and his men crouched behind the rooftop railing on every side of the building. Their hearts pounded in the quiet prerain. There was no fog. If only there had been fog, the flares would not have worked.

"Sir!" a guard called across the rooftop. "We hear something."

Elwell ran to their location overlooking Saratoga. He could hear it too. Engines. "Have you seen them?"

"No, we can only hear them."

He spoke into his headset microphone. "Hartmire, this is Elwell. We hear trucks approaching. No visual confirmation yet, but they're not far away."

"Stay on the roof," Hartmire replied. "Get your men on the Saratoga side. Be ready to fire. Lauer, can you hear the trucks?"

"We just now heard them."

"Get your men to cover on the Saratoga side of the building. Be prepared to fire at the first sign of a hostile vehicle. If they're here, they mean business."

"Ten-four."

"Klepac, forget Dubrow for now. Take your men to the parking garage and get into two trucks. Be ready to drive from the parking structure into a firefight. When they hit us, I want to hit them harder in return."

"Ten-four."

"Remaining guards in the building, return to the main terminal room. You'll join me in protecting the consultants and DoD contingent. This room is the heart of our operation."

Elwell heard a different noise. Instead of the high-pitched labor of truck engines, it sounded like a tractor. He heard treads grinding across pavement. The engine paused, then accelerated, then paused again, idling loudly like a bulldozer at a construction site. Elwell's mouth went dry.

"Hartmire, they've got a piece of heavy equipment."

Hartmire took a quick breath. "What kind of heavy equipment?"

"Sounds like a tractor or a tank."

"Jesus Christ. Can you see it?"

"Not yet. Wait a second, something's coming out of the trees in the neighborhood. It's a tank. Oh hell, Jules. They're driving a tank at us."

"Stay your ground. Fire on any people you can see."

The main terminal room at The Lair was located on the side of the building opposite the Saratoga neighborhoods. Nonetheless, a tank would demolish the entire building in two, maybe three shots.

The guards in the room—who also wore headsets and heard Elwell's report—stared at Hartmire in horror.

"Everybody," Hartmire said, "we need to evacuate to the basement. There's a tank approaching the building."

"What?" Kleewein said.

"No time for disbelief. Let's go! Everybody to the basement."

The terminal room cleared in record time. Pritchett grabbed his milsat radio. Chairs overturned as consultants and terminal operators stood and charged for the doors.

Mark ran to the conference room to grab Grandma Solvang and the kids. "Come on!" he yelled. "We're being attacked!"

Hartmire guards led the way to the stairwell, down past the parking structure, into the cold basement. Mark and Jeremiah helped Grandma Solvang. Alyssa held Kleewein's hand.

"Recluse to Lair, come in Lair," Pritchett's radio cackled.

"Who is that?" Hartmire demanded.

"The SEAL team." Pritchett spoke into the radio. "Lair, go ahead Recluse."

"You must evacuate the building immediately," McCrostie said. "There is a T-63 tank and two trucks with soldiers and tripod-mounted machine guns heading your way."

"Ten-four. We're evacuating."

Hartmire spoke into his headset, eyeing Pritchett the whole time. "We are moving out the back side of The Lair into the field. We will work our way onto the hillside for cover in the trees."

Klepac, Lauer, and Elwell copied the message. The consultants and DoD contingent streamed up the stairwell out the door into the parking structure. Klepac and his men sat in two pickup trucks idling, pointed at the gate. Hartmire guards led the brain trust past them through the rear door.

The guards ran everybody across the wet green field behind The Lair. They cringed in the wide open, expecting shells to drop around them at any moment, or machine gun fire to strafe them from a hidden cluster of soldiers in the trees.

No shells or bullets came. Hartmire kept everybody running onto the hillside, farther up and away from The Lair. They crouched behind trees and rocks. Below to the right, they saw two trucks and the tank thunder out of the neighborhood.

"Dad, is that a tank?" Jeremiah asked, eyes wide.

"Yes."

None of the civilians had never seen a tank before. Nineteen tons of steel rolled heavily on two tracks. The khaki, green, and gray camouflage pattern on its body seemed straight out of a *Newsweek* photo, not something they would see in Saratoga. It was twice as long as a truck. Its turret turned toward the building as it drove relentlessly forward. The tank's 85-millimeter cannon could blow the faces off Mount Rushmore, and it was aiming at The Lair.

"Where's an M1 Abrams when you need it?" Pritchett asked.

The trucks drove around the sides of the tank. Tripods stuck to the roofs of the pickups and two men operated machine guns. They blasted the building in a cloud of bullets and debris. Elwell gave the instruction to fire. The meager pop and crackle from the rooftop was lost in the roar of the machine guns and the tank's rolling cacophony. The Chinese saw Elwell's men, and pointed the machine guns at the roof.

Two violent bursts of bullets flew from the machine guns at a rate of 700 rounds per second. Elwell's men were blown back from the edge of the roof, gaping, bloody holes ripped into their chests and heads. Elwell fired two shots in return before taking a round in the neck and another in the forehead. He died before he hit the rooftop beside his men.

"Do you have a clear shot?" McCrostie asked Dietz.

"Not yet." Dietz stared down the length of the Dragon missile launcher. "They haven't cleared the surrounding buildings yet."

"Neither do I."

McCrostie watched through the binoculars. The trucks opened machine gun fire at the building. Bits of glass and cement flew in all directions.

The guards on top of the building returned fire. McCrostie shook his head. Bad move. He knew what was coming.

Seconds later, the rooftop erupted into a blast of cement dust, shattered wall braces, twisted metal, and dead bodies. A second burst of shots finished off the last few men.

"They're coming into range," McCrostie said.

Dietz nodded. "They won't be around much longer."

Hartmire yelled into his headset. "Elwell, come in! Are you okay? That looked pretty bad." Nothing came in reply. "Elwell, come in!"

The machine gun fire started again. From their position in the trees, the brain trust could hear the front of the building tearing to pieces.

"Klepac and Lauer, come in!"

"Still here," Lauer said. "We're shooting when we can see past the dust and glass falling. It's not having much effect."

"We're ready to go when you say," Klepac added. "It sounds like living hell out there. Just give the word."

"You don't stand a chance against those—"

His voice was cut short by a sudden blast of force. Two enormous streams of white smoke shot like lightning down the hillside. They curved to the right at the last minute and exploded into the tank. Fire and parts filled the sky on the other side of the building.

"Holy shit!" Lauer screamed across the radio. "What the hell was that? Jules, are you there? Something just blew the tank to pieces. There's nothing left!"

"Klepac, go now!" Hartmire yelled.

Two pickup trucks drove from the parking garage, guns blazing.

"Fire, fire, fire!" Klepac yelled to his men over the radio. They drove straight at the Chinese, who were still off guard from the surprise explosion of their tank.

Klepac's guards killed the machine gunners first and then fired ruthlessly into the beds of the trucks. The drivers tried accelerating out of the line of fire, but Klepac and his guards followed. The hostile drivers carried a cargo of dead bodies.

They whirled around the street in front of The Lair, trying desperately to get away. One tried driving onto the sidewalk and blew a tire against a fire hydrant. Klepac's own truck immediately pulled beside the hapless driver, finishing him off in one volley.

The other truck drove around the scene and started toward the Saratoga neighborhood. Klepac's second truck ground its gears turning around. It looked like the enemy truck would escape.

Just before it rounded the corner to disappear into the neighborhood, another streak of white smoke rocketed down the hillside, made a sharp right turn, and blew the fleeing truck to a million pieces.

"Reload!" McCrostie commanded after the last truck exploded. "I don't want any surprises coming out of the neighborhood."

Dietz was a step ahead of him. He promptly reloaded after each shot. He and McCrostie were down to their last two Dragons. If more than two ground vehicles emerged, Sweeny and Archer would use the Stingers to attack.

McCrostie continued monitoring through his binoculars. Everybody on the roof was dead, a few on the ground were injured from debris, all hostiles were dead. It appeared to him that everybody inside the building had escaped to the hillside in time.

"Looks like I was wrong," he said. "It wasn't another boring day after all."

"Klepac, Lauer, Elwell, report," Hartmire said into his headset.

"Klepac here. Everybody is fine. All hostiles killed. We're checking the bodies for identification. We will also claim the machine guns."

"Lauer here. I have several injured men, but nothing too critical. We suffered from falling glass and debris from the building. I'm more worried about Elwell than anything. They took heavy gunfire."

Hartmire feared the worst. "Elwell, come in."

Pritchett's radio crackled. "Recluse to Lair, come in."

"Lair," Pritchett said hoarsely. "Go ahead."

"Is everybody alive and well?"

"The critical management team is fine. We haven't confirmed the health of all guards yet."

McCrostie's voice didn't come right away. There was a hesitation, a long pause, a gathering of thought. "Roger. We'll keep watch from up here." Another pause. "I wish we'd been able to fire sooner."

"Roger that, Recluse. Thanks for the help."

Hartmire sprinted back to The Lair. Elwell hadn't responded yet. There wasn't any movement on the roof.

Klepac's men parked the trucks in the garage while Hartmire ran past to the stairwell. Halfway up the first flight, Vince Dubrow bounded directly into him.

"Oh no," Dubrow said in a high voice.

Hartmire pulled his pistol and placed the barrel on Dubrow's forehead. "You come with me. We're going to the roof."

They emerged into the cool air, the smell of gunfire and explosion still heavy. Hartmire guards lay in heaps across the roof. Some of their mouths were agape, some eyes open, some peaceful looking as babies.

Every one was dead.

Elwell lay crumpled against one of his men, a thick pool of blood under the hole in his neck. His face was drawn, almost sad. Jules Hartmire bit his lip.

"You," he snarled at Dubrow, "come with me."

He took the trembling officer to the back edge of the roof overlooking the field. He clutched Dubrow's hair and jerked his head toward the roof.

"Do you see this?" he yelled. "Do you see all of these men? They had families. That one over there, Eric Elwell, was my friend. Do you see?"

Dubrow nodded, tears streaming down his cheeks.

"Do you know why these men died here today? Do you? Because you sold out your country in its greatest time of need. People are without electricity, and medicine, and food. China is invading Pearl Harbor. This building was busy with people trying to save the United States. And you told their enemies where to find them so that my friend and all of these men would die trying to save them! Has that sunk into your brain yet?"

Dubrow nodded. More tears squeezed onto his cheeks.

"Good," Hartmire said, leveling the pistol on Dubrow's forehead. "Then you know why I'm going to kill you."

He pulled the trigger. The bullet sent Dubrow flipping end over end to the grass below, where his body would be left to decay.

The rain clouds finally gave way, cleaning blood from the streets of Saratoga and the rooftop. Hartmire carried Elwell inside. Other guards had arrived to carry the rest of the men. The squeak of wet footsteps echoed down the stairwell.

Jules Hartmire wept.

Klepac entered the main terminal room, eyes wide, heart still pounding. His left forearm bled from bomb shrapnel that flew into the open truck window.

"Hartmire," Klepac spoke into his headset, "we have an enemy radio. They're asking for a report."

Hartmire walked in, wet from the rain, eyes red. His chest rose and fell in sturdy breaths. Elwell's blood soaked his sleeves and hands. "Tell them everybody is dead and that we're coming for the rest of them."

Pritchett walked over. "What's going on?"

"All your people are dead," Klepac spoke into the radio. "We're coming for the rest of you."

"Careful," Pritchett said. "You don't want them killing everybody inside The Keep. They're desperate."

"More than thirty of their people are dead," Hartmire said. "They're down to two pickup trucks. They can't threaten this position anymore. If they think we're coming there, they'll evacuate. There's no longer a reason for them to remain."

"It's dangerous."

Hartmire stepped closer, showing his hands to the group. "This whole business is dangerous." He turned to Klepac. "Tell them we destroyed their tank with missiles, we killed all their men, and we're coming for the rest of them."

Klepac delivered the message.

The radio crackled. "You will never get the code solution if any harm comes to us."

Mark called from his chair. "Tell them we've already got people at Legacy Conversion. The solution is ours."

Klepac repeated it. The radio remained silent.

"Tell them we're going to the airport to missile their plane," Hartmire said. "That'll get them moving."

Chau thought quickly. They needed to leave right away, but they couldn't lose the diversion of the He Zhang battle group. The U.S. was not scared enough yet. They needed more convincing so they would concentrate on the incoming ships.

"Schwager, gather the men and go to the trucks. We need to leave for the airport."

"What are you talking about?"

"They destroyed the tank and two assault trucks. They are

coming here and to the airport to destroy the plane. We must leave now or we will lose everything."

"They're bluffing."

Chau looked into Schwager's unknowing eyes. The deep ravines on the man's cheeks were perpetually filled with moisture, creating shiny lines like open wounds. "It does not matter if they are bluffing. There is no reason for us to remain any longer."

"What about the gold?"

"The gold is going to ships. We can just as easily coordinate the effort from another location."

Schwager realized at once that he was not in control. There was no longer an American component needed in their plan. The demands had been delivered, the U.S. resisted, and Chau was leaving. Schwager did not trust Chau. He felt uneasy about leaving the country with Chau. "We should kill everybody at this site."

"No time." Chau was already heading for the door. His personal guards followed. He spoke Chinese into a radio. Schwager caught up.

"What did you say?"

"I told the battle group to move forward at full speed and immediately engage. The U.S. does not believe that the group intends to attack. The time to strike is now. America is still crippled, still needs the code solution."

"And they still have the gold."

Chau managed a last look at Schwager. So pathetic. They would keep him around for the time being, just in case his connections were needed again. But after that his life wouldn't be worth a boat load of gold. It would be worth a single bullet.

"Correct," Chau hissed, "they still have the gold." The rest of the sentence he spoke under his breath.

"And they always will."

April Pennington finished plotting the latest data from her brief satellite glimpse of the He Zhang. She measured the distance between dots.

"Uh oh," she said, double checking the distance against previous measurements. "Pete," she called across the room, "they're speeding up again."

"How much?" he called back.

"A lot. They're heading to flank."

"Same course?"

"Yes. They're driving to Hawaii. I think they mean business this time."

"So do I. Pearl Harbor managed to pick up a radio signal from the U.S. mainland." He spoke loudly across the room while he continued pulling tiny bits of data from the few satellites orbiting above the China seas.

"I thought communications were entirely down."

"They were, but they're slowly getting repaired. They didn't catch the whole signal, but they intercepted part that said to immediately engage."

She looked at the dot spacing. The He Zhang was coming just north of Wake Island. Only 2,300 miles to reach Hawaii. At full speed, which seemed to be twenty-five knots according to earlier readings, the He Zhang would reach Hawaii in a little more than three days. She walked to Dubridge's work station.

"Pete, they'll reach Hawaii in three days."

He looked at her, his face a collection of strain. "I know. And that's not all we have to worry about."

"What else?"

"Take a look at this." He pointed to grainy satellite photos. "This one is the East China Sea, just off the coast of Tanshui, Taiwan. This one is the Taiwan Strait off Changhua. This one is the island of Quemoy."

The photos spoke for themselves. Pennington had never seen such a display of force. Warships filled the sea at Tanshui and Changhua. At Quemoy, ships lined the coast, and vehicles covered the shore. "They invaded Taiwan while we weren't looking."

"We couldn't look for a while because of our blind spots, then you're right, we just weren't looking. We watched this He Zhang group speed up and slow down until its final push to Hawaii."

"We had our priorities straight. Defending against an invasion of our own land is more important than defending Taiwan."

"Maybe. But it's not just Taiwan. Look at Spratly." He slid two additional photos into view. "This is near the Trident Shoal, and this is between Thitu Island and Subi Reef."

There were so many ships around the islands that the photos looked almost like land shots. The resolution was grainy—as it always was on the second-tier and third-tier satellite networks—but Pennington could see a Hegu fast attack boat and a Jianghu guided missile frigate. The other ships were just shapes nearby. Lots of shapes.

"Do you think we're too late?" she asked.

"I don't know. I don't see how we could have been on time. We still haven't dealt with the He Zhang. Whoever planned this sneak attack did a brilliant job."

"I need to call everything in. I'll report the acceleration of the He Zhang and the invasion of Taiwan and the Spratly Islands. This is not going to be a fun call to make."

Susan sat at her terminal, the men in plain clothes watching her every move, the terminal operators in front of her typing away. She could no longer tell what they worked on. She didn't recognize any of the screens.

"Yes?" one of the men said into his headset.

Susan looked over her shoulder. The man listened intently, nodding, eyes concerned. He looked to the others, then spoke into the microphone. "Follow me."

The plain clothes men and terminal operators stood and grabbed Susan. The guards from the back of the room ran forward. "Come on," one said to Susan.

She jerked from their grip. "I'm not going," she said defiantly. The room froze. "I have real work to do."

A guard put a pistol to her forehead. "Get moving now."

"No. My place is here. This is my company and these are my people. I don't have to flee."

The guard pushed the muzzle hard. "If you don't get—"

Susan heard a crackle in the guard's earpiece. His expression changed. "We're on our way," he blurted into his microphone. They all turned and ran from the room.

Susan looked around at the consultants, all of whom looked at each other and to their managers. Nikolaas Groen caught Susan's eye. He smiled at her and exhaled long.

Susan fell into her chair at the terminal. She brought up a note screen and fired a note to everybody on the S3D network.

Hostiles left lower terminal room at once. No monitoring. We have
control of The Keep.

"They're leaving," Kleewein said. "Susan is back on line and just
sent this note." He showed his screen to Mark, Pritchett, and
Hartmire.

"They'll go to the plane," Hartmire said. "We've got to stop
them."

"You can't stop them," Pritchett told him. "You need to get these
people back to The Keep, if it's safe. The He Zhang has accelerated
again. They'll reach Hawaii in three days. We have got to get this
entire organization working on the military."

"We can't let Schwager get away," Mark said.

"We're not planning to." He picked up the milsat radio. "Lair to
Recluse, come in."

"Recluse here. Go ahead."

"Hostiles have left Solvang headquarters. We assume they're
heading to the plane to hightail it out of here. It would sure be nice
to keep that from happening."

"Roger, Lair. It sure would. What do you have in mind?"

"This area seems clear now. Hartmire guards will oversee the
safe transport of the executive team to their headquarters. Can you
get to the airport and make sure the C-130 never sees flight?"

"That's affirmative. She's at San Francisco airport. We can be
there in forty minutes."

"You'd best get moving. The hostiles are already en route."

JANUARY 25, 2000

Billy Stamp was tired. His eyes seemed to have sunk far into his
head, dark around the edges. Even with the extra help from the
nation's top hardware teams—Mercury, Atlantic, Lucent, Texas
Instruments, and Analog Devices—they were still days away from
a fighting military. Now the latest reports from Guam said they didn't
have days. Robek had called another briefing. Everybody was sure
the Admiral would send the emergency battle group to sea as is.
That prospect left Billy aghast.

He stood in the Combat Information Center on the *Chosin*. The

CIC housed the ship's warfighting brain, where officers would normally tabulate radar contacts and incoming missiles and torpedoes in the water. At this rate, a pair of binoculars out the window would reveal more information.

Captain Lewis Bailey walked in. "How are we coming along?"

"Slowly." Billy was tired of sprucing up his answers. They were working their hardest and it was still slow going. There was nothing he could do about it.

"Are the backup missiles on the way?"

"Yes. They should be here this afternoon."

"Thank goodness. It's doubtful that we'll have any of the newer models functional."

"That's true. At this point it's doubtful."

Bailey squinted at Billy. "Are you all right, son?"

"I'll be fine. I'm just frustrated."

"We're all frustrated. Admiral Robek called another briefing and I've got a bad feeling about it. Why don't you walk over with me?"

"Thank you. I will."

The now-familiar briefing room in Pearl Harbor didn't fill with chatter as it had at the first meeting. The excitement had worn off. Y2K meant long hours, trial and error, greasy compartments on ships and submarines, and an increasingly high risk of going to war with no way to fight. The situation had become all too real.

Admiral Robek and Rear Admiral Macey stood at the front of the room. Billy left Captain Bailey and walked to them.

The Admiral whispered to Billy. "Mr. Stamp, it looks like we'll be taking you up on your offer to accompany the ships to sea. That time is at hand."

"I knew it would be. I'm prepared to go."

"Most of your crew needs to stay behind to prepare the main battle groups."

"We're also flying in my east coast counterpart. He's been at this job even longer than I have."

"Dan Van Lan," Macey said.

"Yes. He'll lead the repairs in port while I'm at sea."

Admiral Robek looked admiringly at Billy Stamp. There was no way the young man could know what it meant to be at sea. But he knew that it would not be good, and he was going anyway. Billy reminded Admiral Robek of so many other young men he'd known in his career. They were the world's finest, yet few people would ever know their names.

He walked before the assembly. "Good morning. You all know by now of the latest reports from Guam. The He Zhang battle group has accelerated to flank speed on a direct course for Hawaii. Ladies and gentlemen, we are out of time. The civilian work crews assigned to the forward battle group will remain with those ships. They are the destroyers *Ingersoll, John Young,* and *Harry Hill;* the submarine *Olympia;* and the cruiser *Chosin.* The rest of the ships in port will undergo further repairs. Hopefully, the initial battle group will dispatch with the threat and we will have months to continue the repairs. However, in case additional ships are needed, the work in port will continue at the current emergency pace. William Stamp will be heading out to sea on the *Chosin.* He will be replaced in port by his superior, Daniel Van Lan, who arrives this afternoon."

The room looked at him in stern concentration. "The forward battle group departs at 1300 hours, full speed toward the He Zhang. If all courses and speeds remain constant, that places contact at around 0900 hours day after tomorrow. We have limited communications in place. That's all I have. Let's wish our departing sailors fair winds and following seas."

The room broke apart, faces grave. Brosseau remained seated next to Morey. "You need to head into battle at 1300 hours today? That's ridiculous. Are you ready?"

Morey held his chin. "We've made some progress, but no, we're not ready by any means. I need to steer my torpedoes the entire way to the target. Not a single Mk 48 works. We're reduced to battery-powered Mk 44s on 3,000-foot guidewires. We have no active sonar, and our passive sonar is audible only. No computer signatures, no lines to compare, no database of known readings, nothing! I'm blind in the water."

Dan tested the code from Legacy Conversions again at the NMCC. Satisfied that it was the right material, he transferred it to Pearl Harbor over the Solvang satellite network.

He typed a quick note to Billy and copied the rest of Solvang on the S3D account.

> I just sent the files from Legacy Conversions. I tested all of them onsite and again at the NMCC. All appear to work! This is a major leap forward for satellite capabilities in the Pacific. Start work on implementing these files immediately. I will be in Pearl soon to help.

JANUARY 24, 2000

Hartmire, Lauer, and Klepac drove cautiously to The Keep. Mark looked at his building and wondered what they would find inside. It looked as it always had: monolithic, hard working, a distinct do-not-disturb exterior. He needed to get inside to Susan.

"Wait here," Hartmire said to Mark and the other civilians. "We don't know what we'll find inside." He signaled to Lauer and Klepac to move ahead with a group of guards. They entered through the front.

"Hartmire, come in," Klepac's voice said on the radio.

"This is Hartmire, go ahead."

"Everything appears to be secure. Consultants are still working in the terminal rooms. The executive suites are empty. Lauer is checking upstairs. A few more minutes and we can officially reclaim this place as our own."

"Excellent."

"This is Lauer. All's well upstairs."

"Good. Place your men in their traditional posts. Klepac, meet me at the front entrance with your men. I want a full escort to the executive work area."

"Roger."

"Dad, I don't want to go in there," Alyssa said.

"You remember this place," Mark said, stooping to carry her. She was no little girl anymore, but he could still hold her like one. "It's going to be okay. We're all with you now. No more bad guys." Even Jeremiah moved closer to his dad.

Inside, they walked through the haunted corridors. They seemed to vibrate with the screams of those who had died. The blood and gunfire could not go away as cleanly as the terrorists.

Klepac double-checked the executive suites. All clear. They

would post guards at the glass doors just in case. Other than that, it could be business as usual.

Mark went to the PA system. He flipped the switch and tapped twice on the microphone.

"This is Mark Solvang. Your executive team is back at the helm." His voice rolled through the hallways into terminal rooms, under doors and over carpets. Speakers above keyboards and monitors delivered the rich voice of Solvang's president.

A cheer pressed the walls of The Keep. Susan stood at her workstation, looking around, gesturing everybody out of their seats. She yelled until tears came from her eyes. Nikolaas Groen charged forward from the back of the room, hugging Susan and screaming for joy. They made it. All systems were go.

Susan ran from the room up the stairwell. She threw open the glass doors to the executive suite and ran to Mark. He enveloped her and fell to the ground, laughing at his own clumsiness. Grandma Solvang and the kids patted at Susan's frail figure as she broke into tears. Mark kissed her.

The SEAL pickup truck screamed up the 101 freeway toward San Francisco airport. McCrostie navigated while Archer drove. In the bed of the truck, Sweeny and Dietz manned the Stinger missiles to destroy the C-130. On the off chance that they caught the hostiles still in ground vehicles, the two remaining Dragons sat loaded and ready to fire.

Rain pelted the two men in the bed of the truck. They wore raingear and barely noticed the water.

The 101 freeway was empty the entire way to San Francisco airport. Archer squealed around the corner of the offramp. He tore past the usual passenger loading zones to a gate broken open by another vehicle. It lead to the runways.

McCrostie was afraid they were too late. If the Chinese maintained radio contact with the C-130, it would have been running and ready to depart the moment the trucks arrived. With no other planes competing for runway space, it would take less than two minutes to get airborne.

McCrostie saw the huge transport plane turning around the far end of the freeway. Once she made the turn, she gunned her four turboprops and shot down the freeway. With no cargo for the ride home, the C-130 would climb at a rate of 1,900 feet per minute.

The pickup roared down the taxi strip perpendicular to the runway. "Stop!" McCrostie said. "The Stingers have a range of three miles. We'll get a better shot from here."

Archer applied the brakes. The pickup came to a halt in the showering rain, jerking everybody forward. McCrostie ripped the center window open. "Fire!" he commanded.

Sweeny and Dietz stared down the length of their launch tubes. The rain obscured their vision. Droplets bounced from their lids, stuck like glue to their eyelashes. They blinked rapidly.

The C-130 angled sharply higher into the sky. It was already half a mile away, obscured by the thick cloud cover. She would disappear in less than eight seconds. They would each have only one shot.

The plane banked back toward the airport, then turned suddenly, violently in the opposite direction.

"They see us!" McCrostie shouted. "Fire!"

Neither tube growled, telling Sweeny and Dietz that the infrared seekers had not locked onto the target. Turboprop engines don't generate much heat like a jet engine or hovering helicopter.

The men fired anyway. The gas generators popped the missiles ten feet into the air. The motors ignited and the twin needles of destruction shot toward the C-130 at supersonic speeds.

The instant the big plane veered from its gentle curve to a course taking it away from the airport, the loadmaster manually launched a storm of aluminum chaff and ten flares. He took no chances. The already cloudy sky filled with shiny aluminum and hot bursts of fire. The plane climbed higher into the cloud cover, everybody's teeth clenched, hands braced.

The four men watched their missiles race quickly toward the cargo plane. The bright flares burned much hotter than the turboprops on the C-130. One Stinger broke from its course. The other broke in the opposite direction.

The missiles screamed angrily for a target. They nosed down, shot through flares, then exploded into the earth. Dirt and fire burst 500 feet into the air. Shockwaves from the explosions rolled across the valley, shrinking to distant crackles. The sound of propellers came faintly through the clouds.

McCrostie sighed. "Damn."

"The reports about electricity and telecommunications have everybody's spirits high, as they should," Mark said to the lower terminal room. "But we can't sit back and enjoy it yet. The situation with China is more pressing than ever. We're immediately transferring all code processing from civilian tasks to military. Dan Van Lan is flying to Pearl Harbor to assume Billy's role while Billy goes to sea aboard the *Chosin* missile cruiser. We have more than one-hundred consultants steaming to war, trying their damnedest to ready the ships for battle. They're working on the weapons and radar all the way up to engagement. That's how bad it is. You can see why we need the entire capacity of The Keep devoted to military work."

"Absolutely."

"This is the nation's most powerful code processing facility," Mark thundered. "If anybody can take that old military software and turn it into a war machine, it's us. We're working with the best hardware companies. The latest to join the crew at Pearl Harbor is Intel. Trimble is already there working on guided missiles and satellite tracking. The whole nation is involved in this."

Kleewein stepped in. Enough motivation. The consultants needed details. "We need to begin modifying *Solvang2K* to work with old military languages like TACPOL and NELIAC. To this point, progress in Pearl has been slow because the teams are handling a lot of the code manually. Pearl Harbor is going to begin sending batches of code for conversion. We need to have some teams working on that. Nikolaas, you're the man for the job. If you need additional resources, tell me immediately. We're going to run this show like a highwire act, balancing everything we have against minute-by-minute demands."

"I don't understand why we don't just nuke them," Nikolaas said. "I thought we had a B-52 waiting in Louisiana."

"We'd love to," Mark answered. "But it's not ready yet. The slowdown comes from the bomb delivery system. They need to rebuild it."

"When will they have it done?"

"Not before Billy's battle group engages."

JANUARY 25, 2000

Donald Brosseau stood on the dock with Morey. The *Olympia's* civilian crew carried the last of their replacement supplies onto the submarine. Morey's regular crew had been reduced by forty men to make room for the civilian engineers. The sailors would trade off on twelve-hour shifts instead of six.

"Maybe it'll all blow over," Brosseau said. He'd never seen his former college roommate so hopeless.

"It better, or we're all dead."

"Maybe it won't come to battle. I talked to Billy Stamp earlier. He said they'll be able to do a lot with this latest batch of equipment." He gestured to the engineers carrying boxes of components down the hatch.

Morey nodded. "Doesn't this just kill you? What I wouldn't give to drive my submarine as she sailed on December 31. I could clear out the Chinese myself."

"I know."

The last of the work crew climbed down the ladder. All sailors were aboard. Tug boats waited along the inner harbor. The three destroyers and the *Chosin* looked majestic in the mid-day light. Their flags still blew in the breeze. They still looked foreboding and strong.

"You'll be in good company out there," Brosseau said.

"Wish you were coming along," Morey replied. He started to put his hand out, but then stepped to his old friend and hugged him hard.

"I'll be here when you get back. I still owe you a beer."

They managed to smile. Commander Morris Ferdelle turned on his heel and walked across the hull of his submarine. At the hatch, he turned for a last look at Commander Donald Brosseau. They gave a crisp salute. Morey gave a final thumbs up to his friend, then disappeared into the submarine.

Brosseau checked on the *Helena*. The work crews carried boxes similar to those he saw delivered to the *Olympia*. The difference was that his boat was getting fixed while safely in port. Morey's boat was getting fixed on the way to battle. Brosseau decided to leave the work to his XO for a few minutes.

He hiked up a bluff near the water's edge to sit beneath a palm tree. He wanted to be alone to drink a can of Coke and watch the ocean, as he'd done so many times with Morey.

He watched the *Chosin* leading the battle group from Pearl Harbor. Her colors flew proudly as her hull parted smooth water. Even from the hillside, Brosseau could see the bold 65 on her bow. Her twin masts looked like crosses rising from the confusion of equipment.

The destroyers followed behind and to the side of the cruiser. The *Olympia* brought up the rear, a bullet in the ocean, the smoothest of her companions. Brosseau could see men's heads on the sail, looking with binoculars as they drove. He knew one of them was Morey.

He wanted to yell so his friend would look. They intended to go boogie boarding together during this rendezvous in Hawaii, but Y2K moved too quickly.

Morey and his men pulled the hatch to dive almost as soon as they left the harbor. The sub sank gracefully into the ocean, water washing over her bow, whirlpooling around the sail and dive planes, then covering the last piece of black metal. A swirl in the Pacific was all that remained of the *Olympia,* then even that was gone.

Brosseau sat until the ships sunk into the horizon. The four shapes were not seen by viewers of CNN. The only pair of eyes watching the forward battle group leave Pearl Harbor belonged to Donald Brosseau.

Dan Van Lan expected to find a busy scene at Pearl Harbor, but nothing like this. Nobody walked, they all ran. They carried boxes and computer screens and machine guns and torpedoes and missiles from one place to the next. A constant hum of communication from radios and yelling voices electrified the air.

A stadium of people clamored around every ship, twisting wrenches, typing on laptops, directing people with their hands. On the far side of the base, missiles launched into the air and out to sea on test runs. The crews methodically monitored each flight, then proceeded to tweak the next missile to compensate for any failure. They launched it, and tabulated the results. When they finally found a working recipe, they documented it and delivered it to the implementation teams.

According to Billy's last report sent to Dan that morning, more progress had been made in the previous two days than during the time since New Year's Eve. The base had finally reached a critical mass of people with the right knowledge and the right equipment.

The forward battle group was already gone. Dan's first order of business was to make sure that Pearl Harbor could communicate with the five boats steaming toward the Chinese.

"How does it look?" Dan asked Carl Albright.

"Like we still have work to do."

January 26, 2000

Pete Dubridge checked the satellite coordinates and calculated the time to engagement. "We'll have partial coverage of the conflict," he told Pennington.

"How partial?"

"One second-tier satellite. We'll get four, maybe five shots of the engagement."

Billy sat in the CIC onboard *Chosin*. Finally, they had some good news. The old Mk 44 torpedoes would have active pinging search capabilities. All four surface ships reported the same success, and Billy assumed that the *Olympia* would also succeed in the repair.

The group's Seahawk helicopters would also prove useful, after all. The Navy had been able to restore basic flight operations.

"When the helos return," Captain Bailey said, "we'll put two Mk 44s onboard each one. If they pick anything up, they can drop two fish in the water right there."

Billy nodded. "Good idea."

"How are the satellite communications with Pearl?"

"We've done our part. We're testing every twenty minutes. So far we don't have a connection."

Bailey didn't reply. He looked forward across the pale ocean. Teams of men carried boxes and wheeled carts across the deck of his ship. The *Harry Hill* sailed on his port side, the *Ingersoll* and *John Young* on his starboard. The *Olympia* lurked somewhere in the waters ahead.

Billy still wore a headset. "This is Stamp in CIC. How many Mk 44s are going to be ready in the next hour?"

After a pause, an engineer replied. "Ten. We can do about ten an hour."

"We'll need two on the Seahawk. She can drop them on an enemy sub if she finds one." Billy flipped the communications button and watched the needles in front of him. They didn't spike forward. He needed that connection. They needed The Keep to process more software code. "Come on, Dan," he said to himself. "Talk to me."

"Test both simultaneously," Kleewein instructed Dan from The Keep. They just completed the redundant connection to the S2 satellite network.

"We're testing now," he said. "The needles are spiking into the red, yellow, green! So far, so good."

"Now call Billy."

"Pearl Harbor to *Chosin,* come in," Dan said.

"*Chosin* here," Billy replied. "I was beginning to worry. You never write, you never call. Was it something I said?"

Dan laughed as the room around him boiled into a cheer. "No, cutie pie, it wasn't anything you said. I just hadn't paid my phone bill. Do you need any code taken care of? We can transfer over this same connection."

"Yes. If you're ready, we've got lots of onboard radar and sonar contact software that needs work."

"Send away."

Billy turned to Bailey. "We have a satellite connection. I'm communicating with Pearl Harbor."

The captain nodded. That was good news, but not great news. The ocean stretched before him. Somewhere out there steamed an untold number of enemy ships with weapons superior to those scraped together by his crew. He had a bad feeling about what they'd be communicating back to Pearl.

With all its brainpower and technology, The Keep still could not fix the onboard code in time. Nikolaas Groen ran his work team ragged before finally throwing his hands in the air.

"There's nothing we can do in half a day," he told Mark.

"You're giving up?"

"It's not giving up, it's prioritizing. We can't have those forward ships fixed in time. They'll have to fight with what they've got regardless of whether we keep pounding the code. Therefore, I'm switching to ships back at Pearl. At least we have enough time to actually make progress there. We might be able to fully fix a few of them. Then, if the worst happens, at least we have a backup plan."

"Don't say that," Mark told him.

"Well, that's how I see it."

Mark picked up the satellite phone to dial Billy. He put it down. There was no use delivering bad news as they went into battle. "That's how I see it, too," Mark told Nikolaas. "Switch your efforts to the ships still in port. But don't talk to me about the worst happening."

JANUARY 27, 2000

The Seahawk helicopters hovered above the dark ocean just sixty miles from the Chinese battle group. They dipped their sonar transducers into the water for a hint of submarine noise. A battle group almost always had submarines with it. The Chinese have nuclear attack submarines and Captain Bailey assumed they would use them. They might have sent their old diesel subs instead. Those were harder to find underwater because they run on batteries, which are quieter than nuclear reactors.

"We've got nothing," a pilot called back to the *Chosin*. "Their subs must be running really wide. It's a straight shot to the battle group."

"Roger that," the antisubmarine warfare officer replied. "Keep searching. They've got to be out there somewhere. Any radar on the ships yet?"

"There's a little buzz bearing zero-two-zero."

"We've picked it up as well," added another helo. "Bearing zero-four-eight."

The antisurface warfare officer ran the triangulation quickly on his calculator. He turned to the captain. "That puts the radar contact at ninety miles from us."

"Arm the Harpoons," Bailey said. "If we know about them in this weakened condition, they definitely know about us."

"I've got a photo download from Guam," Billy said. "It will be here in less than a minute."

"Sir," the warfare officer said, "we're within range of primary Chinese antiship missiles."

"YJ Strike Eagles?"

"Yes sir, and the bigger HY Silkworms. If they have helos in the air, they can target us." YJ stood for Ying Ji, a 165-kilogram warhead; HY stood for Hai Ying, a 500-kilogram warhead. Both were less sophisticated than their American counterparts. They did not suffer from broken digital guidance.

"Arm the Standard missiles and get men on deck with those machine gun mounts."

"Aye, Captain."

"Here is the photo." Billy handed it to him.

Bailey examined the latest from Guam. It was the most revealing shot yet. "They've got nine ships," he announced. "I count four destroyers, two frigates, and three fast attack boats."

"That's a handful, sir."

"Yes it is."

The call came from Chau himself. Gong Shufang, captain of the Chinese Luhu class destroyer, cleared his throat and picked up the radio. "Yes, Mr. Chau."

"Do you have the Americans?"

"We have detected them on helicopter radar. They are moving toward us steadily. Is it time to turn back?"

"No. You are to attack."

"I beg your pardon, sir?"

"You are to attack."

"Sir, that was not the plan."

"Correct. This is not going as planned. They do not believe that you will attack. It is time to show them the power of China!"

Captain Shufang looked at his officers, all of whom stared at the radio. They heard Chau's commands. Had they known they were going to war, they would have brought a bigger battle group.

Submarines would have been a start. A few planes wouldn't hurt, either. "Have they refused to sign a contract?"

"So far, they have."

"Sir, the Americans are a sophisticated military. Perhaps we should—"

Chau's cool voice sliced through the skipper's protest. "Exactly why they are injured, Captain, and we are not. They have not become desperate enough to pay. You need to convince them that the threat is real."

"Sir, the threat was never supposed to be real."

"It is now, Captain."

Shufang felt a sandbag form in his stomach. There would be no contract. The plan called for them to turn back immediately upon either the signing of a contract between the U.S. Department of Defense and the American firm, Legacy Conversions; or a clear signal that there would be no contract. The Chinese would then establish communications with the Americans and "discover" that the destroyer conflict in Chinese water was a mistake. The He Zhang would sail home, unscathed and much richer.

Now Captain Shufang understood that *the* plan had never been *Chau's* plan. He looked at the faces of his officers. What were his options? If he turned back to China against Chau's command, he would be executed for treason. If he sailed against the Americans and lost, he would die. If he won, he would return as a hero and enjoy a private account filled with He Zhang money. The only choice was combat. Hard, fast, unrelenting and hopeful for a victory. Imagine! Victory against an American force.

His officers stared at him, waiting for a response. Captain Shufang knew his battle group had been sacrificed. Only two things could outweigh the value of so many ships: Taiwan and Spratly. They had to be the reason. Shufang wanted Chau to know he knew. What could it hurt? He would either be dead or one of Chau's most valuable partners after the engagement.

"How is Taiwan, sir?" he asked smoothly. His eyes had gained a confidence few men could muster when dealing with Chau. A severe reduction in options does wonders for assertiveness.

"Taiwan, Captain?"

"Yes, sir. I believe you heard the question. How is Taiwan?"

Chau exhaled a lungful of cigarette smoke into the radio. "She'll be waiting for you upon your return, Captain. Fight with everything.

Pound the Americans. This is your opportunity. Do not let anger cloud your judgment."

"We will attack the Americans with everything in our power. We will win, and we will return to a unified China."

The radio fell silent. The officers waited for Captain Shufang to speak. He sat down, pulled a cigarette from his pocket and lit it.

Oh, that Chau.

Shufang sucked smoke into his lungs. Chau's plan was brilliant. Something in Shufang's background allowed him to admire Chau's machinations, even if they included a lowly sacrifice of Shufang and his men. Reclaiming Taiwan would go far to place China in the superpower seat of the twenty-first century. Chau could control China itself within a matter of years. Serving as Chau's minister of defense would be a charmed life.

Captain Shufang stood suddenly, flicking the cigarette out the window. "You heard Mr. Chau," he yelled. "We're going to battle! Arm the Eagles and the Silkworms!"

"Nothing." Billy threw the radio piece down. "I still can't establish contact with the Chinese." The two battle groups were less than fifty miles apart, dangerously close for comfort. "I've tried every available satellite channel. Either they're not responding or Solvang can't talk to them."

"Could be either," Captain Bailey replied.

"We're picking up strong radar, sir," the antisurface warfare officer reported. "They're running rice screens and Thomsons and cross slots. You need sunglasses to see through it all."

"They've fired! Fangs in the air!" cried the antiair warfare officer. "Sixteen targets bearing roughly zero-five-five, forty-five miles and closing, sir."

"How are the electronic jammers?" Bailey asked Billy.

"No Aegis coordination. The Raytheon can't lock on to jam individual targets. It can only create a swirling confusion."

Billy couldn't breathe. It felt like all the air had left the control room. The *Chosin's* Aegis system could have handled sixteen incoming missiles on autopilot. Captain Bailey now needed to do its work himself.

"Fire the SAMs! Sound the warning system to the machine gunners. Left full rudder, flank speed. Get the chaff rockets ready!"

Billy stood out of the way, incredulous. Somebody had actually fired missiles at them? Through the starboard window he watched the *Ingersoll* and *Harry Hill* turn wildly off course. Sailors braced themselves behind the machine gun mounts. A buzzer blared across the deck of the *Chosin,* alerting everybody to their battle stations.

Standard missiles launched in streaks of gray smoke from the deck. The SAMs screamed away, accelerating past 2,000 miles per hour.

One immediately dipped below its course into the ocean. A column of water exploded into the air. "What the hell happened?" Bailey screamed. The *Chosin* shook from its own missile.

"Targets at thirty-five miles, sir."

"*Ingersoll, Hill, Young,* get your Sparrows ready to fire," Bailey yelled into the radio.

"Roger that, Captain," came a voice speaking to all ships. "They're loaded and waiting for the incoming to reach nine miles."

"In the meantime, fire the Harpoons," Captain Bailey yelled.

Billy watched the destroyers careening through the water. The ends of their quad boxes blew apart. Harpoon missiles skimmed close to the ocean surface.

"Targets at twenty-five miles, sir."

"Two down!" the antiair warfare officer yelled, excited but at the same time wanting more. He waited a few moments. "Fourteen targets at twenty miles."

"Fire the chaff rockets!"

"Firing."

"Engage the jammers!"

Billy switched to a headset radio. Rockets filled the air with showers of aluminized Mylar confetti. The shiny particles rained across the ships.

"Dan, this is Billy. We're under attack!"

"How are the weapons performing?" Dan asked.

"Not well. One Standard missile dropped immediately into the ocean. We had sixteen missiles coming our way. Only two were downed by SAMs. We've still got fourteen incoming!"

"Jammers and chaff?"

"Both active."

"What about the Sparrows?"

"They can only launch when the missiles are within nine miles."
Dan's voice squeaked. "Hang in there, Billy."

"Keep listening for detonation," Morey ordered. "I want to know if our ships are hit."

"Yes, sir." The sonar tech sat with his eyes closed, listening to a headset.

They prowled twenty miles in front of the *Chosin* formation, crawling along slowly as the two battle groups neared each other. They had deployed the towed array and listened to everything on the hydrophones.

The sonar men wrote signals by hand, calculated distances, estimated speeds. The navigation crew plotted direction vectors.

Morey stood in the red battle lighting. This is not how he wanted to fight. They had no missiles. They were out of torpedo range, especially guidewire electric torpedo range. There was nothing he could do but listen to the battle and pray for the American surface ships.

His veins pressed hard against his skin.

Billy could see the missiles angrily homing in on their ships, tiny dots in the sky.

The Sparrow missiles flew from the destroyers in a cloud of smoke. They zipped in wild trajectories confused by their own ships' Mylar in the air. Columns of water rose as several Sparrows dipped into the ocean. Others exploded into the air, obscuring the incoming targets.

"Four down!" the antiair warfare officer reported. "Ten targets at five miles."

Ten more. Billy couldn't comprehend it. Machine guns rattled from the deck of every ship.

The missiles grew bigger. One broke from the pack to chase fluttering Mylar. Another veered away, tricked by the swirling confusion of the makeshift radar jammers.

"Eight targets at two miles."

"Damn," Captain Bailey said.

"Sixteen new targets, sir! Bearing again zero-five-five, forty-five miles and closing."

Through the smoke, Mylar fragments, and machine gun blasts, the front wave of eight Chinese missiles exploded into the decks and hulls of the *Ingersoll* and *John Young*.

The first missile into the *John Young* blew metal and fire across the ocean. The second missile blasted through bulkheads and crew quarters. The remaining blasts seemed almost unnecessary. The *Ingersoll* caved in at the middle, its back broken. The bow and stern of the *John Young* stuck at odd angles from the water as it sank. Men fell from the siderails. There wasn't even enough time for firefighting. Most men were killed by the blasts.

The *Chosin* rocked in the shockwaves. Billy held a rail as he watched the *Ingersoll* sink. The *John Young* soon followed.

"Fire the SAMs!" Bailey yelled. "Keep firing until they hit something this time." More missiles streaked from the *Chosin,* two of which immediately careened into the ocean. "How are the Harpoons coming?"

"All but four have disappeared from radar, sir."

To port, the *Harry Hill* fired another volley of Harpoons. They flew away toward the Chinese battle group.

Billy spoke again into the headset. "Dan, two of our destroyers are sinking. They were decimated by eight missiles."

"Eight missiles into two destroyers?" Dan asked. "Jesus Christ."

"Yes, they went down fast. We have sixteen more on the way. Our defenses didn't work, we don't know if our offenses will either. Missile radar isn't working well. Some SAMs and Sparrows dropped immediately into the water. The radar jamming could obviously use some work. With eight missiles hitting their targets, something sure as hell went wrong. It's the radar seeking that needs help, radar in general. If our Phalanx system had worked, we could have shredded those eight missiles."

"I know. I've got it all and we'll use it on the rest of these ships in Pearl."

"Make sure you do it."

"We have detonation!" the sonar called out.

"Our ships or theirs?" Morey asked.

"Ours, sir. It's bad. We've counted eight hits. We can hear water rushing inside. They're sinking."

"Sons of bitches. Keep listening."

"Four hits!" the *Chosin's* antisurface warfare officer yelled. "All four Harpoons have detonated."

He watched the ancient radar display for a disappearing contact. The forward starboard ship took every missile.

"Incoming missiles at twenty-five miles," the antiair warfare officer reported. "SAMs should be detonating soon." He waited ten seconds. "Three down this time, sir. We have thirteen targets at twenty miles."

The *Chosin* and her one remaining destroyer fired another round of Mylar chaff. Billy saw the Sparrows on deck of the *Harry Hill* ready to fire again.

Billy spoke into the headset. "Dan, the Harpoons seem to be working better than the SAMs. Four of them made contact."

"How many were fired?"

"I don't know."

"Fine. We'll inspect all the missiles." Dan felt useless. "I've made a notation that the Harpoons did reach their targets."

The antisurface warfare officer looked up from the display. "One confirmed kill, sir. An enemy ship just disappeared from radar."

The Sparrows flew from the destroyer. There was so much noise around Billy that he barely noticed the launching of missiles anymore. Frustrated machine gunners had already begun firing toward the incoming missiles, hoping to fill the air with a wall of bullets.

"Sir, two more missiles just fired!"

"Launch the SAMs," Bailey commanded. His jaw was set. Billy could tell that the captain was not hopeful.

Columns of water rose along the path of the Sparrows. Errant radar units sent an occasional missile into the ocean or off on a wild path into the sky. Few exploded into the oncoming missiles. Not good enough.

"Two down. Eleven targets at five miles."

The machine guns fired desperately at the tiny dots. The missiles grew larger in the sky. One dropped into the water chasing a Mylar fragment. The machine guns didn't kill a single missile.

"Brace yourselves!" Bailey yelled. Every man grabbed something. Billy reached to the bulkhead rail.

The first missile hit the forward deck and filled the sky with fire and debris. Four more followed within a second of each other, another into the forward deck, two into the superstructure, and one into the stern.

Billy had never felt such force in his life. His hand was ripped from the bulkhead and his body thrown across the CIC. Fire burst through the compartment, searing Billy's face and arms. He smelled singed hair and molten steel. Men on fire ran wildly, screaming, unable to extinguish the clinging, melted materials burning them alive.

Fire sprinklers doused the ship with saltwater. Billy staggered to his feet, holding the defunct control panel to stand. Blood ran from his nose and ears. The bulkhead he held before the explosions was no longer there. It had been replaced by a gaping, fiery hole.

"Damage report!" yelled Bailey. Blood ran from his ears and through the torn fabric of his clothing.

"Everything!" replied an officer standing near Billy. "No readouts on any equipment."

Billy looked outboard. The *Harry Hill* was sinking quicker than the first two destroyers. She took five missile hits; the others had taken only four.

Billy couldn't feel his left arm. He looked down and saw that it was broken. He remembered the two additional missiles on their way.

"Sir," he said to Bailey. "There were two more."

"We're going down anyway. Nothing we can do."

The captain, officers, and Billy looked for handholds to steady themselves. The ship listed so far to the starboard side that Billy thought they would fall straight into the ocean.

The dying *Chosin* stayed upright, but horribly misshapen.

The men watched out the window as the two final missiles came into view. There was little to obscure their paths. The Mylar had fluttered into the ocean. The machine gunners were all dead.

Captain Bailey pounded his fist. "In any other year..."

The HY missiles packed two-and-a-half times the power of the five YJs that crushed the *Chosin*. The extra power combined with the ship's weakened condition ended matters quickly.

The missiles separated slightly as they reached their target. They rose high, arched down, and blasted the *Chosin* into four pieces spread a quarter mile apart.

"The *Chosin* and *Harry Hill* are going down, sir."

Morey nodded. Every U.S. ship was lost. There was nothing but open sea between the Chinese and Pearl Harbor. He knew that Pearl was working on additional warships. They would have to be better prepared than this forward battle group.

"What are the Chinese doing?"

"They're steaming along. Quite a bit slower than before, but still moving toward Hawaii."

Morey thought. They were still out of range of the Chinese group. There was no way his sub could take out the eight remaining ships before being killed herself. If he could maneuver deep under the Chinese, he could follow along in their baffle noise. They have poor sonar. There was a good chance that he could hide the whole way to Pearl.

The big question was enemy submarines. They hadn't detected any, but that didn't mean they weren't there.

Morey made up his mind. He refused to sit idly while the Chinese invaded. They had now killed six U.S. ships, including the two destroyers in the South China Sea.

"We have a kill, sir. The Chinese are down to seven boats."

Morey turned to the Nav. "What is their speed?"

"Moving at eighteen knots, sir. Same direction."

"Diving officer, make our depth 800 feet." He turned to the XO. "You take the conn. Ahead two thirds, stay below the thermal layer. Change depth if you have to."

"Aye, sir."

"We're crawling right under them, gentlemen. Parasite mode."

12

LIGHTS IN
THE DARKNESS

JANUARY 28, 2000

So many people covered Pearl Harbor that Dan wondered if anybody was left on the mainland. Jet after jet delivered supplies and brainpower from all over the country. Texas Instruments brought new radar homing devices.

Admiral Robek had examined the results from the forward battle group's engagement. "Can you have Aegis fixed?" he asked Dan directly.

"On one ship."

"You're sure?"

"Sure enough that I'll sail to sea with it."

"Dan, Mark wants a full update." Albright handed him the phone.

"Mark, the situation here is an utter disaster. Billy Stamp is dead. He died in combat while trying to ready U.S. ships for battle with the Chinese."

"Oh my God," Mark gasped. He reported the news to others in the conference room. A stunned silence followed.

"The Chinese are steaming closer. Admiral Robek needs to send a carrier battle group to intercept the Chinese group. The most potent fighting system in the Navy is Aegis. I need to get it fixed by the time we leave tomorrow at noon."

"What do you need from us?" Mark asked quietly.

"Complete dedication to the task. I'm going to battle tomorrow, and I need your help!"

"We're behind you, Dan. Start sending the code. I'll personally see that it gets taken care of."

The Keep exploded. A newspaper room before deadline looked tranquil by comparison. Consultants yelled back and forth, slammed desktops, and pounded on keyboards.

At Barksdale Air Force Base in Louisiana, Operation Pacific Plunge airmen finished testing their hydraulic launch system. The two B-52 bombers were ready to go. They would each carry a nine-megaton B-53 nuclear bomb. The Air Force crew finished just in time. They received word that the Chinese battle group had sunk three U.S. destroyers and a guided missile cruiser.

"We've got to get these birds in the air," said the colonel in charge of Pacific Plunge. He called Admiral Robek.

"Admiral, this is Colonel Tolleson at Barksdale. Our birds are ready to fly. I wanted you to be the first to know."

"That's a relief. I'll wait to hear the official announcement from the Secretary."

"Yes, sir. That should come shortly. Good luck."

Tolleson hung up and called the Secretary of Defense. "Mr. Secretary, this is Colonel Tolleson at Barksdale. Operation Pacific Plunge is ready for engagement."

JANUARY 29, 2000

Commander Brosseau and his XO sat in the middle of the briefing room. It was 0500 hours and they hadn't slept all night. Their sub, the *Helena,* was selected to accompany the next battle group. They found out about it late the previous night and stayed awake to monitor the repairs. Eighty civilian engineers came onboard. Most of the sub's crew slept in base housing to make room for the extra bodies.

Everybody knew the fate of the forward battle group. All ships were dead and probably the sub as well. There was no official word on the *Olympia.* It was so often that way with submariners. Their job is hidden, and their fate remains a mystery. Brosseau hoped that Morey was still out there. He refused to give up on his friend.

"Ladies and gentlemen," Admiral Robek began, "the time of reckoning has come. We have assembled a more powerful battle group to engage the Chinese. This battle group will be ready for combat on our terms. Civilian and military crews here and on the mainland have worked continuously for the past two days to prepare six boats for battle. They will be ready.

"The aircraft carrier *George Washington* now has operable elevators to lift aircraft onto the flight deck. Her four Phalanx cannons are operable. Her air wing normally consists of eighty-five aircraft. On this mission, it will consist of seventeen.

"We have four EA-6B Prowlers to provide powerful jamming. The forward battle group suffered from barely functional jamming equipment that allowed their every move to be monitored by the Chinese and allowed incoming missiles to find our boats. That will not happen this time.

"Eight F/A-18 Hornets and two F-14 Tomcats will provide air attack. Hughes was able to repair the digital radar combat system on both planes, though the Tomcat will have a shorter detection range on this sortie. Hughes is working on additional units for future engagements, should there be any. The Hornets will carry Harpoon missiles to attack the enemy ships. The Tomcats will carry Sparrows and Sidewinders to provide air-to-air defense for the Hornets. We don't anticipate trouble in the air, hence the emphasis on the surface strike capabilities of the Hornet.

"The cruiser *Port Royal* will have full use of her Aegis weapons system. She will be joined by three Arleigh Burke class destroyers along for the ride. They are the *Russell,* the *Paul Hamilton,* and the *Hopper.* Though the Aegis weapons system will not work on these boats, they will be linked to the *Royal* and fight with full coordination. Each ship carries repaired Standard missiles and Harpoons. All six Phalanx cannons work.

"The *Helena* attack submarine will lead the charge. She leaves port earlier than the main battle group to give her time to sneak in and position herself. She will have full sonar processing capabilities, but will need to use Mk 44 electric torpedoes.

"The Chinese battle group is proceeding much slower than before. We assume that the ships are injured from the prior engagement. They are currently 1,050 nautical miles from Pearl. The *Helena* leaves today at 0600 hours, the rest of the group leaves at 1400 hours. The estimated time of engagement, depending on the behavior of the Chinese, is tomorrow at 1200 hours. That will be a mere 500 miles from Hawaii, people. We must win this engagement."

He took a step, hands clasped behind his back. This next part of the briefing was tricky.

"We have a backup plan."

The room perked up, all eyes glued to the admiral.

"Two B-52 bombers will fly from Barksdale Air Force Base at 2100 hours our time. Each will carry a nine-megaton B-53 nuclear bomb. The planes will circle the engagement at high altitude, prepared to end the Chinese threat without question. At this stage, the B-52s represent a backup plan only. Our battle group is the primary engagement, most likely the only engagement. Are there any questions?"

"Sir," asked a captain. "Will civilian work teams ride with the battle group again?"

"Yes. Though all systems will have been tested prior to departure, the civilian engineers will accompany the ships with spare parts just in case. They will also communicate weapons performance to teams in Pearl Harbor and the mainland."

Admiral Robek surveyed the room. Everybody looked worried. They didn't feel ready for war. "That's all I have. Let's go sink some boats."

Tom's neighborhood gathered at the Ortiz residence. Debbie Ortiz ran the biggest family on the block and was best equipped to handle the crowd. Everybody brought the food they had on hand, any toys for the children, and plenty of pots, pans, silverware, and extra clothing.

An Ortiz cousin arrived in a gardening truck. An enormous pig stood in the back. Four men guided the pig to the backyard with a stick. Behind the shed, they slaughtered it, ran a spit through its body, marinated the meat, then assigned children to spin it over the fire pit. A plume of smoke rose to the sky. The backyard filled with the scent of barbecue.

Tom stood with Munoz, Butler, and Woo in the backyard. They ate from plastic plates. "I can't believe they brought a band," Butler said. "Such a party at a time like this."

The Ortiz cousins shook maracas and played guitars while others sang. Kids played by the shed. Couples danced on the patio. The sun peeked through the clouds to provide a tour brochure scene of Los Angeles.

Woo swallowed his bite. "As long as there aren't any more riots and shooting, I could get used to this life."

"Same here," Tom agreed. Adelle walked over with a tray of beers for the men. The beer was another gift from the Ortiz clan. They were a regular portable restaurant.

"And you know something else," Tom said after Adelle had gone, "I don't think I've been this close to her in a year."

"Come on," Butler told him. "Now you're gushing."

"I may be, but I'm telling the truth. I couldn't stop thinking of her when we were in Koreatown. I thought we were going to die, but I didn't care about myself—I thought about her living without me and eventually forgetting me and marrying some other guy. She took care of me for the six days I was in bed."

"Now she's bringing beers to you," Woo added. "Things are definitely looking up."

They heard a helicopter buzzing somewhere in the distance. Everybody looked to the sky. Its rotors beat the air, coming closer to the party.

"Who could that be?" Tom asked. He set his plate down and stood to look. Over the line of houses came the Bell 47 like a giant dragonfly. It hovered above the street. The pilot and copilot looked through the curved glass to the party in the Ortiz backyard.

"Those are the guys," Munoz said. All four officers now stood by the fence, looking at the Bell 47. The guitars stopped playing and the couples stopped dancing. Everybody walked to the center of the yard to look at the helicopter.

"No kidding," Tom yelled above the noise. "It's them." He signaled with his arms for the helicopter to land. He pulled his badge from his back pocket and ran to the front of the house, holding it up for them to see.

The two heads inside turned and said something to each other. Then the pilot gave Tom a thumbs up. The Bell 47 settled onto the street. The engine cut back to an idle and the rotor slowed down. The two men stepped out and walked to Tom and his three partners. A crowd of people came around the house.

Tom put out a hand. "You probably don't recognize the four of us, but we recognize you."

Murray took the hand and gave a firm shake. He and Martinez shook the hands of all four officers.

"I recognize you," Martinez said.

Murray looked closely at the men. "You're the ones from Koreatown." He remembered the repeated warnings, the rush of the crowd, the horrible slaughter. Now, looking at their faces, he even remembered the way they stood in their riot gear, shields in flames, weapons drawn and ready for war. That was a grim day. In all his years on the force, Captain Murray Teft had never seen anything so devastating as the massacre at Koreatown. And he'd seen a lot through the years.

He understood that it was the only option they had. The press would certainly not understand. The department would not understand. If they knew what happened that day, even family members would not understand.

Cops who opened fire on a crowd like that—no matter what the circumstances—would lose their jobs. Murray had been around long enough to know that.

He switched his eyes from Tom to Martinez and back to the four officers again. "On second thought," he said, "I've never seen any of these men in my life."

Martinez looked over at his boss. "Come to think of it, neither have I."

Tom smiled. He put an arm around Murray, showing him the way to the backyard. "Just in case I never meet the real guys who helped us out, allow me to treat you and your copilot to some fresh barbecued pork."

"I'd like that," Murray said. He smelled the pig smoke that had alerted him and Martinez to the fire. "I'd like that a lot."

The He Zhang battle group moved slowly. Thank God, Morey thought. It was impossible for a submarine to follow fast moving surface ships without being detected. Motoring along slowly and quietly is what the *Olympia* did best.

The sub remained safely below a thermal layer where the sound of its screw and power plant would reflect off the warmer surface water, away from the Chinese sonar. The *Olympia* drove quickly at first to position herself in front of the battle group, then slowed to a near stop. Morey turned the sub's nose toward Hawaii and let the He Zhang ships cruise over top of him.

"Make our depth 350," he commanded. "Speed zero."

The screw quit turning and the massive attack submarine drifted upward to 350 feet, the depth of the surface thermal layer in that area. Under normal conditions, Morey could have extended a sonar mast thirty feet above the sub into the top thermal layer to listen to the ships while the body of his sub remained safely tucked below the thermal layer. But the sonar mast was broken. He needed to stick the nose of the sub into the upper layer, where his main sonar dome could hear the He Zhang momentarily. Then he would sink quietly deeper into the ocean.

"All seven ships, sir," the sonar reported.

"Direction and speed?"

"Still east to Hawaii, cruising at six knots."

Considerably slower than before. "Do you hear any sign of injury?"

The sonar listened. "No, sir. Engines sound normal, screws are turning smoothly. Unless it's something I can't hear, the ships are fine."

"Take her down," Morey said. "Sink below the thermal."

With forward movement, the planesman would push forward on the dive controls, angling the sub to a lower depth. But they weren't moving. They sat still at the edge of the thermal layer. To sink, they dribbled water slowly and quietly into the ballast tanks until the sub grew heavier and sank under the layer. Then it was safe to drive forward slowly.

"Forward two knots. Make your depth 600."

One knot, two knots. The planesman angled to 600 feet. He evened the submarine to cruise at that depth. They were reasonably deep under the ships to increase speed.

"Six knots."

The screw turned slightly faster. The Olympia glided through the water at six knots, immediately behind the He Zhang, hidden in a layer of cold water and the noise from seven Chinese warships.

In the open sea, they didn't need to worry about touching bottom, which was good since their contouring system was broken.

At two hours into the second day, something changed.

"Conn, sonar. The Luhu is dropping back." The Luhu was the group's most capable ship.

"Entirely?"

"Can't tell, sir. Her engines are still cooking, but she's slowed a lot. I won't be able to hear her for much longer."

That was strange. Why would the flagship of the group drop back? It made Morey nervous. Could be that the Luhu had better sonar than the others and was removing herself from the group to get a fix on the submarine. Did the Chinese hear them?

"Speed zero," Morey said. "We'll drop back with her and see what she's up to."

They drifted to a stop. "She's turning, sir. Can't say for sure from this depth, but looks to me like she's headed home."

"This is just the Luhu?" Morey clarified.

"Yes, sir. The rest of the battle group has steamed ahead."

What was the Luhu doing?

"No sounds of injury at all?"

"No, sir. She sounds fine from this depth."

"Let me know when her course has steadied."

"Aye, sir."

They sat still for nearly five minutes, during which time the Luhu destroyer made a complete about-face and began steaming back toward China.

"There she goes, sir. Bearing steady on a course for China."

Now what? They were still too close to the main battle group to fire on the Luhu without alerting the others to a sub in the water. They couldn't sink her discreetly from their present position.

They could follow the Luhu home for a ways and sink her when they were out of range of the main group. But they'd never be able to catch up to the main group in time. Following the Luhu meant killing only the Luhu and hoping that the next American group could dispatch the six Chinese ships on their own. From what Morey saw yesterday, he didn't want to chance it.

"Maintain our bearing. Make our depth 1,400. Ahead eight knots. When we catch up to the group, resume our previous depth and speed."

"Aye, sir."

The *Olympia* dove to a quieter depth and accelerated to chase the main battle group.

"We'll let her go," Morey told the XO. "Much as I hate to do it, she's no longer a threat. The other six are."

The XO nodded. "Smart choice, sir."

Two civilians entered the back of the conn. Morey turned to them. "What is it?"

"We have good news," one said. "We've been able to repair two Mk 48 torpedoes. You should be able to fire them without the guide wires."

"Active homing works?"

"On two of them. There's no inertial guidance, but the Hughes digital homing sonar works."

"Excellent job," Morey said with a smile. He walked over to pat them on the shoulders. "Any chance that you can fix more of them?"

"Unfortunately, no. We would have been able to, but somebody grabbed the wrong parts box. We've got Sparrow missile guidance units sitting down there instead of torpedo parts."

Morey shook his head. "At least we have the two. Go have yourselves a snack in the galley. It's on me."

The Mk 48s are the standard attack sub torpedo. Their pump jets drive them at fifty-five knots. They can attack from twenty miles away and deliver a 650-pound warhead. The backup Mk 44's, by comparison, needed to be fired within three miles of the target and only delivered an 85-pound warhead.

Morey returned to the conn. "Did you hear that?" he asked the weapons officer. "We have two Mk 48s fully enabled. Make sure they're racked up and ready to fire."

"Aye, sir."

"We've got a little something special for our Chinese friends, courtesy of the former U.S. Navy."

"Former, sir?" the XO asked.

"The one we remember from 1999."

Dan Van Lan met Captain Ira McCain after Admiral Robek's briefing. McCain commanded the aircraft carrier *George Washington*. He wore freshly pressed khakis, a pen clipped between the top and second buttons of the shirt. The tiny silver clip betrayed the captain's penchant for detail. He was never without a pen to take a note.

"Looks like we're ready to go," McCain said. "Aegis is up, Phalanx is humming, I'm feeling good."

The carrier air wing commander, Captain Mauer, looked up to the flight deck. "We've got only seventeen birds. It's a sparse part of the air wing, but small and deadly."

"I believe so," Dan said. "This battle group is much better prepared than the last."

"I've admired the efforts of your company," McCain said. "Your tests show we're ready."

"We are ready."

"Which makes me wonder why you're out here. You don't need to be. Let me remind you that there's a battle at the end of this boat ride."

"I'm here to see our efforts work. I want to see with my own eyes the victory that Billy never saw."

"And you're damn well going to see it."

McCain was a full head taller than Dan, thinner and much more confident. Dan looked at the patches of gray above McCain's ears and the prominent nose on his face. It was fitting that he commanded the *George Washington*. He walked forward with the urgency Dan pictured on Washington's face as he marched the Continental Army south to Yorktown.

"I knew Captain Bailey on the *Chosin*," McCain said.

Mauer nodded. "So did I."

"I knew Billy Stamp on the *Chosin*."

That was all they said about their friends. They did not expand on the sadness, the anger, the will for vengeance hardened at the base of their skulls.

Murray and Martinez partied with their fellow officers and the Ortiz family until nightfall. They ate their fill of barbecued pork, danced with the señoritas, and even played a little kickball with the kids. It became clear early in the afternoon that they would be staying for awhile, so Murray turned off the helicopter in the middle of the street.

But now it was time to head back to work. Murray looked for Martinez. His copilot had wandered back to the firepit for more pork. Even with all the people picking away at the meat, three-quarters of the pig was still waiting to be eaten. Martinez cut two slices for himself and returned to Murray's side.

"Scarf that down," Murray said. "We've got to get going. It's night time. Fire watch season."

Martinez nodded, chewing quickly.

"Are people still rioting?" Tom asked.

"Not rioting," Murray said. "But they're burning homes for fun. We can't get fire trucks there, but there's always the off chance that we can save somebody's property."

Martinez dropped the plate into a plastic trash bag and wiped his fingers. "I'm all set."

"Gentlemen," Murray said, "thanks for the hospitality. Let's do it again sometime."

Murray and Martinez walked around the house to the Bell 47. They started the engine and waited for it to warm up. The rotors spun slowly, gained momentum. The kids came around the side of the house with flashlights and lanterns to watch the helicopter take off. Murray waved goodbye, not sure if they could see him or not.

They climbed above Encino, the field of darkness extending in all directions. The San Fernando Valley lay quiet between its hills. No cars on the freeway, no lights in the homes. An occasional orange flame was all that broke the field of darkness. The glow of the Ortiz barbecue pit shrank in the distance. They flew along the Hollywood freeway back toward LA.

Murray banked the 47 over Laurel Canyon. They climbed above the hill and angled forward into Hollywood.

Without warning, Los Angeles exploded into a million lights. Street lights, house lights, spotlights, building lights, colored lights, white lights, Christmas lights, dock lights, ship lights, big and little lights of all types poured illumination into every crack of the city.

Murray yelled to Martinez. "Look at that, buddy! Would you look at that!"

Murray flew low over the city, watching the activity. People ran out of homes, waving their arms and beaming from cheek to cheek. Restaurant signs lit up, freeway billboards, and even the Hollywood sign came back into view.

"Look at them," Martinez said. He pressed his face against the glass of the 47.

Women held children in their arms, smiling at the frolic around them. It was like nobody had ever seen lights before. They stared at them in wonderment. They leaned against the street poles, feeling them as if they channeled some mysterious force unknown to man.

"This is incredible," Murray said. "I haven't felt like this in a long time." He thought a moment. He looked at Martinez. "You know, I don't think I've ever felt like this."

"Me neither."

Gary Maris finished dealing the cards around the table. It was another fine night after a great dinner. He was content, and he was about to win another evening of poker against the women and Rob Hansen.

The lanterns burned cozily from their perches on the kitchen counter. They'd settled on that as the best place for them. From the center of the table, they cast too harsh a light. Besides, putting the lanterns in the kitchen left extra room for the evening snacks. Gary reached his hand into the bowl of peanuts. He was glad they had stocked plenty.

"Does anybody else think the iodine in the water is going to stain our teeth?" Claire asked.

"What do you mean anybody else?" Patricia asked. She rearranged her hand of cards. "Do you?"

"Yes. I was looking in the mirror today and I think my teeth look brown. What are people going to—"

The house filled with light from everywhere. The kitchen fluorescent blared down on top of the lanterns. The hallway became a photon expressway, light pouring from its mouth across the floor where the children slept. The television blared back on to the same station Gary and Patricia watched on New Year's Eve. Only colored bars showed on the screen and a loud blare from the speaker jolted the children awake.

The refrigerator cranked back to life. Gary ran to the television and punched it off. The kids sat startled, looking at the adults, wondering what had happened. Danielle's stereo blasted the house from her bedroom where one of the kids had pushed it to full volume.

"Turn that off!" Gary yelled to her. She ran upstairs to silence the loudspeakers.

Everybody sat back down, noticeably disturbed. Gary dropped his hand of cards face down and looked at the kids in the bright light. Why was it so bright in the house? Did they really use that many lights before New Year's?

He stood and switched lights off around the kitchen and living room. He walked upstairs, flipping light switches everywhere. The house returned to its former darkness, the way it was supposed to be. Gary walked downstairs again.

He sat at the table. From its brief moment back on, the television screen glowed faintly in the darkness. Gary stared angrily at it.

"Rob, could you help me, please?" They both stood. Gary led Rob to the television. They picked the TV off its stand and walked to the front door, dragging the cord behind. Danielle opened the door.

"Right to the sidewalk," Gary said.

They walked across the grass to the sidewalk, stopping where the trash truck used to come.

"I'm assuming this is where he'll start coming again," Gary said. "Now, lift as high as you can go."

They strained, pushing the weight upward until they held the box above their heads. The women and children watched from the front doorway. Now that the streetlights were back on, they could see the scene taking place.

"On three, release and back away," Gary directed. "One, two, three!"

They let go of the box and let it crash on the sidewalk. The glass shattered and two of the plastic sides cracked off.

Gary rubbed his hands together. "Looks like trash to me."

They walked back up the grass to the front door where the women waited. Gary led the way back to the kitchen table, still lit gently by the lanterns. Everybody picked up their cards.

"Let's see," Gary said. "I dealt, so it's your turn, Danielle. What will you bet?"

JANUARY 30, 2000

The *Helena* shot through the ocean at thirty-two knots, far ahead of the main battle group. Captain Donald Brosseau's crew had tried the sub's new sonar computer. She worked. They could process sounds against a database of known signatures. In all ways but their electric torpedoes, they were able to fight like the good old days— one month ago.

They left Pearl eight hours ahead of the surface battle group. That gave them enough time to maneuver close to the He Zhang and wait for engagement. When the ships scrambled to defend against the surface assault, Brosseau would strike from below.

They came within thirty miles of the Chinese.

"Make your depth 300, speed four knots."

Brosseau wanted to stay in the top thermal layer to hear the ships as far away as possible. He would hear them before they would hear him, then he would drop into colder water to sneak under them.

"Conn, sonar. We've got firm confirmation on six ships, sir."

Brosseau furled his brow. "Six? There are seven of them."

"We're only picking up six, sir."

"Could the other be lost in the noise?"

"Doubtful. Our sonar is at full performance. If we can hear six of them, we'd be able to hear seven."

Maybe the forward group killed three of the Chinese ships, Brosseau thought. A thin smile appeared on his lips. "Make your depth 700."

"Depth 700, aye."

The *Helena* nosed her powerful shape into the cold waters of the Pacific. The layer of warm water above her would hold the sounds of the He Zhang ships and make it harder to hear them coming. That meant the ships would also find it hard to hear the submarine, and they didn't know she was on her way.

"Slow to two knots."

The screw relaxed its assault on the water, spinning gently behind the sub. Water flow slowed over the hull, enhancing the sonar's capabilities.

The navigator plotted the course and speed of the He Zhang ships. They had slowed to two knots. If the He Zhang remained constant, the *Helena* would be within range of the ships in eight hours, right on time.

Brosseau turned to his XO. "I'm getting a bite and taking a rest. You have the conn."

"Aye, sir."

Brosseau walked to the galley for a sandwich and cup of coffee. He returned to his stateroom. He downed the sandwich in four bites, soaking each mouthful in coffee. He lay back on his rack, thinking.

He felt sad about Morey. He was sure his friend had died. How could the *Olympia* have survived when so many others had gone down? At thirty-nine years of age, Morey had never married. He had joked to Brosseau once that he was married to the ocean. "She's a big woman to love," Morey had said.

Brosseau smiled and closed his eyes. Maybe there was hope for his friend. Sleep came at last.

He jolted awake to the sound of knocking. He stood and tore open the hatch. It was the XO. "Sir, we're nearing the battle group. We also have a contact beneath the ships. You should come see."

Brosseau splashed water on his face and walked quickly to the conn.

"Contact in the water, sir. Dead ahead. We're holding for a fix."

Brosseau's muscles tensed.

"Nuclear attack sub, sir. Range, nineteen miles. Still running the signature check."

"Slow to one knot."

"Conn, sonar. Contact dead ahead, sir."

Morey snapped his neck toward sonar. "Range?"

"Can't say yet. We're holding for a fix."

"Slow to one knot. Make your depth 800. Ready the torpedoes."

They listened in the dark. The water flow over the hull slowed to a faint swish. Sinking deeper under the cavitation of the He Zhang battle ships quieted their surroundings even more. Morey winced at the single pop of the hull under pressure. He hoped the Chinese didn't hear it.

"Contact at eighteen miles, sir. She's coming our way."

Silence.

"She's nuclear, sir. Sounds like a 688 to me."

Morey let out a lungful of air. "She's one of ours."

"She's one of ours, sir. We'll have an ID in a moment."

Brosseau let out a lungful of air.

The repaired sonar computers on the *Helena* converted the sound into digital form and filtered out noise. They were left with the raw signature of a submarine that they could instantly tell was an American 688. In a moment, they would be able to tell which one.

"It's the *Olympia,* sir!"

"Morey! I'll be goddamned."

The sonar computer aboard the *Olympia* was broken. Morey relied only on the ears of his sonar chief to identify the contact as one of their own subs. But he had no reason to doubt. A second battle group from Hawaii would probably be preceded by a submarine. He wondered who it was.

"Resume speed at two knots." They had to keep pace with the Chinese ships, below their soft gray underbellies.

"Two knots, aye."

"What's the sub doing?"

"She's slowed to a crawl, sir. She's in our same thermal layer. Probably waiting for the ships to steam overhead."

No, that wouldn't be smart. This late in the game, the Chinese would start sending helicopters ahead with sonabuoys. The American sub had better go wide and come in from the side.

"She's turning, sir. Looks like she's going wide."

Morey grinned.

Dan wouldn't have traded places with the Chinese for anything in the world. All around him on the *GW,* men acted with steel confidence toward a well-understood objective: to kill the Chinese that had killed American sailors. There was no attempt at concealing that desire. They came to sea to kill. As Captain McCain put it, "We're going to show them where our other boats went."

Still hundreds of miles from the Chinese battle group, the Prowlers and Hawkeye needed to get airborne. The Hawkeye's propellers cut the air on deck, grinding and gnashing in their desire to reach the sky.

The airmen exchanged hand signals. Steam puffed through the catapult track. At the final signal, the catapult shuttle thrust forward, pulling the 52,000-pound aircraft 310 feet. Two seconds later, she shot from the edge of the flight deck at 165 miles per hour, climbing viciously toward the clouds. She would watch the Chinese ships and report every move back to the battle group.

The four Prowlers followed shortly after. Steam poured across the flight deck following their launch, wispy in the cool morning air.

Dan sat in the bridge at the satellite communication center, safely out of everybody's way. He looked to the *Port Royal* and *Hopper* sailing to the *GW's* starboard side. Their wakes churned white immediately behind them, gradually deepening to the blue of the ocean. The ships looked like comets streaking ahead of their tails.

He looked to the port side of the ship. The *Russell* and the *Paul Hamilton* motored over the water, their own comet tails extending back toward Hawaii. The pointed hulls of the ships tore through choppy water, mesmerizing in their grace, frightening in their power.

Adrenaline pumped through Dan's body. The steam rising from the flight deck cast a medieval quality over their charge across the ocean. He heard war drums beating in his head. They announced to the world that the United States of America was coming, and she was not pleased.

13

TRIUMPH

Mark put the phone system through the PA. The entire work force packed into the huge lower terminal room. Mark, Kleewein, Susan, and Pritchett sat at a table in front of the legions of consultants. They wore headsets to talk to Dan during the engagement.

"Can you hear us?" Mark asked.

"I can hear you," Dan said from the bridge of the *GW*.

Mark took control of the communications. Jeremiah and Alyssa sat beside him. "We're at a table in front of the entire emergency consulting team. Everybody's in the lower terminal room. You're being piped through the PA. We're all with you."

"Is everybody really there?" Dan asked.

Hundreds of consultants yelled encouragement. Some crossed their fingers that the code they tested would work in real life. There was always a possibility of failure.

"Yes," Pritchett added, "and we even have satellite coverage of your progress, thanks to the installed code from Legacy."

"Glad to see my trip to Boston wasn't wasted," Dan said.

An overhead projection screen faced the crowd from the side of the room. Every fifteen seconds, it updated with the latest image from Guam. It switched between the American and Chinese battle groups, like some perverse form of sports coverage. There were few clouds in the air above the Pacific, allowing for clear monitoring of the engagement.

"Is everything working?" Pritchett asked.

"So far, we're fine," Dan said. "The Hawkeye and Prowlers are in the air. All took off without a hitch. The fighters are crouched on deck, ready to spring when it's time."

"Excellent," Mark replied. He smiled each direction down the row of faces beside him. "Hey, we have a surprise for you."

"Oh, what might that be?"

"Both coasts have electricity!" The room burst into cheers again, underscoring the good news.

"Are you serious?" Dan shrieked. He lowered his voice when Captain McCain shot an angry look at him. "Are you serious?" he repeated more quietly.

"Yes! It happened last night. Phones are going to be operable on a limited basis tomorrow morning."

"That's excellent. We're wrapping this little shindig up."

"Damn right about that," Pritchett said. He eyed the satellite screen. It showed the Chinese ships en route.

"Sonabuoys forward, sir!" Morey's sonar chief sounded urgent. The clock had been ticking for hours with no indication of battle. Now they were getting worried. Quiet seas aren't always a good sign.

"Range?" Morey requested.

"Three miles."

The sonabuoys wouldn't pick up the *Olympia* from her hiding spot beneath the battle group, but they might pick up the other American sub. She'd gone wide hours ago and Morey's sonar crew lost her sounds. But if there were sonabuoys ahead, there might be sonabuoys farther out in any direction.

"Sir, we've got a submerged contact bearing three-four-five. It's a faint signal, but getting louder."

"The American sub?"

"Probably. I can't hear clearly enough yet to say."

"Keep listening. I want to know where our guys are."

Captain Gong Shufang sat uncomfortably on the bridge of the Luhu destroyer. The coterie of officers around him did not know what to feel. They were pleased to be heading back to China, but not sure that leaving their six sister ships to deal with the Americans alone was an honorable decision.

Captain Shufang claimed it was. They were needed back in Chinese waters. Reunification was at hand and an extra Luhu destroyer would be helpful. The other officers could at least hide behind the fact that the decision to return home rather than engage another American group was Shufang's alone. They did not turn their backs on their countrymen. They just followed orders.

"Captain?" an officer said. "Mr. Chau is on the radio."

Shufang was not afraid. He saw what the Americans were capable of doing to heavily armed Luda destroyers. Even in a crippled state, the United States Navy was no pushover. He knew that the Americans would not stay crippled for long. The next battle group from Pearl Harbor would be much stronger. Better to return home and get a piece of the victory.

He dragged on his cigarette. "Yes, Mr. Chau?"

"You are returning to China."

"That is correct. My services are needed in Taiwan."

Chau breathed angrily at the other end of the radio connection. "That was not my order. I told you that Taiwan would be waiting when you returned."

"Mr. Chau, if China is to reunite, she must fight the battle in her own waters. The decoy is over. They don't know about Taiwan and Spratly. Your plan worked, Mr. Chau. My early return to China does not change the success."

Chau breathed but did not speak.

"Besides," Shufang continued, "don't you want the captain with six American kills under his belt to join your side where it counts most? Peasants you may sacrifice. But not great warriors."

Chau laughed, the hacking, windy sound coming through the radio in spikes. "So, you have become a great warrior, Captain. Then it's with open arms that I will welcome you back to China. We will need great warriors, men who know strategy and can think one step ahead of their commander. I look forward to your arrival." The radio went dead.

Shufang slowly placed the receiver back in its clip. He dragged on his cigarette. The sky met the ocean on the horizon before him. Somewhere past it lay China.

"Mr. Schwager," Chau said from his building in Hong Kong. The city bustled around them, noise of pushcarts and vendors leaking through the windows. Chinese soldiers as still as statues lined the walls of the room, watching the business proceedings of the He Zhang commander. "I have much work to do."

"Yes, I can help however you need."

Chau smiled and stood. He walked next to Schwager, slid an arm around his shoulders. They strolled nonchalantly to the window looking across Hong Kong's busy streets, the primitive exchange of goods unaffected by the Year 2000. "You can help however I need?"

Schwager nodded. His facial ravines glistened in the window. He didn't like the feeling of this new arrangement. He hated what he'd seen of Hong Kong. It wasn't home. He couldn't follow the chatter, couldn't deduce anything from voice inflections, couldn't even make sense of the body movement. He was vulnerable in Hong Kong, and Chau was not the man to be vulnerable around.

Things had not gone well. He knew they would receive no money from the United States. Now he began to wonder what his place in Chau's organization would be. Head of arms trading? Chief of tariff hopping?

It still bothered him that Chau didn't seem concerned by anything. He'd spent millions funding Legacy Conversions and paying for everything Schwager needed to coordinate coders in Hawaii and the Pentagon. Why didn't he care that it had all been wasted?

"What kind of help might I need from you, Mr. Schwager?"

"I don't know."

Chau raised his sparse eyebrows. The dark freckle on his lip rose and fell with his expressions. "You see, that is precisely the problem. I do not know either. You have already helped more than you can imagine."

Schwager didn't see how. Chau must have intended sarcasm, but it was hard to tell with the Chinese. Schwager needed to say something to calm him. "I realize that things didn't go as planned, but there have to be other opportunities."

Chau patted the American on the back, then stepped aside. They both looked out the window, several feet apart. Chau gave a slight nod to the men behind him. "The sad thing for you, Mr. Schwager, is that things *did* go as planned. The Americans have focused their efforts on the mock invasion of Hawaii. In the meantime, we have mobilized the forces we need to take Taiwan and the Spratly Islands. I was never interested in money, Mr. Schwager. I thank you for your assistance."

Schwager turned a puzzled look at Chau, but never had a chance to respond. A heavy cloth bag dropped over his head and tightened at the neck. He reached up in a panicked attempt to release it, but there were too many arms around him. Strong hands pressed over his mouth through the bag. Other hands lowered him to the floor, chest down. They wrenched his arms and legs to the center of his back, tying them together and then several times around his torso in a compact package. They tied a rope around the space where his mouth gaped inside the bag. Aside from a few muffled squawks between the time the hand lifted from his mouth and the time the rope tied securely in place, he made little noise. They slid him into a larger canvas sack with handles along the edges. Four men held him in the air and waited.

An old Chinese man walked to Chau. "How much for this one?"

"No charge, my friend. He comes as a gift with one request."

"Yes?"

"He must never be seen again. I would have preferred to kill him. But you are an old friend and deserve your fun. I know you will honor my request."

The old man bowed. "Yes, Zhan Qiao Chau. You can rest assured that nobody but my people will ever see him again."

Chau watched the old man turn and walk from the room with his men and their new parcel. He looked at the odd shape in the canvas bag, laughed, and lit a cigarette. The poor bastard would never understand what had happened.

The Hawkeye circled above the ocean. "That's affirmative, Captain," the pilot said. "They're at 150 miles, still cruising slowly. From all the Prowler jamming up here, I doubt they could detect a string of deep sea oil rigs off their bow."

The Prowlers flew far from each other to achieve maximum coverage. Their powerful tactical jamming systems created an umbrella of noise over the field of engagement. The Chinese would have almost no chance of seeing the activity of the American battle group. Their missiles would have a difficult time finding targets within the cloud of electronic noise. The combined jamming of the four Prowlers was so ferocious, it could even impede communication between the Chinese ships.

The lead Prowler pilot radioed back to the *GW*. "This looks about as ripe as it's going to get, Captain. I'd let 'em rip."

"Sir," sonar called to Morey, "it's definitely the American sub. Same sound we picked up before. She's coming toward us, getting louder. Bearing still three-four-five. Depth around 700."

The sub was joining the *Olympia* beneath the Chinese ships.

"How long until she's in range?"

"Not long, sir. Maybe four minutes."

Four minutes later the sonar reported again. "Sir, the sub has cut her engines. She's prowling with us."

"Range?"

"Nine-hundred yards, just off the port side of the group."

"Where are those sonabuoys?"

"Still bobbing ahead, sir. The others gave out by the time they reached the battle group. They're looking everywhere but down, sir."

Morey wanted it to stay that way. The *Olympia's* situation was precarious at best. At the first sign of detection, he'd need to call a right full rudder and charge out of there at flank speed. It would be so noisy a kid with a tin can and string could follow their movements. But it would be their only chance. Depth bombs and torpedoes would rain down. At only 700 feet beneath the ships, the explosives would reach them in less than fifteen seconds.

Still, there was no other way to play the situation. The *Olympia's* electric torpedoes had a guidewire range of only 3,000 feet, and the ships were noisiest right behind their own screws.

Morey bit his thumb. Where was the surface group? They had better strike soon. The Chinese would get tired of hearing nothing from their sonabuoys and then they'd start looking other places. He hoped they wouldn't look down.

McCain waited until they were only forty-five miles from the Chinese ships, the same distance that the forward battle group had been when the Chinese fired. He left no room for mistaking the intention of his battle group. They came to settle a score.

"Let's feed some fish," he told the XO. Word spread from the bridge to primary flight control to the commanding officers of the *Port Royal,* the *Hopper,* the *Russell,* and the *Paul Hamilton.* Electricity filled the air. Dan stood at the back of the bridge, wearing the satellite receiver headset, watching out the windows of the *GW's* superstructure. Men scurried around the deck of each ship.

"Here we go," Dan said into his headset.

"That's a go!" Captain Newell announced to the combat information center of the *Port Royal.* "I don't want to give them any lead. It's Aegis time. Weapons free!"

"Weapons free, aye," came the immediate response from the antiair officer. "She's fully automated, sir."

The ship crouched, her claws extended, ready to pounce on the first sign of movement.

Yellow shirts directed the first four F/A-18 Hornets onto the catapult tracks. Dan watched a green shirt hook the plane nearest him to the cat shuttle. The man kicked the nose tow bar into place then attached a second bar just aft of the nose tire. The two steel bars would pull angrily against each other until the rear one released, allowing the front bar to catapult the plane off the ship.

A jet-blast deflector panel rose from the flight deck behind the hornet. It would redirect the hot exhaust into the sky where it could not harm crewmen.

A green shirt held a sign in the air with numbers across the front: 47,000. It told the pilot what weight they were setting the catapult to launch. The pilot confirmed the figure to be accurate with a quick thumbs up. Too little pull on the cat could sling the plane over the edge into the water. Too much would slide the pilot's face to the back of his head and possibly damage the Hornet.

The green-shirted hookup man gave a rolling signal and pointed forward to the yellow-shirted plane director. The yellow shirt signaled brakes off, full power.

Here's where much of S2's work paid off. The Hornet's launch sequence was automatic, preprogrammed into the flight control computer. The computer hadn't worked just three days prior. Now it did. The pilot would ride passively until the Hornet left the flight deck. Dan saw the man push his helmet back against the headrest, bracing for launch.

The Hornet's afterburners ignited, blasting against the deflector, shaking the flight deck like an earthquake. The restraining steel bar trembled and hummed, holding the fighter back. The green-shirted hookup man leapt to safety.

The pilot saluted the catapult officer. The officer acknowledged, squatted for a last look at the launch path, then pointed two fingers down the deck.

The restraint bar released.

The Hornet screamed past 310 feet of deck in two seconds, departing the ship at 150 miles per hour with a loud clunk. As quick as it seemed to Dan, the next fighter was already in position before the first had reached the sky. Steam rose from the cat track as the shuttle returned to the nose of the next plane.

All eight Hornets and two Tomcats reached the sky three minutes after the go signal. They grouped into the wind, then roared away toward the Chinese.

"We're picking up serious radar," the forward Hornet pilot reported. "They're trying their best to punch through the haze."

"Two helos!" cried a Tomcat pilot. "One bearing three-five-five, the other bearing zero-one-two. Looks like antisub work."

"Roger," said the other Tomcat pilot. "Let's help our shark in the water. I'll take the starboard."

"Roger, I'll take the port."

The two Tomcats broke formation, peeling left and right of the group as they dove to lower altitude. They accelerated to the two Harbin helos from the Jiangwei frigates. Each fighter launched a Sidewinder missile into its oblivious helicopter target. The helos exploded. Two balls of fire plummeted to the ocean.

"Splashes in the water," sonar reported to Brosseau. "Hissing sounds, sir." The sonar chief glanced at the display. "Missiled helicopters, most likely."

"Ah," Brosseau thought aloud, "the sonabuoy droppers. That must mean our birds are in the sky." He wondered if Morey's crew heard the splashes. He didn't know the extent of the *Olympia's* sonar capabilities.

"The *Olympia* is opening her torpedo tubes, sir."

Brosseau smiled. His friend's sonar wasn't so bad after all. It was time to move in. "Weps," he said to the weapons officer, "let's do the same."

"Aye, sir."

"Prepare to fire and flee," Brosseau commanded.

The eight Hornets separated for the kill. They swooped low for the targets, the air around them buzzing from intense Chinese radar and jamming from the Prowlers.

"Arm the Harpoons," came the order.

They closed to less than five miles. At that range, even jammed radar detected the planes. Men on bridges could see the American attackers homing in.

That's what the flight wing intended. They could have launched their Harpoons from thirty miles away and never come within range of the Chinese. But the Americans wanted the enemy to hear the scream of afterburners, see the launch of Harpoons, feel the sting of Vulcan cannons across their decks.

The octuple launcher on the Luda and the sextuple launchers on the Jiangweis filled the sky with antiair missiles. The Prowler jamming confused most of the missiles, sending them on paths across the ocean where they would run out of fuel and sink. Four of the SAMs were smarter. They turned their tips at the Hornets, accelerating to 900 miles per hour over the short distance.

The Tomcats were ready. They flew directly above the Hornet attack wing, their Sparrow air-to-air missiles set to go after a flick of each pilot's thumb. Four Sparrows nosed away like swimmers at the starting gun. They intercepted the Chinese SAMs in a shower of sparks and debris.

"Four up, four down," reported the Tomcat wing commander.

Captain Newell bared his teeth. The folds of his skin separated into a growl as the bulldog of a skipper monitored the progress of battle. The planes had neared the enemy fleet and would soon drop their Harpoons. He wanted to make sure ship-launched Harpoons got to play too.

"Fire away!" he yelled into the *Port Royal* radio. The destroyers responded as if they were waiting with their fingers on the buttons.

Starboard of the *Port Royal,* the *Hopper's* two quad canisters exploded in rapid-fire mode. Eight Harpoons shot from the deck, roaring past the bow to descend to sea level for their closing approach. It would be very hard to see them coming on radar, harder still to thwart them with counter missiles.

Out the port window, eight trails of smoke drifted above the *Russell* and eight above the *Paul Hamilton.*

Captain Newell's face watched the twenty-four missiles skim out of sight. "We just sent twenty-four messengers of death," he crowed. "The planes will drop another sixteen."

He turned to face his officers. "That's forty missiles among six ships. Each one packs a 500-pound warhead. I think it's safe to say they'll get the message."

The Hornets blazed ahead. "On my count," the lead pilot said. "Three, two, one, bombs away." The two Harpoons below each plane broke free. They sank to just above sea level, then accelerated toward their victims.

Chaff rockets burst above the Chinese ships. The destroyer, two frigates, and three fast attack boats whirled in radical turns, frothing the water behind them in a mad attempt to break the Harpoon missile locks. Sixteen Harpoons raced to their enemies. The Prowler jamming prevented Chinese equipment from confusing the Harpoons.

"Fangs in the air!" the Hornet wing leader cried.

The ten fighter planes watched a wall of missiles rise from the Chinese launchers and settle into their own course toward the *Washington* battle group. The fighters would have fired, but they were too close to the ships. The enemy missiles flew under them, moving ever faster toward the American ships.

The Chinese had entered the stage where they had nothing to

lose. They needed to activate every defense and every attack available before they were crippled by the incoming Harpoons. They began launching and shooting wildly into the air. The six ships became a 10,000-ton floating shotgun, blasting everywhere in the hopes of hitting something before it hit them.

"Damn!" the forward Hornet pilot yelled. He squinted his eyes to see better. Chaff fogged the air. In the confusion, a SAM came out of nowhere and ripped the Hornet apart.

"Hornet down!" reported the wingman.

Machine guns rattled in all directions. The nine remaining planes roared past the ships. One Tomcat flew directly through a stream of bullets. They tore through the fuselage, ripping apart the wing base and fuel tank. He banked hard to the right, losing altitude.

"I'm hit! I'm hit!"

He sank lower in the air, closing the distance between his plane and the twin cannons on a Houjian attack boat. He saw the barrels shaking ominously. Another stream of bullets tore into the Tomcat, shredding the outer skin and breaking the plane apart at high speed. He ejected too near the water, crashing into the rock-hard surface less than a second behind his dead Tomcat.

He never felt any pain.

"They're churning everywhere, sir!" Morey's sonar chief reported. "Changing course, accelerating, firing everything they've got."

"It's showtime," Morey said. They heard the other sub open her four torpedo tubes as well. A total of eight torpedo tubes sat agape under the Chinese ships. "We were here before the other sub, so we'll lead the charge."

"Sir, splash-down bearing one-four-seven."

Morey knew it was one of the fighters.

The *Olympia* steamed on the starboard edge of the Chinese group while the other sub steamed on the port. Morey hoped the other skipper would fire and break left while he fired and broke right. So far, they'd been thinking on the same wave length. He'd see if it continued. "Right full rudder!"

"Right full rudder, aye."

"Sir," sonar called. "Another splash-down, this one bearing two-seven-nine."

Morey winced. "Make your depth 300 feet!" he called.

The planesman pulled back on the controls. The *Olympia* climbed through the thermal to warmer water, closer to the surface where she could hear everything in stereo. The lighter water pressure would use less of their air to launch the torpedoes, and also lessen the time to contact. The move was daring and deadly—exactly how Morey felt.

"Sir, our fellow sub is climbing as well."

Who was the other commander? Morey pictured in his mind the two cylindrical submarines rising underneath the ships, torpedo doors open, ready to blast and run in opposite directions. If people could only see the artistry of submarine warfare. "Fire control, let 'em rip!"

"Set, fire!" the officer called. The cabin pressure changed, popping the ears of everyone aboard. "Four launched sir, reloading."

"Sonar, what are they up to?" Morey called. He should have been more patient after all his years of training.

"Still dancing and running, sir."

"Can you hear enemy torpedo launches through the noise?"

"Not sure, sir. I haven't yet."

That was not comforting. "Fire two more sets of Mk 44s. Then load the two Mk 48s and finish these bastards off. Let's get a move on!"

"Second set launched," Brosseau's weapons officer announced. The *Helena* already faced away from the Chinese on their port side, ready to reach full speed out from under the ships.

"Enemy torpedoes in the water, sir!" sonar cried. "We've got six contacts."

"All ahead flank!"

"All ahead flank, aye."

"The *Olympia* has accelerated as well, sir. She's tearing the other direction." Sonar paused. "She's also diving sir."

Good idea, Morey. Brosseau didn't flinch. "Make your depth 800. Fire control, let's get that last set out."

"Ten seconds to go, sir."

"Depth bombs released, sir," sonar called. "Mortars fired as well. This is getting to be a nasty place."

Jesus Christ, Brosseau thought. The Chinese fought below the waterline exactly as they fought above: all-out weapons blitz. When they go down, they go down fighting.

"Find me a path, sonar."

"Looking, sir." The sonar chief watched the display, a tool that their sister sub lacked. Contacts dotted the area everywhere. Bombs sank from above, torpedoes swam after them, and mortar charges plunked the surface of the water in a close radius around the battle group.

"No clear shot, sir. Course bearing two-seven-zero would take us between two mortar charges. It's the best I can do."

"Set course at two-seven-zero!"

"Last set launched, sir," reported the weapons officer.

"Good. Get some noisemakers in the water"

"Aye, sir."

Sonar called again. "Three torpedoes on our course, sir. I can't hear much at this speed." Their screw churned frantically behind them, creating enough cavitation to carbonate a year's worth of club soda.

"Range?"

"One-hundred yards."

That was horribly close. They normally tracked incoming torpedoes from thousands of yards away. These three were swimming inside the same stadium.

"Noisemakers ready?" Brosseau called to weps.

"Yes, sir."

"Get ready to fire them starboard side. Left full rudder!"

Everybody held on as the *Helena* turned sharply to a new course.

"Make your depth 1,400!"

The nose dropped toward the seafloor.

"Straighten her out."

The wild turn relaxed and the sub speared deeper into the ocean.

The weps fired three noisemakers to swim back toward the torpedoes, intercepting them on the submarine's previous course. The sub went left, the noisemakers went right. Stupid torpedoes would prefer to follow the noise in front of them. In this situation, that would be the noisemakers, not the *Helena*.

The sonar chief ripped the headphones from his head to spare his ears. "Sir, explosions everywhere! I can't tell what's what."

Everybody held on. There was nothing more they could do at

that point. They couldn't hear distinct targets through the noise of exploding torpedoes. There was no time for another course change. Brosseau wiped his brow.

"Can't hear a damned thing, sir!" Morey's sonar chief held the headphones away from his ears. "The whole ocean is exploding."

Steady as she goes, Morey thought.

They'd fired their noise makers, dropped to a lower depth, charged along at high speed. He hoped they weren't heading straight into a mortar charge. The one thing he had working in his favor was inferior Chinese weapons. They used stupid torpedoes and weak mortars. If the *Olympia* had been below a group of former Soviet Navy ships, she'd already be a deepwater salvage project.

"Fire the Mk 48s!"

The weps issued the command. "Both 48s fired, sir. Swimming to the surface on active homing."

Before the explosions began, the sonar crew was able to hear the other sub launch twelve torpedoes. His own sub also launched twelve. With the addition of the last two 48s, which packed eight times the punch of the electric 44s, the two subs had sent twenty-six torpedoes at six Chinese warships.

Morey saw the scene in his mind, the only place anybody could see it. He knew the American surface group would unleash a swarm of Harpoons at the ships, some from the Aegis system and some from the planes. He saw the Chinese ships, whirling in wild course changes, churning the water white around them. Lines of missiles filled the air, closing from above. Lines of torpedoes filled the water, closing from below.

It would be quick.

"Fangs in the air!" announced Newell's antiair warfare officer. "Twenty targets, group bearing zero-seven-five, forty-five miles and accelerating, sir."

"Excellent," Captain Newell said. "Here's where we do nothing and watch Aegis protect us."

The tactical display in the combat information center showed the incoming missiles as dots. Eight careened off the monitored boundary.

"Jamming took care of eight, sir. We're down to twelve targets, still bearing zero-seven-five. Range is thirty-five miles."

Without warning, the vertical launch systems onboard the three destroyers activated. Standard missiles rose from the deck of each ship, obscuring their paths in billows of smoke. They flew away noisily. A minute and a half later they exploded.

"The SAMs killed ten more, sir. Two targets bearing zero-seven-nine. Range is twenty miles."

Chaff rockets scattered Mylar above the battle group. Not a single ship broke course.

"Targets at one mile, sir."

The missiles zipped toward the bow of the *Port Royal*. One missile suddenly veered sharply away to chase a piece of Mylar into the ocean. Water exploded 500 feet into the air.

The ship's starboard Phalanx cannon spun to life. When the missile came within 1,600 yards, the six-barreled Gatling gun unleashed hell. Dan had never heard anything like it. The pneumatic cannon spewed seventy-five bullets a second, each one made of twenty-millimeter armor-piercing Tungsten. The Phalanx radar tracked its outgoing stream of bullets along with the incoming missile to bring the two together.

The lone missile disintegrated into a smear of metal and wires and fins. The residual cloud flew above the ocean at 900 miles per hour, falling into the water bit by bit like chum bait.

Captain Newell made a fist. "Yes."

The Hornets and Tomcat watched the doomed Chinese ships. They stayed safely out of machine gun range, surprised by what it had done to their friend.

"Two seconds to impact!" a Hornet pilot said.

The air-launched Harpoons fell slightly behind the planes when they descended to sea level. When the planes banked away from the SAMs and machine gun fire, they had just enough time to whip around.

The sixteen Hornet Harpoons slammed into the Chinese hulls. They penetrated into the bowels of the ships, then exploded without mercy. Sailors flew from the ships, arms flailing on some, others didn't have any arms left. Fragments of metal created new chaff in the air. Fire spread between the six ships.

Seconds later, the ships exploded from underneath.

"What the hell was that?"

"Our shark in the water." The pilot laughed. He didn't know how extensive the assault from below would be. The first volley of eight torpedoes cracked the hulls of ships. Then came another volley, further rending the frames and boiling the ocean water in huge wrinkles. A third volley of torpedoes blasted the remains of the ships in every direction.

"Holy smokes!"

Morey's Mk 48 torpedoes came last, each one scoring the most powerful shots of the battle. It was mere luck that the mighty 48s both homed in on one of the smallest enemy ships, a Houjian fast attack boat. The Houijian's beam was only twenty-eight feet. The torpedoes were twenty feet long.

The torpedoes exploded almost simultaneously against the Houjian's belly. Combined, they detonated 1,300 pounds of high explosive warheads. The ship rose from the water, then sank like a heavy screen door.

The twenty-four Harpoons from the destroyers didn't have much left to hit. They skimmed into the floating chunks of ships that burned atop the ocean, blowing them into smaller pieces that sank quickly. A few men clamored aboard life rafts.

The Hornets and Tomcat screamed overhead. The water looked like somebody had just turned on a Jacuzzi. Bubbles rose around the debris, boiling and churning as air pockets escaped from sinking ship compartments.

"Sir," a Hornet pilot radioed to the *Washington*, "I'd like to report on the state of the Chinese battle group. However, we can't seem to find any Chinese battle group."

Morey was knocked off his feet by the mortar explosion. The *Olympia* swam away from the Chinese torpedoes directly into the ring of mortar charges. The charges all detonated at once.

"Damage report!" he yelled from the floor.

The officers scrambled back into position. Sonar clipped their headsets back over their ears. "Hull is intact." That was the most important thing. "Looks like the main sonar dome is shot. She can't hear a thing, sir."

There's a big loss, Morey thought. "We made it this far on partial sonar, I guess we can make it all the way on even less. Was that a direct hit?"

"No sir," sonar replied. They looked at the contacts they tracked by hand on charts. "We swam between two of them. That was an outer blast ring."

"Slow to two knots, make your depth 300 feet, deploy the towed array."

They slunk along in the warm surface layer of the Pacific, listening with their string of hydrophones in the water. "Nothing but popping and fizzing, sir. They're all dead."

"Not a single contact?"

"No, sir."

Wow, Morey thought. That must have been quite a show.

"Well, what are we all so quiet for?" Morey shouted. The conn cheered. It was one of the few times their CO had ever encouraged noise.

Morey laughed. "Get that galley cranking. Nav, set course for the shortest distance to Hawaii. We've got some sun tanning duty on the way."

"You got it, sir."

"Sir," sonar called. "We've got active pings bearing two-seven-zero."

The atmosphere chilled.

"Torpedo?"

"No, sir. Sounds like the friendly sub."

The crew breathed again. Morey raised a relieved eyebrow at the XO. "They must be verifying that we're alive."

"They're up to something, sir. Just a minute." The sonar wrote dots and dashes on the paper in front of him. "Morse code, sir. This is a novelty."

"What are they saying?"

"One moment." The crew looked toward sonar, waiting, a little nervous. The party was momentarily on hold. "Sir, if I've got my Morse right, it says, 'I still owe you a beer.'"

"I'll be damned!" Morey laughed. "That's Brosseau on the *Helena.*"

He wasn't too surprised. He knew few other skippers who would have followed his own instincts as closely.

The B-52 navigator answered the satellite communication signal. "Pacific Plunge One," he said.

A steely voice came through the headset. "The Chinese have invaded Taiwan and Spratly. The President wants a show of force. Proceed with the operation."

"Copy, but there's nothing left for the operation. According to our scanners, the battle group was destroyed."

"Negative. One ship broke from the battle group, a Luhu." The voice gave the location.

The navigator looked at his screen. There was a dot, the tiniest of dots steaming toward China.

"You want us to complete the operation on a single ship?"

"Affirmative. Proceed with the operation on the single runaway ship."

"Roger. Operation Pacific Plunge active." He checked his watch. "With no further notice, Operation will be complete in one hour and forty minutes." The Luhu hadn't had a chance to go far.

The B-52 duo cruised across the Pacific. Plane One adjusted its altitude to the predetermined level. At one minute to drop, the navigator confirmed the go.

"Operation Pacific Plunge, Pacific Plunge One, sixty seconds from execution. Confirm go-ahead."

"It's a go," came the reply.

Pritchett answered the satellite call. "Yes, sir. I see. Thank you for the call, sir."

"Who was that?" Mark asked above the cheering. The Keep went berserk when the final wave of missiles connected, ending the He Zhang invasion once and for all. Now the room was awash in champagne and long overdue celebration.

"We're proceeding with Pacific Plunge." Pritchett dialed the satellite phone to Guam. "This is Pritchett at Solvang. I want coverage of the fleeing Luhu." He hung up.

"What are you talking about?" Mark asked. "It's over. There aren't any ships in the water."

"There's one that got away."

"So we're dropping a nine-megaton nuclear bomb on it?"

"There's more to the story," Pritchett said, a deadpan look on his face. "Lots more to the story. Let's just enjoy the victory, shall we?"

The wall screen switched from the swirling waters of the He Zhang wreckage to a lone ship. The shot zoomed closer every fifteen seconds, revealing that the ship was indeed the Luhu that got away. The satellite backed up until the ship was surrounded by miles of ocean, viewed at an angle from her starboard side.

The lower terminal room of The Keep quieted. People sipped their champagne and watched the screen, unsure of why the surveillance had begun again. Most had never seen the Luhu before. They had no way of knowing it had been part of the initial He Zhang battle group.

"What's going on?" Dan asked from the *Port Royal*.

Mark answered into the microphone that would speak to Dan while also informing the room. "We're watching live footage of Operation Pacific Plunge."

"Pacific Plunge?" Dan asked. "There's nothing left to plunge. We already wiped them out."

"The seventh ship."

Everybody fell silent. The footage from Guam updated onscreen every fifteen seconds. A shot appeared with a black dot at the top. The room had fifteen seconds to gasp and watch the unchanging image. It clicked to the next shot with the bomb closer to the unsuspecting Luhu ship.

"I don't understand—" somebody started.

"Shhh!" said a dozen other voices.

The next screen showed the biggest blast any of them had ever imagined. A column of white water half a mile wide rose 18,000 feet into the air. It mushroomed at the top where it fell over its outer edges in a spectacular shower of white fingers. Nobody breathed.

The next screen showed the column detached from the surface of the ocean, taking on a life of its own. It turned out to be hollow. One-hundred-fifty-foot waves rolled outward from the center point of the blast. A huge empty dish appeared where the ship had once been.

The next screen shocked everybody. The base of the water column now hovered 1,500 feet above the Pacific. The ocean had filled in the empty dish carved from water. The most awe-inspiring part of the shot was the tsunami now coming closer to the satellite camera angle. It looked the entire ocean had rolled into a single wave.

The final screen showed a wave the size of city buildings rolling away from the blast. The ocean surface at the point of detonation had returned to normal, aside from the unusual cloud hovering overhead.

The satellite screen clicked off. Operation Pacific Plunge was a success. After a minute during which nobody knew what to say, a daring voice cried out, "Take that!"

The room broke into laughter. Glasses clinked, smiles beamed, and the celebration of a hard-won victory could finally get underway.

February 1, 2000

Pearl Harbor had become a Luau. Tugboats pulled the *Washington* battle group slowly to the docks, crowded with sailors and civilians. Fireworks shot high into the air. They reminded Dan a bit too much of chaff rockets.

The cheers rolled across the water. Captain McCain stood on the bridge, surrounded by his men and an unscathed battle group. He turned to Dan. "Well, Mr. Van Lan, I hope we gave you a memorable tour."

"Yes, sir, you did."

"What now?"

Dan looked around the harbor. The twin sails of the *Olympia* and the *Helena* led the last hundred yards to the docks. Men atop each signaled back and forth to each other like they were old friends. Beyond the battle group, hundreds of ship sterns and submarine sails shrank into the distance.

"There's still a lot of work to be done, sir. The *GW* is a mighty ship, but she can't defend the world on her own. She doesn't even have a complete air wing yet. I think my job is secure."

McCain chuckled. He looked up and down the harbor as well, following the gaze of every officer on the bridge. "Yes, if it's job security you want, Mr. Van Lan, you certainly chose the right field of work."

Commander Brosseau wrapped up a few paperwork details in his state room. There was plenty to be done to the *Helena,* but not right away. His men needed a rest. He sent them all ashore to enjoy the party that he knew would follow.

"Sir, will you be all right?" the XO asked.

"I'll be fine. Enjoy the party."

"Enjoy the party, aye." The XO smiled, then walked away.

By the time Brosseau climbed the ladder, a familiar face waited on the dock. Morey stopped, dropped a sea bag, and snapped a salute. Brosseau returned the gesture. The two men hugged.

"I had a hunch it was you," Morey said.

"I had a computer signature that it was you."

The two of them walked up the dock. Pearl Harbor felt more like a resort than a base. Everybody smiled. The running around had a distinctly different flavor than it had the last time they'd walked the docks.

"You're kidding me," Morey said. "Did they actually fix your sonar computers in time?"

Brosseau nodded. "The only thing we missed out there were Mk 48 torpedoes. Other than that, we were good to go."

Morey smiled smugly.

"What?" Brosseau asked.

"We had a couple 48s. Fired them, too. From what I already heard from one of the pilots, we lifted a fast attack boat out of the water."

"We were hauling too fast to listen." Brosseau looked at his friend. "How did you get 48s? You left before we did and we weren't able to get any."

"I fed my civilian teams lots of spinach."

"All right," Brosseau said. "Enough sub talk. The surf has been amazing and we have a boogie boarding weekend ahead. What do you say we cut out of here right after the debriefing?"

"I say, yes sir."

January 30, 2000

"I don't care what else needs to be done," Mark yelled into The Keep's PA system. "Everybody go home. Lay in the grass or walk along the beach somewhere. Go anywhere but here. No computers. No code. No life or death emergencies."

The terminal room cheered. Consultants milled around Mark and his kids. "Let's go to my house to celebrate," he told them.

"Let's do it," Susan said.

"Mr. Pritchett, would you like to come?" Mark asked.

"I would love to, but I've got quite a lot to do yet. If you don't mind, I'd like to use The Keep to make phone calls."

Mark smiled. "The military's work is never done."

Pritchett smiled in return. He could have elaborated right then, but it wasn't the time. Mark would find out soon enough. "No, it isn't. Enjoy yourself over the next couple days."

Most of the cars in the lot still didn't work. Gasoline hadn't been delivered to stations yet. Food wasn't on grocery shelves, either. But there was electricity. Mark's family, Nikolaas Groen, Hartmire, Lauer, and Klepac all divided themselves into pickup trucks. They arrived at Mark's home fifteen minutes later.

"Everybody inside so you can see this," Mark said. The group paraded into the living room. They looked at him. He placed his finger ceremoniously on the light switch.

"Count down with me. Five, four, three, two, one, light!" He flipped the switch, filling the room with light from three lamps.

The S2 escapees settled on chairs and couches and floor. Most of them hadn't been inside a home in a month.

Susan stood to retrieve the coffee pot. "It's broken," she yelled from the kitchen. She walked back into the living room with the manual.

"What's wrong with it?" Mark asked.

"I'm reading. I think the problem is right here in the introductory text."

She read aloud. "This intelligent coffee machine is controlled by a powerful computer chip to provide you with the freshest, richest cup of coffee in the morning."

JANUARY 31, 2000

Gary Maris watched another car filled with neighbors returning home. He wondered where they'd spent the last month. The quiet of Y2K lifted. Kids screamed in the cul de sac. He already braced himself for the sound of gunning engines in the upcoming week. Surely, the boyfriends couldn't be far away.

Patricia slid her arms around him from behind. "What are you thinking about?"

"How to pull the plug on Portland again."

"Not looking forward to work?"

"Not looking forward to any of it. I'm sure the mailman will have lots of fun material for us to sort. I know Brysco will be a complete mess. The girls are already checking their makeup to see what they need at the store. The whole damned machine is cranking into action."

Patricia squeezed her husband. "We don't have to join it."

He turned around. "I'm glad you said that, because I was thinking the same thing."

"You already killed the television."

"Yes I did," he boasted.

"I can live by lantern light for a bit longer. If you want to play cards by the woodstove every night, I'll join you. If you want somebody to walk down to the creek with you to fetch pails of water, I'll go. If you want to cut our own wood for the stove, I'll help you carry it."

He hugged his wife to his chest. "You're the best, Patricia. You really are. There's no better cave woman in the world."

"There is one request I'd like to make."

"Anything."

"May I at least use the toilet?"

JANUARY 30, 2000

Tom awoke under a blanket in the Ortiz backyard. Adelle's spot beside him was empty. She stood by the fire pit. They'd already stoked it for the morning. It smelled like another party on the way.

He stretched and crawled from underneath the blanket. Davis, Butler, and Woo slept nearby, each under his own blanket rolled against the fence. He walked to Adelle.

"Good morning," he said.

She kissed him on the lips. "I'm scrambling some eggs for you. I know you like those when we camp out."

"You remembered. It's been a long time since we camped out."

"I know." She scraped the bottom of the pan, turning the eggs over to cook the other side. "Maybe we should start going again."

"I'd like that."

She slid the eggs to his plate, leaving a third for herself. "Come on, there's juice on the patio."

They walked together to the table full of juice. People moved quietly around, grabbing their breakfast and returning to their camping areas. Tom and Adelle sat in a pool of sunshine at the edge of the patio.

They ate their eggs and drank their juice. The birds still sang. Tom looked up at them, remembering the days he gazed through the window from his bed while Adelle tended him. Terrible days. But the birds were there. As long as the sun rose and fell, the birds would sing.

Tom put a hand on his wife's leg. She scooted next to him and laid her head on his shoulder.

February 2, 2000

Pete Dubridge double checked the photos. "April, come look at this." She walked over.

The photos were the clearest yet, all of Taiwan. Dubridge had worked for hours getting shots of the inner shoreline, main transit routes, and city streets. He spread twelve photos on the table in front of them. "Look how many there are."

Her face turned gray. "Oh, Pete, this is bad."

Armored personnel carriers rolled along Taiwan's roads. Tanks filled the cities. Helicopters hovered above homes.

"Bad?" Dubridge said. "That's one way to describe it. You might also describe Hitler as rude."

14

ONLY THE BEGINNING

FEBRUARY 3, 2000

The phones rang constantly as more civilian problems arose. Consultants and managers wore their headsets all morning, coordinating requests for help against their available resources.

Mark convened his managers in the conference room for a full report.

"The phone system has already overloaded again. Radio, television, and newspapers issued a statement from the telecommunications industry that assigned calling times to different areas of the country."

"Insurance is so overwhelmed with claims that it cannot provide immediate financial relief. Banks are still a shambles, as is the stock market. The exchanges are closing."

Mark nodded. "People are lining up at banks again. This is almost worse than before. At least in the initial stages of Y2K, there was no economy to worry about. People didn't need money. Now there's an economy creeping back onto the scene and people need money again."

"We've got a train collision back east," Kleewein reported. "The engines are running, but the computerized track switches aren't all working. They found that out the hard way."

"Same thing in Japan," Susan added. "Two high speed commuter trains collided from faulty switches."

Amid the confusion, Pritchett walked to Mark. "We need to hold another briefing."

Mark looked at Pritchett. He feared the appearance and the tone. "All right."

Pritchett stood at the head of the table. "The military needs to take top billing again." He tossed a stack of photos in front of him. "These are the latest from Guam. I think they tell the story better than I could. You can see exactly why we elected to drop the bomb on the fleeing Chinese ship. Something's brewing over there, and we missed it."

"What do you mean we missed it?" Nikolaas Groen asked. "We were rather busy at the time."

"And that was no mistake. Andrew Chen at the CIA has constructed quite a file on the situation in China. He's flying here now to present it in person."

"No," Susan said. "This can't be happening. We're right back where we started."

"I'm afraid we may be. The picture unfolding before us sends chills through everybody in power. The circumstances surrounding the He Zhang attack coupled with these developments in Taiwan and the Spratly Islands make one thing clear. We were sent a decoy to keep us busy. That battle group did not have submarines. It did not intend to fight. It was merely a show of force."

He pointed to the photos. "The fight was happening over there. That was the real invasion."

Mark still held industry reports in his left hand. Included in them were accounts of new riots in Los Angeles that erupted when people could not get their money. In his right hand, he held a photo of Taipei. Tanks rolled past office buildings while soldiers stood nearby.

"My God. This is only the beginning."

ORDER PAGE

⌨ **Internet:** www.Y2KBOOK.com
Email: orders@y2kbook.com

☎ **Telephone:** 1-800-829-5723

Y2K—It's Already Too Late is available in paperback or on tape:

Paperback (384 pages)	$17.95
Abridged Audio (2 tapes, 180 minutes)	$16.95
Unabridged Audio (9 tapes, 810 minutes)	$39.95

❑ Check ❑ Visa ❑ MasterCard ❑ AmEx ❑ Discover

Please be prepared to provide your credit card and shipping information when contacting us.

Orders received by 4:00 PM mountain time ship the same business day. Order soon before your phone is dead, your computer shuts down, and the lights go out. You will still be able to read after the meltdown. Remember candles and lanterns for nighttime reading.

From all of us at Jason Kelly Press, good luck in the days ahead.